PRAISE FOR MAUREEN LANG

"[*Look to the East*] teems with conflict. . . . Lang's novel is a cautionary tale as well as a romance within an exciting framework of war, secrets, and blissful reunions."
PUBLISHERS WEEKLY

"A story of love and courage that uplifts and inspires. Lang brings an element of inspiration and beauty to the story that renews the reader's faith in mankind and the power of love."
FRESHFICTION.COM

"Maureen Lang's novel is a must-read for all historical romance fans!"
STORY CIRCLE BOOK REVIEWS

"*Whisper on the Wind* shouts God's goodness to His followers, even when His plan seems unknowable. . . . Lang has done an excellent job drawing her reader into World War I and the stories of the brave souls who fought and perished on both sides."
AUTHOR'S CHOICE REVIEWS

"The characters are well written and well-rounded in this tale of romance and suspense."
ROMANTIC TIMES

"A moving book with a suspenseful plot that has a twist of romance."
TITLETRAKK.COM

"An excellent historical read. . . . The plot is clever and will keep you guessing."

RADIANTLIT.COM

"*Springtime of the Spirit* is rich with politics, war, secrets, faith, and love. Any woman with an affection for historical romances . . . would enjoy this finely-woven tale."

CHRISTIANBOOKPREVIEWS.COM

"A heart-wrenching love story."

LIBRARY JOURNAL

"Lang masterfully weaves historical facts and figures with postwar promise and love."

ROMANTIC TIMES

"History, politics, passion, loyalty, and danger swirl together to create an intriguing story. Historical fiction fans and others will enjoy this compelling novel's undercurrent of danger and romance, beautifully combined with a riveting plot and likable characters."

FAITHFULREADER.COM

"This story is bound to pique the interest of historical buffs if only because it's written by an award-winning author with a demonstrated knack for reeling in her readers. . . . I have no doubt anyone who reads this book won't be disappointed."

HISTORICAL NOVEL REVIEW

BEES IN THE BUTTERFLY GARDEN

Bees in the Butterfly Garden

MAUREEN LANG

Tyndale House Publishers, Inc.
Carol Stream, Illinois

Visit Tyndale online at www.tyndale.com.

Check out the latest about Maureen Lang at www.maureenlang.com.

TYNDALE and Tyndale's quill logo are registered trademarks of Tyndale House Publishers, Inc.

Bees in the Butterfly Garden

Designed by Stephen Vosloo and Beth Sparkman

Edited by Sarah Mason

Published in association with WordServe Literary Group, Ltd., 10152 S. Knoll Circle, Highlands Ranch, CO 80130.

Unless otherwise indicated, all Scripture quotations are taken from the *Holy Bible*, New Living Translation, copyright © 1996, 2004, 2007 by Tyndale House Foundation. Used by permission of Tyndale House Publishers, Inc., Carol Stream, Illinois 60188. All rights reserved.

Scripture quotations marked NIV are taken from the Holy Bible, *New International Version,*® *NIV.*® Copyright © 1973, 1978, 1984, 2011 by Biblica, Inc.™ Used by permission of Zondervan. All rights reserved worldwide. www.zondervan.com.

Library of Congress Cataloging-in-Publication Data

Lang, Maureen.
    Bees in the butterfly garden / Maureen Lang.
       p. cm. — (Gilded legacy)
    ISBN 978-1-4143-6446-9 (softcover)
    1. Upper class—Fiction. 2. Boarding schools—Fiction. 3. Family secrets—Fiction. 4. Thieves—Fiction. 5. New York—Fiction. I. Title.
    PS3612.A554B44 2012
    813'.6—dc23   2012004757

Printed in the United States of America

18   17   16   15   14   13   12
7   6   5   4   3   2   1

To my sister Tina—
do you remember when I was seventeen years old
and you introduced me to my
first historical romance?
This one's for you.

ACKNOWLEDGMENTS

PERHAPS NO BOOK ever written has been the exclusive product of a single mind. I know my books come from a compilation of material and input. I could not have written the advice in Madame Marisse's handbook without the wonderful examples of Victorian life found in such sources as *The Essential Handbook of Victorian Entertaining*, adapted by Autumn Stephens and published by Bluewood Books; *The Essential Handbook of Victorian Etiquette*, from the original works of Professor Thomas E. Hill between 1873 and 1890 and published by Bluewood Books; and *Manners and Morals of Victorian America*, by Wayne Erbsen and published by Native Ground Books and Music. All other introductory chapter quotes are also fictional, meant to enhance the setting and era.

I'd like to thank my critique partner, Siri Mitchell, and my first readers, Victoria McChesney and Laura Palmere, whose evaluations always give me the courage to keep writing. And my agent, Rachelle Gardner, for her perceptive insight into Meg's character. Rachelle's input saved me countless hours of pondering and rewriting! I also wish to thank my wonderful Tyndale partners: editors Stephanie Broene and Sarah Mason for their discernment, encouragement, and friendship; Beth Sparkman for her amazing designs; and Stephen Vosloo for his photographic and Photoshop skills, inspiring me to work harder with the hope of the content living up to the loveliness of the cover. Also, thank you to Babette Rea and Maggie Rowe for their work and support on the marketing end to distribute this book far and wide. Finally I'd like to thank my readers for supporting this dream that takes so many talented people to put together. Thank you!

Therefore, dear friends, since you have been forewarned, be on your guard so that you may not be carried away by the error of the lawless and fall from your secure position.

2 PETER 3:17, NIV

PROLOGUE

A young lady of impeccable decorum never appears outside her
home unchaperoned, uncoiffed, ungloved, or unhappy.
Madame Marisse's Handbook for Young Ladies

FREEZING RAIN PELTED Meg Davenport. Though her cloak was
thoroughly sodden, along with the hem of her gingham skirt, she
refused to think about her misery. *This is my last chance. All the
blasted rain in the sky won't stop me now.*

A glimmer of warm hope stirred inside when she peered ahead
instead of watching her own slippery steps. People, horses, carriages. She'd jumped from the back of a farm wagon nearly a mile
ago when it had turned off the main road, and here at last was her
first destination—the roadhouse near the train station.

Meg hurried into the modest one-story building, squeezing
through the crowd but keeping her hood so low that she could
barely scout an opening in the room. Though she wanted to, she
wouldn't dare remove her wet cloak. She'd promised herself not to
take any risk of being seen, at least not until reaching safe anonymity
in the thick of New York City.

So she clutched her travel bag to her chest and pressed on,

hoping to find a spot against the wall. She didn't worry her satchel would be grabbed as much as she feared that dropping it would mean certain trampling in an effort to retrieve it.

It was warmer in here than waiting outside for the train; there was no doubt about that. But the smell of the place almost sent her back out anyway. Besides the odor of smoky wood from a fireplace and burnt onions from the kitchen, smells of many other sorts came from those who, like her, had sought shelter from an icy April rain. Such smells as Meg had never, in all her fourteen years, been subjected to. Unwashed bodies simply weren't tolerated, even among the school staff with whom Meg was rarely allowed to mingle. How long would she have to wait for the train to take her on the next leg of her journey?

Journey. The word tripped her thoughts. *Flight* was more fitting. Fleeing to New York City, where she would be free to do as she pleased, dress as she pleased, eat as she pleased, talk to whomever she pleased. In short, free to *be* whomever she pleased. She'd saved enough allowance money from her father to be entirely independent, at least for the few days it would take her to find employment.

Finding a spot near the fireplace to dry out her cloak would be impossible, judging by the cluster of people already doing the same amid the flicker of firelight casting them all in silhouette. So she followed her nose instead, hoping a place nearer the kitchen might provide preferable odors to those from the press of people. Warmth from the stoves would dry her cloak just as nicely.

Whatever sustenance the roadhouse offered held little appeal to Meg. She'd eaten a full breakfast shortly after setting out, of cold but tastily spiced beef on the same pure-white bread she'd enjoyed ever since Mrs. Hale had been hired as head cook some years ago. Her specialty was baking. A hard-cooked egg and a flaky blueberry muffin had followed, all washed down with the tea Meg managed to carry in a pouch she'd stolen from one of the school's liverymen. The container had an odd scent to it when she'd first added her tea, something along the lines of the peach cordial that was kept under lock and key. But as Meg had taken her first sip from the pouch, she hadn't minded the flavor the tea acquired from whatever dregs were left behind.

Meg still had a bit of food left. Another sandwich, a sourdough biscuit, and some of the most flavorful cookies served by the exclusive Madame Marisse's School for Girls. They were, in fact, created from a recipe each girl was awarded upon graduation, to be given to whatever kitchen staff awaited her. A signature teatime addition only alumnae of Madame Marisse's were known to serve. If Meg had a mind to, she could probably sell the ones she'd wrapped in a napkin to any one of the roadhouse patrons and make enough money to buy a full meal right here and now.

But she only clutched the bag closer as she found a free place by the wall and pulled back her hood just enough to assess her surroundings.

Her gaze froze on a familiar figure. Mr. Pitt, the oldest, grouchiest liveryman who ever lived. The very person from whom Meg had stolen the pouch she'd used for her tea.

She was ready to bolt when she realized he hadn't seen her. She heard some of his words through the din of the crowd because he was speaking over the noise himself.

"About this height." He held up a hand, just below his own rounded shoulders. "A girl. Fourteen. Blue eyes. You wouldn't miss that—the eyes, I mean."

But the woman he addressed, wearing an apron and a servant's cap, only shook her head, then moved away with a mug-laden tray balanced on her palms.

Meg pulled the hood lower again. Blast her eyes to make her so easily identifiable—just like her father's. Blast him, too. It was his fault she had to run away. He was the one who made sure she stayed in that blasted school.

Blast, blast, blast. It was a word Madame Marisse had more than once reprimanded Meg for using.

Blast . . . *everything.*

The door through which she'd entered was on the other side of Pitt. There must be another way out . . . perhaps from the kitchen.

But no sooner had she slid into the kitchen than a woman raised her voice, shouting nearly into Meg's ear.

"You can't be in here, dearie. Have a seat, and we'll serve you as soon as we can."

Then the serving girl ushered Meg out, making sure the door swung closed behind her.

Meg stole another glance at Mr. Pitt. He was already looking around; even if he didn't see her face, she knew that when he spotted a girl of the right height, cloaked and alone, it would mean the end of her dreams. Her heart pounded and heat rushed to her limbs, preparing to transport her away.

But she froze; too many people made running impossible.

The nearest table offered barely a single spot of clear space, and there was no empty chair in sight. Meg crouched at its side as if she were part of the group seated. She could see only a portion of the table itself, too afraid to pull back her hood to see the faces of those she joined.

"Mama! Who's that?"

Meg spied the child next to her, who pointed one wobbly finger her way.

"Shh! Hush!" Meg tilted her head back to see beyond her hood: other children and adults—parents, no doubt, and grandparents, too—all staring at her. Clearly she needed to speak. "I—I wonder if you would permit me to join you?"

Her perfect diction did little to impress them; she saw that immediately. She must appear to be the invader she was, though this was hardly a private table.

Perhaps she could crawl *under* the table—

But it was already too late.

A hand from behind cupped her elbow while another pulled back her hood.

"Don't you think you've gone far enough this time, Miss Meg?"

Perhaps if the room hadn't been so crowded, Meg might have sprinted away. Perhaps if Mr. Pitt hadn't such a strong hold on her arm, she might have succeeded.

Or perhaps if she thought she could get away—though every previous attempt to escape had failed as well—she might have resisted.

But today's venture had been her best effort, and she'd promised herself it would be her last. Her heart—the very heart that had thrummed at the thought of escape—now sailed to the lowest corner of her being. Trapped.

She'd gotten farther than ever before; there must be something to be said for that, anyway.

Blast.

Part One

1

A young lady who attains the grace of self-discipline rightfully earns the admiration of others. Indeed, her place in genteel society will not be won without it.

Madame Marisse's Handbook for Young Ladies

MEG DAVENPORT STOOD barefoot on the warm, loose garden soil. She watched a butterfly hover on a breeze above the garden as if it danced before a banquet, contemplating which nectar to sample first. Yellow celandines, purple coneflowers, or red verbena? Not far off, the sweet briar rose beckoned, trimmed with a skirt of pinks and zinnias. All planted under Meg's direction to attract butterflies of every sort.

She knew this butterfly. As a caterpillar he had, along with so many of his butterfly siblings and moth cousins, undoubtedly been hosted among the clover beds or colorful sweet peas that festooned the white columns of the gazebo where Meg often sat. But while many of the moths and butterflies boasted shades of black and white and gold and orange, this one lit a delicate shade of blue as the sun blended its sheer wings with the summer sky. How she wished she could fly like him, beyond the walls of the school, and see what the world looked like from a butterfly's view. It had been so long since she'd let herself dream of such things that she'd nearly forgotten how.

Perhaps it was as silly a whim for herself as for this pretty blue butterfly. He wasn't as adventurous as the others. She'd seen him before and knew he rarely floated beyond the edges of the garden.

She bent to remove another weed, although if Madame Marisse were still alive, she'd have quietly but firmly directed Meg back to the gazebo to merely enjoy what even she had called "Meg's garden." Even with the school nearly empty for the off-season, there were others employed to do such menial tasks as pulling weeds. But Meg enjoyed the satisfaction to be found in keeping the garden pure of anything but what she'd intended for it to present. Besides, the earth was softer than any carpet beneath her toes.

"Meg!"

Hazel Hibbit beckoned, but beside the stout school matron bustled her sister, Beatrice. Meg smiled, far from alarmed. The Hibbit sisters were forever distressed about something, perhaps more often now that Hazel had become the matron. Meg added the weed to the others she'd collected and set to the side for the gardener to remove, then stepped back onto the grass.

"A message!" Hazel called.

"Yes!" Beatrice added. "For you!"

Curiosity stirred, Meg held the puffed flounces that trimmed the bottom of her silk day dress out of the way to wipe her feet on the downy lawn. Obviously it wasn't a letter from a former schoolmate, an invitation to a soiree, or even a note from some prospective beau. Such things wouldn't have warranted any more attention than to be left with the others upon her silver card holder by the door.

Only a message from one person would hasten Hazel's step and add a bloom to Beatrice's cheeks. It must be from Meg's father.

"Open it, child! Look, it's bordered in black."

Meg reached for the sealed envelope. Indeed, the stationery was outlined in black, though her name was written neatly in the center where the paper had been left white. She tore it open, seeing it was dated that very day.

June 7, 1883

Dearest Meggie,

I write to you today with a heavy heart and unsteady hand. Your beloved father passed on to his reward this very day. I will, of course, see to all the arrangements of his burial.

Please be assured he did not suffer but breathed his last in the peacefulness of sleep.

Respectfully,

Ian Maguire

"He's dead." Meg's words, like her heart, were untouched by the news. So it was over. Her hope that he would one day arrive knowing how to be a father to her, or to share with her anything of the family to which she was bound by blood.

"Your father?" Beatrice's voice was usually high-pitched, but just now piercingly so. "He's—he's gone?"

Meg nodded, folding the note and slipping it back into the envelope. She walked past the sisters, back to the three-story house that had once ranked among the finest Federal estates on the hills between Boston and New York. For the past twenty-five years, this home had been one of the most expensive, exclusive schools in New England. One that taught European grace and manners to the next generation of accomplished wives and mothers, all under the far-reaching umbrella of Christian love. Even after Madame Marisse died two years ago, the staff had carried on in her absence so that it was still regarded as one of the finest schools along the East Coast.

Beatrice fluttered behind Meg, taking one of her arms. "Oh, dear, we're so very sorry for the news!"

"Yes, of course we are," Hazel added, reaching for Meg's other arm. "How sad the world has lost such a gentleman."

Indeed.

Meg stepped up to the porch that served as the entrance to the back of the school, walked past the sunroom, where she and countless others had learned not only the art of watercolor and charcoal drawing, but the art of conversation and genteel manners. Here they had been taught how to be demure yet confident, all the while reminded of the delicacy of a woman's constitution and the greater delicacy of a woman's reputation. She passed the music room, where she'd learned not only to sing and dance and play piano, but the history of musical elements as well, because Madame Marisse had believed in the depth as well as the breadth of knowledge—at least as it pertained to becoming an asset to a husband. And she continued past the sitting room, where she had rested after lawn tennis or horseback riding or long afternoon walks. Or had spent time with the mundane to the profound, from idle embroidery to discussing the greatest literature known to man. Where she'd prayed with other students and the staff alike in English as well as French. Because Madame Marisse had believed in educating the whole person, physically, intellectually, and spiritually.

Meg passed all the rooms in which she had been a student, a friend, a protégé. But never a daughter.

In the front hall, at the foot of the stairs, she turned back to the sisters. "Thank you for your concern, but I wish to be alone for now."

"Oh yes, of course," Beatrice said.

Meg put a foot on one stair, then another, realizing for the first time that she'd left her shoes in the garden. But they didn't matter now.

"But . . ."

One hand on the polished walnut handrail, Meg turned back.

Hazel looked up at Meg with the oddest expression, one of uncertainty rather than sympathy.

The look disappeared as Hazel turned away. "It's too soon, my dear. Never mind. Go upstairs, and we'll talk when you're ready."

"Pertaining to what?"

Hazel faced Meg again. "Pertaining to your father, dear."

"There is nothing to be said."

"You'll want to go to his funeral, of course," Beatrice said.

Meg shook her head. "Even if I did, I wouldn't know how. That boy—" She amended her thought of him; the last time she'd seen Ian Maguire, he *had* been a boy, but surely he was as grown as she by now. "A Mr. Maguire will be attending to all of the details."

Hazel pulled at the bottom of her cuirass bodice, which shifted despite the finest of corsets beneath. It would fit even tighter by the end of summer, during which time Hazel annually added a few pounds, eating quantities she would never permit herself—or others—to consume while school was in session. "Yes, well, that isn't exactly what I meant, but we needn't discuss anything right now."

Meg descended the two stairs she'd mounted. The school was newly quiet with only her and the sisters there, besides the reduced year-round household staff.

"If there is anything to be said regarding my father's death, Miss Hibbit, you might as well tell me now. Has it something to do with my place here?"

"Oh no, of course not!" Beatrice spoke before Hazel could, shaking her head and taking one of Meg's hands, patting it. She was as wont to be thin as her sister was to be plump. When the students returned in the fall, one sister would eat with those whose diets were curbed, while the other ate with those whose diets were embellished. At the end of every summer they were able to provide guidance and personal example for those girls who had to work at becoming the ideally sized debutante.

"Your position is secure as long as you like," Beatrice added. "Madame Marisse made that so very clear, you know, before . . . well, before she passed on."

Meg turned her eyes back to Hazel, and as so often happened when Meg leveled a gaze at anyone, man or woman, Hazel let her own stare linger. It happened because of the color of Meg's eyes; she knew that. The eyes she'd inherited from her father. Eyes that people simply wanted to peer into.

Hazel took Meg's other hand, leading her from the hall and back toward the wide, curved threshold into the parlor. It was a large room appointed in the finest fashion: furniture designed by such famous people as Phyfe, Lannuier, and Roux; side chairs and sofas and a pair of French ladies' desks trimmed with inlaid mahogany; and nearby, a rococo center table of marble and rosewood offering an inviting surface for a silver tea set imported from London.

Hazel headed to one of the desks. "I wonder if you might think this a bit sudden, considering the news has had but a moment to make an impression."

Meg stared at Hazel, wondering if the older woman truly believed her own words. Did she think Meg's lack of emotion was simply because her father's death hadn't sunk in yet? Did she expect Meg to mourn a man she barely knew? Other women might not have been immune to the charms of John Davenport, but unlike them Meg had never once wanted to simply stare at his handsome face.

"What is it you'd like to say about the matter, Miss Hibbit?"

Hazel looked from Meg to the desk beside her, the one used only by the staff. Meg expected, one day, that she would use that desk. Knowing there were few other options for her future, Meg had decided to transform this school from a luxurious factory of wives and mothers to an institution that could offer women more choices: to be instructors or lecturers, doctors or lawyers, or anything else they wished. It wasn't the kind of future she'd envisioned as a child—one in which she made others' dreams come true as she ignored her own—but with so little choice left open to her, it would have to suffice.

Hazel withdrew a key from her pocket. "Please, make yourself comfortable. Perhaps Beatrice could summon some tea."

Meg could hardly sit, let alone drink tea. "What is it you want to share with me?"

"I have a letter for you." She opened the desk as she spoke. Meg had seen the interior a thousand times or more: little compartments neatly holding bills and records, a small inkwell, pens and tips, stationery and envelopes. Nothing unusual. It was, in fact, the perfect model for students to reproduce while studying household management.

But then, after Hazel withdrew a small stack of envelopes, she pushed the edge of the corner compartment. In one surprising instant the rear wood piece dropped down. A shadow appeared, from which Hazel drew another lone envelope.

Holding it in her thick fingers, Hazel turned back to Meg. "It's from Madame Marisse regarding your father. We were instructed to look at it if you were ever at death's door. Otherwise it was to be given to you upon the day you left our school or the day your father died. Whichever came first."

How silly of Meg not to have had some kind of premonition of this. But she hadn't; Meg was completely, utterly stunned that Hazel knew something concerning her father that she did not.

"A letter from Madame to me, about my father. Do you know what it says?"

Hazel shook her head.

Meg took the envelope, instantly disappointed in its weight— or rather, the lack of it. Surely it was a short letter.

She didn't open it right away. Instead, she stared down at the familiar script. So precise, so feminine. The perfect handwriting, as perfect as everything Madame Marisse had done. As controlled as Meg had learned to be.

Meg broke into the envelope, withdrawing the paper inside. She recognized at once the school stationery, upon which was written a few meager lines and a New York address.

The address below is to be used to contact John Davenport, should anything happen to Meg. If there has been any change, the proprietor of this business will know where Mr. Davenport can be reached. Only to be used in the most dire of circumstance.

Meg allowed the sisters to read the words over her shoulders.

"Well, then, there is no reason for you not to attend his funeral," Beatrice said. "You have means to contact his estate now."

Hazel nodded. "We'll accompany you, of course."

Meg shook her head. "No. I'll not be going."

She folded the letter, slipped it back into the envelope, and crumpled it with the other one, the one from Ian Maguire that had revealed her father's death. Then she walked from the room.

It wasn't until she was up the stairs, down the hall, through the very last bedroom door, and inside the perfectly decorated room that she fell to her knees, pressing those letters to her breast. And then she burst into tears.

2

A young man worthy of a lady's attention must be impeccable in manner and dress. He must be humble yet confident, strong yet sensitive to his ladylove's nature, and above all else, he must put the needs of others before his own.

Madame Marisse's Handbook for Young Ladies

NEAR PEEKSKILL, NEW YORK

IAN MAGUIRE RUBBED the soft fur behind Roscoe's ears. He needed the comfort of the massive dog just then, if only to steady his hands after writing explicit instructions for the undertaker who waited nearby.

He could barely read his own writing. But there they were, directions for the stonemason on what was to be inscribed upon John's headstone.

> Behold and See as You Pass By
> As You are Now so Once was I
> As I am Now You Soon will Be
> Prepare for Death and Follow Me

Ian had nearly begged John—Skipjack to those who knew him best—not to order such words to reside over him until the end of time. Not to bring such a dour warning out here to the country air they loved, the air that had served them far better than that stinking cloud hovering over New York City.

But John had been insistent. He'd changed in the last few months of his life, had acted as if he'd known death would summon him sooner than any of the rest of them suspected. The inscription itself gave no clue as to why John had presumed the quickness of death, other than the fact that it might be imminent for anyone—something Ian would rather not consider.

It was all Kate's fault. She'd changed John with her new talk of hellfire, God's judgment, and all that. She might have kept it to herself if she'd known John's heart had been brittle as glass. The stress of life had proved too much for him.

Ian folded the instructions and handed the page to the undertaker, who would see to all of the details. With it he sent enough money for the cabinetmaker to build a proper coffin—the newer kind, with lining—and for the stonemason to brick over the grave as an extra precaution, even though John would be buried here on Ian's own property, a safe distance from the city. No physician's experiment would John be.

Ian returned to the bedroom where his friend's body waited. Roscoe followed, the tips of his nails sounding a familiar tap on the uncarpeted floor. Pubjug was in the room, watching over the body alone for the moment. If Ian didn't count Kate, he and Pubjug would miss John the most.

Served Kate right not to be here when John died, though it was a shame his last moments had been in a borrowed bed. That was Kate's fault too, having recently thrown John out of her flat. Until they could be wed, of all things! After all this time.

Ian saw Pubjug seated on the chair near the bedside, arms folded, legs sprawled. Barely awake. Ian jabbed his shoulder when he passed.

"I's watchin', Pinch," Pubjug said, calling Ian by a leftover nickname that only he—and John—ever used anymore. "He ain't moved a mite, not a mite."

"It's all right, Pubjug. You can go now. I'll watch over him for a while."

Even as Pubjug left the room, Ian knew it was no use. John didn't need to be watched over anymore. Ian believed the doctor who'd said John was dead. He no longer breathed. Ian had placed his hand under John's nose often enough just to make sure, ever since he found him when Roscoe started howling that dawn, alerting Ian that something was amiss.

Now Roscoe took up the place he'd been coaxed away from earlier, on the bed and close to John's cool body. The undertaker would be back shortly to shave and redress him, pack his body in ice to preserve it as well as he could before moving him down to the ballroom, where even now furniture was being rearranged and the dining table brought in. Ian hoped John would look better than he did at the moment, with a few days' stubble on his chin and his mouth frozen open.

No one could see him this way. They should see him as the man he'd always been in life: strong, handsome. Though no longer charming or decisive or confident. So confident he could make someone believe up was down or the other way around if he wanted. All that was gone now.

Ian ignored the pain in his gut as he thought once again about the note he'd sent with Keys that morning—the one that was to be delivered first thing. Why had he done it? Why had the first note been to her? It wasn't because John had said to take care of Meggie, because that hadn't, in fact, been his most urgent instruction.

No. John had indeed told Ian to take care of her . . . but to do it from afar. Just as John had done all his life.

And yet visions of Meggie had come to Ian all morning. Surely she would be sorrowful over her father's death. Perhaps she would be unable to keep herself away, despite the purposeful lack of invitation to help with the details of her father's burial. Perhaps she would come here at last, and they could mourn their loss together.

"I don't care what he said. I'm going in there."

The sound of protest barely registered before the door burst open and there, obviously hastily coiffed, dressed in her habitual red, stood Katherine Kane, called Kate. For a woman nearly ten years older than Ian, she had been a lovely counterpart to John's own youthful good looks. No doubt the reason that, together, they had profited so well from unsuspecting prey. They'd been too difficult for mere mortals to resist.

"John!" Kate brushed past Pubjug, who looked helplessly toward Ian before backing out of the room and closing the door.

Roscoe greeted her with a wagging tail and submissive ears, along with a little whimper as Kate approached John's side. She brushed the top of the dog's enormous brown head in an acknowledgment of their shared suffering, but it was barely more than a graze.

If she saw Ian, she ignored him as she fell at John's side, a torrent of tears already dampening her unpowdered cheeks.

Despite his best intention, Ian was unable to remain cool in light of her grief. He watched her stroke John's face, his hair, his brows; she tried closing his mouth, which remained stiff and unyielding against her effort. She uttered words Ian couldn't decipher, except *no, no* and *too soon.*

Then she pressed her face to John's chest, deep sobs racking her body.

Ian let her cry. But not for long. He pulled her from the bed, and for a moment she turned to him, nearly forcing an embrace as if to extract some small comfort. Ian let his arms fall around her, but even as he did, she backed away.

"Why didn't you send word to me sooner? I had to find out

from Dice, and he said Keys had the list of those who were to be told. I wasn't even one of them!" Her words were barely out before Ian felt the imprint of her palm against his cheek. "How dare you! How dare you try controlling this, the way you've tried controlling everything else lately!"

Roscoe whined again, leaving the bed to stand between Ian and Kate. Ian wanted to rub the sting from his face but refused to give Kate the satisfaction. Instead, he rubbed Roscoe's ear, but the action wasn't calming enough to stay his tongue. "Maybe if you hadn't banished John from the only bed he's known for the past three years, you would have been the one controlling who heard the news."

If she had a retort, she caught it between pursed lips. New tears appeared, and she turned back to John's body. She sank to his bedside, bent close enough for her own tears to dampen his cheek.

"You know why," she whispered, not to Ian but to the body in front of her. "You know it was right for us to part, if only for a little while. We were to be married, weren't we, darling? This very week." She put her head on his chest again. "But you've gone on without me."

Ever since they'd met, she'd been able to make John do just about anything she wished. Precisely why Ian and the others disliked her. The vision of him as their leader had blurred with visions of her.

Kate continued to cry, and Ian wanted to tell her to go, to leave him alone with his own grief.

Instead, he left the room, taking Roscoe with him. There were still details to be seen to if they were to have visitors both tonight and tomorrow.

Because once word of John's death circulated through New York, Ian was certain he would be juggling more than just a few visitors at a funeral.

3

It is generally unwise for a lady to travel without an escort. In emergencies, however, the wise traveler will arrive well in advance for ease of departure, use baggage of the best quality to avoid breakage in transit, avoid wearing such fabrics as velvet or lace (known to attract dust), and be careful not to draw the attention of strangers.

Madame Marisse's Handbook for Young Ladies

NEW YORK CITY

ALTHOUGH THE SHOP was in a respectable neighborhood, south of New York City's exclusive Ladies' Mile, where Meg had often shopped at the Marble Palace, Macy's, and Lord & Taylor, she knew a moment of hesitation as the driver directed the hansom to the curb. But Meg refused to acknowledge her whisper of fear. This was New York! And even though she was here alone for the very first time in her life, this was the city she'd once wanted to claim as home.

Peering through the carriage window, Meg saw the sign identifying Yorick's Household Goods. The wide plate-glass display windows on each side of the threshold showed off wares beneath an awning protecting the goods from the sun.

Meg swallowed, but her mouth remained dry. All those times

she'd been the one to set an example for other girls at school haunted her now. Certainly some families, even upstanding ones, allowed their ladies to shop without a chaperone, but this simply wasn't permitted among the girls from Madame's school, not even for Meg as an exemplary student. Just taking the train into the city and then the carriage ride here—alone—had been an infraction Meg hadn't been willing to commit since she was fourteen years old. Since then she'd succumbed to the life she'd been dealt: as the favorite, most accomplished student at Madame Marisse's. The one who was good at being good.

Any time for hesitation was long past. She'd made up her mind last night, only hours after receiving word of her father's death. And this morning, before either Hazel or Beatrice had arisen, Meg had packed a bag—much as she had that early morning four years ago. Only this time she hadn't thought about taking any food, and she'd asked Mr. Pitt to take her to the train station. If her father's laying out lasted the customary three days, she intended to stay at least another day. So she'd dressed in the one black gown she owned, reserved for occasions such as this, knowing she would play the part of the grieving daughter. She also left orders for her darkest burgundy gown to be dyed black as quickly as possible so she would have another gown to wear during her period of mourning.

Leaving her bag on the seat beside her now, she asked the cabbie to wait. Then she saw herself into the shop.

A little bell jingled when she pushed open the door. It was a surprisingly quaint feature for a specialty shop, since she knew most of its northern neighbors had clerks greeting customers. But she could tell there was a need for the bell here. Not a clerk to be seen. With such poor service, it was no wonder this shop couldn't earn a spot closer to the more fashionable real estate up Broadway.

She looked around. While the view from the street had been common enough—household and sewing goods neatly displayed—inside the shop was something else. The first shelf she viewed shared its goods with a thin layer of dust, as if it had been quite some time since anyone had tended to the inventory, let alone been interested in a purchase. How on earth had her father made enough money to support her at Madame Marisse's with such humble business interests?

She eyed another door behind a plain oak counter. "Pardon me?" she called. "Is someone here?"

No answer. She looked around again, noting the limited choices, the general lack of attention to detail in each display. She was nearly tempted to rearrange a set of dishes when the door at the back of the shop opened and someone emerged, a tall man who looked surprised to see her. He was finely dressed—his attire included gloves and a fedora—and he did not offer any help. Instead, he walked past her and out the front door.

Meg looked again at the inner door. It was ajar.

"Pardon me?"

A moment later another man peered around the edge of that door. She saw his white cap of hair first, then wrinkle-shrouded eyes that widened upon sight of her. He disappeared before she could say another word, finally opening the door wide enough to pass through while he pulled away an apron that had hung around his neck.

"May I help you?"

Meg nodded. "I hope so. Are you the proprietor here—or a clerk in his service?"

He didn't look directly at her; rather he looked around the store as if checking to see that nothing had been disturbed. "I am the proprietor," he said. "Mr. Thomas Yorick. How can I help you?"

"I came because you are my only means to contact my father, an investor in this shop. John Davenport."

He gasped—she was quite sure of it, though he hid it well with

19

a little cough. Instead of looking around anymore, he turned his gaze on her. He had to look up to see her face, and his white brows rose, lifting some of the wrinkles around his faded hazel eyes.

"Your father, did you say?"

"Yes. John Davenport."

Now those brows fell, gathering in the middle. "And who are you, young lady?"

"My name is Margaret Davenport, but my father always called me Meg." *Meggie,* she silently amended but wouldn't say that name aloud. She'd always hated when he'd called her that, such an affectionate and familiar form of her name, as if he'd known and loved her. "I received word yesterday . . . about him . . ."

She stopped speaking because he leaned closer to study her, and she in turn leaned back to maintain a standard distance.

"Yes, you have his eyes, just as he said you did. Blue stolen straight from the sky." Mr. Yorick grinned, and different wrinkles appeared on his face, on his upper cheeks—deeper on one side than the other, making that grin appear lopsided. "Blue of the sunniest day."

"My hired carriage is waiting outside, and I was told you have my father's household address. I intend going there now."

The man was already shaking his head. "No, no, you needn't trouble yourself. He's not here in the city, you know." He was already turning, and Meg's heart sank to her stomach for fear of being sent away without completing her mission. She knew her father wasn't here, not in spirit anyway. But in body, at least. She would say good-bye to him and remember him in death, perhaps more fondly than she had while he lived. And perhaps, just seeing his home, she would gain a glimpse of what her life might have been had he truly acted a father to her.

The proprietor glanced out the shop window. "Do you have the means to travel outside the city, miss?"

"I'm familiar with the train schedules."

"Very good, then." The man withdrew paper, ink, and a gold-tipped writing instrument from beneath the counter. "Go to the station at Chambers and Hudson, to pick up the Hudson River train. Buy a ticket to Peekskill. Have you traveled the Hudson line before?"

She nodded. Every so often she had taken the Hudson line for student outings to explore historical sites from the Revolutionary War.

Mr. Yorick blew on the ink before handing her the paper. There was no name attached to the unfamiliar address he'd written.

"And this is where my father's funeral will be held?"

"Yes. I received word about it yesterday afternoon. You'll be traveling on your own, then?"

She nodded again, determined to hide the fact that this was the first time she'd traveled by herself any farther than a few hours' distance from her school.

He eyed her as if reading the truth. "You might as easily get off at Croton, but it's a bit farther by carriage from there. Take the train as far as Peekskill; you won't regret the extra expense."

"You'll be going, then?"

"To this address? Oh, I should say not." He winked. "It's a bit closer to Sing Sing than West Point, if you know what I mean."

She nodded, though his words—and wink—meant nothing. If the address was closer to Peekskill than Croton, what had that to do with either Sing Sing or West Point? But she didn't ask because he looked a bit too amused over his own choice of words.

Meg turned away, and as she reached the door, he called after her, "My condolences."

As she settled in the carriage, an unjustifiable feeling of sadness came upon Meg. Her stomach grumbled from lack of nourishment, but she'd been unable to eat and even now had no desire for food. This was a journey she had to make, although she wasn't sure why. If money were love, then John Davenport had loved her well. But if love were smiles and embraces and companionship, then he'd loved her not at all. Why honor his passing?

This should be an adventure, if nothing else—at long last she was beyond the school and on her own. What was she mourning? A father she'd barely known?

She'd never understood the fascination he'd stirred in Hazel and Beatrice. Even Madame Marisse must have been moved by his charm; otherwise she never would have taken in Meg. Not when admission into her school normally meant a thorough exploration of background—and not just of bank accounts, but of pedigree. Other than money, the only things in Meg's past were questions.

Meg remembered the day she'd vowed to never again inquire about her father and whatever lineage she'd inherited. She'd been nine years old, and her father had brought Ian Maguire with him to visit her. It wasn't long after that Meg had made her first of several attempts at escape. Not to run to her father, but to run away from the life he'd designed for her.

Why should her father need her—or love her, for that matter—when he had a surrogate son upon whom to lavish all his affection and attention? Though the two had barely exchanged a word in her presence—the boy was as awkward as her father had been—Meg knew. She knew whatever place she might have once held in her father's life had been filled. By Ian Maguire.

The carriage slowed at the train station, drawing Meg's attention from her thoughts. Folding the paper and stuffing it inside the fringed pouch she carried, she withdrew enough money to pay the cabman. Then she took her satchel and went in search of the ticket office.

Nothing stood in her way now. Meg could finally discover her past—and with that knowledge, better plan her future.

A lady in the company of strangers while traveling will not be
considered unrefined should she partake of polite, though guarded,
conversations.
Madame Marisse's Handbook for Young Ladies

MEG STARED OUT the window of the train car, ignoring again the
emptiness of her stomach and the heaviness of her heart. She wished
she'd paid more attention the last time she had taken this train route.
All she'd noticed was the river, how it widened and twisted, how the
trees grew alongside. The outings she'd enjoyed with other students
had taken her only as far as Hastings, some twenty miles outside the
city. Up to that point, she did recall a few things, like Tubby Hook
being Inwood's old name and some of the history associated with
Fort Washington. And Yonkers, where one of her former schoolmates had said her family owned a summerhouse.

Soon Meg would reach her destination—although once there,
she had no idea what she would do. She supposed the length of her
stay would depend on what she found at her father's home. During
the past four years, she'd accepted her fate, knowing her past, present, and future were bound up in the school. But the farther the
train took her, the more she felt like that fourteen-year-old girl
again, the one she'd banished so many times in the last few years.

A rattle at the train vestibule door drew her notice. A man

walked the aisle slowly, so slowly that Meg's eye wasn't the only one drawn to him. He looked at each passenger as if to catch their attention like some kind of friendly host: nodding, occasionally greeting some, winking at the child two seats in front of Meg. She turned her gaze back out the window, but when he neared her seat, he paused altogether.

"Good afternoon, miss."

Meg nodded with the barest of glances. She'd never minded speaking to strangers with a gaggle of girls behind her, but alone—and to a man, even one nearly her father's age—wasn't at all proper.

The man did not move on. He was garishly dressed, with a jacket so purple no gentleman ever would have chosen it. And the hat! A British pith helmet, as if he'd just gotten off a sailing ship from some faraway colony.

To her dismay he steadied himself by grabbing the back of the seat in front of her. "You going far up the line, miss?"

Without answering, she softened her rudeness by issuing the tightest of smiles. If he were any kind of gentleman, he would receive the message to leave her alone. Of course, if he were any kind of gentleman, he wouldn't have spoken to her in the first place. Why hadn't she spent the extra money for a seat in first class, where other passengers could not wander in?

A conductor entered, announcing the next stop at Tarrytown. The man lingering by Meg's seat had to step aside to let the conductor through, but instead of moving on, the older man took the seat on the other side of the aisle, directly across from Meg.

"Sing Sing's next, you know. Ever been there?"

Meg lifted her chin, still staring out the window.

"The city gets their ice from Rockland Lake. Nice, fresh." He mimicked a shiver as preamble to his next word. "Cold."

She chanced a glance around them, wondering if someone else might engage the man instead. But the mother and child traveling together were silent, and so was the couple sitting in front of him. She knew there were others behind her, but no one responded. They must all have known, like she did, whose interest he wanted.

Rather than looking out the window on his own side of the car, he stared beyond Meg at the landscape on her side. "Lots of quarries along here. Yes, indeed. Enough to build an entire prison at Sing Sing. Five stories high, one thousand cells. Built by inmates, you know."

That, evidently, piqued the interest of the gentleman in front of the man speaking.

"Do you work for the railroad?" He threw the inquiry over the back of his seat.

The man laughed. "No, sir; no, I don't."

"You sound like a travel guide, that's all."

"Well, I could tell you a thing or two about the places we've passed, that's for sure."

He prattled on, talking mostly about Sing Sing. Meg couldn't help but listen, even if she'd wished otherwise. There was no other noise in the train car, and she hadn't thought to bring a book for diversion. By the time the track entered the tunnels beneath the prison's yard, she, along with anyone else who might never have traveled this far on the line before, knew what to expect.

The travelogue continued as the man talked about the aqueduct at Croton, but it was the name that piqued Meg's interest. Croton . . . she wanted the stop after that one.

Despite her best effort at cool confidence, when the conductor announced Peekskill, Meg's pulse fluttered with excitement. She was almost there, where her father never wanted her to visit.

Without looking at the man who'd shared so much information about the route, Meg found her way to the vestibule. But as she waited for the conductor to open the door and lay out the step, the very man she'd been ignoring stepped past her and offered a hand down to the platform.

"Thank you," she said but neither took his hand nor looked his way. Between her own stiff limbs from sitting still so long and an effort to avoid him, she nearly stumbled—yet that was preferable to sending a message she had no wish to issue. She gripped her bag and reticule, confident she could take care of herself.

Meg walked toward the station office to inquire about hiring a driver to take her to the address she'd been given.

"Going to the Davenport funeral?"

Meg nodded at the man emerging from the ticket office; he wore a sturdy cloth apron and a leather visor, which he tipped her way.

"Needn't hire a driver, miss." He pointed to the end of the platform. "See there? A carriage is just around the corner, here at every arrival from the city and meets every departure back. They'll see you safely on your way, and without charge."

Meg followed his gaze, spotting a matched pair of horses that were no doubt hooked to a carriage behind them.

"Thank you," she said.

"Anything else I can help you with? Carry your bag for you?"

"No thank you."

"My condolences, miss." Then he turned to greet others from the train.

Meg stepped forward in time to fall in line with the talkative man in purple. Only now he was strangely quiet, walking beside a stout man even older than he. The other man was dressed finely from a silk-ribboned top hat to white spats on his dark leather shoes, carrying a shiny black walking stick in his gloved hands.

By the time they all stopped beside the waiting carriage, Meg's heart settled somewhere around her waist. It was obvious they were headed in the same direction, and she could avoid looking at them no longer.

"Good day," she said.

The talkative man removed his pith helmet, then bowed, revealing a balding head. He nudged the older man at his side. "Didn't I tell you, Brewster?"

The man he'd addressed as Brewster looked mildly perturbed—though not surprised—at the elbow the other had used. He tipped his own hat Meg's way. "Will you be accompanying us to the Davenport wake, miss?"

She reluctantly raised her gaze to meet the inquiry, only to see his eyes momentarily widen.

"You needn't answer, my dear," the older man said softly. "Surely you must be his daughter. I'd begun to believe you were nothing more than a figment of John Davenport's renowned imagination, but now I see it's true."

"Just as I told him." The purple-decked man winked. "I spotted you right off, which is why I kept an eye on you on the train. We knew your father." He put a hand over his heart. "Loved him like a brother."

Meg shifted the grip on her bag's latch from one hand to two, so neither hand would tremble and she would not have to offer the contact of a handshake. "You knew my father well, then?"

"Of course," Brewster said. "He was one of my closest advisers."

"Take your bag, miss?"

Meg started at the question, issued from so close by. She hadn't seen the driver alight from the box seat atop the carriage to stand before her, palm outstretched. She handed him her bag, which he placed on the driver's seat before offering to help her into the open-sided carriage. There was no need to pull out a step; the carriage was nearly level with the platform.

Meg settled herself inside, taking the side facing forward. It wasn't long before they were all seated, the train now chugging away while the carriage driver urged the horses on in the opposite direction.

Brewster smiled from the seat directly across. "Permit me to formally introduce myself. My name is Alwinus Brewster, and it's my great pleasure to meet you at last, Miss Meggie Davenport."

The other held out his hand. "And I'm Jamie. Just that, just Jamie."

She took his hand. "You were very . . . informative on the train."

He nodded. "I try to make time go faster, and the only way I've ever done it is by talking. Have you ever tried it, miss? You were sure quiet on the train."

"Pardon my companion, Miss Davenport." She noticed Brewster shift the tip of his cane to place it on the other man's foot. "Youth can no longer be his excuse, I'm afraid. He's never been very bright."

"He certainly knew a lot about the route."

"Yes, he can memorize facts and dates, but when it comes to the subtleties of society, I'm afraid he's at a distinct disadvantage. My apologies if he is disrespecting your grief. Such a shame about your dear father. We all thought him robust as a horse. But who can tell what havoc life causes a body? Particularly the life your father lived."

She wanted to ask what he meant but knew she couldn't. What kind of daughter didn't know the havoc her father faced, if others such as this man knew? She wouldn't have him thinking her lack of knowledge about John Davenport was her doing. The blame for that rested entirely upon her father.

"He did love the risks, didn't he?" Jamie said. "I recall the time he placed five hundred dollars on a horse over at Jerome Park. Five hundred! But don't you know, he won. Walked away with more money in his pocket that day than I'd made pinching in a year."

He stopped abruptly, evidently because of the pressure put on his foot by Brewster's cane.

Meg offered a tight smile and diverted her gaze from them both. While it might be admirable that Jamie pinched to save his money, she wondered if that was how her father amassed so much of his own.

But in spite of the censuring thoughts she'd been thoroughly trained to have, a sudden and unbidden excitement erupted at the thought of gambling. What would it feel like to hand over five hundred—five *hundred*—dollars, just like that? And then to have a thousand, or even many times that, returned? What must it be like to have the freedom to do something so foolish and have it rewarded anyway?

She looked out the side of the carriage as they passed through the town of Peekskill, where a row of awnings shaded various businesses and restaurants. It wasn't the money that seemed so appealing; rather it was the risk. What must taking such a risk feel like?

Habit told her to force such thoughts away. A person could hardly prevent thoughts introduced by others; it was what one did with such thoughts that proved to be improper or not. And dwelling on whatever exhilaration gambling might offer was decidedly not proper.

Mr. Brewster, opposite her, had stopped talking altogether yet kept the cane on his companion's foot. He seemed to sense her lack of interest in conversation, but she knew he'd misunderstood the reason entirely. Let them think grief gave her leave for rudeness, when it was really no more than ignorance about her father and his life. Soon the only thing she heard inside the carriage was her own gurgling stomach.

Beyond the town, houses spread out to green landscape, and she soon realized how remote her father's home must be. She refused to reveal either uncertainty or fear, even when it had been several long minutes since she'd seen a house or gate, and ruts and potholes began to pock the road.

When at last the carriage turned onto a private lane, dense trees on either side prevented much study of the land. She guessed only that the terrain led somewhat upward. Then the trees parted to a final curl in the lane, revealing the house at last. The mansard-style roof gave away the mansion's age as neither new nor old. With its three-story size it could easily have earned a place along Fifth Avenue in New York, but because it was here—far more secluded than "cottages" in such places as Newport or even Yonkers—she wondered what her father had been thinking when he'd purchased it.

But mostly she wondered why he'd never wanted her here. Certainly there had been more than enough room for her.

Only one other carriage was visible in front of the prominent entryway. A laurel wreath hung on the front door, warning visitors death had come to this home. So it was the porch just to its left that seemed most inviting. Iron chairs, a table—and, just now, a cluster of people watching the carriage approach.

Meg wasn't sure who spotted whom first. She wasn't sure what drew her eye to him; he wasn't much taller than any of the others, and his clothing unremarkable. A standard three-piece suit, dark as the occasion called for. Perhaps it was his hair: thick and black, neither straight nor curly but something in between, clean but not neat or oiled, and a bit too long.

He stepped off the porch to greet the carriage, and once his gaze met hers, it stayed. With eyes the exact color of blue she'd always preferred over the color she had: not the shallow, pale blue of morning sky, but rather that of a sunset, dark and endless, unfathomable.

Ian Maguire.

Immediately she wished she didn't find him attractive; she knew the weakness a pleasing face could inspire in others and wanted no such thing to touch her, especially regarding him.

The carriage driver reached Meg before Maguire could, for which she was grateful. She knew he would have offered her a hand, and she wasn't sure she would have taken it.

"Meggie!" The welcome in his voice told her he was oblivious to her stiffness. As soon as she reached the ground, he took both of her hands. His delight was clear, although on such an occasion she thought she wasn't the only one who might think his happiness odd.

"Mr. Maguire." She tried pulling her hands away, but he held fast.

Then the shadows behind her drew Maguire's gaze, as well as an immediate frown from his handsome face. He freed her hands at last but didn't free her altogether. Instead, he looped one of her hands over his forearm and stood slightly in front of her as if to separate her from the two she'd arrived with.

"Brewster. Jamie." No further formalities were exchanged, from either end. "You'll allow Miss Davenport to go in first, won't you? For a visit alone with her father?"

"Of course, of course," Brewster said. He tipped his hat at Meg. "It was a pleasure meeting you, Miss Davenport, and sharing the ride."

"Thank you."

Maguire was already leading her away, placing his own hand over hers on his arm. "This way, Meggie."

She wished he wouldn't call her that. She'd hated it on her father's lips, and it felt even more unfitting from this man. So friendly, so intimate.

Meg had little time to assess the others still on the porch, beyond a vague recognition that only one woman stood among them. Even the servant with a beverage tray was male.

It occurred to her as she followed Maguire that this was the first time in her life she'd been in attendance at an event in which she, as a girl or as a woman, was in the minority. The sound of men's voices seemed so unfamiliar to her, so foreign and almost exotic.

The arched entryway led into a long hall. To the right was a glass door that would open to the porch she'd noticed. On the left was another door, this one closed; it was tall with insets carved like a basket. The rest of the hall was a mix of marble flooring and dark wood paneling that widened at a central rotunda.

At the far side of the rotunda's curve, Maguire led her to a large, empty room that would probably serve as a ballroom during more festive occasions. There were a few chairs set up near a large fireplace on the outermost wall, between two tall, open windows. Flowers were arrayed in front of them, perhaps to disperse their aroma upon any breeze in hopes of dispelling the scent of death that met her. Because there, on another far wall, was a table skirted in dark purple with a coffin on top.

Her father.

Maguire let go of her hand and stood nearby like a submissive schoolboy. His watery gaze caught hers. Meg looked away, the void in her heart a stark contrast to the sorrow she saw in him. She sucked in a breath of the perfumed air and stood as tall as her five-foot frame allowed, then approached the body for her farewell.

His face looked strange to her, not at all as handsome as he'd been in life. She'd never seen him in repose but doubted this was how he'd looked even then. His jaw was oddly set, his pallor appalling. She'd only ever seen him in the school parlor—once or twice a year, sitting stiffly, always igniting a single question in her, one she'd never asked aloud: Why had he bothered to visit?

She wanted to ask him that now, demand to know why he hadn't just sent the money to school without ever coming to see her. It was obvious he'd never had any affection for her, had probably never approved of her at all. If he had, wouldn't he at least have wanted her company?

Her hollow stomach lurched, and she thought she might be sick. Surely it was only the smell, not just from her father but from the pungent flowers surrounding him. Scents so strong she suddenly wasn't sure she could enjoy her expansive gardens at school ever, ever again.

And then everything went blank.

5

The true lady represents both beauty and health. It is not
uncommon, however, for even the healthiest of young ladies
to swoon. Swooning should never be used to demand attention
or stir unnecessary sympathies.

Madame Marisse's Handbook for Young Ladies

IAN KNELT AND scooped Meg's head into his lap. Then he lifted her
altogether and crossed the room, passing the flowers and the windows and fireplace, reaching the three-story rotunda in the very
heart of his home. He passed to the other side, knowing the library
and billiard room were unoccupied but opting instead to take her
upstairs. There were six rooms up there, only half of which were
comfortably furnished and only one of which he absolutely could
not take her to—it was, in fact, kept locked at all times.

But rather than taking her to John's room—there was something repugnant in the idea of laying her on the bed in which her
father had so recently died—he took her to his own room. It was
the largest, after all, even larger than the guest room her father
had used.

He'd forgotten he'd shut Roscoe in there, who greeted them
with a wagging tail. Ian ignored him, settling Meggie on the bed
and shooing the dog away when he tried taking a place next to her.

Ian poured a glass of water from the pitcher at his bedside. "Meggie?"

She seemed half-conscious, offering him only a little moan in response.

"Would you like a drink? Water?"

She turned away, eyes still closed, forehead puckered in a frown.

Roscoe squeezed closer, shoving aside Ian's arm and nearly causing him to spill the glass of water. He replaced the glass, then reached for the dog, who was busy getting to know Meggie by pressing his nose directly in her face with a friendly lick.

"Oh! Oh!" Meggie sat up, brushing a hand over her cheek.

Ian hauled Roscoe away, wishing he'd had the heart to train him better. He told the dog to sit but knew the animal had no idea what such an order meant. "This is Roscoe. He's harmless."

"Dogs," she said, "are made for the out-of-doors."

He offered no argument, although he quite firmly disagreed. "I'm sure you're right about that." He held the dog back when Roscoe made another attempt to acquaint himself with this new visitor on the bed he so often shared with Ian. "But today he'd be more of a nuisance, with all the guests in and out."

"Has he no chain, no shed?"

Ian eyed her. How could Meggie not like dogs, when it was her father who'd taught him they were the only living things that could really be trusted?

"He's a barker . . . well, unless he's comfortable, that is. And he's comfortable here."

She looked around for the first time. He took in the room too, trying to see it as she might. The heavy drapes were closed, but light seeped around the edges, providing a dim view. She was surrounded by plenty of down-filled blankets he kept handy, even now when the days were warm. His wardrobe, which he'd forgotten to close, stood off to the side. It held all his clothes, neatly hung. Beyond that was the open door to his bathroom, and he wondered if she was impressed by such a modern convenience. Surely she could see the parquet flooring and the towel he'd forgotten to rehang; it was draped on the side of the polished mahogany frame surrounding the porcelain tub. He followed her gaze around the rest of the room, to the desk between the two windows, full of records Ian shared with no one. Opposite that was the fireplace, and above that the landscape oil that had been left behind by the former owner of the house.

He thought the place neat enough, especially considering he hadn't expected any company.

"Is this my father's room?"

He shook his head.

"Yours?"

No sooner had he nodded than she swung her feet to the floor, inviting Roscoe to lurch forward. Ian held him back again.

"This is quite a large room for a secondary," she said, but when she tried standing, she must have done so too quickly because she sank back down to the blanket as if dizzy.

"Look, you're obviously overwrought. Can I get you something? A sandwich? Perhaps it would help to eat something."

Meg nodded. "Yes. I'm afraid my head is still spinning, but this room—you, being here—isn't helping in the least. Could you send up a maid with something light? I'm afraid in my haste to arrive, I forgot to eat."

Ian understood a lack of appetite; he'd barely eaten anything himself since finding John the day before.

He led Roscoe away, though Roscoe clearly didn't want to leave the newcomer and cried when Ian grabbed him by the scruff and made sure he followed. He put the dog in another room—the guest room John had used—and went in search of someone in the kitchen.

Apart from the blanket offering the faint scent of an animal, the room was quite pleasant. Too dark for Meg's taste, of course, but with the little light illuminating it, she could see the wallpaper was fine quality, complementing the design in the velvet curtains. She used the bathroom, noting that it was decorated tastefully too, if a bit stark. Other than the tile, it was plain and lacked any hint of the toiletries she was so used to seeing: bottles, oils, perfumes, various size mirrors, and so on. This one offered a single mirror on the wall, a cup for soapy cream, a discarded blade for shaving, tooth powder and brush.

Back in the bedroom, she opened one of the drapes. The house, as she suspected, was on something of a hill. In the distance she saw the river beyond a multitude of green trees. The yard was nearly barren but for hardy grass, and she couldn't see the porch at all from this angle.

She supposed it wasn't odd that Maguire would have such a large room here, in her father's home. He'd been the son her father never had. She turned to look at the room again. *This might have been my room, had I been a boy.*

"Meggie?"

She turned at the gentle voice, seeing a woman entering with a covered tray, a small cup and teapot rattling on the edge. But she was no servant; she was the woman Meg had spotted on the porch, properly dressed in black.

She was lovely, Meg noticed as she neared. Perhaps a bit old to be Maguire's wife, but she didn't look the right age to be his mother, either. A sister? Yet there was no family resemblance at all.

"My name is Kate, and I've brought you a little something to eat. Are you comfortable here at the desk, or would you like to move elsewhere?"

"Is there another place I can go where I won't have to see anyone else?"

Kate nodded, leading back over the threshold, tray still in hand. She went to the opposite end of the hallway, around the hollow rotunda, to a small room where sunlight beckoned from a dazzlingly bright sunporch. It overlooked a considerable segment of the outlying countryside, past the trees surrounding the house, to the river beyond.

Settling the tray on a table between two comfortable chairs, the older woman invited Meg to sit as she stacked a couple of books out of the way. The tea was tepid but tasty. Meg couldn't tell if it was hunger or if the food truly was exceptional, but she quickly ate the lobster salad and chicken pie. She would have preferred eating alone, but the woman lingered nearby, pushing open one of the windows—it was on a hinge like a miniature door—then peering out. After a while she withdrew a handkerchief from her sleeve, one Meg noticed was incongruously red.

Meg heard voices from below. Male voices again, somber. She couldn't hear well enough to tell what they said, but it made her pause just the same.

"How well did you know my father?"

Kate dabbed one eye, then left the window for the seat nearest Meg. There were circles around her golden-brown eyes, and though her matching golden-brown hair was swept up in a chignon, it looked as though she hadn't taken much care in the styling of it.

"We were to be married this week."

"Oh!" Meg's fork slipped from her hand, falling with a clatter to the porcelain plate in her lap. The news effectively killed what little appetite she had left. Meg put the remainder aside, letting it sit on the table between them. She lifted the teacup instead, because having her hands suddenly free only reminded her of her awkwardness. "Then you must be far more saddened by his death than I. You must also know that my father and I hardly knew one another."

One of Kate's arched brows rose. "I believe he knew you very well, Meggie. He loved you so much and was proud—"

Meg replaced the teacup with a clank and stood, taking the place Kate had left vacant at the open window. From here she could almost make out the conversation rather than just a deep-pitched rumble from below.

"If you think it'll somehow make me feel better to hear such words, Miss . . . What did you say your name was? Miss Kate . . . ?"

"Katherine Kane, but please just call me Kate."

Meg started to, but the friendly acknowledgment died before reaching her lips. "I barely knew my father, and I see no reason for you to pretend he knew anything about me."

"But it's no pretense!" Kate stood, approaching Meg. "He knew everything about you, Meggie. Simply everything! How you excelled at your studies from spelling to botany—imagine that, botany! I didn't even know what it was until your father told me. He also knew that you couldn't be beaten at tennis, and that when Lady White-Somerset-Stewart visited Madame Marisse from England and was asked to name a Harvest Princess, she chose *you*. Awarded to the girl who best combined all the qualities of a lady." She pressed the red handkerchief to her nose, eyes closing momentarily before gazing at Meg once again. "He even attended several of your chamber music concerts at the school."

To busy herself, Meg returned to her chair and took up the tea again. She didn't want to believe Kate, but how could she not? Why would she lie, and how else could she know about some of those things?

"He attended my concerts? But he never, *ever* came to see me—"

"Did you or did you not find a yellow rose in your viola case after several performances?"

"Left by Madame or one of the staff . . ." A secret admirer had been her most fervent wish. But her father? Impossible.

Meg set aside the tea again. "If my father attended my concerts, why did he never want to see me? Or talk to me? Only one thing has ever been clear to me: he didn't want me. He chose a surrogate son instead."

"Nothing could be further from the truth."

The statement came from behind them—and from a distinctly male voice. Ian Maguire moved around to stand directly in front of Meg's chair.

"Your father loved nothing more than he loved you. Everything he did, he did for you."

Meg raised half-veiled eyes to him. "And that's why he lived here with you rather than me. Why he left me to be raised in a school."

"Not just any school!" Kate insisted. "Madame Marisse's is one of the finest schools in New England. Anyone schooled there has achieved the pinnacle of society's training."

Meg stared down at her hands, folded firmly—desperately—in her lap. If her fingers didn't cling to each other, she was sure they'd be trembling.

"Look at yourself, Meggie," Maguire added, his voice little more than a whisper. "You're a lady, just as your father hoped you would become."

She would have stood again, but Maguire hovered so close to her chair that to rise would mean brushing up against him or at least touching him in order to push him away. So she stayed seated, hands clasped even more tightly. "I won't deny my father provided well for me. But loved me? Hardly. Having kept spies around me all my life doesn't speak of love so much as a desire for proof that he was getting his money's worth for my education."

"Oh, Meggie," Kate sighed. "There are so many things about your father you don't know. The things he did to provide so well for you—"

"What you need to know, Meggie," Maguire cut in, "is that your father loved you. Take it from us, who knew him best."

She smiled tightly. "That's rather hard to believe, Mr. Maguire, given my father's history with me—or lack thereof."

"But you're here," Kate said. "Surely you mourn his passing?"

Meg held Kate's gaze. "I came to see if I might like him better dead than alive. And I find I don't, after all."

Cruel words, especially spoken before two people who obviously *did* love him. But seeing this house, hearing them say her father was capable of loving someone, only made his absence from her life that much worse. So Meg didn't regret her words, even as Kate's eyes widened in horror and Maguire's brows gathered in concern.

"There is something you should know," Kate said.

"Yes." Maguire spoke, though Kate appeared to have wanted to continue. "Your father's greatest hope was that once you finished school, you would be happy to remain there until choosing to marry one of the young men you met through the school's social events. He hoped your life at school would have provided the foundation you needed for a proper, happy life."

Return to school. Return to school. It was all she ever heard!

Suddenly the next step in her future became startlingly clear. What reason did she have to return to school? To spend another summer with the Hibbit sisters and reduced staff? No other student lived there year-round, the way Meg had ever since she could remember. Even if Meg's future remained the same as it had been two days ago, even if she eventually joined the staff at Madame

Marisse's the way she'd always expected to, there was absolutely no reason to hurry back.

"I'm sure you do have your choice of suitors," Maguire went on.

"Without a family to present me properly? I don't think you understand the circle that frequents Madame's." Meg looked past Maguire and Kate, her gaze taking in the sunporch and, beyond, the view outside again. There was no reason she couldn't spend the summer *here*. It was her father's home; therefore she had some right to it. Didn't she? "Pedigree is nearly as important as money." As she spoke, her mind formulated plans having nothing to do with the conversation. "Sometimes it doesn't have to be an old pedigree, but one's family mustn't be a mystery."

"Madame Marisse assured your father there were eligible gentlemen vying for your attention, even two years ago—"

This time Meg herself interrupted Kate. "There is no reason to begin that future immediately. No one is waiting for me, and I have no wish for anyone in particular to be waiting for me."

"But that's where your life is, Meggie," Maguire said in that same soft, somehow disconcertingly gentle voice. "Everything you know is there. Where else could you possibly go?" He bent over her and slipped his hand under her elbow to help her rise. "I can see you're feeling better, so you might want to visit your father again. After that I'll take you to the train myself and accompany you back to the school. Because—" his dark-blue gaze held hers— "that's what your father would have wanted, and it's my desire to do exactly as he would have regarding you."

She stood but pulled her arm from his light grasp. "While I would appreciate it if you'd take me back to my father's side, I must tell you I have no intention of returning to Connecticut today. At the moment my plans are indefinite." Coward! Why hadn't she told them what she meant to do?

Their astonished stares nearly made her stomp her foot,

demand to know why she should do anything they wished. She was eighteen years old and could go where *she* wished. And what was so outrageous in wanting to spend time in her father's home, anyway? To be in her father's life—even if he was no longer here? Especially since he wasn't here to say no?

"Listen to me, Meggie." Maguire leaned toward her, once again too close. "I can't let you leave without knowing exactly where you intend to go."

She stepped around him, not caring that her shoulder brushed his in order to get to the door. "You have nothing to worry over, Mr. Maguire. I intend staying right here in my father's house. It must be mine now, anyway."

6

It was important to me that my lawyer—and through him, the jury—knew I was not just a thief. I was every bit a gentleman as well.

ALEXANDER "THE GENT" DIBATTISTA
Incarcerated for fraud and bank robbery
Code of Thieves, compiled from interviews of temporary
residents of Tombs Prison, New York City, 1873-1875

"MEGGIE!"

The entreaty came from Kate, but it was Ian who caught up with Meggie first, in only two long strides. At that moment he wasn't sure if he felt admiration or exasperation. Irritation, at least. Meggie was the prize of John's heart, the symbol of everything fine and worthy and precious. Here was someone to be protected at any cost—protected from the harshness of life. From the truth.

But as much as he might have unwittingly wanted her here, she was turning out to be a nuisance. She'd become the beautiful young woman he'd once dreamed she would be, with eyes he was sure were even bluer than John's and hair as dark as licorice. But she shouldn't be here. She should have stayed in Connecticut, being a good little girl at school, learning all she needed to know so she might one day become the grand lady with a respectable future John had always envisioned.

He should tell her the truth, at least some of it. He knew Kate would if he didn't. He stood in front of Meggie, effectively blocking her path.

"This house isn't your father's, Meggie. It's mine."

Meggie looked at him, brows now raised over those two blue pools. She looked from him to Kate, then back again with something he'd never expected to see in her eyes. Suspicion.

"Yours? Entirely?"

He nodded and saw that Kate did the same. For once, he and Kate seemed to be united.

"Did he . . . leave it to you, then? Instead of to me?"

Kate took one of Meggie's hands, something Ian wished he'd thought to do first. "Ian bought this house nearly a year ago. Your father lived in the city, with me."

"How . . . convenient," Meggie whispered. Then she took in a breath, her petite shoulders rising as if in determination not to change her ridiculous plans. "I'll go to the city, then, at least for a few days. I'd like to see where he lived."

She looked uncertain, and Ian thought that a good sign. Perhaps she wasn't nearly as determined as he'd feared. Besides, so long as Kate didn't invite Meggie into the dregs of John's life, she would never be the wiser to how he'd lived.

"New York isn't the place for you, Meggie," Ian said. "Your father would have preferred you to stay in the clean country air of Connecticut. At school."

He took Meggie's arm again, this time looping it through the crook of his, relieved when she didn't resist him. He'd dreamed often enough of having her beside him, and for the moment he intended to enjoy it. He even put one of his hands over her soft one, as if the one that rested beneath his was there by her design rather than his own.

Her skin was as inviting as he had imagined it to be. Ian had always known she would be beautiful—he'd known since she was nine years old that she'd grow up to be lovely. But when she was older and he and John had secretly attended several of her chamber music concerts, he'd gotten a good look at just how beautiful she'd grown to be.

It had been John's idea to leave a yellow rose backstage, but it had been Ian who'd always left it for her. Inside the instrument case with her name on it, or in the little cubbyhole where it was stored, so he knew he'd left it somewhere she could find it.

Downstairs, Ian kept a close eye on Meggie as he delivered her once again to the ballroom, where her father was laid out. He and Kate waited with her until the room cleared—a new mourner had arrived whom Ian recognized instantly as one of Brewster's younger brothers. Then Ian escorted Meggie closer while tipping his chin Kate's way.

He knew she understood: leave Meggie alone, but make sure no one else interrupts. She walked from the room.

"Will you be all right, Meggie?" He used the same gentle tone he summoned when feeding meat to ill-trained guard dogs in order to slip past them. "I'll stay if you like."

She shook her head without looking at him, then left for the table upon which her father lay.

Ian wanted to stay but knew he shouldn't. Not only for her sake, but also because of those waiting on the veranda. He followed the path Kate had taken a moment before.

Most of the mourners would miss the man they affectionately called Skipjack, but Ian also knew a number of them had already begun assessing things, before John's body was either cold or buried. They were looking between Ian himself and Brewster, as if wondering which of them would take the role Skipjack had left vacant.

Ian was determined that man would be him, and it was none too soon to start making that clear. Letting Brewster take the reins of the men he'd worked with so many years would lead down a path Ian had no wish to travel. It had been John who restrained Brewster more than once, away from excess, from violence. Crime was one thing, John used to say, greed another. And while Ian couldn't claim himself free of avarice, he'd never once been impressed by Brewster's willingness to let force take the place of clever and careful planning.

In the hall, Kate stopped him.

"I'd like a word with you before you go outside." Her voice was low but with a hint of urgency. Fine. He had a few things he wanted to say to her too. Things that probably couldn't wait.

Chin high, eyes defiant, Kate stared at him a full moment as if in preamble to whatever she was about to say. "I want Meggie to come to the city with me, and I don't want you to interfere."

Ian looked over his shoulder to make sure the words hadn't been overheard before taking one of Kate's arms, nearly pushing her into the library. "Are you insane? The last thing John wanted was for Meggie to know about him, and if you think you can keep the truth from her and be a friend at the same time, you're deluding yourself."

Kate was already shaking her head. "You heard her, Ian! She doesn't believe he loved her. Maybe the only way she *will* believe it is if we tell her the truth."

"No! We'll do it John's way, the way he's always handled his daughter. That was his decision, not ours."

"But she must be told of the risks he took, the sacrifices he made—and his intention to make the best of his legitimate investments. As soon as he was able, he was going to invite her into his life, just as she's obviously always wanted."

That was news to Ian. Not that John hadn't hinted at going clean—his living here at Ian's for the last few months before intending to marry Kate had been evidence enough of that. It had been a move that stirred unexpected thoughts in Ian's own life—of his father and how he'd have wanted Ian to do the same had he still been alive.

But it didn't matter. John hadn't been allowed the time to prove his good intentions, and all that was left was evidence of the kind of man he'd always been. The kind not good enough to be a lady's father.

The kind of man Ian was too.

"It's out of the question," he said. "I won't have it."

"*You* won't! Who do you think you are, anyway? Have you assigned yourself John's role before he's even buried?"

Ian put his face directly before Kate's, reveling in the moment when doubt took the place of her anger. "It's me or Brewster. And you don't want him telling everyone what to do, do you?"

Her eyes narrowed and her mouth tightened, the intimidation he'd stirred a moment ago quickly fading. "He *won't* be telling me what to do, nor will you. John was hanging up the Skipjack name; you know it as well as I do. It was the Skipjack way of life that killed him."

"A way of life you were happy enough to live for more years than I have."

"To my everlasting regret, yes. And to John's, too. He was going straight, Ian. You can't deny it."

"Going, perhaps, but never gone."

Kate's face softened, and now it was her turn to lean forward. "It can't possibly do any harm for her to know. She already thinks badly of him. It can only help."

"No. She goes back to the school. I'll see to that myself. Today."

Then he turned his back on her, walking from the room with only one destination in mind. As much as he wanted to return to Meggie, he knew he couldn't ignore much longer those who stood on the porch. Even now, Brewster was no doubt campaigning for the confidence of men Ian couldn't afford to lose.

Meg stood over her father's body, no longer dizzy. For the first time she saw something familiar in him. Most of his face—the odd set to his jaw, the lifeless curve of his brow, the sallow color of his skin—belonged to someone, something, else. But his nose was the same, perfectly centered, neither too large nor too small. It was his, all right. Unchanged.

"It doesn't matter what they said about you loving me," Meg whispered. She'd once convinced herself she'd outgrown her need for a father, but somehow seeing him this way reminded her of what she'd missed, and it pierced her soul.

It was too late for him to hear what she had to say, but words spilled from an overfilled fountain deep inside. "I wanted so little from you, things you could never give. Never once did you *tell* me you loved me or that you were proud of me. Did you think the money would say it for you? I'd rather have had the words."

She wanted to touch him, his hands that were so peacefully folded across his chest. The single memory she had before living at the school was of him tossing her up into the air, catching her safely in his strong arms with those same hands. Where had that father gone, the one who'd rejoiced in having a daughter? What had she done to make him shut her away?

She took a step back, still facing him, words she'd wanted to say for years now refusing to be stifled. "I'm finished being that perfect student, that perfect young lady. There's no hope of pleasing you now, so I might as well do as *I* please. At last."

Meg turned away, shoulders so stiff they ached. Without looking back, she walked from his side, so fast and firm that the heels on her shoes tapped against the floor, no doubt hard enough to nick the wood.

But she made it no farther than halfway across the room. It was as if her father called to her, using words Maguire and Kate had just spoken. He knew about her studies; he knew about her being Harvest Princess. He'd left the roses.

"Why?"

She hadn't realized she'd nearly screamed the word until it came back to her in an echo.

Meg fell into one of the nearby chairs, and tears pricked her eyes—tears that made way for the torrent that followed.

She didn't hear the light footsteps behind her until the edge of Kate's skirt came into view. Perhaps Meg should resent this woman who'd been allowed to share her father's life—at least as much as she resented Maguire—but when Kate took the seat next to Meg, drawing her into a gentle embrace, any desire to feel that resentment dwindled away.

"I wanted him to love me." Her voice, garbled with tears, was barely recognizable even to Meg herself.

"Shh, now. He did, Meggie." Meg felt Kate stroke her hair as if she were a child. "He loved you, and I can prove it to you."

Her words penetrated Meg's tears, slowing the spigot inside.

"You can't." Meg wiped her eyes with a handkerchief Kate supplied. This handkerchief was black, although a red one still peeked out from Kate's pocket. "I don't care if he knew every last thing I did. Nothing could convince me he loved me. It's too late, don't you see?"

With a glance over Meg's shoulder as if to make sure they were alone, Kate shook her head. "John didn't think himself worthy to be your father." Kate looked at the table now, at the box holding Meg's father. The older woman seemed to fossilize before Meg as a frown set premature creases into place. "I suppose you already believe him unworthy, but that wasn't his intention."

Meg spared only a glance her father's way. "He never gave me the chance to see if he was unworthy or not! His absence proves. he wasn't a good father."

"He was a better father than you think, considering how he made his living. You cannot discount his protection of you."

"Protection from what? I know about the gambling, Miss Kane. Jamie mentioned it in the carriage. And while I'm sure a number of families sending their daughters to Madame Marisse's would have been scandalized to learn such a thing about him, it's hardly an illegal way to make a living. That was no reason to banish me from his life."

"You were to be raised a lady, like your mother. Someone he never thought himself worthy of, either, really. You never knew, Meggie, that she was from London, did you? The daughter of a gentleman, and your father wanted you to be just like her. He knew he couldn't raise you properly, so he found the finest school in all of New England to do it for him. All he needed to do was supply the money, and he did."

"And so he gambled. Is that all?"

Kate looked from Meg to her father, then to the door that led from the room. The hesitation lasted long enough to make Meg wonder if whatever she had to say was the truth or just being made up for Meg's benefit.

"His fortunes are . . . complicated, Meggie. They came from various sources." She caught and held Meg's gaze. "Not a single one, at least initially, was legal."

Meg nearly laughed. "What are you saying? That he was a thief?"

Kate nodded.

"That *is* what you're saying? He was . . . he *was* a thief?"

"Shh! Keep your voice down. He never wanted you to know—"

"And I doubt he can hear you now."

"No, but Ian might, and he didn't want me to tell you the truth. If it's the only way to bring you some kind of peace with your father's memory, then so be it. Your father wasn't proud of the things he did, but it was the only thing he knew how to do and he did it well. You don't remember—how could you?—when he partnered with his old friend Brewster. They conned their first mark together. It came too easily to both of them, but especially to your father because people have always been eager to trust him. With Brewster's help, your father made enough money to present himself as a gentleman and pay Madame Marisse to keep you for years. He never stopped working. He had to earn enough to keep you there."

The words swirled in Meg's head until they made no sense at all. Her father with the smiling, guileless blue eyes . . . a thief.

She would have stood, paced, moved to relieve some of the nervous energy building inside her, but she had been left without a trace of strength. Her hand smoothed a small wrinkle on her gown, a gown made of the finest black silk money could buy.

Purchased with money stolen from someone else.

Something in her throat stabbed at her painfully—gall, anger. Shame.

But just as instantly, another moment of realization exploded inside her. So much made sense now. No wonder she'd always lusted after what she should not have—not material things, but things outside the rules, freedom to do as she pleased. No wonder she'd had to stuff aside every rebellious thought, eke out the perfect behavior expected of her. Rebellion was in her blood! She was more her father's daughter than her mother's, after all.

"How exactly did he get that money, then? What kind of 'marks,' as you call them?" Were people suffering because of her? Had he stolen from others who'd had to do without just so she could live a pampered life?

"I don't think he would've wanted you to know details, Meggie. Just know that he had a reason to keep his life separate—and a secret—from you."

Meg shook her head. "I need to know, Miss Kane. I need to know who he stole from, if he left anyone in desperate circumstances—because of me!"

"Oh! No! No, no, Meggie, not at all. Your father was the kindest, most generous man I've ever known. He was more apt to give to someone in need than take, believe me!"

"I'm sure whoever he stole from wouldn't think so highly of him."

"He only outsmarted people who could well afford to lose. He's never even had a warrant out for his arrest, he was so careful."

Another realization. "Is that why he refused to be seen at any of my concerts?" Meg whispered. "Because he cheated some of the same families I went to school with? Is that why he chose that school—because of the many *marks* connected to it?"

"Never intentionally, my dear. He wouldn't have wanted it to touch you in any way. There was only one family from your school he might have risked targeting, but he never had the opportunity."

"Which family was that?"

"It doesn't matter, does it? I hardly remember, anyway. The fact is your father loved you. Surely you believe that now?"

Meg sighed. "I don't know what to believe. I might have thought him an incompetent father, but at least I thought him an honest one." That uncertain sigh was chased by a gasp. "You do know what this means, don't you? If I thought I had few marital options before, they've narrowed all the more with what you say. What sort of future have I, except one my father forbade me to have? And, oh! If only I'd known all these years what a liability I've been to Madame Marisse's. A whisper of this could mean the end of the school's reputation. And it would be my fault!"

She stood, anger fueling her now, and stared at her father's body. "No! Not mine. It would all be *your* fault! How could you?"

The path to the scaffold can be approached from many angles.
General poaching, pickpocketing, impersonation of another with
the sole purpose of stealing his pension are just a few crimes that,
along with murder itself, demand the death penalty.

An Informal Look at the Penal Codes of London and
  New England

Ian set his gaze on Brewster. Upon Brewster's arrival, there had
been a gradual but noticeable shift, as if by unspoken request the
men took literal sides on the porch. One half was filled with men
who sided with Brewster, the other with men behind Ian himself.

He wondered if anyone else noticed that those who sided with
Ian were the ones he knew still possessed a heart.

"Skipjack never had a part in the venture I'm planning," Ian
began.

"Then perhaps you ought to run the plans by me," Brewster
said, "if Skipjack didn't have an eye on them."

"I don't think that's necessary." The words rippled in the silence
from one end of the veranda to the other.

"So it's come to this already, has it?" The brogue Brewster took
such pains to hide in the city sometimes showed itself among them.
"The pooka wants to be me new partner; is that how it is now?"

Ian refused to be irritated by the reference to childish stories of mischievous Irish fairies. Age had nothing to do with competence. "I have no plans to take Skipjack's place as your partner." Ian took a sip of the drink in his hand. Smooth and watered down to keep his head clear, but whiskey all the same. He'd skipped breakfast and lunch, so there was little left to stand in the whiskey's path to Ian's brain.

"If you've no thought to take his place, then things will remain as they've always been. As such, you might tell me what you have in mind before the doing of it."

"Your partnership with Skipjack is dead, Brewster. It'll be buried with him by this time tomorrow. And I've no plan to take up his half. What I do from now on I do of me own accord. I need no one's approval." Sometimes Ian's own brogue had a way of surfacing.

If anyone so much as swallowed, Ian would have heard it—it was that quiet. Even the birds in the nearby wood that a moment ago had whistled and cooed suddenly fell silent.

Brewster swished the drink in his glass, a smooth movement that seemed to say Ian's challenge hardly warranted a reply, let alone a counterchallenge.

"What you do on your own is up to you, Maguire." He consumed the last of what remained in the glass, then neared a table to discard it, bringing him two steps closer to Ian. "But if you do it without my help, you take the risk for yourself. None of my men will be involved—before or after, no matter the outcome. No protection from me. Is that clear to you now?"

Ian's lack of a response said enough.

"I needn't refresh your memory, do I, Ian?" Brewster fairly whispered now that he was nearer. "I could have saved those men, all three of them, had they only come to me before their last attempt."

No, Ian needn't be reminded. The last time a handful of men had decided to break free of Brewster, they'd ended up ambushed by a competing gang; three of them hadn't survived the street battle.

If the reminder was meant as a subtle threat, Ian was willing to call his bluff. Brewster might shed more blood than either Ian or John ever had, but there was no questioning his loyalty to John. Ian was willing to wager Brewster would no more bring him harm than he would Meggie.

There was only one real problem: how many men, without Brewster's protection, would be willing to stray from his control?

Brewster left the porch, going to the carriage that waited for anyone who wanted to be taken back to the station.

As Ian expected, several other men left the porch as well. They wouldn't all fit in the carriage with Brewster, and so they started to walk.

Ian faced those who remained: six. Fewer than he'd hoped, but nothing to scoff at—until he saw that one man was missing upon whom he'd been counting. The cop who played a pivotal role in his plan.

His gaze flew to the retreating men. All he saw was Keys's back.

Ian had to force himself to hold steady his glass. His mind already raced, ineffectively trying to reassure him. There was still time to convince the man back to Ian's way, and convince him he would.

Ian's future depended on it.

8

To hearken one's ear toward a conversation one hasn't been invited to partake in is to prove oneself of the lowest moral character. If such a basic rule of manners might be compromised, what else might one do?

Madame Marisse's Handbook for Young Ladies

MEG SAW MAGUIRE enter the large ballroom from the veranda, once again struck by his looks. His dark hair was in sharp contrast to the vivid blue of his eyes. Eyes so different from hers and her father's, yet striking in their own way for their depth and darkness. And skin so healthy she wondered how it would feel to the touch—his wouldn't be soft like hers, but surely it would not be rough, either.

She snapped her eyes away.

"You'd best allow me to handle telling him our plans," Kate whispered before taking Meg's hand in hers to lead her forward. "But not yet."

Together they met Maguire at the first row of chairs in front of her father's body. "Meggie will of course be staying for the funeral tomorrow afternoon."

Maguire's blue eyes showed a hint of surprise, then a bit of regret. The surprise was so fleeting she couldn't be certain it had been there. He looked from Meg to her father, and once again his sadness was all she could see.

"Very well. Supper will be served soon, if you would like to rest or freshen yourself for that. I'll show you to a room upstairs."

"May I stay in my father's room? Where he stayed while visiting here, that is?" Meg's request surprised even herself. Yet she couldn't deny a stubborn wish to know her father despite his failures, the same force that had brought her here to begin with. Somehow, learning he'd been a thief hadn't quenched her thirst to know what her life might have been like had he allowed her even the slightest place in his.

"If you wish."

"I'll be staying as well, Ian," Kate said, following them from the room. "But I'm sure you can accommodate both of us."

Maguire didn't respond, just walked ahead without looking back. Meg looked at the back of his handsome head, at the way his hair followed a perfect pattern: wavy in some spots, straight in others. Thick and so long that it touched the collars of his shirt and jacket.

Then she realized something she hadn't considered before. He was her father's *partner*, his protégé. That meant he could be only one thing: a thief.

She placed her hand on the wooden railing once they reached the stairs on the other side of the impressive, three-story center hallway. She needed the aid to steady her step.

How could she never have guessed, never even have suspected there was something nefarious in the way her father had withheld information about himself, about their family? Surely Madame Marisse had never suspected, or she wouldn't have jeopardized her school by taking in Meg. Or had her father's charm blinded Madame Marisse so much she didn't care to know the truth?

No wonder Maguire found it easy to follow her father's footsteps. One glance from those eyes and women probably just opened their purse strings, no questions asked. When he stopped at a bedroom door, Meg walked around him, leaving plenty of room, refusing to look into those eyes that had no doubt fooled many women before her.

The room that had been her father's wasn't as large as Maguire's. Still, its accommodations were plush, with a generously sized bed . . . upon which lay that huge, slobbering dog. It greeted them with a whimper as it beat its tail against the bed.

"Off you go, Roscoe," Maguire greeted with a friendly tone. "That's a good boy." Though the dog jumped from the bed, he came immediately to Meg in another attempt to get to know her better. She took a tentative step back, unsure how to act around an animal so large, even one she suspected might be friendly.

Maguire pulled Roscoe away and aimed him at the door. She was pleasantly surprised the dog did as directed, as if eager to be free of the bedroom.

Then Ian turned to Meg. "The bathroom is through that door, and there is another bedroom beyond that. You can stay in there, Kate."

There was no reason for him to linger, yet he did. Rather than following the dog out, Maguire closed the gap between himself and Meg, stopping so close that she took another step back. Could he not tell she wished to keep a respectable distance between them?

He took one of her hands in his. "I think it's all still a bit of a shock to you, Meggie. In time you'll grieve your father properly because you'll realize he was a good man. One who would have welcomed your love above all else."

She pulled her hand from his, wanting to scoff at the pronouncement. A good man! Considering the source of the compliment, she disregarded it altogether.

But even as he walked from the room at last, Meg watched him. All these years she'd been made to follow every rule in existence, while Maguire—at her father's side—had been allowed to break any one he chose.

The fourteen-year-old girl still inside suddenly wished she'd been able to switch places with him, if only for a day.

Ian finished his whiskey, this time undiluted. He shouldn't have poured another, but it was too late now. He stared at John's profile, half-expecting him to sit up and tell Ian the same thing he always said when anyone around him was tempted to drink too much. *No cheating. Life is what you make of it, so don't miss it by getting drunk.*

Surely he'd understand this time, though, and condone the escape Ian needed, if only temporarily. Having Meggie here wasn't helping him with his grief at all; if anything, she made it worse. He'd thought they could mourn John's loss together, but she didn't even miss him! That much had been clear when Ian had looked into her eyes, the same eyes she'd inherited from her father. Ian swore they'd turned as gray as a winter sky when he'd tried coaxing a bit of mourning from her.

He shouldn't be wasting time thinking of her. Instead, he would do as John had always done, at least before Kate and her new faith got to him. Ian would focus on the job at hand.

Dickson, specially employed at the bank for over a month now, fed Ian the information he needed on a regular basis. Floor plan, schedules, security measures, average number of banknotes, and—most importantly—the kind of safe the bank used. An exact replica of which Ian kept in the locked room upstairs right now. The unholy thing had been hard enough to get up there! Ian already knew where Dickson should drill the preliminary holes and was surer than ever he could be in and out in less than seven minutes.

Losing Keys could delay the date of the heist. The targeted

bank was on Keys's beat, and the last thing they needed was a real cop looking out for predawn activity along that stretch of city block. It would take months to get a replacement.

But the job meant more than ever now; Ian couldn't fool himself into thinking otherwise. Nothing less than a quick success would set him free of the threat Brewster posed—not only to claim a portion of any job Ian cared to do, but to call on Ian's talent wherever Brewster thought necessary. Ian couldn't wait months for that freedom.

"Supper, sir."

The pronouncement came from Ian's most trusted servant, standing at the door closest to the dining room. Tupp, who acted as butler, valet, right-hand man, and trusted message runner.

Since Ian didn't employ a single female servant, he took it on himself to go upstairs to let Meggie know dinner would be served.

He knocked softly on her door, wishing he wasn't quite so eager for her to answer. Nothing had changed that boyhood secret hidden in his heart ever since setting eyes on Meggie nearly a decade ago. She hadn't changed either, except to grow lovelier. She was still the image of perfection John had so lovingly placed on a pedestal, right from the start. It had proved impossible not to love her simply because John had.

But the Meggie on that pedestal had been little more than a figment of John's imagination—worse, she'd become a figment of Ian's. Today proved he knew nothing of her and that he would do well not to try knowing her any better.

He tapped again but received no answer. Perhaps she'd fallen asleep. He should go downstairs, instruct the cook to hold dinner until later. But his own stomach—empty but for the whiskey sloshing about—demanded some kind of sustenance. He'd been mostly ignoring food since finding John in this very room.

Ian tried the doorknob, and it twisted easily at his touch. He'd never had a sister, hadn't lived with a woman since the day his mother died on the boat from Ireland more than a dozen years ago. Even so, Ian knew the last thing he ought to do was open this door.

He pushed it out of the way—only to find the room empty.

Quiet voices through the bathroom joining this room to the next drew Ian's attention. Instantly his heart bludgeoned the walls of his chest. Why had he left her alone with Kate, of all people?

In three long strides he was at the bathroom threshold, but there he stopped, thankful that he'd somehow managed to make no noise despite his panic. If by some miracle Kate had kept silent about Skipjack, there was no need for Ian to blurt the truth in a groundless accusation.

Without a trace of compunction, he leaned in to hear what they said.

"Did that man—Brewster—know my mother, too?"

"Oh yes. John told me it was Brewster who rescued her from homelessness after her first husband died. I think she must have been quite something to turn her back on everything she knew— her family, her homeland, every friend in the world—for the man she loved. And he was just a footman. She could have married a man of high standing."

"But he died, this footman she ran off with to marry?"

"Your father said after your mother's first husband was killed in a carriage accident, she intended to return to England and beg her family's forgiveness. But she met Brewster, and he offered to help her—without reciprocation, if you know what I mean. Of course, Brewster was married back then, but he never did anything without expecting something in return. From what I learned, Brewster's wife and your mother became great friends. After they both died—Brewster's wife in childbirth—it was one more thing that Brewster and John shared. Their grief."

Ian knew that much was true. He leaned comfortably against the doorjamb.

"So my father and Brewster have been friends for a long time, and my parents met because of him."

"Yes, that's right. Speaking from personal experience, once your father fell in love with your mother, it was only a matter of time before she returned the feeling. He's impossible to resist."

"Do you think they loved each other truly, Kate?"

"Of course! It's entirely possible to fall in love more than once. Your father proved that when he fell in love with me."

"Then perhaps you'll fall in love again too."

Ian couldn't see them from where he stood behind the door; he only heard a light laugh, and it twisted him inside. That they could sit and talk so amiably, even laugh, when John was downstairs waiting to be buried—it made him sick.

He might have turned, found his way quietly back out to the hall to tap on Kate's door, but Meggie was talking again and he couldn't help listening.

"I know so little of either of my parents. I might at least know my father through you, Kate."

Ian knew Kate would be all too eager to answer that entreaty. This conversation had gone on long enough. Too long, in fact. He burst through the bathroom, every sensible thought, any hope of caution or calm, banished by hot, whiskey-enhanced anger.

"I think you know enough about your father, Meggie. That he took care of you all these years because he loved you."

Both women sprang to their feet, and some small, rational part of him was glad to see they hadn't adjusted any uncomfortable clothing for an intended nap but had been sitting on the two chairs in front of the window overlooking the river. They might summon enough anger over the interruption to match his, but at least embarrassment over a loosened corset wouldn't add more fuel on their side.

"How dare you!" Meggie scolded, her cheeks flushed, blue eyes glaring. "No gentleman would listen at the door. You, sir, are most certainly no gentleman."

To his private disgrace, he had to struggle to remain standing stiff and tall after his sudden entrance. His head was spinning. "I never claimed to be one."

She stood not two feet from him, her face less lovely while looking at him with such contempt. "You smell of alcohol."

"What of it? If you possessed the shadow of a daughter's heart, you, too, might turn to comfort where it could be found."

"He was more a father to you than he ever was to me! Why shouldn't you mourn him more than I? I'll only miss his pocket-book because that's all I ever knew of him!"

How he wanted to shake her for renouncing John, but he'd never touched a woman in anger in all his life and wasn't about to start now. And then his anger suddenly deflated. She was right. How could she have loved him, when all John had allowed between them was a figment of both their imaginations? The real tragedy was that the figment she'd created of John hadn't been nearly as appealing as the one John had created of her.

Anger dissipated, Ian turned away. "I came to announce dinner."

"You might have knocked on the door instead of sneaking in," Meggie said to his back.

If she was still hoping to continue their fight, he wanted none of it. He did not turn to face her as he said, "I tried." Then he moved out of the room, leading the way down the stairs.

9

The true colors of ladies and gentlemen are revealed at every meal.
Madame Marisse's Handbook for Young Ladies

DINNER WAS SERVED on the veranda that stood atop a freshly mown hill sided by trees outlining a path to the Hudson River below. The wide expanse instantly brought Meg visions of gardens. If this house needed anything, it certainly needed that.

Maguire sulked through most of the meal. Meg wanted to gloat, but when she saw his gaze travel to the door that led to the ballroom, where her father's body awaited burial, she felt chastised. He wasn't sulking; he mourned her father. That dog was in there too; she saw him through the glass. Lying at the foot of the table upon which her father's body lay.

Halfway through the meal, another gentleman joined them, although the manner in which he plopped a bottle of something near his plate, then sat down without so much as a greeting, made her wonder if she'd used the term *gentleman* too generously. He'd half filled his plate before she realized no one, not even Kate, was going to make a proper introduction.

"My name is Meg Davenport, sir." She offered the traditional bow of her head, waiting for him to introduce himself in return.

He grunted with the slightest of nods.

Meg looked from Kate to Maguire. Neither said a word, just continued eating.

She looked again at the man. "And you are . . . ?"

"Pubjug's the name." He took a bit of meat dangling from his fork and added, "Sorry about your father, miss. He was my best friend."

She looked away from the sight of the man's full and working mouth. "Thank you, Mr. . . . Pubjug."

"Just Pubjug. It's a nickname. We all have them, you know."

"Like a . . ." Maguire seemed to search for a word, though it was clear he wished this man, Pubjug, hadn't shown up at all. "A club."

Pubjug laughed. "A club! I like that, Pinch! I earned my name at a little bar in the Bowery when I was just a boy. The place were run by a coupl'a John Bulls, so we called it the Pub as if it was in England. And I once drank an entire jug of—"

"Pubjug knew your father longer than any of us did," Maguire interrupted. "They were childhood friends."

Pubjug nodded, unfazed over the interruption. "Your pa and I grew up in the same neighborhood, over on Fifth Street in the Bowery. I still live there, mostly."

Meg's heart skipped. "So you knew my father's family? His parents . . . my grandparents? Brothers and sisters?"

"He ain't got no brothers or sisters, least not'ny more. Had a sister once, but she died in a fire. 'Bout killed John's ma. She never could dance after that. Always got winded and short for breath, on account of the smoke she took in trying to save her little girl. Shame, too. My pa said she was the finest dancer at the hall." He offered a brief laugh that was altogether amused. "'Course she'd have had to give up the dancing anyway, after John's pa quit tendin' bar in the dance hall."

The food in Meg's mouth went tasteless. Her grandmother a dancer—someone who *danced*, in public! Visions of a half-clad woman pirouetting in front of a bunch of gawking men filled her mind. And with the full approval of a husband who poured liquor!

"Your father came from humble means," Maguire told her, though the statement ended a bit more gently than it had begun.

Meg had countless other questions but for a long moment could only stare straight ahead, oblivious to anything in front of her. She came from a long line of those who cared little for any of the rules she'd been fed from the earliest days of her life.

"You said my grandfather left the dance hall. Why? For other work?"

"Went to work at the mission hall till the day he died," Pubjug said.

"From the dance hall to the *mission* hall?"

Kate nodded and took a sip of the water in front of her. "That's part of the reason your father was so interested in what I learned at a revival meeting that changed my own life."

"If you'll excuse me," said Maguire, who swiped at his mouth with a napkin, then stood with a shove to the chair beneath him. "I trust you'll limit the conversation to happy memories, Kate."

He fairly stomped to the door of the ballroom but opened it only long enough to call to his dog. Then the pair walked away.

Never, not at school and not even in the homes of any fellow students, had Meg sat at a table where people came and went without the slightest consideration of etiquette.

"He don't like to listen to the things Kate likes to talk about," Pubjug said before taking a long drink directly from the bottle he'd brought. "'Specially when she brings up the revival meetin'."

"Unfortunately it's true." Kate watched Maguire walk off.

Meg spared a glance at Maguire as well. "Perhaps he has a guilty conscience." Providing he had one, of course.

"Guilt? Perhaps a little. But it's more than that. He's like a spurned lover when it comes to God." Kate smiled at Meg. "Only

I wonder why Ian believes God did the spurning, when it must have been the other way around."

Ian threw a stick and Roscoe shot after it, trotting back proudly but not letting go when Ian reached to reclaim it. He didn't have the energy for a tug-of-war. In times like this he contemplated training the animal, but such notions were usually short lived. More than one encounter with a guard dog had left Ian with an understandable fear of trained dogs. He guessed turning Roscoe into a soldier—even for protection—wouldn't be easy on either end.

Ian lifted one foot to rest it on an old tree stump by the water's edge, staring at the river flowing by while petting the dog's sizable head. Roscoe played his part well enough. He was a faithful, affectionate companion, and that was all Ian expected of him.

"Well, boy, it's back to the city after tomorrow. If I can't convince Keys to flip back to me, we'll have to work on someone else to take his place."

Police training took three months. Even if Ian found someone tomorrow to put on the job for his purposes, it would take too long. If he didn't go through with this break-in quickly, Brewster could easily call himself John's replacement and everyone but Ian would likely accept it.

But if Ian went through with this heist, and if it went as well as he expected, even Brewster would have to admit Ian didn't need him. Working side by side with Brewster—each with their own men— was fine with Ian. It was submitting to him, running every idea by him the way Ian had done with John, that Ian hoped to avoid. There was only one John Davenport, and Brewster was no equal.

Ian walked along the river, picking up more sticks and throwing them rather than wrestling away the ones Roscoe retrieved. Other images invaded his mind—some he wished to throw away as easily as he did the sticks. But Meggie's face was like a boomerang, returning between every thought of John's death or the coming burglary.

The sun had sunk low on the horizon before Ian tracked back to the house. Tomorrow afternoon would be here soon enough, and before then he needed to come up with some way to persuade Keys back to his side. A bigger share might work; Keys's greed was as famous as his caution, something Ian could understand. Money was security, status, the blood of life. If Ian could buy Keys's loyalty, it would be worth it.

By the time he reached the veranda, all trace of dinner had been cleared away. He let himself in through the ballroom door and paused by John's side, knowing by tomorrow at this time his friend and mentor would be buried, forever beyond Ian's sight. Roscoe plopped at his feet.

"Good-bye, my friend," Ian whispered. "And thank you."

At last he turned, following the spill of light he spotted coming from the parlor. His first thought was to hope Meggie might be there. And even as he reined in that hope, his footsteps hastened when Kate's familiarly stern voice was met with laughter. Though Ian had never heard it before, he instantly recognized that laugh as belonging to Meggie.

"I'll have no part in such a thing! It's not a game," he heard Kate say.

Another laugh from Meggie met Kate's words. "Why not? Where else could I ever learn such a talent?"

Ian stopped at the threshold. "What kind of game?"

Kate stepped in front of him. "Ian, I'm glad you've returned! Maybe you can talk some sense into her."

"Now I know something's wrong. You're never glad to see me, Kate, and I didn't think you believed I possessed enough sense to spare for anyone else. What's going on?"

"I's showin' her how to lift a purse, Pinch. Same as I showed you."

Ian looked past Kate, past Pubjug, then on to Meggie with growing horror. In that moment he knew he had no hope, not a trace, that she was still ignorant of her father's occupation. Desperate to deny it, he kept his voice calm and his hands at his sides. "That's an old game, Pubjug. Something Meggie's father wouldn't approve of her learning."

He looked at her again, seeing her gloat in all-knowing confidence. By contrast, in the corner of Ian's vision, stood Kate. Looking as guilty as she no doubt was. Why had he left Meggie alone with them?

An explosion of anger shot through him. Marching past Meggie, he stood toe-to-toe with Kate. "You've betrayed his memory. Betrayed *him* by telling her."

"I haven't! Meggie had a right to know. I'm convinced John himself would have wanted her to know so she wouldn't doubt his love."

Ian spun around to face Meggie again. "Are you assured of that love now? Have you seen the light, changed your mind about him? Or do you think the worst of him instead?"

Meggie squared her shoulders, and her gaze met his without a hint of cowering. How was it that she could replicate that look in her eye, the same one her father had used when he wanted his way, without ever having been taught by him to do so?

"At least I understand why he kept his secrets—and what's more, I understand myself better than I did this morning. Kate did the right thing in telling me, and I can only believe it wasn't my father you were trying to protect, or me, but yourself."

The words had the power to pierce Ian, had his heart stood still long enough to receive that piercing. He leaned toward her the way he always did when he wanted to reinforce his words. "I haven't given a thought to myself since your father died, which is more than I can say of you."

If she was insulted, she didn't show it. "If you're worried I might have you investigated for whatever crimes you're guilty of—and my guess is there are many—then you can rest assured I'll keep my mouth shut."

"Trying to teach me honor, Meggie?"

"Given your eavesdropping earlier, it's a lesson you obviously need to learn."

He ignored her jab and shot his next words at Pubjug. "What were you thinking? Is that any kind of thing to teach little Meggie?"

Meggie huffed. "Little Meggie! Which reminds me—my name is Margaret, but I'm called *Meg*, not Margaret and certainly not Meggie. I'll thank all of you to remember that." She glared at Ian. "And why are you scolding Pubjug, anyway? It was my idea."

"Oh, now, Miss Meggie—er, Meg," Pubjug said, "that ain't true. I was the one that said it might be in your blood, same as you got your papa's eyes."

"It doesn't matter whose idea it was," Ian said. "It ends right now."

Meggie gasped. "Why, you pompous, overbearing, meddling reprobate! You have no right to give orders to me or to Pubjug."

He used a stare that made many men cower, but she stood unwavering.

"You haven't the stomach for your father's life, *Meggie*." Then he turned to address the others. "I suggest we all go to bed. Tomorrow will be another busy day."

Pubjug started to shuffle from the room, and even Kate turned away. But Meggie stayed where she was. "How dare you dismiss this before it's even begun! Pubjug, come back here. Show me what you were going to show me."

"It's probably best that we end the day," Kate said gently. "It's been tiring for all of us."

"And I . . . don't . . . I don't like arguing." Pubjug's old eyes never attempted to meet Meggie's gaze. "So good night, then."

He left the room somewhat quicker than he'd tried before, and Kate went along with him.

"You might have them bullied," Meggie said to Ian, "but you won't do that to me."

Ian caught her arm and put his nose almost to hers. "You're going back to Connecticut tomorrow, Meggie, to count every garment and comb and jewel your father ever gave you as the loving gifts he meant them to be. Then you're going to contact each one of the acquaintances you made at that fancy school and beg them to introduce you to any and every eligible, wealthy bachelor they know so you can be securely settled in matrimony for the rest of your life. That's what you're going to do. And you're not going to play any more ridiculous games with Pubjug. Do you hear me?"

"Oh, I hear you, Maguire." She ripped her arm from his grasp. "Just don't expect me to listen. I'll be going to New York City and staying with Kate."

Meg nearly smiled at yet another look of astonishment on Maguire's handsome face, finding she enjoyed surprising him. Between his menacing tone and the fierce look in his eyes, Meg might once have stepped back. If someone—anyone—had treated her in such a way just last week, she'd have melted into a puddle of eager-to-please capitulation.

But everything had become so clear today. No wonder she'd resented each of her eighteen years of following rules, eighteen years of being forced to behave in a way that was never her first thought. Eighteen years of doing as *others* expected instead of pleasing herself. Knowing each of her forebears had very likely done exactly as *they* pleased, breaking whatever rules *they* wished, why shouldn't she?

"And how long do you intend to stay with Kate?" Maguire's voice was so steady that she marveled at his control.

"Indefinitely."

His brows gathered. "That's not in your best interest, Meggie. What of your place at school? Friends?"

"All of that is over. It must be. I couldn't possibly jeopardize the school's reputation more than I already have."

"How can it matter now? Your father is dead, and you've never done anything wrong—"

"The school accepted funds that were illegally gained. Obviously there was not a glance at my heritage, even though it's believed every girl admitted must withstand a rigorous investigation. I won't risk the school further by adding so much as a day to my residence there."

"You won't find a suitable husband living with Kate."

"Who said I was looking for one?"

"Every girl your age—"

"Not me."

He raised a finger directly in her face. "Look, I'm not accustomed to being cut off midsentence. You'll listen to me—" She opened her mouth again, but he was already shaking his head and raising his volume. "You'll listen to me, and you'll heed what I have to say. Even if Kate convinced you she knows what your father wanted for you, I have a pretty good idea of it myself. You have as much obligation to listen to me as you have to her."

She crossed her arms. "Very well, Mr. Maguire. Had I shown up at his door while he was alive, what do you suppose he would have told me to do?"

Despite his own claim a moment ago, he appeared somewhat flummoxed. Definitely a good sign.

But his hesitation didn't last long. "If marriage is out of the question—for the time being—he would have wanted you to continue schooling. If not at Madame Marisse's, then elsewhere. He wanted you in school until you chose a husband."

While Meg knew there were a handful of colleges that allowed women, and several finishing schools she might consider as well, all she saw now in such a choice was a life according to someone else's rules. She would never be free to do as she pleased if she went from being a student to being a teacher.

Besides, no institution in the country would accept someone whose education thus far had been paid for by money gained as her father's had been. Not any institution where reputations mattered, at any rate.

"No, Mr. Maguire. I'm finished with school. For good." Meg unfolded her arms, brushed away the wrinkles in her sleeves that had formed while she'd clutched herself together, and attempted as conciliatory a smile as she could muster. "After the funeral, I'm going to Kate's. As I said, for an indefinite period of time."

Then she followed the same path from the room that both Kate and Pubjug had taken before.

10

It is socially imperative that a funeral not only honor your beloved deceased, but fittingly reflect the status of a life well lived.

Madame Marisse's Letters to Young Wives, NO. 12

". . . SO LET US remember we shall be reunited with John on that day when we, too, leave behind the burdens of the flesh and run into the arms of our Savior. The very Savior who offers abounding grace and unconditional love, who throws our sins away as far as the east is from the west. We commit the body of our brother John to the earth, ashes to ashes, dust to dust, in sure and certain hope of the resurrection to eternal life, through our Lord Jesus Christ. . . ."

It was over. Her father's body was lowered into the ground, although the gravesite still awaited closure.

Meg walked away, twisting her handkerchief between tense fingers. She saw Kate stay even as others waited for her to go. It was the custom for only men to witness the final interment, but this was one rule Meg didn't care to break. She didn't belong there; Kate did.

Nearly everyone had cried except Meg. She saw Maguire's eyes well up more than once. Even the older man, Mr. Brewster, had the sparkle of one tear make a path down his cheek while the minister spoke. And Kate's constant sniffling bespoke her immeasurable grief.

Meg told herself she'd cried over her father last night; surely that was more than he deserved, having abandoned her since she was four years old.

But the truth was those tears had been shed not for her father, but for herself. Perhaps he'd believed that by not allowing her in his life he'd spared her from the less than noble truth about him, but the end result was that she'd never known him. And now she never would.

She could have walked along the edge of the hill, toward Maguire's house and away from this newly designated plot. Instead she descended that hill, away from the house, away from the others. Let the rest of them take comfort in one another; she didn't know them and didn't need their company. She didn't belong with them in their grief.

Her father's death meant certain change for her, more than she'd ever expected. If he were here, she might have asked him what he thought she should do, just as she'd put Maguire to the test earlier. Why had her father deposited her into a social circle that would never, ever accept her if the truth about him were uncovered?

The water rippled in the early-afternoon breeze, and she crossed her arms, reminding herself she was used to being alone. Her father's death might have changed her future, but it hadn't changed her past—a past that had taught her solitude.

"I wish it could have been different."

Meg didn't have to look behind her to know the voice was Maguire's.

She didn't turn from the water. "So do I."

"Look, Meggie—" He drew in a breath as if to stop himself. "I want to apologize for last night. For all of yesterday, actually. I've been less than pleasant to you, and I didn't mean to be that way. It's part of grief, I suppose, being a bully to someone who doesn't deserve it. I never meant to be that way, especially with you."

He stepped beside her, and she glanced up at him, thinking she'd been somewhat of a bully herself—though she couldn't attribute it to grief.

"If he were still here, alive and able to speak to you," Maguire whispered, as if he supposed her thoughts were like his, unable to consider anything but her father, "he would tell you that he always loved you."

Meg wanted to trust his words—how she wanted to—but everything she'd believed of her father wouldn't let her. "I want to grieve him, but I realized during the service that I don't know how. I never knew him." She faced Maguire. "But you did. You knew him as I should have."

He nodded, but the look on his face was wary at best. She wasn't surprised; she resented him and made no secret of that. But for the moment she put that aside. "You might be the only one who can help me to grieve for him, Mr. Maguire. What was he like—as a father, I mean? Will you tell me?"

He studied her, as if trying to figure out if she were laying a trap for him. Then, evidently deciding to take her at her word, he took a step closer and gently wrapped her arm through his to stand beside her as if they were a couple, staring out at the river together.

"Your father put a roof over my head when I was twelve years old. He made sure I went to school and that I learned everything I ought to have learned." He tilted his head toward her and grinned. "He helped me to lose me brogue, don't you know. And he saw that I dressed and behaved in a way that didn't leave me open to ridicule or mark me as a target. I tended to be on the scrawny side when I was younger."

She smiled because though he was considerably taller than she was, he wasn't much more than average height for a man. And anything but bulky.

"Being Irish and scrawny is a dangerous combination in New York, but your father taught me how to read others—to understand them enough to know when to keep my distance or to trust a friend."

"Or . . . take advantage of a mark?"

He frowned. "Yes. But he was a good man despite some of the things he did. He was generous with what he had, protected me when I needed it, told me I was wrong when I needed to know that too. He wasn't a model of virtue in the way you would define it, but he wasn't without virtue, either. He loved well, and believe it or not, he lived generously. Everything he earned, he gave to you, or to me, to Kate, or to countless others he knew in need."

"Like Robin Hood." She hadn't meant to sound snide, but she wasn't as devoid of that tone as she would have liked. For a moment she wondered what it would have been like for the children of a real Robin Hood. Would they have welcomed knowing their father robbed from the rich to give it all away, especially if they never had his company because he had to hide himself from them? Would it have consoled them to lose him to a greater cause?

"I know your relationship with him wasn't ideal, Meggie, but he arranged for you to be raised better than he could have done himself. He wanted you to have the best choices and to make a better life for yourself."

"Better than yours?"

He stopped, facing her with an all-too-serious look on his face. "Most definitely."

Meg sighed, knowing she would have to believe that or she would never know peace. "Thank you, Mr. Maguire."

He slid his arm from hers only to catch both her hands in his. "If I learn to call you Meg instead of Meggie, can you learn to call me Ian instead of Mr. Maguire?"

"That, Ian, is acceptable."

He led her away from where they stood, releasing one of her hands but keeping the other securely inside his own. Surprisingly, she had no desire to pull away, even if she did warn herself not to think too much of such contact.

They walked along the water's edge, which seemed far away from the house and all the visitors in it. Meg found herself wanting to stay where she was instead of joining anyone else, and not only because she didn't want to be with the others. She didn't want Ian to leave her alone.

"Why did my father take you in? Where were your parents?"

"We'd come over on one of the immigrant ships, the five of us. My parents, two brothers, and me." With his free hand he rubbed the back of his neck. "My parents were all that was left of their family after the hunger, but they did all right for us. My father was willing to leave it behind, though, to partner in a mission he'd been invited to join. He wanted to be a preacher, and New York City was to be the mission field for all the Irish who'd come before us."

"You didn't want to talk about such things when Kate brought it up last night."

His brows drew together. "Because it was all some kind of hoax conjured up by a God with a twisted sense of humor, if you ask me. My father left Ireland to do God's work and died before he could offer a single day's effort. The God my father wanted to serve took my father, my mother, and my brothers and left me behind. The scrawniest, most useless and irreligious of the bunch."

"I'm sorry, Ian," Meg whispered. She'd been raised to believe God was sovereign and good and wanted only the best for everyone. But that same God had never answered any of her prayers about letting her know a real family, so she had nothing to offer Ian as comfort. "When did your family . . . die?"

"On the boat. Typhus. Half the people on that boat died, and they almost didn't let the rest of us land. We were shipped to a holding cell for months, to make sure we weren't bringing in the sickness." He sighed, facing the water again. "I would have been shipped back, being an orphan, but I was healthy and old enough to work, and a stranger vouched for me so I could work in a sugar refinery. Only I hated it, so I ran away. Straight into your father."

"And he took you in . . . like some kind of Fagin, turning you into his Artful Dodger?" She recalled the novels she wasn't allowed to read, consumed late at night after the school staff had long gone to sleep.

"I was already stealing—I tried stealing his wallet, in fact. He made me stop pickpocketing altogether, until Pubjug . . . well, let's just say I know Pubjug is capable of teaching you what he taught me, too."

"My father didn't want you to steal?"

Ian offered a smile that appeared halfhearted. "He didn't want me to get *caught*, and until I learned how to do it properly, that was a near certainty. Your father wanted to teach me other ways of doing business, too. Some honest, some not."

She glanced back up the hill, at the large house few people could afford. "So your house—it's all from money you stole?"

"Not all of it. I'm pretty good at gambling, and I've made an honest investment or two. Like your father." Ian, too, looked back at the house. "I suppose we should join the others," he said. Then he caught her gaze. "But I'm glad we were able to talk this way, Meg. Your father wanted all of us to hold you in a special esteem—you've been sort of our hope for everything good in the future. That's why I want you to have a happy life."

Was she to be some noble symbol of virtue—she who'd resented that whole good life? "Aren't you happy?"

He looked around them. "When I'm away from the city, I am."

They walked up the hill, and somewhere along the way Ian dropped her hand with an apologetic smile, as if he'd just realized he still held it. But as they approached the veranda, he took her arm again, leading her inside through the now-empty ballroom. Guests milled between the hallway in the center of the home and the dining room—where she assumed the table now laden with food was the same one that had held her father only that morning.

Kate greeted them.

"There you are." She kissed Meg's cheek. "I was wondering what happened to both of you."

"We had a chat." Meg offered a glance Ian's way. Certainly there was nothing wrong in having had a private discussion about her father. And that's all it had been.

"It appears to have been a truce talk."

"That's because we didn't discuss what will happen after the guests leave this afternoon." The pleasant look on Ian's face disappeared with his words. "When I take Meg back to Connecticut."

Then he walked away, and the truce seemed to be over.

Those of the female persuasion must strive to develop a quick sense of discernment so that a young lady may accurately assess who is worthy of her attention, friendship, respect, or trust.

Madame Marisse's Handbook for Young Ladies

"AND HOW ARE you doing this afternoon, Miss Davenport? I hope the pain of saying farewell to your father hasn't weighed too heavily upon you."

Meg diverted her gaze from watching Ian, who remained oblivious to her as he conversed with another man across the dining room. She'd heard others talking about some kind of job Ian was working on, and she could only guess that was what he discussed so earnestly now.

She looked at Mr. Brewster, who'd approached just as Kate left to see off the minister and his wife.

Brewster was near her father's age, perhaps a year or two older if the gray hair along his wide, rounded forehead was any indication. His brows were gray as well, thick and close set, over brown eyes that slanted slightly downward and lent authenticity to his expression of concern.

Meg had no desire to pretend grief. "I'm sure those of you who were closer to my father will miss him more than I shall."

"I offer my help in any way you need, should there be anything

I can do. I'm more than happy to be of assistance. Your father would have expected nothing less of me. We were like brothers, so please consider me family, as he did."

Meg considered his words. "You . . . worked with my father, then?"

"Regularly."

"And you were in his confidence?"

"In everything."

"Then I'd like you to tell me something." She glanced again around the room, first at Ian, who was still in conversation, then at the door through which Kate had disappeared. "Did my father place me in the school where I was raised so he might have access to wealthy people? Was that his goal?"

Brewster appeared both surprised and amused by her question. "Your father, my dear, dear Miss Davenport, placed you in that school because he wanted you to grow up exactly as you are. A lovely young lady with limitless opportunity."

"Limitless, Mr. Brewster? I know those in Boston or New York with new money are more forgiving than those with old, but everyone has a pedigree. Mine has been hidden for a reason, kept a strict secret from anyone in legitimate society who has expressed the slightest interest in me."

His gaze roved her face, her hair, even briefly skimmed the rest of her in a way that might have made her uncomfortable if she allowed herself to think about it very long. "You're a vision of loveliness. That ought to go a long way in reducing curiosity about family backgrounds that make little difference."

"I've always been taught it's impossible to make a silk purse of a sow's ear."

Brewster laughed loud and boisterously, out of place with the rest of the somber room. "You're hardly a sow's ear, my dear."

"Something funny?"

Ian's voice was closer than she'd expected, just behind her. He stood next to Meg and placed a hand at her elbow, as if by doing so he claimed not only the right to touch her, but to defend her.

Meg would have preferred keeping this conversation between herself and Brewster, hoping to find her first—and so far only—ally. But she decided there was no place to go but forward. "We were discussing the opportunities my school acquaintances might have provided to someone such as my father . . . or you, Ian."

"What kind of opportunities?" Ian's question, quietly spoken through barely moving lips, couldn't have been issued with more tension. Perhaps the approach of several others, Pubjug among them, had something to do with his obvious frustration.

Even Brewster looked surprised. "That's not precisely our topic."

"Oh, but that's where the discussion was headed, wasn't it, Mr. Brewster?" Meg looked at the curious faces surrounding them. "I'm sure anyone present would be very interested in knowing the people I know. Some of the wealthiest daughters of New York and Boston are among my very closest friends."

Her words were only a slight exaggeration. . . . Well, if she was completely honest, at least to herself, the statement was an utter fabrication. She'd cultivated few friendships over the years. Never before had she found lying as simple as she did just now. Obviously such behavior *was* in her blood, just as she suspected.

A whisper of caution crossed her mind; perhaps she was too eager to offer up those daughters she'd grown up with, that endless parade of debutantes and debutantes-to-be. But the hesitant voice attempting to speak in her mind was not nearly as loud as it might have been within the sanctuary of her school. Her father had traded her real heritage for that of a lady. Hadn't he realized hiding such a history didn't mean she could be part of the society he'd longed for her to claim? As far as she saw it, she had only one option: to inherit the society in which her father had belonged. If there was justice in the world, her father could see her this very moment, and she could prove once and for all that she'd have been every bit as valuable to him as Ian Maguire was.

Pubjug's snicker drew her eye. "Oh, we got ways of getting to all the wealthy families we want. Servants come and go easy enough and are easy to plant inside, too." He rubbed his chin. "There's one family, one we all knew was connected to your school. Brewster dared sendin' in a scout once, even though John said no. But it didn't do no good because they ended up no use. There ain't a soul here who wouldn't give up a year or two a their life for a shot at that Pemberton money."

Pemberton . . . Pemberton. Of all the names she'd expected, she recalled that one with some distaste. Both Pemberton daughters had been residents of Madame Marisse's at one time or another. One just a few years older than Meg herself, and the other a few years younger. The older one was the very image of haughtiness. But it was the younger Meg most preferred forgetting. Meg had been instrumental in having the girl expelled for all the rules she seemed intent on breaking.

"I know them well." Despite the memory of the girls, Meg reminded herself that her involvement in the younger sister's inevitable expulsion had been behind the scenes. Just as quickly, she recalled their mother expressing an interest in Meg's talent for garden design, once she learned it had been Meg who'd designed the garden around the gazebo at the school. "In fact, I have a standing invitation to visit the Pemberton family any summer I wish." Only a slight overstatement . . .

The reaction around the circle was so visible it sped her pulse even faster. Brewster lost his smile of simple enjoyment and studied her intently. Pubjug's jaw dropped, while others exchanged curious, serious glances. Ian glowered.

"That's very nice." Ian took one of her hands in his and slipped his other palm to the small of her back. Meg heard a couple of whispers spout up around the circle, but Ian spoke above them as he attempted to lead her away. "But we're not at all interested in any of your connections."

"Aren't we?"

The two words instantly quieted everyone else.

Meg looked at Brewster, ignoring the warning she detected from Ian. "Is there a specific reason you would like someone to befriend the Pemberton family?"

Brewster's brows rose. "Surely you've heard? Surely you know about the Pembertons?"

"I know two Pemberton sisters, Claire and Evie. I know their money came from their grandfather."

"The Pemberton gold, Miss Meg!" Pubjug nearly shouted. "You ain't heard a that?"

Although Meg had seen more students come and go at Madame Marisse's than anyone not on staff, she had to admit money—or at least the measure of it—had never sparked her interest. Certainly she'd heard rumors about where the Pemberton money had come from; she even knew the Pembertons were among the richest of the families connected to the school. But whether those riches came from gold, goods, or gifts of inheritance, she'd never cared.

Rather she'd learned from Madame's example to separate families into the three groups that made up high society: those who valued wealth, those who valued ancestry, and those who valued cultivation. Because of their obvious ease with their own money, Meg had put the Pembertons in the camp that valued cultivation above all else. Which of course made Evie Pemberton's expulsion all the more disastrous. She'd been thrown out of a school offering the very commodity they most wanted to either attain or keep secure.

"The fact is I'm well acquainted with the Pembertons. If my father were here and I expressed an interest in working with him, I see no reason why he would have refused me. So now I extend that offer to those of you who worked with him."

Ian chuckled, but the sound was unsteady, a bit too breathy. "Just what sort of help could you be offering, Meg? To leave the door unlocked so one of us might sneak in and clean them out?"

"Yes, of course." Too late, she realized he'd been joking. "Or whatever you need."

If Ian had been about to speak, Brewster spoke louder, commanding everyone's attention. "That's very generous of you, Miss Davenport. But quite a shift in direction for you, wouldn't you say?"

"A shift made the moment I learned the secrets my father kept from me all these years. I have no more right to be an accepted member of polite society than any of you do. He had only one legacy for me, and I have no qualms about receiving it."

"Spoken like a martyr if ever I heard one," Ian said.

"Then you would be willing to have these friends of yours turned into victims of a crime?" Brewster asked. "One in which you play a part?"

Meg refused to be afraid of what she'd just volunteered to do. "I can't believe anyone here would actually harm another person."

"We avoid violence at all cost." Brewster spoke with what she could only call an amused smile.

She couldn't help but be relieved. "Then if you would simply be lightening the considerable Pemberton coffers, I see no reason not to do something my father himself would have wanted to do."

"This is the last thing your father would have wanted." Ian's gaze wandered the circle much as Meg's had, then settled and remained on Brewster. "Every last one of you knows John never wanted his Meggie to be involved in any of this. He wanted her to live the happy, comfortable life he designed for her."

"She's too young to be merely comfortable." Brewster aimed a wink directly at Meg.

She smiled because he was precisely the ally she needed. And his words so clearly spoke for her. Who wanted to be comfortable? Not Meg. Comfort was all she'd known her entire sheltered life.

She might have spoken, but Ian took her hand so suddenly, fairly pulling her from the dining room, that she would have had to make a scene to resist. None of the others protested, although Meg saw Brewster's interest follow her from the room.

In the hallway, Ian nearly collided with Kate. "Come with us, Kate."

Ian still held Meg's hand, although she had to admit his grip felt more like a grown-up's hold on an errant child than the gentle touch of an equal he'd used when they stood at the water's edge.

But the prospect of imminent battle neither deterred nor intimidated her. She hadn't felt so hopeful since the day she'd set out to run away from school all those years ago.

Ian led the two women to the library on the far side of the rotunda. He seldom invited anyone into the library—it was, in fact, the holy of holies in this house that was a sanctuary to him, so far from the city. The walls were lined with shelves that he imagined would be full one day. As it was, after only a year of occupancy, they were still mostly empty.

But there was a couch in the center, where he took Meggie. She did not sit, and he guessed he would have to push her into it to see her comply. Tempted as he was, he did not.

"That was the most foolish act of bravado I've seen." He let go of her hand but stood over her, closer than ever. If she wouldn't sit, she would have to withstand his face nearly pressed to hers.

"It wasn't meant to be. I was in complete earnest."

"What happened?" Kate demanded, joining the little huddle Ian had established.

Sensing his closeness to Meg wasn't intimidating her in the least, though it was inspiring unwanted feelings inside him, he turned away and threw his hands up. "She offered to join in with Brewster!"

"And with you," Meg added softly. A glance told him what he suspected: she'd said the words with a smile. A gift he knew he'd have to spurn, though it addled him just the same. Her smile stirred something in him he'd be hard-pressed to deny . . . as did the Pemberton gold.

"Meg!" Kate's reaction was exactly as he expected, the precise reason he wanted her here. "You can't possibly know what you're proposing, especially with Brewster! Not to mention what it would have done to your father. Just what, exactly, did you offer?"

"Only to spend time with the Pemberton family in New York and see what I can do to . . . Well, just to see if there are any opportunities . . . Oh, I don't know exactly, except that Pubjug said they have some kind of gold, and it occurred to me that I might easily find out where such a thing is kept and provide an opportunity for someone to simply . . . take some of it."

Ian felt her gaze on him, and he couldn't resist returning it. "It's what you do, isn't it?" she added with such sweetness in her incredibly blue eyes that he nearly wanted to nod along and let her do as she insanely pleased.

He commanded his gaze away, knowing hers was lethal to him. Combine that with images of the purest gold in the country, and he could very nearly be overwhelmed. "First of all, you haven't the faintest idea of how we do what we do, and I have no intention of enlightening you. Second, you don't know a thing about Brewster. He just lied to you, and you didn't even know it."

"Lied? How?"

"Let's just say avoiding violence at all cost isn't anything he worries about." He glared at Meg anew. "And there is nothing you could do to convince me you have the stomach for what you just volunteered to do."

She neared him, and this time it was she who stood a bit too close for comfort. "Then let me enlighten you. First of all, I'm strong and smart enough to learn about whatever it is you do. And you have no idea of my stomach's capabilities. All of your suppositions lack one thing: knowledge. About me, or about anything I might have in common with my father."

"As you've said since nearly the moment you stepped off that carriage, you barely knew your father. You have nothing in common with him. He made sure of that."

She shook her head. "There is a German proverb that says the apple doesn't fall far from the tree. I have my father's blood; you can't deny that."

"No, I don't deny you're his daughter, but I do deny you're anything like him, apart from the color of your eyes. Why would you even suggest leaving the life your father wanted for you?"

"I can't go back!" She hurled the words at him, and in that moment he knew she believed what she said.

He grabbed her arms, giving her a gentle shake. "You can! No one has ever suspected your connection to a man like your father. If you choose any one of the many beaus that must be flocking after you, no one will ever be the wiser. You have complete control over your future, Meg. None of us would ever betray John's memory or have any reason to hurt you by doing so. You can make a clean break from all this."

"And what should I say to this beau when his family asks about *my* family? Even if by some miracle they didn't care, what would I say to my own children, who will no doubt ask one day where I came from?"

He loosened his hold on her, gently rubbing where he'd gripped her arms, then let her go altogether. "Parents keep secrets from their children all the time. Besides, the way you were raised, it's almost as if you'd been adopted away from whatever your father was or did."

"Not quite. His money paid for every year of my education and everything I own. Without him, I never would have met all the beaus you think I have."

"But you do have them? Choices, I mean?" He found himself wanting to know the answer but unwilling to explore why.

She lifted one shoulder. "None that I care to think about." Then she smiled at him, and it was the kind that made him want to simply stare, she was so lovely. "I can't permanently go back to school now that I know the truth, Ian, but I will agree to return long enough to pack my bags. Oh, and to take one sheet of stationery boasting the school emblem. I shall address it to Mrs. Dolly Pemberton of Fifth Avenue, New York, and graciously accept her generous invitation to host me for a summer. This summer."

Ian looked past her earnest face to beseech Kate, whose expression held all the dread Ian felt. He hadn't expected to partner with Kate in anything, but in this he knew he had her full support.

"This is what I want you to do," he said to her. "Take Meg to Connecticut; make sure she packs up every single belonging she owns. Then meet me in New York, at the shipping office in Battery Park. I'll book passage for both of you on whatever sailing ship will take her away from here. Far away. Europe or—or China, on any ship that's sailing tonight, to anywhere."

It was the last thing he wanted, never to see Meggie again, but he knew even as he heard his own words this was precisely the right thing to do. For her own sake. If Brewster believed Meg could be of use to him, there would be no stopping him.

"Kidnapping is illegal," Meg said in such a merry tone of

voice that his eyes ricocheted back to her. Then she offered an embellished frown and a *tsk*. "But I don't suppose that would deter you, would it?"

She was laughing at him! Thought him joking! Ian had half a mind to wrap her in a burlap sack and take her out of the country himself, to some undisclosed location where she would never find her way back to New York.

Except he had a job waiting to be carried out. . . .

Ian glared at her. Never in his life had he expected little Meggie to be so much trouble.

Meg almost felt sorry for Ian, seeing his genuine dismay over her decision to pursue the way of life that was so obviously her only choice. She hadn't expected him to resist so vehemently; after all, she was only validating his own choices by offering to join his ranks. What could he find wrong in that?

She was sure she could change his mind, but a rap at the door stopped any further attempt. The sound of the knock had barely drifted away before the door opened and Mr. Brewster stepped over the threshold of the library.

"I came to see if I might be of some assistance." He held a cigar so naturally in one hand that it seemed almost an extension of the appendage. He approached Meg. "I'm sure Ian—and Kate—have tried talking you out of joining forces with us. I came to add my own advice, since I knew your father at least as well as either of these two."

"We don't need your advice, Brewster," Ian said. "Meg has decided to withdraw her offer to you."

"Of course that's best." He laughed and took a puff from his cigar. "Did you think I would say anything else?"

Kate stepped forward, and Meg noticed the woman hadn't stopped wringing her hands since she'd followed them into the room. "So you *don't* want Meg to learn anything about the Pemberton gold bricks?"

The astonishment in Kate's question matched Meg's disappointment. Could she find no one who would allow her to do as she pleased?

"I came with another offer entirely." Brewster fished in an inner pocket, withdrawing a small card from his vest. "Have you heard of the St. Denis Hotel, on Broadway and Eleventh? I happen to reside there, at least most of the time, and the assistant to the manager is a very good friend of mine. If you need a place to stay—quite a nice place, I might add, fit for no less than presidents of this great nation—all you need do is ask for Mr. Marshall and show him this. He'll make sure you're well taken care of and have every expense forwarded to me."

Meg reached for the card, not because she intended to take such charity, but because he was kind enough to make the offer.

But Ian stood between Brewster's outstretched arm and Meg's open hand before the transfer could be made. "That won't be necessary, Brewster. Meg already has other, more viable options."

Brewster leaned around Ian to give Meg a wink similar to the one he'd aimed at her earlier. He replaced the card in his pocket. "My, my, you have quite the protector in this young man. Only I have no idea what he thinks he's protecting you from. I was your father's partner before Ian ever came along. You've nothing to fear from me."

Meg had no reason to disbelieve him, yet it was obvious both Kate and Ian were wary of the man—making her wary as well.

"Thank you for the offer, Mr. Brewster. I'll keep it in mind as I decide what to do."

"Whatever you decide, Miss Davenport, I hope you'll allow

me to keep in touch. I want you to know I'm at your disposal for whatever needs you might have. In honor of your father."

He bowed slightly and, with another puff of the cigar, walked from the room, leaving behind only a pale cloud of smoke.

With him went whatever energy Meg had for arguing. She knew what she must do and had no intention of letting Ian or Kate deter her.

She looked at Kate. "I'd like to stay with you in the city, at least for a couple of days."

The concern on Kate's face did not lessen. "Until you're welcomed by the Pembertons?"

Meg knew any honest answer was the last thing either of them wanted to hear, so she refused to reply. "May I stay with you? Or not?"

Kate neared her, taking her hands. "Of course you may." Then, over Meg's shoulder, she said to Ian, "As I see it, I'll have these few days to stir up some sense in her."

"I haven't seen evidence she has any."

Meg would have laughed away the insult, except she knew Ian believed his pronouncement.

She would have to prove him wrong.

12

A young lady properly raised and tutored should not be ambitious. She should accept where her Creator has placed her. However, if her circumstances are altered due to a family relocation, increased fortune, or marriage plans, such changes in life must be thoroughly explored and planned, then carefully and cautiously executed.

Madame Marisse's Handbook for Young Ladies

THE HIBBIT SISTERS fussed and cried, expressing how worried they'd been over Meg's absence these past few days. They barely spared a glance at Kate until Beatrice's tears had been brushed aside and Hazel's pleasure to see Meg was replaced by her familiarly stern face—sternness familiar at least since she'd taken over as matron.

Meg had made the proper introductions, but once they learned she intended to take up residence with Kate, they eyed the woman with a mix of suspicion and curiosity.

Keeping her explanations vague, Meg told them about her father's funeral, about Kate's engagement to him, about her plan to stay with Kate, at least for the foreseeable future. When the sisters protested over such a sudden departure, Meg reminded them she'd have been leaving the school in the fall anyway—if not for marriage, then for college or finishing school before returning for a staff position at Madame Marisse's. And that this place, after all, was a school and not a home.

It hurt them to hear Madame Marisse's called less than a home; she saw that on their faces. What else had this school ever been to her, all these years, if not a home? But there was no alternative. She had to inflict such pain if she was to sever her association with them—for their own good.

They abruptly eased their inquisition, offering a tense farewell, and the tears in their eyes were of a different sort altogether than when they'd greeted Meg with such welcome relief.

A moment after Ian's knock, one of the two maids Kate employed opened the door, smiling a friendly greeting and revealing small, off-white teeth that had gaps between each and every one. She had a mole beside her left eyebrow that he recalled pulled upward whenever her brows moved. But he could not, despite some effort, remember her name. Alvira? Anna?

"Miss Kane ain't . . . that is, she *isn't* here at the moment, sir."

Although he'd met this maid before, she was relatively new and no doubt another young rescue project Kate had brought home since "awakening from her sinner's slumber," as she'd once put it. The kind of slumber Ian had been enjoying ever since he stepped foot on American soil.

"Yes, I expected her not to be at home yet. She told you, didn't she, that she is bringing a guest? John's daughter, Meg Davenport. I've come to wait for them."

"Oh, sure, she sent a message telling us to dust one of the spare rooms. Do you want anything while you wait for 'em?"

Ian looked around the cramped parlor, half of the items knick-knacks John had purchased for Kate, and the other half just as unnecessary. But that was Kate, always cluttering up a room to show off the money she didn't have growing up.

"No," he told the maid, "don't go to the trouble. I wanted to go through John's belongings, to spare Kate from doing it."

"I . . . I guess that'd be fine, Mr. Maguire. So long as you run by Miss Kane anything you might take or get rid of."

Ian found his way to the hallway that led to the three bed-chambers, knowing each had its own unprecedented private bath closet.

Kate's apartment house had been her idea. She'd once owned what even he had recognized as a stunning town house; the rent alone could have fetched twenty-five hundred a year. She'd brought it to John as spoils of her lifestyle prior to knowing him, no doubt an indulgence from some old sot who'd died and bequeathed it to her rather than to his own children. Ian didn't really know. But she'd sold the town house for a hefty sum and had this three-story house built with her profits, complete with six apartments, two per floor. French flats, she called them, to attract a reputable clientele and further distinguish her building from even the best boarding-houses or tenements.

The building was situated on the very edge of the respectable part of Manhattan, far enough from the old, worn downtown but not close enough to the higher-scale, expensive uptown in which she would never fit no matter how much money she earned.

He opened the wardrobe to all of John's clothing, instantly besieged by a wave of grief. Maybe it was too soon to do this. Surely Kate wouldn't care how long John's clothing hung here.

But he hadn't just needed an excuse to be here when they returned; he was looking for something important to him.

No sooner had Ian found what he'd been looking for than he heard voices from the parlor. He entered the room at the same time the maid arrived from another direction to greet Kate and Meg at her side. Behind them was a man laden with a suitcase and two hatboxes, no doubt full of Meg's possessions.

"Ada," Kate said to the maid, "please show this man where to take our guest's belongings, won't you? Another man will be up any moment with the rest."

As she spoke, Kate looked at Ian. Pulling off her gloves, she narrowed her eyes at him. "I'm not surprised to see you, but I expected you tomorrow. We've already eaten."

"I came only to help clear away some of John's things. And to look for something in particular."

Kate's eyes widened. "You needn't trouble yourself about that. I'll see to it." She glanced Meg's way. "Meg can help. It'll be good for us."

Eyeing Meg, who hadn't stopped looking at him since she'd entered, he extended a smile as he let the chain linking fob to watch dangle between his fingers. "That's fine. I have just one request, which I'll make to you, Meg, as John's only legal heir." He opened his palm to reveal the watch he'd just found. "This was your father's, and I'd like to have it as a remembrance of him. If it's all right with you, of course."

Meg did little more than glance at the watch before giving him a smile that, to his own consternation, created a stir in his heart. "That would be quite all right, as long as Kate doesn't mind."

"Not at all. But Meg has a bit of unpacking to do now," Kate said stiffly. He had to admit they were uncomfortable partners, he and Kate, but like it or not, they had the same goal for the time being.

"Perhaps you ought not unpack everything, Meg. You might find you want to return to school, after all."

"That is exactly what I've been telling her," Kate said.

Meg turned to face them, her arms folded in defense. "I completely agree about not entirely unpacking. I'll be sure to leave folded what I intend taking with me to the Pembertons', once they extend their invitation to me for the summer."

Ian shot a startled look at Kate. She'd let Meg send that note? There was no possibility of dissuading her?

Kate lifted a helpless palm. "She hornswoggled me! Left some kind of hint with the two schoolmarms that I might join their attempts to keep her at school if I only knew about the school's charm. They nearly kidnapped me to show the school's highlights, while she pretended to pack. Only she wrote the note instead. I didn't know she'd left it in the school's post until after we'd left."

Ian's gaze returned to Meg. This task might be more of a challenge than he'd expected, but he had no intention of giving up. It made staying in the city all the more important, even though his other demands would keep him busy.

More boxes and a small crate arrived just then, and Kate followed the path the maid and the first luggage-laden man had taken—leaving Ian alone with Meg. Just the opportunity he'd hoped to gain.

"I'm glad we have a moment, Meggie—Meg," he amended, wishing again that John's old, affectionate name for her wasn't indelibly burned into his consciousness. "I came to discuss something with you."

Her gaze met his, and he was sure he saw more than a bit of interest there. Perhaps it wouldn't be so difficult after all, even though what he was about to propose probably wasn't what she expected.

"As your father's closest friend—"

"Something Mr. Brewster claims to be as well."

Ian reminded himself not to be troubled that she'd interrupted him. Now that she knew he didn't like such a thing, she might employ the habit more often. It's what he would have done himself.

"Be that as it may," he continued, "I was—without a doubt—your father's closest confidant when it came to you. I realized after you left with Kate this morning that I haven't fulfilled the role your father left to me. I've failed to consider what you must be feeling, having lost your father."

He lifted a hand before she could speak. "I know your relationship lacked . . . time spent together . . . but it occurred to me that you might worry because your father was your only provider. I was too caught in my own grief to see how uncertain your future must seem without him. I apologize for not seeing your side of things."

She studied him as if trying to determine the level of his sincerity, but he knew she wouldn't find him lacking there.

Still, she might need more convincing. "Your father asked me to look after you if anything ever happened to him. So as your guardian—"

A flash in her eyes cut him short before her words did. "Guardian! You're barely older than I am, and if you think you have any authority over me, you'd better reconsider so ridiculous a thought."

"It isn't ridiculous at all, not if that's what your father wanted."

"There can be absolutely no legal grounds for you to assume such a role—"

"Can't I leave you together for two minutes without it ending in a squabble?" Kate waved them to hush as she bustled to the center of the room, stepping between them. "I won't have voices raised, not here in my own home where my neighbors might hear every word."

Ian sent a scowl Kate's way, even though the exasperation wasn't entirely her fault. He was sure if he'd been left alone with Meg a bit longer he could have convinced her. Now that Kate was here, he would have to recruit her help.

He breathed in deeply, unused to having his patience so tested. "Meg misunderstood, but it was partially my fault for misspeaking. I meant only that Meg must realize her future isn't as uncertain as it feels right now. If she won't go back to the school, and she won't seriously consider marriage, then the only option is for me to hire a chaperone—pardon me, Kate, but one with an unsullied background—and set her up in a place of her own for the summer. Until—" now he eyed Meg with as fierce a look as he could muster—"the finishing school of your choice welcomes you into its halls this autumn."

The smile she sent his way held not a hint of gratitude—or compliance. "So I'm to be a kept woman this summer, instead of accepting the gracious invitation of one of my old schoolmates? How is that preferable, at least as far as polite society goes?"

"Kept woman!" He was shocked she'd ever heard such a term. "I only agreed to pay your rent, not anything else."

"Even a casual investigation into such a situation would be embarrassing at best, a scandal at worst."

To his chagrin, Kate was nodding now. "Since I've had a little time to think about the situation, Ian, it might be best if she does go to the Pembertons' after all, if such an invitation arrives as easily as she expects."

His jaw went slack. "What? You can't possibly want her to feed Brewster—or even me—the information she's offering to acquire."

"Of course not. Listen to me—we're partially to blame for allowing Brewster anywhere near her, and it's our job to protect her. At least at the Pembertons' she won't be within Brewster's easy reach. Beside that, as you said, she hasn't the stomach for her father's way of life. Perhaps she needs to learn that for herself."

From the corner of his eye he saw Meg take on a now-familiar stance. "Please stop discussing this as if I'm not in the room. And stop doubting my capabilities." She turned to fully face Ian, with a change in her expression. Instead of anger, her face reflected something more along the lines of an entreaty. "If the Pemberton gold is as desirable as Pubjug and Mr. Brewster seemed to think, then why won't you accept my help?"

Ian's mind was racing ahead. If there were any way to succeed at getting even a portion of the Pemberton gold—without endangering Meg—he would readily agree. It was, after all, the *Pemberton* gold! But what could he do? Use John's daughter, risk her future? Kate was right. Believing herself capable of doing something and following through with it were two different things altogether. He nearly patted Meg's head just then, he felt so much wiser than her. "All right, Meg. You go to the Pembertons' for the summer. But if by the fall you haven't learned anything of any interest, you'll agree to go to the finishing school."

She offered a slow blink. "I'll consider it."

If that was the best he could do, Ian was prepared to accept it. He had the summer to make her see reason.

13

It is no less than the poorest measurement of a young lady's moral, intellectual, and spiritual strength should she allow herself to be kissed before standing at the altar.

Madame Marisse's Handbook for Young Ladies

FOR TWO DAYS, Meg went nowhere and saw no one. Ian checked in only as warden over Kate, Meg's prison guard. She knew something else demanded his attention, perhaps whatever job she'd heard he was planning. She wished someone would tell her about it but didn't dare ask for fear their refusal to answer would be yet another example of how little they'd welcomed her into their midst.

On the morning of the third day, Meg left her room to find Kate not only up but dressed as well, including a small hat and a short cape. She was dressed entirely in black but for the startlingly red gloves she was just pulling on.

Meg hurried closer, ready to turn in an instant to retrieve her own outerwear. "Are we going somewhere?"

"You'll be staying here, my dear," Kate said as she tugged at the second glove. "I shouldn't be gone more than an hour. Feel free to continue reading the book I began last evening."

Meg sighed. "I'd really rather come with you than stay behind, Kate. Here I am living in the city, and the only thing I've seen is this flat."

"But we're in mourning, darling. It isn't as if we should be going all about town."

Meg was well aware of the rules of mourning, from the assigned time period for her as the daughter of the deceased to which clothing she ought to wear for each segment of time, including jewelry or lack thereof.

It was Kate who seemed to need a reminder of the rules: even now, the gloves were all wrong, and another red handkerchief stuck out of her sleeve. Everyone knew burgundy didn't come until much later in the process—but these items on Kate weren't even that sedate shade. They were stark, vibrant red. The handkerchief was probably not even made of cambric, though Meg couldn't be sure without a closer look.

"Your rebellious nature is showing, Kate," Meg said, gesturing toward the gloves.

"It's all right to break some of the rules, darling Meg," she said softly. "Besides, I have my reasons. I wear red to remind me of what my Savior did for my forgiveness. The rules you seem intent on breaking, however, shouldn't be broken."

Finished with her gloves, Kate left her apartment without further consideration of taking Meg along.

Upon entering the white hotel's basement café, Ian removed his hat and scanned the tables. Dressed in his black suit, complete with an armband to indicate his mourning, Ian was neither under- nor overdressed for the Lower Fifth Avenue address. Keys had chosen the spot well.

He found Keys at a corner table. The long-faced, thin man was easy to spot even in plain clothing. He'd already been served coffee.

As Ian took a seat opposite, he accepted a cup of his own from an eager waiter but leaned forward without taking a sip.

"Well? Have you had a change of heart?"

Keys had a perpetually crooked mouth that gave the impression he was either smirking or smiling. Only the look in his eyes offered a hint at defining which was which. But at this moment he appeared, at least, not to be smirking.

"Not even a how-do-you-do?"

Ian was without patience, even though he needed Keys. "Consider it said. You can't really prefer working with Brewster instead of with me. I've never wanted us to be a gang, one with rules all its own—of Brewster's making."

"I see you're wearing Skipjack's pocket watch. What time is it, anyway?"

Ian sat back, exasperated. Without touching the timepiece, he said, "A little after ten o'clock."

Keys rubbed his chin, then caught Ian's glance. "You know, none of us would've chosen Brewster over John. But you're just a mite young to be calling orders."

"That's just it! I won't. I intend doing things the way John always did. You mind your business; I'll mind my own. I only want you to work with me on this one job, Keys. After that you're free to do whatever you like. You think Brewster won't be expecting more from you than just one job? He wouldn't have to know until it's finished."

At Ian's last words Keys's face took on a definite smirk, not a smile at all. Once the job was done, everybody in New York—at least on their side of the law—would know who did it.

Keys shrugged, taking a long sip of his coffee. "So you've been keeping a pretty close eye on John's daughter, I hear. Even tolerating Kate for it."

Ian tasted his own coffee without answering.

"Meggie seems eager to join our little gang. Why not let her?"

Ian stared at the other man. "Didn't you know John at all? It's the last thing he wanted."

"Yeah, well, John's gone, isn't he? And she appears old enough to make decisions for herself. Old enough," he added, his expression changing to a smile, "for a lot of things."

Keys's attention to the ladies was notorious. Unlike Ian, Keys didn't seem to care how many vices he let get the best of him. If the man weren't such a reliable, standard fixture on the police force—reliable for the wrong side of the law—Ian doubted they would be friends at all.

"Listen, Keys, I'm glad you contacted me. I have a revised proposition about the job coming up." He lowered his voice further, passing his hand over the edge of his mouth as he continued to speak. "You come in with me on this deal and we'll switch shares. I'll take yours; you take mine."

Keys leaned back, studying Ian for what felt far too long a moment. Then he bent forward again, resting his forearms on the table between them. "What time is it now?"

Distracted, slightly annoyed, Ian took out the pocket watch, vaguely wondering if Keys had his eye on that as well. Something Ian wouldn't be willing to part with.

"Ten twenty."

"Then I'd say you better not lose any time getting over to Kate's."

"Why?"

"Because Kate's not there, leaving little Miss Meg all alone. Brewster was going to walk in a few minutes after Kate left."

Ian stood so quickly that the table between them rattled their cups. "We'll settle details later, Keys, but thanks."

Then he ran to the nearest trolley, realizing only after he'd jumped aboard that he'd failed to shake hands with Keys to seal the deal.

Never mind. The information Keys had imparted was seal enough.

Meg poured the tea Ada had just delivered to the parlor, feeling very much in control even though this was the first time in her life she'd hosted anyone other than classmates or school staff. Here she was, almost entirely independent, entertaining a man all by herself with only Ada somewhere nearby, just in case she was needed to take the dishes away.

"You'll allow me to be frank, Mr. Brewster?"

"I wouldn't have it any other way."

"You've come here stating your concern over my welfare because of your affection for my father. Yet when I saw you in the company of both Kate and Ian, who also profess great affection for my father, it was as if there were some barely hidden animosity between the three of you. Can you tell me why?"

He reached into a pocket of his vest and withdrew, then replaced a fat cigar as if changing his mind about smoking. "I can tell you my version of it, if you like. But my guess is Kate and Ian would each have their own—equally mismatched."

"Let's start with you, then."

"It's Kate. When she demanded so much of your father's attention, we naturally began to resent her. For a time it wasn't so bad—not bad at all, in fact. We largely ignored her influence on John because her ideas rarely included the rest of us. We missed his company for the time she demanded, but who can blame a man for wanting to enjoy the company of a beautiful woman who loved him? The Jack Frost started when she reformed. There's nothing worse than a reformer in the family, Miss Meg. It would be fine if people kept newfound beliefs to themselves, but they so rarely do. Abandoning her talent for our games was one thing. But trying to reform the rest of us was the final, cutting stroke."

"If it were only what you just described, I would think you and Ian would be allies of a sort. Why aren't you?"

Brewster set his teacup on the low table between them, a look on his face hinting relief to have put aside any pretense of wanting to drink from it. "Now let me be perfectly frank. Ian wants to take your father's place in our little family, but he's just a whelp. Your father wasn't even in the grave before Ian told the rest of us what he wanted to do. That's why I came to you."

Meg's heartbeat picked up a notch. Neither Kate nor Ian would take her seriously, but obviously Brewster did.

"For all practical purposes," Brewster continued, "Kate is out of the picture now. She wants nothing to do with our ways anymore, and I say good riddance to her—so long as she keeps her mouth shut about anything she knows, I'll leave her be. From what you said the other day, I have a feeling you'd like some connection to your father, a sort of posthumous relationship now that you know the truth about him. Well, Kate can't be that connection. I can be."

"What about Ian?"

His face screwed up with annoyance. "What about him? How sincere was his grief over your father if he was making plans to sway men to his side even as your dear departed was lying neglected in the other room? Ian Maguire is for himself and himself only. If you want to know anything about your father and how he lived, I'm the one who not only has the knowledge but is willing to share it. To Ian, I'm afraid you're nothing more than an inconvenience, someone in the way of his next job."

He reached into his vest again, but instead of withdrawing a cigar, he took out a small card Meg had seen before.

"This is the card from the gentleman I told you about, from the hotel over on Eleventh Street. The St. Denis, do you remember? If you truly want to be your father's daughter, you'll leave Kate to herself and Ian to his own selfish interests and strike out on your own. Here is the means for you to do so."

She eyed the card. "I am my father's daughter already, Mr. Brewster. Exactly what that means, I'm not yet sure. But I would be no more independent should I turn to you instead of to either Ian or Kate."

"You would be if you were my partner, just as your father was. You promise to do your share, and I see no reason why you shouldn't accept a small token of help from me in advance, with the expectation that your help in the future will more than earn whatever pittance you cost me now."

She ignored Ian's words ringing in her head, warnings that this man didn't care if he avoided violence or not. Brewster looked to be on the gentle side, by all Meg could see. And with his obvious affection for her father, surely he was no danger to Meg.

"I assume you'd like me to give you whatever information I could about the Pemberton gold?"

He sighed and puffed as if he'd drawn in smoke from one of his cigars. "That's appealing to be sure, and of course I'd be open to whatever information you could share. What I think would be of more immediate help would be establishing an understanding between the two of us."

"What kind of understanding?"

He laughed with such delight that she realized he loved his work, if she could call it that. "Simply for us to trust one another. You have a trusted position among the rich, my dear. I might devise any number of ways to gain a fortune from your invitation and introduction to those you know."

"Aren't you forgetting that I'm in mourning? If I'm welcomed by the Pembertons, I could hope to be enfolded into the family to some extent and listen for clues about the whereabouts of their gold, but any parties they attend, or even host, would not be something I'd be allowed to enjoy."

He eyed her closely, a small smile on his slightly rounded face. "Mourning is largely self-imposed, and as you've stated yourself, you hardly knew your father. Who would be the wiser if you decided not to follow some rather useless customs anyway?" He winked, then raised a chubby palm as if to erase what was obviously a scandalous suggestion. "In any case, surely a visit from someone like an uncle to you wouldn't be out of the question? You provide the invitation, my dear, and I'll do the rest."

She might have asked what that would entail exactly, but the door to the apartment burst open so suddenly that blood shot through her veins to propel her to her feet, ready to flee.

There stood Ian. Out of breath, a look of such distress on his face Meg was certain he'd been chased by the law.

"Ian! What is it? What's the matter?" She looked beyond him, fully expecting a helmeted, club-wielding, blue-uniformed officer in his wake.

He closed the door, then let his gaze settle on Brewster. "*This* is the matter. What did he ask you to do, Meggie?"

Somehow the name wasn't bothering her as much as it once did, knowing it only slipped out when he was distracted by something else.

"Why, nothing . . . specifically. We were only discussing possibilities. Whatever is the matter with that?"

Ian took Brewster's hat from the table where it had been left, handing it to him. Brewster stood with far less suddenness than Meg had done, in no apparent hurry to accept his hat.

"This is no concern of yours, Maguire," he said. "Meg is free to direct her own life, in any way she chooses."

"Not if she wants to respect her father's wishes. Get out, Brewster."

"Ian! How could you be so rude? This isn't even your home."

Just then the door broke open again, causing Ian to buck out of the way. There stood Kate, a look of similar alarm on her face. Meg would have thought it funny if she weren't so irritated with their obvious displays of overprotection. The last thing she needed was a pair of eager guardians to replace the school staff who had hounded her for the last fifteen years.

Brewster accepted his hat before Kate said a word. But not before sending Meg another wink and a glance at the card he'd left on the table between them.

Meg offered an embarrassed smile. "Thank you for your visit, Mr. Brewster. And my apologies for how it has ended."

He bowed and tipped his hat. "No apology from you is necessary. If you want his confidence, lass, you might offer to help him with the bank job he's planning. Good day to you all."

The moment he left and closed the door behind him, Meg turned to Ian, wide-eyed. "Is it true? About the job you're doing? It's a bank? Can I help?"

He looked at her as if she'd taken leave of every shred of sense she'd been born with. "Forget everything he said to you, Meg. I mean everything."

She glared at the two standing before her. "I don't care what you think of Mr. Brewster. He was right about one thing: I'm free to direct my own life."

They both made such instantaneously loud protests that she couldn't understand either one of them. Ian put a hand to Kate's elbow, and for the moment her objections quieted, letting Ian continue with his.

"Alwinus Brewster is anything except generous. If he offered you something, you can be assured it's because he expected something in return."

"He admitted that much. All he wants is access to the kind of people I've known all my life. Something I've been offering all along."

"Yes, and he'll swindle them or cheat them or use them without a single thought for where it leaves you in the end. Think, Meg! Do you really want all of New York society shunning you for the blight you could bring them? Or to go to jail as an accessory?"

"Why should anyone go to jail? You've lived your way of life for quite some time, and Mr. Brewster that much longer. I'd say he's been at least as successful at evading the law as you've been. As my father was."

"That's only because New York is as corrupt as it is rich."

Kate, who'd taken off her gloves, looked between the two of them. "Brewster may be able to keep you from jail if it suits his purpose, but it wouldn't protect you from loss of any place in decent society." She set aside her hat. "I'm going to the kitchen to see about lunch. Ian, I will give you exactly fifteen minutes to talk to Meg, and after that I'll take my turn at it. Maybe together we can make some progress."

"I'm honored to be a project worthy of your time," Meg called after Kate.

Meg was glad Kate had left her alone with Ian. As much as she'd once been jealous over the time he'd spent with her father, she now saw Ian Maguire altogether differently. As exciting as it would be to work with Brewster, she had to admit she would much prefer cooperating with Ian.

And she'd decided just how she would convince him.

Smiling, she took her seat again on the sofa. "Mr. Brewster didn't even take a sip of the tea, Ian, so if you'd like his cup . . ."

He plopped on the seat opposite her, shaking his head. "No. What I want is for you to agree that it's a crazy idea for you to even consider working with that guy."

"All right. I won't work with him."

The look on Ian's face froze, until a grin started to form on his handsome mouth. He sat up straighter, leaning slightly forward. Then one skeptically dipped brow ruined the look. "Just like that?"

Meg sipped her own tea but, finding it cool, set it aside. She smiled again at Ian, having been around enough flirtatious girls to know the kind of smile that was most effective. "Not if I can work with you. As little as I knew about my father, I do know you were closer to him than Mr. Brewster could have been. I think my father would have been pleased if we worked together."

"Oh no, he wouldn't have. Not at all."

"Well, he no longer has a say. In fact, even if he were alive, he wouldn't have a say. He would know he never earned the right to think I'd listen to any of his advice. So. What do you say? Whatever plans Brewster might have had for the prime pickings of New York society can be had by you instead of him. Surely you're as clever as he?"

He rubbed his palms on his knees, then stood, turning his back on her. Meg stood as well, surprised at how easy it was to play this game. She rounded the table, breaking every rule of etiquette by coming up behind Ian, standing far closer than she'd ever stood to a man, and putting a gentle hand on the back of his shoulder.

"Ian," she whispered, "wouldn't you like to work with me?"

He turned to her with a look torn between panic and interest. Then anger flashed in his dark-blue eyes. He didn't back away, but she might have wished he had when he grabbed her by the arms in a less than romantic way.

"Stop! I know what you're doing. You can't work with me, Meg, or learn any of the things my way of life can teach you. If your father were alive, he'd have my hide. . . ."

Instead of accepting his words, she saw only his struggle, and it was to that she appealed.

"Ian." His name came so smoothly to her lips, so naturally. She'd meant only to use it the same way she'd used the coquette's smile a moment ago. And yet she found herself enjoying the entreaty more than she'd expected. It felt so perfectly right.

Suddenly it wasn't so much control she felt as . . . a lack of it.

This is madness.

And heaven.

It wasn't the first time Ian had imagined taking Meggie into his arms, but even as he knew that was precisely what he was about to do, Ian knew in some small and still shrinking part of his mind that it was the last thing he should be doing.

She was clearly using him to get her way, manipulating him to suit her own naive wishes.

But he didn't care.

His lips came down on hers gently, increasing in pressure when he found what he fully expected—complete and utter surrender.

"Ian." His name came off her lips again, breathless, happy, like no other sound he'd heard. She put her hands on either side of his face, her eyes as light as ever and full of eagerness. "This changes everything, doesn't it? We'll be partners now?"

He wanted to promise her anything but knew that in a few moments, when he wasn't quite so foolishly dizzy and giddy, he'd have to follow through on whatever he said in reply.

"I . . . can't." Never were two words more difficult for him to say. But once said, they gave him strength—strength enough to pull himself out of her all-too-willing arms.

This was Meggie. Meggie, whom John had placed on so high a pedestal that it couldn't be Ian who made a mere woman of her.

She folded her arms again, but this time it was as if she were hugging rather than defending herself. "I don't understand. Didn't you want to kiss me?"

"Oh, I wanted to, all right." No sense lying; she wouldn't

believe him anyway, when the kiss had already revealed the truth. "But there's something you ought to know about me, Meg. I only trifle with women."

She loosed her arms to put a hand to her forehead. "What does that mean?"

"I never allow myself emotional involvement—but I often take advantage of favors sent my way. I don't lie to women with promises of undying devotion."

"How honorable." Ice couldn't be colder.

"I never pretended to be honorable. If you're bound and determined to get involved in your father's way of life, I can't stop you. But I'm not going to make a fallen woman of you too. I won't help you there."

Her shoulders stiffened as if shrugging off the embarrassment of a rejection. Rejection! If only she knew every word he'd just spoken was a lie. All she had to do at this moment was come near him again, and any noble intentions would be immediately forgotten. He'd dreamed of her for too many years to be strong for very long.

"All right. No personal entanglements. You've said you can't stop me from taking up my father's way of life, so at least that's understood."

He shook his head at her assumption, risking all good sense and grabbing her again, this time by the shoulders. "Think, Meg! This isn't just one decision. You're making a hundred decisions right here and now. A thousand. If you go through with this plan to use the Pembertons or help steal their gold, every decision you make—every day—will be based on what you decide right now. Every word you speak, every action you take, will be a result of this decision."

"I've made up my mind. So in what way do you want to be partners?"

A gasp from the threshold drew Ian's attention. Kate stood there, her mouth agape. "What are you saying? Partners in what?"

"Yes, let's discuss my options, shall we?" Meg clasped her hands in front of her as if she were about to make an oration, obviously not at all vexed by Kate's disapproval or Ian's reluctance.

Her voice, though, was a bit too eager to push that kiss behind them in favor of this new, business-only partnership. Something Ian wasn't quite ready to do.

"What are you discussing?" Kate demanded. "What sort of partnership? This is absurd; you both know it."

A tap at the door sounded just as Meg started speaking. "I know no such thing. Shall I answer that?"

But Ian was already moving toward the door, and he opened it wide. A boy stood there, one hand holding out a note and the other displaying an empty palm. Ian slipped him a coin as he accepted the envelope.

He turned to Meg, looking anything but pleased. It took no more than a glance at the expensive linen envelope, emblazoned with a *P*, to know from whom the note had come.

Meg met his frown with a triumphant smile before she even opened it.

This note was as good as gold—as good as the Pemberton gold. Her past was behind her and the future ahead. The note made it so.

Written in the same perfect script Meg herself had learned, she read the words from Claire Pemberton.

My parents' departure for Europe has delayed my response to your interesting and most unexpected note. What a delightful gift it would be for Mother if upon her return awaited the garden she always hoped you would design. So

*yes, do come, Meg. At once. Please let me know if you
need transportation and I'll send a carriage for you.*

Meg refolded it into the envelope, then looked at the waiting
faces before her.

"My invitation has been offered. I'm to come at once."

"At once?" Kate repeated. "Surely there's no hurry. You've just
lost your father!"

Tapping the edge of the envelope with her forefinger, Meg shook
her head. "Actually I'll be keeping that to myself. Claire never met
my father. No one but the Hibbit sisters knows that my father
recently passed, and they're far away in Connecticut with little connection to any of the families here in New York, at least throughout
the summer. I intend keeping my father's death to myself."

"But why would you deny such a thing?" Kate cried. "It's like
denouncing your father!"

Ian folded his hands behind his back, glaring as if he were
some kind of schoolmaster and she an errant student. "Because
she doesn't want her visit limited. Is that it? No wish to follow the
rules of mourning?"

She looked away, raising her chin and returning his glare.
"You'll thank me when I deliver the information you need."

"That's just it, Meg—I don't need it! I'm working on something else anyway and couldn't devote any time to whatever it is
you think you can accomplish."

"That's fine. It'll probably take some time for me to learn much
in any case. I welcome not having the pressure of any immediate
demands." She moved away from them both. "Still, I ought to get to
the Pembertons' as quickly as I can. I'll send a note telling them I'll
arrive in the morning. Would you mind fetching a messenger, Ian?"

"Find one yourself." He retrieved his hat and put it on, leaving
without another word.

14

Collusion for illegal gain is punishable by fine, imprisonment, or in some cases, death.

*An Informal Look at the Penal Codes of London and
New England*

IAN SHOVED HIS HANDS into his jacket pockets, determined to walk off his anger. Nothing was going as it should. If John had known how much trouble his daughter was, he might have sent her to a school of an entirely different sort. One with bars on the windows and matrons who long ago would have crushed that obstinate spirit of hers.

Even as such thoughts crossed his mind, Ian knew neither he nor John would have wanted such a thing. Not for Meggie. She was Skipjack's daughter, through and through.

Ian stopped short, nearly colliding with a suddenly immovable object in front of him. Keys.

Perhaps the day wasn't a total loss. At least he might finalize their deal.

"Brewster's waiting for you. In there." Keys pointed with his chin to the tall carriage standing by across the street. Then he tipped his hat and started walking away.

"Aren't you coming?"

"Can't. Got a shift tonight."

"Wait!" Ian took a step closer, lowered his voice. "Do we have a deal, then? What we discussed earlier?"

Keys eyed him, the slightest smile curving one corner of his marred mouth. "Sure." He glanced at Brewster's waiting carriage before studying Ian again. "Why not?"

Then he turned away, leaving Ian to approach Brewster on his own.

"Step in, won't you?" Brewster greeted from behind the door, opened no doubt by Jamie. All Ian could see was the sleeve of one of his gaudy suit coats. This one was green with a stripe of orange.

When Ian was settled, Brewster sent him a friendly smile—effectively doubling Ian's guard.

"Can we take you anywhere? Uptown? The Bowery, perhaps?"

"I'm staying in the Village for now. You can take me to Washington Square." That was close enough. No need for Brewster to be able to find him too easily.

"Jamie," Brewster said, "go up top and direct the driver."

A moment later they rolled down the avenue, and Ian cast his gaze out the window despite knowing Brewster studied him closely. Ian let him do so for several minutes, not caring if the entire ride was shared in silence. Better, in fact, if it was.

"For as long as I've known you, boy, you've never been an idiot. Until now."

Ian offered Brewster a halfhearted smile. "Because I refuse to partner with you?"

"Because you refuse to partner with her."

Ian folded his arms. Discussing the possibility of working with Meg wasn't something he cared to do, especially with Brewster.

"John wanted her to be happy," Brewster went on. "I've known her only a week, and already I can tell she wasn't happy in the life he wanted for her. In any case, she'd be no less happy than she is right now if she worked with us."

The cocksure smile on Brewster's face set off a spark of anger in Ian, but sitting at countless card tables had taught him control. "Us?"

"Your little rebellion won't last, Maguire. What are you but a lost-and-found whelp? Meg wants to take risks, the same as her father. If she tells us how to access the Pemberton gold, there will be plenty for all of us."

Ian turned his gaze from Brewster, doing his best to seem bored with the entire idea. If only it were true.

"Don't get in the way of letting her do what she wants," Brewster added softly. "I'll see that you don't, if it comes to it."

"Sounds like a threat," Ian said, careful to tinge his voice with amusement rather than intimidation—though he knew the kinds of tactics Brewster used to carry out his threats.

Brewster said nothing, offering neither admission nor denial, and they fell back into silence. Ian had no desire to change that until they reached Fourth and Eighth.

He pounded on the roof of the carriage. "You can stop here."

As the carriage slowed and Ian moved forward, Brewster extended the handle of his cane until it reached Ian's chest. "Think about it, Maguire. The only thing standing in the way is your own misguided attempt to fulfill something John himself might not have wanted. If he knew she desired to be her father's daughter, he wouldn't have thought himself unworthy."

Ian opened the carriage door, and Brewster withdrew his cane. As Ian descended to the street, he heard Brewster bang on the side of the carriage to call his attention.

"Neither would you be unworthy of her anymore, Maguire."

Ian didn't look back. Those same words—ones he'd been forcing away for days now—echoed in his mind until that was all he heard.

Part Two

15

It should be unnecessary to state that sincerity and honesty are required in all things, so long as your sincere honesty is in the best interests of others. If not, then by all means seek the virtue of silence.

Madame Marisse's Handbook for Young Ladies

FIFTH AVENUE, NEW YORK CITY

MEG WAITED WHILE the driver of her carriage mounted the stairs of the white marble home on the corner of Fifth Avenue and Thirty-Fourth Street to announce her arrival. Her luggage was in tow, but she would wait for a Pemberton servant to collect it rather than ask the driver of the hired cab to do more than he'd already done.

She dismissed any trace of embarrassment. Perhaps she should have accepted the offer Claire had made to send a Pemberton carriage, but she'd been hesitant about letting even a Pemberton liveryman know where she'd been living so recently. The only hired carriages that strolled Fifth Avenue were for gawkers, even now in the off-season. If Fifth Avenue knew the real reason she'd arrived, she would deserve such judgment—or worse. Instead, her heart pumped with excitement. It might be too late to prove her father wrong about being any value to him, but it wasn't too late to prove it to herself.

A Pemberton manservant arrived at the side of the carriage, addressed her by name, then gave orders to another servant about her belongings. He then led Meg into a wide foyer lit only by sunlight filtering through high-set leaded and stained-glass windows. Passing a set of doors that were carved like fish scales, she was taken to a full yet uncluttered parlor, a room replete with elegant furniture and original artwork that somehow managed to be unpretentious in both design and display.

The butler did nothing more than announce her name before a familiarly graceful figure came forward with hands outstretched.

"Meg! How wonderful that you've come." Claire Pemberton grabbed Meg's hands and pulled her into a quick and unexpected embrace. Meg hid her surprise. If Claire wanted to pretend they'd been the best of friends, it suited Meg's purposes to let her.

Claire called back the retreating manservant. "Please tell my brother to come down, won't you, Mr. Dunlop? He'll want to meet our houseguest."

"It's so good of you to take me in, Claire." Meg looked around the drawing room, seeing beyond the Persian carpets, the mahogany and teak furniture, past the deep forest green upholsteries and golden accents to wonder if here, in this room, might be a hidden safe or a passageway where the famous Pemberton bricks were kept. Who knew! For all Meg could guess, she might be standing above the gold right now.

"The timing for your visit couldn't be better. Nelson and I have decided to stay here in New York this summer, since Mother and Father are traveling. We wanted a quiet season, but no sooner had we agreed than I wondered if it might not seem too quiet. Having you here swept away every doubt that we chose correctly."

Claire, as always, was a portrait of loveliness. But Meg had always thought her beauty cold, her blonde hair nearly white as snow, her skin flawless but stiff—like cream left out on a winter porch—and her eyes a shade of glacier blue.

"I'm happy to be here and to offer ideas about the garden, of course. It's a garden here in the city, then?"

"Oh yes, a tiny space compared to the one at Newport. I'm afraid since our gardener retired, the courtyard here has become more like a slice of jungle than a garden. I'll show it to you after tea. I'm sure you're parched!"

Just ahead of a maid laden with a tea tray arrived a slender man Meg knew from more than one social occasion through school.

"Do you remember my brother, Nelson? Nelson, this is Meg Davenport, whom I told you about the other day."

Nelson was the reverse of his sister, the antonym of her beauty. Meg always thought it odd how two so opposite visages could come from the same family, and yet there was a shadow of similarity. Nelson's hair, though thin and lifeless, was as white as Claire's. His eyes—small while Claire's were large—were hazel but might shine blue, if the lighting were right. And his skin was a waxen pale in comparison to Claire's pink-and-white luster, lending him a fragile look. But there were rumors at school about Nelson's power in the courts and his reputation for justice that left little room to think him weak.

There was nothing weak about his smile. He exuded genuine welcome, echoing Claire. Relief over their glad reception allowed Meg no room for secret compunction about the reason behind her visit.

"I know we've met before," Nelson said, "though you probably don't remember me. As I recall, your dance card never had an empty spot at school functions."

Claire laughed. "Yes, that's true. Speaking of our school dances, look! I had our cook bake Madame's cookies, to celebrate our little reunion."

They chatted on so cordially that Meg wondered if she'd come to the right Fifth Avenue mansion. Surely this wasn't *Claire* Pemberton, who spared barely a dozen words for Meg that last year of her residence at school? Both she and Nelson treated Meg as if she'd been adopted into the family—something she wouldn't have guessed possible given the school's treatment of Evie Pemberton. Surely neither one knew Madame had depended upon Meg as a reliable source to verify some of the trouble Evie caused, resulting in the youngest Pemberton's expulsion.

"So your parents are traveling?"

Claire nodded. "Paris for the last of spring, Italy for the summer, then back to Paris before coming home for the fall season."

"And did Evie go with them?"

Both Claire and Nelson erupted in laughter.

"Mama wouldn't dream of subjecting passengers in an enclosed vessel to Evie!"

Nelson picked up his tea. "No, she's here with us. Claire has been given strict authority over her. So far, she hasn't been a whisper of trouble."

"But then we have the entire summer ahead of us." Claire's perfect face took on a frown. "I'm afraid I have a confession to make; Nelson insisted I be perfectly frank. Of course he's right; I value honesty above all things . . . only . . ."

Meg's pulse quickened over the words, knowing an honest confession was something she could not offer, either. So when Claire averted her gaze, Meg did, too.

"Well, here's the truth," Claire continued. "One of the reasons I was so happy to have you hasn't anything to do with Mother's garden. It has everything to do with Evie. We've decided to skip the summer season because of her. You must remember what trouble she's always been, and I didn't want to risk having sole authority over her at Newport of all places. You knew her for more than a year at school and must have had more success than I've had reining her in."

"But she was expelled!"

"Only after her *second* year. As one of the older students, nearly in charge, you lasted a full year with her and then some. I wasn't there to see how you managed."

"Evie never did confess what she'd done to get herself expelled," Nelson said, "and Mother refused to tell us. What did the little terror do?"

Meg wasn't sure how much to divulge, if she was to share the same roof with Evie. While she didn't recall Evie being particularly gruesome with most of her mischief, the final straw had been leaving raw chicken parts atop wardrobes in the rooms of the two most popular girls. The stench had been as noxious as it had been mysterious.

Her dismissal had happened only a year ago, not so long past to hope that maturity had rid the girl of her mischievous ways . . . or squashed a wish for revenge against anyone who might have played the slightest role in her humiliating departure.

"Let's just say her sense of humor and adventure didn't endear her to the other girls."

"Spoken like the social diplomat you were trained to become." Claire was smiling now, her confession evidently having been good for her soul. "Far better than I ever learned, I admit."

"But we do still hope you'll redesign Mother's garden," Nelson said. He glanced toward one of the tall windows at the back of the room, through which Meg saw the edge of a yard full of greenery. "I'm eager to see what you can do with the area, here in the city. It has only a few hours of sunlight due to the high walls, so God will have to help. Our gardener retired last year, and Mother hasn't hired anyone to take his place yet. But we do have Mr. Deekes, our butler. He'll purchase whatever you recommend and follow your instructions for planting. Will you be needing anything else?"

"I've brought my books—sketches I've done through the years, full of possibilities. I thought I might show them to both of you for suggestions of what your mother might like."

"We'll be glad to help, of course," Claire said, although her hesitant voice sounded anything but glad. She exchanged a glance with her brother, who gave a small, encouraging nod. "Only I must admit this idea isn't entirely for Mother's sake. It seems our new neighbor next door, Mrs. Mason, hinted about the garden not being up to Fifth Avenue standards. I'm not at all sure she meant it to be a slight, but that's the way Mother received it. So having you here will solve not only the garden, but a rift between neighbors."

"They're new to New York and Fifth Avenue," Nelson added, "which likely accounts for noticing things like standards. In any case, we've gone through a series of neighbors since the one that ended in heartache. We'd like to do what we can to maintain good relations with this new family."

"There was heartache between neighbors?" Meg asked, intrigued but cautious. Had Evie's mischief been so serious that it caused a family to move away?

"Nelson!" Claire chided. "How could you bring that up? And in front of our guest!"

"I assumed Meg knew all about it. Isn't that what schoolmates do, share all of their secrets?"

Meg might have made a flippant remark to ease any hint of embarrassment, but she held back when she noticed the tremble in Claire's hand as she set aside her tea. Evidently this secret was no trifling matter.

"Then I'm glad I've come, Claire." Meg squashed any trace of conscience and added, "So we can get to know one another well enough to share all of our secrets."

Was that gratitude in those once-frosty eyes?

Nelson stood. "I'll leave you both to it, then. Forgive me if I've said anything I shouldn't have, Clairy. And I'll see you both at dinner." He turned to Meg with a polite bow. "It's a pleasure to have you here, Meg—do you mind me calling you that?" He exchanged a quick smile with his sister. "I'm afraid with our parents gone, we've relaxed many of the rules, so I hope you'll allow me the liberty of treating you like a member of the family."

He was gone then, and Meg found herself wishing he'd been able to stay. How lucky Claire was to have such a brother—one who might say the wrong thing but do it so charmingly.

When her gaze fell back on Claire, she found another reason to wish Nelson hadn't left. Claire seemed to have closed up a little, becoming more like the quiet, standoffish girl Meg remembered from school.

"I'm surprised you didn't travel with your parents to Europe, Claire. Did you not want to go?"

She gave a shrug, a decidedly un-Madame-Marisse-like gesture that was somehow still becoming on Claire. "I went to London and Paris last year with Mother, and the long voyage was just enough to make me appreciate our own country all the more."

"What about Nelson?"

"Oh, he couldn't possibly leave for an extended amount of time. He's a lawyer, you know, and in spite of Fifth Avenue disapproval of all the time he spends working, many people—beyond Fifth Avenue—depend upon him." She offered a grin that held a spark of the happiness she'd possessed when Meg first arrived. "Besides, Mother would never leave me here with Evie alone. One of us might not survive, although I'm not entirely certain which of us would be the victim."

Meg looked around, wondering where the mischief maker was at the moment.

Claire looked toward the open door, beyond which the stairway was partially visible. "I suppose I should go and check on her, make sure she hasn't disappeared the way she does sometimes. I'll show you your room too. It's our favorite guest room and overlooks the courtyard that you'll be designing. We thought you might like it."

"I'm sure I will."

"I should tell you, too, that we gather the family and staff together every morning, and you're more than welcome to join us if you like. We meet at the piano here in the parlor at nine thirty. If that's too early, please don't feel obligated. I only wanted to extend the invitation so you'll know what's happening should you hear any voices."

No doubt a planning meeting about meals and the day's engagements, something Meg need not attend since she only planned to tag along with Claire.

As they climbed the stairs, memories of Evie's school pranks made Meg wonder if a quiet house was a good sign or bad.

Claire stopped in front of one of the upstairs doors. "Here we are."

She opened the pristine white, six-paneled door and stepped aside for Meg to enter first.

Meg saw only a glimpse of a room decorated in pinks and greens before a huge gray shadow at the window captured her gaze. Instant fear stole her breath. Wings longer than the length of Meg's arms flapped madly, contrasting with a tail apparently dipped in vibrant red. The large bird hopped precariously along one edge of a sturdy but tipping lampshade. Feathers floated to the table beneath, joining what looked like generous spots of feces.

Upon sight of them, the bird's head lowered and its hefty body went rigid as it stared directly at Claire, eye level.

"Evelyn Annabel Pemberton! Evie, come here at once and take this dreadful creature to the aviary!"

Meg's heart rate calmed once she knew the bird hadn't flown in from the wild. Only then did she realize the window wasn't even open. The bird evidently could not fly anyway, and thankfully its droppings seemed contained in a single area.

A moment later Evie appeared, her light-brown hair loosely braided, with various wisps having escaped a once-neat pattern. She'd grown at least an inch since Meg had seen her last, an appropriate height for a near-fifteen-year-old. But her green eyes shone bright with the same look of pleasure they'd had after any successful antic back at school.

"Oh, did I forget to take you with me?" Her loving words, aimed at the bird, made the gray-feathered pet instantly relax. His head and body went up, and his wings fluttered as if inviting an embrace. When Evie held out her arm, he hopped aboard and climbed up to her shoulder. "That's my pretty baby."

"Pretty baby," the bird repeated. "Funny prank. Funny prank."

Meg couldn't help but laugh. "It seems he's tattled on you, Evie."

She scowled. "He always says that."

Claire pointed a finger at her sister. "That's because anyone who's around you for five minutes knows that's what you do best: your so-called funny pranks. Only I don't think they're funny at all. Look at the mess he made!"

"Hello, pretty girl," the bird went on, this time eyeing Meg.

"You don't have to greet her, Pindar. She's the one who made me leave school."

To that the bird whistled in a decidedly human way.

Evie might have walked from the room, but Meg held out a hand to detain her, despite the bird's proximity. It did have a rather large, black beak that looked capable of tearing into flesh.

"It wasn't my decision to have you leave, Evie."

"We all know who was responsible for your expulsion," Claire said. "You were, Evie. And it's ancient history by now anyway. Apologize to Meg this instant, and then get that bird out of here."

Evie walked from the room, gazing downward, mumbling as she walked. "I don't apologize."

"Apologize," the bird said and repeated the word all the way out of the room.

When her sister was gone, Claire turned to Meg. "You've gotten off lightly. The last time I had a friend stay, she put a snake in the bed. Oh!" She eyed the neatly covered mattress as if an idea had just struck her. "I think we ought to check anyway. I'll have someone up here to clean that table and replace the lamp too. Perhaps we ought to check the closet and the corners and drawers as well."

As they did so, Meg couldn't help thinking that, despite Evie, she might enjoy her stay after all.

16

The difference between bank robbery and bank burglary is whether or not the victimized bank was open at the time of the theft. It is robbery if the bank is open for business, putting the lives of employees and patrons at risk. It is burglary if the bank is closed at the time of compromise. Either criminal act is a felony and not to be dealt with lightly.

An Informal Look at the Penal Codes of London and
New England

IAN LEFT THE BANK, having made yet another deposit—one he would soon withdraw in both an unconventional and illegal way. He walked with a light step until turning onto Broadway. It was there he felt something old and vaguely familiar join him. The weight of a shadow trailing behind.

This was no human shadow. Rather it was something Ian had long ago thought he'd banished. He shrugged one of his shoulders as if to shove it away, but no sooner had he done so than the memory of its origin made it grow even larger. It was a shadow his father had tried to bequeath him—his real father, not the replacement both he and John had established through their friendship. This was the shadow of compunction.

Why be bothered with such a thing now? This wasn't the first bank job he'd planned. Ian's thoughts scattered in search of an answer. Surely by understanding the dilemma, Ian could leave it behind.

The answer was easy. Meg's wish to have better known her father had conjured memories in Ian of his own family. Memories he hadn't allowed himself to ponder for quite some time.

He picked up his pace in a useless attempt to skirt the phantom. His plan for the bank was set. It was bound to be a success with the measures he'd taken, and it certainly could not be abandoned at this late stage anyway. Besides, what harm was done? Brewster might work with those possessing fewer scruples, but Ian limited himself to an etiquette established by Skipjack, one that had steadily averted threat of arrest. Settling for the theft of stocks and bonds for ransom—and not endangering either the public or bank employees in the process—would result in the same freedom John had enjoyed his entire life.

Ian was a master at negotiation, something John had always utilized. With the theft limited to banknotes, the bank often didn't even involve the police. True, it made the banks somewhat complicit in these crimes, but it was worth it to save the embarrassment of having been robbed. Through negotiation they ended up with their stolen notes returned, and Ian with cash that was more or less sanctioned. The banks benefited by tightening their security, so as far as Ian saw it, he did them a favor. More or less.

Ian knew the layout of the targeted bank as if it were his own home. Before this week was out—on Thursday, to be exact—Dickson would stay late on his shift to prepare the supposedly crack-proof safe. He would drill holes with one of the smallest drill tips available, holes that would be indiscernible once he adhered putty to the vulnerable spot. Ian could then compromise the safe by removing a small piece of the drilled metal and inserting a tiny mirror below the combination wheel. He would twist the dial to see which numbers allowed the safe to open. With the holes already drilled, Ian could be in and out in a matter of minutes. All under Keys's watchful beat parade on the sidewalk outside—making sure the street remained safe. For them.

They waited only for the designated day. Soon, not only would Ian's coffers increase; so would his reputation for designing a job without John's—or Brewster's—help.

With the upcoming success, Ian's claim to have little use for Brewster couldn't be denied. He could far more easily refuse anything Brewster proposed after this week.

Including the proposal to accept help from Meg.

Now all he needed do was avoid thoughts of either her or the old memories newly stalking him.

Although Fifth Avenue ran alongside Central Park, the park was too far from the Pemberton mansion near Thirty-Fourth Street to reach by foot, at least by feet confined within fashionable shoes. The afternoon following Meg's arrival, Claire insisted they continue her normal routine by taking a drive to the park and, once there, a walk.

Surprisingly enough, Evie didn't need to be asked. She appeared at the door at the appointed time of departure, looking far neater than she had yesterday with her messy braids and rumpled day dress. Today her maid must have taken great care with Evie's coif, creating curls from a fountain of light-brown hair that cascaded in waves past her shoulders. Her dress, though falling above the ankles, denoting her youth, was clean and attractive with straight sleeves and a cinch waist. She didn't compare to Claire, who looked particularly lovely in the multiple flounces and dainty lace of her turquoise morning gown, but Evie was pretty nonetheless. If Meg didn't know better, at that moment Evie could have presented herself as an immaculate product of Madame Marisse's.

They soon alighted from the Pemberton carriage under the welcoming shade of young oaks and maples inside the low, concrete Scholars' Gate.

"Are there any particular plants or flowers your mother has admired in the park?" Meg asked. "Perhaps we might consider them for the courtyard, if you see any that grow in shade."

"She does love those tall purple flowers," Claire said. "We'll see them along the way."

"Must we always go the same route, Clairy?" Evie moaned.

"There's nothing wrong with taking a familiar path."

Evie looked from her sister to Meg and then issued a smile that was never a good sign from the girl. "Do you know why she always takes the same path, Meg?"

Meg shook her head but, judging by the unprecedented wrinkle marring Claire's forehead, guessed she didn't want it discussed.

"Because she used to walk this route with our old neighbor, Jude Johnson. They were supposed to get married, only Jude left her. A year later, the rest of the family packed up and followed him to Chicago. The last of their belongings were taken away the very day their wedding was to have been."

Meg watched the color in Claire's face heighten, though she made no attempt to stop her sister's words.

"I'm so very sorry, Claire," she whispered. "I didn't know."

"Nobody did," Evie went on, her tone a cheerful contrast to the subject. "She went back to school that last year even though the engagement had just been broken. Didn't you notice how she was? I expect she didn't say a word at school, unless they were the ones no one could avoid: 'Yes, Madame,' or 'No, Madame.'"

"Really, Evie," Claire said quietly, "must you enjoy yourself so much in trying to embarrass me?"

"I'm not trying to—oh!" She cut herself off, waving a handkerchief that had appeared from her palm. Meg followed Evie's gaze to see a young man with an older woman—much older, gray-haired and somewhat frail—walking slowly along a path that would naturally intersect theirs up ahead. "Look, it's Geoffrey!"

"The latest of the new neighbors," Claire said to Meg. "The Masons."

Eyes sparkling, Evie nodded. "Yes, they're the third family to live next door since the Johnsons moved out. They've lived there only a few months, but we hope they stay! People do come and go in New York, don't they? Come along, Clairy! They've spotted us. We don't want to keep them waiting, and you know Nomi doesn't do much walking. She'll be back in that carriage before you know it."

Considering the slow pace of the woman tottering alongside the man, it was doubtful they would reach the intersection before Evie.

"Good afternoon, Geoffrey!" Evie greeted. "How lovely to run into you."

"Hello, Evie."

Geoffrey could not be much older but was considerably taller than Evie, even without the top hat he removed in greeting. A light spring coat broadened his shoulders, giving him the classic look of a gentleman in the latest dove gray. His light-brown eyes were set a trifle too close and his mouth a straight line until stretching into a polite smile. Overall he was strikingly handsome, though, with a proportionate nose and thick hair that suddenly reminded Meg of that dog Ian so loved, with its color of milky cocoa.

Because Evie had reached them first, she was at the forefront of the meeting. Claire made introductions as Meg joined them, and she learned the older woman was Geoffrey's grandmother, whom everyone called Nomi. She was an impressive woman, her thick gray hair perfectly waved beneath a feathered hat—a hat that could have been the inspiration behind Geoffrey's dove-colored coat.

"It's a pleasure to meet you, Miss Davenport," Nomi said. "How long will you be visiting the Pembertons?"

"For the summer. I hope to help them refresh the courtyard garden. Perhaps you might be able to see a portion of it? Claire tells me your house is the closest to hers."

Geoffrey, who upon introduction had politely bowed toward Meg while keeping his hold on his grandmother's elbow, nodded and replaced his top hat. "Yes, we can see the furthermost corner."

"Improving the garden is welcome news," Nomi said, sparing a glance with one raised brow Claire's way.

"So you've an eye for greenery and flowers, I take it?" Geoffrey said to Meg.

"Yes, I do enjoy the colors of a garden. There are so many."

"I do, too," Evie said.

Claire shook her head. "You detest the garden, Evie. For someone without a trace of fear when it comes to birds or snakes or lizards, you have a most unexpected respect for at least one of God's less amicable creations: bees."

"That's only because I was stung and know how much it hurts."

"Speaking of your fearlessness, Evie," Geoffrey said, "how is Pindar doing?"

"Pindar was a gift from Geoffrey," Claire explained to Meg. "He brought him from . . . where, did you say?"

"The Congo, just after my graduation from secondary schooling."

Meg eyed him, assessing his age. He seemed to possess confidence that came with maturity, but that often came with money as well. Certainly his skin was not smooth like a youth's, yet there was something very young about him despite the knowledge that at his graduation he would have been precisely the age Meg was now.

"That explains why the bird speaks French," Claire said. "Though some of his words wouldn't have been any learned at Madame Marisse's."

Meg felt Nomi's gaze on her. "So you're a graduate of the famous Madame Marisse's as well, Miss Davenport?"

"Yes. Please feel free to call me Meg," she said. Might as well join Nelson and Claire in abandoning some of society's rules this summer—along with the others she was delighted to discard.

"Claire is such a spoiler about our wonderful Pindar," Evie said to Geoffrey. "You'll be happy to know he is very healthy and happy and so brilliant there isn't a cage in the aviary that can contain him. Feel free to visit us anytime, Geoffrey."

"Pindar greeted Meg upon her arrival," Claire said.

Geoffrey's gaze had gone briefly to Evie but now rested again on Meg—a gaze she was dismayed to recognize as an interested, exploratory one. She broke their eye contact, feigning shyness. No use complicating her visit with an unwanted suitor.

"I hope you weren't frightened," he said. "He's larger than most house birds."

"Oh, he didn't frighten her in the least," Evie said. "I was right there, anyway, to take him away. His favorite perch is my shoulder. Do you know, I think he'll be able to entirely undo my braids one of these days. Our Pindar is so clever!"

Geoffrey glanced back at Evie, where the look in his eye shifted entirely to one of simple affection. "Tell me when he can braid that hair of yours, and then I'll call him truly clever."

"Miss Pemberton," Nomi said, "won't you bring your guest to our home for supper later this week? Thursday, perhaps? And your brother, if he's available, of course. Perhaps my daughter can give you some suggestions for the garden. We did promise your mother to look in on you from time to time while they're gone, you know."

If Meg were to judge Claire's enthusiasm by her smile, she

didn't feel much in that direction. "We should love to come to dinner, Nomi. Thank you for the invitation."

"My daughter will send a note this afternoon, then. Good day."

They started to walk on, and Evie called after them, "I'll look forward to seeing you on Thursday, Geoffrey!"

Once she and her companions were also on their way, Claire took less care to conceal her dissatisfaction. "I suppose that will please Mrs. Mason, to help design Mother's garden." Then she glared at her younger sister. "And I don't recall your name included in the invitation."

"But of course they meant to invite me! Didn't you see Geoffrey smile at me?"

"It's understood now, in any case," Meg said.

Claire nodded, to Evie's obvious delight—and Claire's just as obvious dismay.

If you present yourself as honest, trustworthy, and a gentleman, those who meet you will likely accept you as such. The true discernment of the average mark is nearly nonexistent.

ALEXANDER "THE GENT" DIBATTISTA
    Code of Thieves

"FOR YOU, MISS," said the maid at Meg's bedroom door. She handed Meg an envelope. "It came just a moment ago."

It was midmorning on Thursday, and Meg had been about to go downstairs, knowing she'd missed yet another of the staff and family gatherings. She doubted such a meeting would offer the kind of information she was looking for anyway. What could the staff know about where the Pemberton gold might be hidden?

Meg unfolded the note eagerly, seeing the masculine boldness of the writing.

> *My dear Miss Davenport,*
> *Please permit me to send greetings from a fond friend.*
> *I hope one day soon our paths will cross again.*

It was signed with a reminder that Alwinus Brewster was ever at her service.

So, he was keeping track of her whereabouts. Surely he guessed she had no need of his offer for protection and must have heard by now that she was working with Ian. If she *was* working with Ian! She still wasn't entirely certain.

Meg folded the note and slipped it into the fireplace. It had been an uncommonly chilly night, and the coal embers were still hot enough to consume the paper and its envelope, too.

Thursday's sunset seemed especially long in coming, marking the predawn hour an eternity away. Ian paced, but it only made time move more slowly. Everyone was in place; he'd done all he could to plan each detail, including addressing potential problems. The bank's janitor would not arrive until five in the morning, and by then Ian and the others would be well and truly gone. A generously paid-off night watchman, who owed his job to Dickson, had allowed a replacement of Ian's choosing to fill in for him until three in the morning. Pubjug would let Ian into the bank and stay until the regular watchman returned sometime later.

Ian sat on the couch with Roscoe at his side. The dog's whimper said he sensed his owner's mood, somewhere between anticipation and anxiety. Not even Roscoe's softest fur could calm Ian's pulse. There was no room for the dog to run, but tugging on an old sock spent some of the extra energy they both needed to rid themselves of.

Soon the fire in Ian's veins would be used to carry out his plans, forever ensuring his independence from Brewster.

Evie led the way up the sidewalk, her eagerness to arrive at the Masons' all too clear. Claire set a more leisurely pace beside Meg, and Nelson brought up the rear like the guardian he was.

"It appears your neighbor across the street is having a party," Meg said, "with every window lit."

Claire sighed. "That's exactly why we put you in the guest room at the back of the house, Meg—so you wouldn't be bothered by the lights in those windows. That's the Fillinghem-Welch home, and poor Mr. Fillinghem-Welch passed on so suddenly his wife hasn't been able to accustom herself to it. She's been hosting parties of imaginary guests every night for the past year, ever since her husband died."

Meg glanced again at the house that looked so merry, with its pearl-hued stone exterior contrasting to the many brownstones along this stretch of the avenue. She'd heard more than her share of strange stories about wealthy New Yorkers, how families came and went as fortunes allowed, but rumors seemed harmless until imagining real people behind such tales.

There was no time to dwell on the image of a widow who drank toasts to figment friends because Evie was already twisting the bell on the Mason door. Soon they were divested of their cloaks and ushered into a parlor, where Meg was introduced not only to Mr. and Mrs. Mason—dressed impeccably to their station—but reacquainted with both Nomi and Geoffrey.

Conversation during the before-dinner interval was pleasant enough, and Evie exhibited rare good sense by keeping quiet. She did laugh a trifle loudly at each of Geoffrey's witty comments, but the Masons had the grace to ignore her youthful display of enthusiasm. Mrs. Mason spoke to Meg about the garden, as expected, but her suggestion to consider removing the dovecote in the corner closest to their home seemed reasonable rather than meddlesome. Meg knew how early doves started billing and cooing.

When dinner was announced and Mrs. Mason directed the procession, Meg was disheartened to learn Geoffrey was to be her escort, signaling their partnership throughout the meal. Evie,

Meg noticed, was seated as far from Geoffrey as the table allowed, between Nomi and Claire.

Meg knew the dinner hour was the most important of a hostess's day. She didn't have to be well acquainted with Fifth Avenue families to realize the newest in the neighborhood wasn't likely to possess a sought-after table. However, she saw no reason the Mason table would not become just that. The conversation rarely faltered, and the food was more than palatable, from the bisque to the chicken croquettes to the pineapple soufflé. Meg could fault neither Mrs. Mason nor her staff, but for one thing: the perfection of the meal suggested a hint of fear that any broken or merely bent rule of etiquette would be irredeemable.

Meg was mulling such thoughts when Geoffrey led her from the dining room back to the parlor, where he leaned close and whispered in her ear. "I must say this is the most enjoyable test I've had all month."

"Test?" she whispered back.

He smiled at her and glanced at his mother, who was sitting in the same chair she'd occupied earlier, as if he knew their time for private conversation was limited. "Mother is working her way up Fifth Avenue society. Perhaps by the time the top of society has returned from Newport, she'll relax a few of the rules."

The Meg of Madame Marisse's school would have been aghast at Geoffrey's blatant honesty. Certainly such an admission was well outside every rule of after-dinner conversation. But the Meg who was her father's daughter chose instead to be amused.

"Your mother is doing a marvelous job."

"Mother is Dutch but not a Knickerbocker; she's from Illinois of all places. She's rich, but even here where money ages so quickly, ours is still a tad new."

A footman arrived to offer wine, which Meg refused but Geoffrey accepted.

Geoffrey leaned close again. "Your being here in New York at the end of June speaks volumes, you know. Rather than at Newport."

"Claire and Nelson decided to stay home this summer, while their parents are traveling."

"And my mother and grandmother attend neither Newport nor Saratoga for lack of an invitation. Father won't build Mother a Newport cottage until she gains acceptance, and Mother is afraid she won't gain acceptance until she builds. You see the dilemma?"

Meg studied him as he took a sip of his wine. He appeared entirely unashamed of his revelation that his family—at least his mother and perhaps Nomi as well—were parvenus of the worst kind, attempting to climb their way into a social class that obviously had yet to open its arms.

"Your honesty is . . ." She'd been about to say *refreshing*, and yet that wasn't exactly what she meant. "Astounding."

"The truth is we're from Chicago, Miss Davenport. Where Mother turned her back on what's considered the height of society there, to try her best at elbowing her way into the toughest society on earth: New York City's. We're not some old, established family or descendants of European aristocracy. All we have is money. I've learned wealthy people can afford big houses, fancy clothes, lavish parties . . . and incredible rudeness. Mother was rude to Chicago snobs and now is on the other end with New York's elite."

He kept his full attention on Meg while the others listened to whatever tale Mrs. Mason shared on the opposite side of the room. "Let my honesty continue to astound you, Miss Davenport. I plan to visit the Pemberton home tomorrow on the pretense of seeing Pindar. Evie rarely takes no for an answer, and so in a few moments when I mention my intention, I'm sure it'll be accepted. But I'll really be there with hopes of seeing you."

With others now laughing along with Mrs. Mason, Meg was

confident no one paid them any attention. "Do you mind if I press that honesty of yours with one rather obvious question?"

He raised a brow as if his consent was given.

"Claire is much closer to your age than Evie. Why is it you haven't expressed an interest in her?"

A golden light brightened his brown eyes. "I would have been happy to give her my full attention from the moment I moved in—at least it would prevent Evie's pointless preoccupation with me. But from the icy shoulder Claire offered and all Evie has told me, the last thing Claire wants is another suitor from the house next door. Any more questions?"

"No, but I do have a warning. If your family truly does have an interest in acceptance from Upper Fifth, then I assure you I will be of no help."

He lifted his wineglass in a toast. "On the contrary, my dear. You're a product of Madame Marisse's. At the very least, you can advise my mother on the many rules of high society."

"The very thing I've escaped by leaving school. So you see, I would bring you no benefit whatsoever."

He leaned scandalously close, making her stiffen. "Let me be the judge of what benefit you might bring."

Two hours later, once the after-dinner interval had elapsed into general conversation and then come to a polite end, Meg left with the Pembertons for the short stroll home. Across the street, the imaginary party at the Fillinghem-Welch mansion was still in full swing, while up the street a few fine carriages rolled along.

They were barely inside their own door before Evie rushed past, chin high, elbows swinging as she stomped up the stairs to her room.

"Best lock your door tonight," Claire said to Meg.

"Why?"

Nelson let a servant take his hat and coat. "I'll speak to her, and if I sense she's up to any mischief, it'll be her door that's locked."

"Whatever are you both talking about?" Meg asked.

Claire took Meg's hand as if to offer fortification. "Didn't you see Evie scowling at you all evening? You were seated next to Geoffrey at dinner, and afterward he did all he could to occupy your attention."

"Oh yes, it's plain that she cares for him." Meg looked at Nelson. "May I come with you to talk to her?"

"Of course."

Evie wasn't in her bedroom, but that didn't seem to surprise Nelson, who then led the way to the front corner of the house. He opened a door to a room where ceramic, cast-iron, and brass pots supported a variety of ferns and tall palms amid intermittent shocks of color from fuchsia or heliotrope. There were several birdcages, most of them covered and quiet.

One cage stood empty, nearest Evie. Pindar, the large gray bird, sat perched on Evie's shoulder. Her back was to them, and when Nelson spoke her name, she refused to turn around.

"Perhaps Evie and I might talk . . . alone?" Meg asked.

Nelson did not hasten to agree as Claire might have, but at last he nodded. "Evie, I expect you to behave yourself. And I remind you again that it isn't only I who would be disappointed if you misbehave. The Lord watches all you do. I want your word you'll not create any mischief for Meg. Do I have your promise?"

Only a shrug ensued, one that briefly lifted the bird on her shoulder, who flapped an ineffective wing.

"Evie." Nelson's voice increased in firmness.

She heaved a sigh. "All right, I heard you."

Pindar repeated the words, followed by something in French that Meg was fairly certain had to do with fish entrails.

Meg waited for Nelson to leave. There were two wrought-iron

chairs near the window, and she walked past Evie with a motion for the girl to join her.

Evie ignored the invitation.

Meg folded her hands. "All right, then, Evie. I'll be brief. I know you don't want to be friends because you blame me for what happened at school. So we'll start with that. It's true Madame Marisse asked me if I'd seen you leaving the kitchen at an odd hour, carrying a sack—we assume containing the chicken. She also asked if I saw you fill those perfume bottles with vinegar. I could have lied or simply refused to speak, but the fact is I did neither. I didn't protect you because I knew you wouldn't have done the same for me or for any other girl at the school."

She let that thought linger between them for a moment before going on. "Do you think you were the only one ever to play a prank at school? Of course you weren't. But you were the only one to do so many and to do them without the protection of friendship. That's what caused your trouble. You didn't take the time to cultivate any allies."

Placing a finger beneath the bird's claws and moving him from her shoulder to the top of the empty cage nearby, Evie took the seat next to Meg. She tilted her head as if to consider Meg with some perplexity. "You're not going to lecture me about how wrong it is to play a prank?"

"I suspect you've known right from wrong for a long time, as evidenced by your brother and sister. But you chose your own way from that very first assignment at school. The pillows, remember?"

Evie smiled with the memory, and Meg was tempted to as well. They'd been assigned to embroider small parlor pillows with a verse from the Bible. Evie had paraphrased a verse from the first chapter of Job: *Naked I came; naked I go.* Hardly an endearing quote from a child whose responsibility was to exhibit modesty above nearly all other things.

"I suppose next you'll tell me you want to be my ally."

"Hardly. What I want is to sleep in peace. And perhaps spare your sister some worry. Why do you do the things you do?"

"If I answer that question, will you answer a question of mine?"

"I'll try."

"I'm good at mischief. I'm clever that way. And everyone always likes Claire but not me, so why not do as I please?" The answer was so quick, so practiced, that Meg wished she'd bartered better, at least to ask more questions about Claire. Then Evie placed her palms on the sides of her seat. "Now answer this question for me: are you falling in love with Geoffrey?"

"I barely know him!"

"All you did was talk to him this entire evening. You should know by now whether or not you *want* to fall in love with him."

At least Meg could answer this one honestly. "I most assuredly am not falling in love with Geoffrey Mason."

Evie relaxed in the chair, folding her hands in her lap. "That's fine. Then as long as you refuse his attention, I won't cause you any trouble."

Meg stood. "I'm glad to hear that, but you do know you can't threaten every girl who catches his interest, don't you?"

"Only for the next three years. I'll be seventeen then, and that's old enough."

"Old enough . . . for what?"

"Anything I might have to do to catch his interest."

Meg wanted to sit again to give Evie a lecture she never would have heard at Madame Marisse's—one about expanding her goals and objectives beyond capturing the interest of a man. But she couldn't give that lecture. Not when she might be guilty of the very same crime.

18

Without exception, the thieves I have met in my long and
illustrious career seek not only to answer their demand for
high adventure through such an occupation as mine, but more
importantly to strike against those stingy bankers, those corrupt
businessmen, those greedy rich men, by divesting them of some of
their ill-gotten gain.

ALEXANDER "THE GENT" DIBATTISTA

Code of Thieves

BY THE TIME THE sun shone brightly above and the deed was long
done, Ian had considered every possible consequence of the burglary. So far, he was certain none of the others had taken time to
consider the fears Ian now contemplated.

They would no doubt celebrate this job for months to come.
After all, a million dollars was nothing to scoff at and would
certainly end any perceived need for Brewster. A successful
job—particularly one with the potential of bringing in so much
profit—would lift more than a few brows. But it was success in
spite of Brewster that would command the most attention.

The hotel room Ian had rented on the edge of the Bowery
was clean and nearly respectable. He hadn't attracted much attention walking in, carrying a nondescript black satchel. Dickson was
already there, and Pubjug and Keys had met them later.

Ian's satchel was full of banknotes totaling over a million dollars. Pubjug, having joined Ian in the vault, had swiped some gold eagle coins as well.

The commercial paper in Ian's satchel was every bit as valuable as what they'd left behind in ignored safe-deposit boxes. What they took would be far safer to exchange with the bank for profit, far easier than selling any goods from a safe-deposit box that their owners could identify. He couldn't hope to cash a single note without being caught—but then, without the notes the rightful owners couldn't cash them either. And thus would begin the ransom dance. For a percentage of the value, Ian would be happy to return the stolen goods to the bank. He knew the bank would be more concerned about the return of property they held in trust than justice being served.

The total amount of their payout had yet to be calculated. Ian had left for the bank manager the customary instructions on how to negotiate the return of the stolen notes. Four hundred thousand in cash for more than twice that in paper was a fair enough price. Such deals were standard practice when those who abided by the law were bested by those who did not.

Ian wasn't in the least worried that someone would finger his crew, although apart from the four directly involved, there were at least that many more who would rightfully suspect his signature on this job. Other than the bonds, banknotes, and gold coin, they'd taken nothing and violated none of the safe-deposit boxes, showing a singular act of restraint. But those who could've identified him lived in the same murky world Ian inhabited and, like all cockroaches, were most comfortable in the sewers of society.

Still, the truth was this job wasn't truly over until the bonds and notes were negotiated, so Ian didn't allow himself the jubilance the others enjoyed. Only after his satchel had been ransomed would he share their triumph. One hundred thousand apiece wasn't a bad haul, not bad at all—well, except for Ian himself and Keys. Ian had agreed to giving Keys 25 percent more, a share he'd originally designated for himself, having planned the theft from the beginning. Even if they had to settle for a bit less, the night would still be a success once the negotiations were completed.

While Ian's bank account would still swell considerably, he would be free to continue as he pleased without interference from Brewster. Money was, after all, the only thing beside his dog that Ian trusted.

And he would have done it all without using Meg—no matter how willing she claimed to be.

Nearly two weeks after she'd arrived at the Pembertons', Meg began to wonder how effective she would be at gaining the information she hoped to acquire. Claire was perfectly sweet, if a bit private, and Evie had thankfully decided to leave them alone entirely. Nelson, the one Meg was sure had the most knowledge about where the famed Pemberton gold bricks might be housed, was rarely at home. No one ever talked about money, the source of their wealth, or even the bank at which they might be storing their gold. Meg knew she could hardly bring it up without casting herself in sudden suspicion.

One thing she'd learned about the Pemberton household was that the servants were far friendlier here than at any other home Meg had visited. She'd also learned that despite being surrounded by the highest-quality furnishings, neither Claire nor Evie went on the daily shopping sprees of many other girls their ages. All they ever did on a regular basis was stroll through Central Park. Admittedly it was a place used almost exclusively by the elite families surrounding the considerable park, but walking there did little to enhance the image of Pemberton purchasing abilities since it was entirely free.

When Claire mentioned that Nelson led the morning meetings she'd described on the day Meg had arrived, Meg decided it was time to join them. It wasn't difficult to rise early, considering all she did in the evening was sit with Claire in the parlor either drawing flowers and garden sketches or reading one of the many books from the Pemberton library. And if she was going to be successful at finding the gold, Meg was beginning to think she would have to befriend Nelson.

"Oh, Meg!" Claire greeted her at the parlor doors. "You've decided to join us this morning. I'm so glad. Come in, won't you?"

Nelson stood beside the piano, with Evie on a window seat nearby. The rest of the room was crowded with the staff: the head housekeeper, a chef and a cook, a butler and a valet, two lady's maids, a parlormaid, a chambermaid, four footmen, a coachman, a stable hand, and a dark-haired girl who curtsied Meg's way and was probably a maid of all work. Obviously when Claire said the staff, she meant the *entire* staff.

Other than a soft whisper or a giggle here and there, the room was quiet. Nelson had little trouble calling them to attention.

"We can leave the doors open this morning," he said when someone went to close them. "We're all present today; no need to keep quiet. We can *shout* today if we like."

Laughter bubbled up from opposite ends of the room over the way Nelson bellowed the word.

"All right, then. Let's begin. Anyone?"

"I had a letter from my sister, asking we pray for her youngest daughter. She's been sick in bed nearly a week now."

"Could we lift my brother in prayer? He's having an awful time since his wife died."

"I know . . . ," started the young maid of all work in a tremulous

voice. "I know all of ye are so generous in yer prayer, always askin'
for others. But might it be all right if I asked ye to pray for me?
I . . . I miss me folks so! And I'm never to see them again, as far as
they be—still back home in Ireland."

A general rumble of compassion erupted, and although one
maid had already placed an arm around the girl, another woman
came closer to offer her an arm of support—none other than Mrs.
Longford, the housekeeper. As Nelson began a prayer, even Claire
rested a gentle hand on the servant's shoulder.

If Meg hadn't been so well trained at hiding any extremes of
emotion, she might have stood with her mouth agape. Instead she
watched as if the sight were common, this mingling of classes both
rich and servant as if all were one family. Never in her life had she
seen or heard of such a thing.

So preoccupied was Meg that she could barely listen to what
Nelson prayed, though she was sure he included all of the requests
made and then some. When he spoke her name, thanking God for
Meg's visit and asking His blessing upon her, Meg blinked, quickly
bowed her head, then folded her hands and joined the rest who
silently prayed along.

It wasn't as if she'd never prayed before. Faith in God was certainly
understood by all who attended Madame Marisse's, and Madame
had made prayer regular practice at school, at least before every
meal. Meg had just never seen it practiced so . . . democratically.

Soon the prayer ended and music started, with Claire at the
piano and Nelson leading a hymn. Thankfully it was one with which
Meg was familiar, Luther's "A Mighty Fortress Is Our God."

By the time the servants went on their way, Meg still didn't
know what the meeting had accomplished. No meals were discussed. No schedules compared. No correspondence mentioned,
no marketing or household needs determined. Nothing productive
happened at all.

All the meeting had really produced was a number of smiles and a few grateful tears. And although Evie had behaved like a quietly angelic youth, she was the first to leave the room. But Claire and Nelson lingered, both coming to Meg.

"I hope you didn't mind," Claire said. "I suppose I should have warned you about the kind of meetings we have."

"Is this something your family has always done?"

"Of a sort," Claire started, then looked to her brother to continue.

"We expanded on it a bit since Mother and Father sailed, but the staff doesn't mind, and we like it this way."

"But when do you tend the day's business? The menus and household needs and such?"

"We discuss all that before the meeting begins. Anyone who has business arrives earlier. Nine thirty is when everyone else arrives, and we officially start the day in a way that brightens everyone's spirits and reminds us of what's important."

Claire put her arm around Meg. "And don't tell Father when my parents return—I hope you'll still be here—but we've raised everyone's wages, though Father was the most generous employer on the block to begin with. It's been more fun than I can tell you seeing how happy it's made everyone."

"That's very generous of you," Meg said cautiously, "so long as they don't tell the neighbors. You'll have to withstand some censure from the other families who don't want to match your wages."

Nelson signaled a servant for his hat and coat. "We've thought of that," he said, "which is why our higher wage is only temporary, until Father returns. Given with the admonition that it's to be kept our own happy little secret."

"You're off already?" Claire asked him. "You haven't even had breakfast."

"I've had coffee. I'm contributing to a procedure that I'm eager to see finished. Another bank was burglarized late last week, a number of bonds stolen. I've petitioned Congress to have them all declared worthless so the bank won't have to negotiate their return." He placed the hat on his head. "That'll show the rascals, won't it? Stealing from a bank shouldn't be a battle of wits, after all."

For the second time since her early rising, Meg mustered all her training to maintain an unaffected facade.

Bank robbery? Surely not . . .

Her heart pounded in her ears, and she had to remind herself to breathe slowly. "Does that mean they haven't caught the person who robbed the bank?"

"Persons," Nelson amended. "And it was technically a burglary, since they came when the bank was closed. Most likely there were several people involved, at least one of whom must be working at the bank. They've been interrogating employees since the break-in was discovered." He approached the door. "Sooner or later they'll figure it out. They most often do, you know."

Then he left, and Meg had all she could do not to run after him and demand to know everything the authorities had discovered about whoever had perpetrated the theft.

But she stayed where she was, offering a silent—and belated—prayer for Ian's protection.

19

You gotta be willin' to take the risk—that's worth somethin', ain't it?
STEVIE "CROW" COBB
> Convicted of bank robbery without stepping foot in a bank,
>> for acting as a "crow" while those inside divested the bank
>> of its holdings
> *Code of Thieves*

WORTHLESS. Every single one. Nearly one million dollars in notes and bonds, which should have reaped at least a third of that total in ransom, was now worthless paper. Suitable for nothing but tinder, confetti, or the outhouse.

Although Ian had already shared the bad news with the others, the truth repeated itself over and again in his mind. No moment, no thought, no action or purpose was without the weight of failure looming overhead. The money Ian had counted on obtaining would not be his after all.

Money that, even with his caution and smaller split, Ian had already thought of as his own. And the power that went with it.

In spite of his certainty that even Brewster couldn't have foreseen or prevented this fiasco, Ian knew he was a failure. To vanquish the feeling, he went on a gambling spree, but even that brought only lackluster winnings. Nothing was as it should be. Not since John's death.

And with each invasive thought of John came one of Meg. Knowing where she was, what she hoped to do, tempted Ian more than ever. Once word of Ian's misfortune spread, it was a near certainty that Brewster would emerge from his lair. He would never let go now.

Like it or not, if Meg was lucky or smart or wily enough to learn anything about the Pemberton gold, she was going to offer that information to one of them.

It might as well be to Ian. There was only one way to forget this latest loss, and that was to replace it with an even greater victory.

Surely the Pemberton gold could erase any trace of this failure.

"Tell me, Miss Davenport," said Geoffrey Mason, who had invaded the garden suspiciously soon after Claire took Evie away on an errand in an open carriage, "what kind of birds do you hope to attract here, without the dovecote my mother objected to? It's not a very large spot."

Meg glanced up from the oversize sketch pad balancing on her hip to take a broader look around the square plot. Most of the greenery had proved to be weeds of one sort or another, although an attempt had been made to add some shape to the growth. She was drawing a replica to see which shapes she might fit into her final design.

"I'm hoping to attract as many butterflies as birds," she said, returning to her drawing. Beneath the tall trees of heaven in the corners, pigweed and mugwort nearly dominated the ground. But amid all that she'd spotted the same milkweed they had at the school, known for attracting butterfly larvae. For receiving only a few hours of sun a day, the weeds were surprisingly healthy.

"But we'll leave the pokeweed because it has berries that birds like. Hopefully by adding a bit of thistle, we'll attract some finches and orioles too." She shifted so that her back was nearly to him as she continued her sketching. Meg had no real desire to let Geoffrey stay too long; she'd planned to use this unprecedented time relatively alone at the house to search for clues about the Pemberton gold.

"What, no crows?"

Meg was unfortunately acquainted with the ways of crows, having seen more than once how they robbed eggs from other birds' nests. "Why would I want to bring to the garden those thieving pests?"

No sooner had the words been uttered than she wondered if she had something in common with the crows.

"Oh, crows are the best of all wild American birds!" Geoffrey said. "I've watched them both here in the city and out in the country, and I assure you they're the smartest birds around. Once I saw a crow drop a bottle of spice seeds it found who knows where. The bottle had a little string around its cap, and the bird picked it up in his beak."

"And you found that admirable?"

"But you don't understand! He had to drop it *three times* to crack the bottle—it was a sturdy little thing. He had to drop it from the correct height and on pavement, not grass. Only then could the bird enjoy the contents. Magnificent intelligence from a bird's tiny brain! You should design a place to leave corn kernels to attract them."

"I think I'll leave the crows to Central Park, thank you. Now, Mr. Mason, you must go. I'd like to finish my sketch, and I cannot do so with you distracting me from my work." Calling him Mr. Mason was not so much an effort to follow the rules of etiquette as it was to place some distance between them. Geoffrey, although good-humored, had become increasingly friendly with his frequent visits—perhaps too friendly.

Instead of stepping away, he reached around her to take the sketch pad from her hands and let it rest on the wrought-iron table behind them. "There is to be a charity ball hosted by the Markinghams, and even my family has been invited. Anyone who is no one in New York will be there, as consolation for not being in Newport. I expect since the Pembertons are in town, the Markinghams have dared to invite them and that you'll be going as their guest. But I'd like it if you would let me—my family, that is—escort you instead."

Despite an appealing affection growing in her heart for Geoffrey, Meg knew she must decline. "But of course you know I can't. What would Evie say . . . or do?"

He glowered at her. "You cannot seriously allow that child to alter your behavior."

"No more than you've done, waiting until Claire rode off with her in the carriage."

He looked away, obviously guilty as charged. "I'll have a talk with her and explain the age difference is too much for me. I should have been more forthright from the start, but the women in my family suggested I might not want to offend a Pemberton, no matter how young."

"Perhaps they're right. You do live next door."

That sparkle in his brown eyes—the one that came with his blatant honesty—glimmered her way. "It's not the Pembertons' proximity; it's their money. And their placement on the social scale my family measures as important. But it's ridiculous. Evie is a child! I shouldn't have to stem my interest in you because of some silly infatuation on her part."

"It's more than that for Evie. She's a very spirited and deter-mined girl."

"One I can't ever imagine taming. I already pity the man she marries—and fear for her children." When Meg took up her sketch pad again, he still remained standing in front of her. "If you won't go as my guest, will you at least promise me the first dance? And more than one after that? Evie won't be present to monitor us."

"But her spies will be; I've heard about that from Claire. Bribed servants who will report everything you do." His look of annoyance was so plain, Meg tried cajoling it away. "My advice to you is to leave the country, find a foreign wife, and return only after you've become a father. Perhaps then Evie will realize you won't wait."

"Go ahead and laugh at my misfortune," he said, at last turning away and retreating toward the leaded-glass doors. He continued speaking as he went over the threshold. "There he goes, the man who could never marry. Why, you ask? Oh, because he's hounded by the devotion of Evie Pemberton." Then he turned back, bowed politely, and wished Meg a good day.

"Don't forget about a place for the corn," he called from inside the house. "It's the crow's favorite food. . . ."

Meg found herself laughing, suddenly sorry she had to send him away. She could see why Evie was enamored with him. Geoffrey was not only handsome; he was witty and willing to talk about things other than himself and his own future, unlike so many men of society. If Geoffrey adhered to one principle in life, it was to be true to his thoughts—and unafraid to share most of them.

She waited a few moments, finishing only half of her sketch. Undoubtedly one of the staff had seen Geoffrey to the door, or at least heard him leave. She was glad he'd left the door open from the garden. She could go inside without anyone hearing, as long as she kept her footsteps quiet.

Meg knew where she wanted to investigate. There were two offices in the house. One, upstairs, belonged to Nelson. She'd seen him going in and out of it often enough and had followed him in there one day under the pretext of asking him about a social engagement they would be attending.

She'd half hoped to find some sort of safe, thinking an upstairs office might be more secure than the office on the first floor. But other than a rather large desk, a shelf of books, and a row of cabinets and various furniture in between, there had been no sign of anything more. Unless, of course, a safe was hidden in a wall. Behind the bookshelves? The cabinetry? A smaller safe behind the single portrait hanging on one of the inner walls?

Or perhaps she might find bank papers there, something to suggest where the Pembertons stored the majority of their gold. But she hadn't spotted anything atop his desk—at least not in plain sight—with the cursory glance she dared while in Nelson's company.

Still, she would save revisiting that spot. Today she would explore the office on the first level, the one belonging to Mr. Pemberton himself. If any clue about the gold was to be found, that was probably the best place to start.

Meg stepped inside the house, gripping her sketchbook to her chest and standing completely still. She did not even allow herself to breathe as she listened. The best servants, of course, were neither seen nor heard, and those employed along Fifth Avenue were certainly among the best.

Earlier in the morning the house had enjoyed the staff's diligent attention: a daily dusting, a polish here and there on a rotation known only to those who cared for the brass knobs and fixtures, and replacements of such things as greenhouse flowers from the florist and the bowl of fresh fruit in the dining area. Luncheon had passed, and dinner was still hours away.

On other afternoons Meg had learned these hours were spent quietly if a visitor wasn't being received or calls weren't to be made. When they were at home, Claire liked to read or crochet, and Evie was most often hidden away in the aviary, likely reading books she did not find in the Pemberton library.

Meg stepped through the dining room, past the small parlor, pausing long enough to glance in the library. Finding it empty, she entered, going to one of the two doors she knew offered access to Mr. Pemberton's private place of business. Her heart sank to find it locked.

She'd practically expected that. Perhaps the other door—the one in the hallway, just out of view from the foyer—would allow entrance. She found her way quietly out of the library, then tiptoed altogether because she had no logical reason to enter a hallway leading exclusively to the office only a Pemberton had a right to visit.

To her great surprise, the door was wide open. She stopped, listening but hearing not a sound. Surely even the quietest maid would make some sort of noise if she were cleaning. The whisk of a carpet brush. The flutter of a feather duster. Meg stepped closer and listened again.

Nothing.

Three more strides took her inside the room. The first thing she saw—a desk—had upon its corner a carved wooden cross, giving her the immediate feeling of standing on the threshold of a sanctuary, a holy and protected place. The room was lit by a pair of high windows, too high to offer a view of the street outside but sending in beams of light that reminded her of rays from above . . . of God watching. She shivered, then shook the thought away.

Turning round to take in the room's entirety, she found one spot of light on the wall behind the door, just now in the path of the sunbeam from the opposite windows. The light fell on a painting that took her breath away, catching her gaze with a force she could not resist.

It was a portrait of Christ on the cross between the two others crucified at His sides. The colors arrested Meg first: the white of His loincloth, the red of His blood against skin that was neither white nor brown but somewhere in between. Gold lettering glimmered on a sign affixed above His head, a head haloed in a crown of gray thorns. All of it was rich and pure, depicting a suffering man upon a suffering earth with its dark skies and angry, tormented clouds. She thought if she could regain her breath, she would smell rain in those thunderclouds above the Lamb of God.

The lighting—from the sky outside as well as the light depicted in the portrait itself—allowed almost no notice of the other two figures on the canvas. One looked away from the Christ, lost in his own misery. But the other's eyes were fixed on Jesus, as if by watching Him, his own pain could be withstood. There was longing in his gaze.

Meg stood still, struck by the beauty—but no sooner had she realized the full impact of the work than another thought threatened to send her running from the room. The eyes looking to the Christ with such hope belonged to a thief.

"It's magnificent, isn't it?"

"Oh!" She dropped her sketchbook, the voice behind her startled her so. She turned to see Nelson.

"I'm sorry if I frightened you." He looked at the artwork, a knowing smile on his face. "I can get lost in it too."

Meg looked around the room, wondering how he could have entered so silently. She was sure the office had been empty upon entering, and the hall door was too near her to have been used without her seeing him.

"Were you looking for something? Someone?" he asked.

She shook her head. "No, I—that is, I was on my way . . . out . . . near the foyer . . . and I saw the open door to this room." She attempted a smile. "Curiosity got the best of me, I'm afraid." She looked again at the painting with the hope of keeping his attention on it rather than upon her. "It's quite something, isn't it?" She wished her voice wasn't so breathless. Did she sound as guilty as she must look?

"I've often wanted to hold our morning prayers in here, just to be near it. But the room is too small to host the entire staff."

Tingles along the back of Meg's neck would surely have her visibly squirming if she did not move. She stepped toward the door.

"Wait," Nelson said, bending to retrieve her forgotten sketchbook. He handed it to her with a smile. "You know you're welcome in any room of the house, don't you, Meg?"

His kind and gentle tone was too much for her. Murmuring a feeble "Thank you," she flew through the doorway, her step not slowing until she was up the stairs and inside her room.

20

It is through fashion that one reveals status, influence, and ability to control oneself both emotionally and physically. Fashion is, in fact, the first and foremost tale that will be told of you.

Madame Marisse's Handbook for Young Ladies

INSTEAD OF WATCHING the maid coil her hair, Meg looked at Evie's reflection in Claire's mirror. The girl was reclining on the bed behind them, staring up at the ceiling while she bounced a foot balanced upon one knee amid a pile of her petticoats.

"When I'm old enough to attend a ball," Evie said to no one in particular, "I'm going to put henna in my hair until it's completely red. I'll go without a corset *or* a bustle, and I'll have flowers sewn into a Chinese silk gown. And I won't wear heels on my shoes, either."

"Red hair!" Claire exclaimed. "Just wear a sign round your neck declaring yourself a complete social outcast."

Evie rolled over to glare at her sister's reflection. "Why shouldn't I be a social outcast? That's what you've wanted to be ever since Jude left. And Nelson is no better, with that work he's always doing. I'm surprised you're both going to the ball tonight, even if it is just because of Meg."

"Evie! Can you ever put a rein on your tongue? We're attending the ball because everyone invited has agreed to donate money to the hospital."

173

She rolled over again, and Meg saw only her profile. "My red hair won't make me a misfit. It'll make everyone talk about me, and I'll be the most popular girl at every ball. Wait and see."

"I like the idea of going without a corset," Meg said. Although she didn't like encouraging most of Evie's wild talk, a positive remark now and then might remind Evie they weren't enemies.

Evie faced the mirror with a challenge in her eyes. "Then why don't you go without one tonight?"

Meg smiled at Evie's reflection through the two maids, one standing behind her hair and another behind Claire's. "My dress is made for a corset. I couldn't wear it without one."

"Try it and see. At least then you'd have people talking about you, too."

"Evie!"

Evie scowled at her sister. "You know, Claire, if someone were to record my name every time you used it, it could fill volumes." She turned her gaze back to Meg; Claire's admonition did nothing to remove the open curiosity growing on Evie's face. "There were all kinds of rumors about your father at school, Meg. Did you know about those?"

Hoping they attributed any increased color in her face to the waving iron the maid used to crimp Meg's hair, she nodded. She'd heard a few of those rumors.

"In all the years I went to school with you," Claire said, her tone far more gentle than the one she used on Evie, "I don't think I ever met your father. But he did visit you."

"Yes. He was a very private man."

"Was? I didn't know he'd passed on. When did it happen?"

Meg's throat constricted, and it felt like a weed from the garden had lodged there—the sticky kind with sharp edges. Accusations from Kate about denying her father echoed in her head. But Meg had no choice except to carry on with her lie of omission, or Claire would be aghast at best and send Meg away at worst. "Some time ago."

Evie pulled herself from Claire's bed. "But did you know everyone said the Miss Hibbits—*both* of them—were madly, secretly in love with him? Girls heard them call him 'that handsome devil.'"

Meg didn't doubt it. Little had she known how close they'd been to an accurate description.

When Claire reached over to place a tender hand on hers, Meg nearly jolted in her seat.

"I'm so sorry, Meg. Does that mean you're all alone in the world?"

The words were true . . . and yet suddenly Ian's face came to mind. He was here in New York City, and somehow he reminded her she wasn't alone. Surprisingly enough, the notion of his connection to her father seemed rather pleasant instead of stirring the old resentment she'd felt for so many years.

She sent a quick smile at Claire. "Not with friends who've been closer to me than family."

Claire squeezed her hand, and only then did Meg realize Claire thought she'd referred to her.

Out of training and the habit of offering the correct response even when not entirely sincere, Meg returned the smile.

Too late, she realized that despite every effort to steel her heart against the Pembertons, her smile wasn't as calculated as it ought to have been.

Ian pulled at the stiff white collar of his shirt, shrugged his shoulders to adjust the fit of his black tailcoat, and smoothed the red silk of his city vest. Never had he longed more for a pair of cotton trousers instead of these pinstripes, a plain black tie instead of a formal cravat, and a sporting cap instead of this top hat. He'd long ago realized discomfort came with wealth. Elevated purpose, nobility of character—which everyone assumed accompanied wealth—seemed like so much nonsense if it was exhibited only through personal inconvenience.

But this wasn't the first time he'd played a gentleman, and he knew as soon as he walked past the threshold of the Markingham home, he would forget the nuisance of fine clothing. In fact, the demands of the evening called for this to be his last thought concerning anything so mundane.

The prospect of seeing Meg again was already doing its job to distract him. This was business, and like it or not she was to be part of it. He'd timed his arrival not too late but certainly not early. She was likely already here.

He'd opted to walk from the Glenham Hotel on the corner of Twenty-Second and Broadway, despite the threat of rain. A brisk walk never failed to aid concentration—and gave him a fair view of the neighborhood. Carriages converged on the block of the Markingham home, making the street all the narrower for too much traffic. Another reason he was glad to have walked.

One carriage caught his eye as it glistened in the gaslight. It pulled out of the congestion, obviously only recently having let off its occupant. The carriage itself was nondescript: typically black, a Quinby coach so common in the city. But the familiar driver revealed who that occupant had been.

Brewster.

Ian hurried inside, eager to scout out the man himself. For a thorough search, though, Ian must first gain welcome. Before his arrival he'd acquainted himself from afar with the host, hostess, and most importantly, their son. Davis Markingham II—the generational tag no doubt added to increase the impression of age to their money. Those who knew him well, Ian had learned, called him—

"Dex!"

Ian issued the bold call to the young man standing between two women on the far side of the crowded foyer—a foyer absent of Brewster, as far as Ian could tell.

The man looked up. His roaming gaze went easily past Ian, only to return with some confusion as Ian approached, hand outstretched.

"Good to see you, old man!" He pounded one of Dex's shoulders, then burst fearlessly into his full act: the first lines of Schubert's song cycle *Winterreise*. Ian was not a great tenor, but he could hold a tune like any Irishman.

After hearing only the first few words, Dex fell to its spell. He joined in with his far superior talent, as loud and marked as Ian had hoped. At the first pause, both men laughed and joined in a hearty handshake.

"Of course you remember me, Dex!" Ian said. "Vandermey, man!" Then he pulled away to bow more formally to the ladies beside Dex. "Ian Vandermey, at your service. I admit I received no invitation for tonight, but when I saw a notice in the paper about your event, I sent a donation to Dex's mother immediately. I explained Dex and I went to school together, and she insisted we surprise Dex tonight. I suppose you've already guessed he made the glee club while passion alone failed to grant me a spot." He nudged Dex with an elbow. "Dex went on to tour with the best of them, and I stayed behind, ever diligent in my studies."

"Vandermey, you say?" Dex was clearly searching his memory—after all, Ian's research had revealed the man had been at Harvard less than seven years ago and should recall it in detail. But Ian doubted Dex would deny what he could not recall, not at a charity ball among those whose social status had yet to make the top tier.

So Ian offered some help. "Yes, you remember, of course, how we cheered at Hamilton Field? You know, at the game! The first football match between Harvard and Yale, in '75! I ought not speak of too many details of the day, considering the ladies, but how we celebrated that victory!"

Ian's laugh was as contagious as ever, and soon Dex joined in, confirming to the women beside them that Ian was indeed his old college chum. Embarrassment over a forgotten schoolmate had no place in high society.

And Ian knew he was in.

Meg left several dances free on her card, feigning delicacy of stamina. Although she'd never been formally introduced to New York society, she did have the stamp of approval by being a Pemberton guest, which therefore put her in demand. Geoffrey was her most persistent suitor of the night. His face had fallen when she told him she'd promised the first dance to Nelson, but lightened when she gave him her second and a claim to another line farther down her card.

Claire introduced her to many suitable and capable dancers, as well as other women to chat with. But Meg noticed the women did not exude much eagerness to spend time in Claire's quiet company, leaving Meg in Claire's semi-isolated realm. Having learned Claire's self-imposed seclusion was likely a result of her shattered heart, Meg was content to stay by her side. She had no desire to meet or impress new people, as these functions were designed to do for someone not already known in such circles. While skipping dances was frowned upon as a failure of the host to provide enough dance partners, this was yet another rule Meg was glad to break.

For the moment, though, Claire danced with a young man whose smile never left his face, even while Claire failed to look his way. She danced in his arms, her pale loveliness undeniable and marred only by her restrained expression. Despite the reminder not to think of Claire as her true friend, Meg couldn't help wondering just how utterly devastated she must have been to remain unhealed after so long.

Meg was tempted to ponder the thought, even as she told herself not to. She was becoming far too fond of Claire as it was. But something caught her eye—rather, someone—simply because of the intense stare aimed directly her way.

A moment later Mr. Brewster stood before her, bowing formally with a smile on his fair-skinned face. "Good evening, Miss Davenport. I trust the evening finds you well?"

"Why, Mr. Brewster!" she said, hoping her face didn't reflect the absolute shock she felt at seeing him. Here! "How nice to see you."

"Likewise. Tell me, my dear, has your visit with the Pembertons been . . . profitable?"

She spared a glance around them, seeing that for the moment the other ladies she had been standing near were either dancing or engaged in conversations of their own. "I've enjoyed myself more than I can say, thank you. And how are you? It appears you need no help in garnering invitations to society events after all."

He leaned close, so close that she caught the scent of peppermint on his breath. "My dear child, who said I had one?"

Meg blinked in an effort to control what she knew to be widening eyes.

"I came to see you, of course," he continued, low, though he'd pulled back his face to a more polite distance. "To offer you a bit of advice that your father's protégé seemed loath to give you. Advice on how best to use your time with such a family as the famous Pembertons."

"And what would that be, Mr. Brewster? Advice that would secure me as your partner rather than Ian's?"

He laughed as if she'd said something witty. "You've no more an obligation to me than you have to Maguire, but to work with him is to work with me. I'm quite certain I'll be able to convince him that we would all be better off enjoying each other's cooperation. It's in that vein I offer you a bit of direction, nothing more. To use as you wish."

She wanted to express her doubt that Ian would so easily work with Brewster, but his offer intrigued her. "What sort of direction?"

"You know only of the gold," he said, glancing once over her shoulder. "But there is something just as valuable in that house, something they won't soon miss should you be wise enough to recognize it."

"What could be more valuable than their—?"

"A seal, Miss Davenport. With a flourished *P*. You find that, and you've found something that someone like your father could put to good use. It's unique to the family name, one with all the prestige that money and integrity can demand. You find that seal, and you'll have the power of the Pemberton name behind anything you'd like to do."

"As in . . . creating fraudulent . . ."

"No need to discuss details now. Such a thing might easily be found in any drawer of an office, not even locked away. Be discreet enough in your aim for it, and they won't know it's missing."

Meg put a hand to her throat, nearly dropping her fan in the process. This was what she'd wanted, wasn't it? To have a partner willing to use whatever her position inside the Pemberton home could provide?

The music ended, and before saying another word, Mr. Brewster took himself away. Barely a moment later, before Meg could contemplate what he had advised her to do, Claire returned. Her cheeks were still pale, with no trace of the excitement some of the other girls had shown after sharing a dance with a handsome partner.

"Who was that you were talking to?" she asked as another dance began and the two stood side by side, watching.

"Someone I once met—through my father."

Claire's gaze went in the direction of Brewster's retreating back, but Meg didn't care to watch. Somehow, here under the lights and in the company of those he was so eager to victimize, he hadn't seemed at all as charming as her father had been. Yet how was he different from him? Not at all.

"May I say something I could regret, then?" Claire asked gently. "But something completely from my heart?"

Meg nodded.

"I'm glad you didn't introduce me to him. I was watching him while I danced, and . . . well, I didn't like the way he looked at you. As if he . . . weren't as old as your father."

Heat rose to Meg's face, though she couldn't deny Claire's words. He might not have been as interested in Meg herself as he was in what she could bring to him, but Claire had been close enough in her assessment.

There was but one thing to do. Make light of it. "He did rather remind me of the snake in the Garden. He speaks with something of a hiss."

Claire laughed but covered her mouth with her fan. "Oh, forgive me for enjoying that!"

"Then I should ask forgiveness for saying it, I suppose." Meg shook her head. "Except I haven't quite so healthy a conscience as you. The farther I am from school, the less those rules haunt me. Now, would you care for some punch? I'm parched!"

"I'd love some, except I'm promised for the dance after this one. Aren't you as well?"

"No, I've agreed only to waltz with your brother or Geoffrey tonight."

They watched the rest of the old-fashioned quadrille, until it ended and Claire's partner arrived to claim his dance. Meg watched them go off, knowing Claire granted her dances out of politeness. Surely she and Claire had something else in common: they both longed for someone who was not here. Well, not that Meg longed for Ian's company the way Claire longed for her former fiancé. Meg only wished to speak with Ian. Let him know Brewster was as eager as ever to work with her, and there was only one way to prevent that. By Ian's agreeing to work with Meg.

She turned away from the dance circle in an attempt to distract herself with her mission for punch but stopped abruptly when someone waylaid her at the refreshment table.

"Ian!"

As if her thoughts had conjured him, he stood before her in perfect image for the evening. Fine clothing, impeccably tied cravat, gloves as spotless as any gentleman's. His hair, though still a trace too long, was so charmingly thick she wouldn't have seen it cut for anything.

"Will you give me the pleasure of dancing with you?"

How foolish she'd been to believe either Brewster or Ian could be barred from polite society. They were free to do as they wished!

Meg reached for the fan hanging at her wrist. While flirting with such an object had not been among the lessons officially taught under Madame Marisse's watch, the language had been mastered by most students anyway. Not a single transmission came coherently to Meg's mind just then, however, so she hoped the simple flutter meant only that she needed the air.

"I would love to dance." She only hoped her feet could keep up with her heart. Her silly, racing heart. She ought to have been this pleased to see Brewster, knowing he at least would welcome Meg's willingness to do what she could. But her heart was acting far too pleased at the prospect of working with Ian instead.

The waltz allowed Ian's hand—though gloved—to take hers,

equally gloved. She entered the dance with movements embedded in her memory, because her mind was entirely engaged elsewhere. She wanted to tell him that Brewster was here, at this very same event, as uninvited as Ian must be. She wanted Ian to know Brewster trusted her to work with him, even if Ian didn't.

But other thoughts filled her mind instead, with far more urgency. Without thought to a single dance step, she let every ounce of her concentration rest on his face.

"Are you well, Ian?" She searched his face for any hint of the grief that had been so much a part of him when she saw him last. Or leftover worry from the bank job she knew he'd been part of.

"I'm well, Meg," he said. "And you?"

"Quite fine." Such foolish, useless words when so many others threatened to make her forget the simplest rule of etiquette. "I'm beginning to believe my father must have been quite an accomplished man." She grinned. "Was he the one to teach you to fit in at such a place as this?"

"He could fit anywhere from Battery Park to the top of Fifth Avenue." He let his gaze linger on her face a moment before adding, "Like you."

She issued a breathy laugh. "But it took the entire staff of an exclusive school to tutor me. Perhaps he alone might have done as well."

Once again Ian's gaze rested on her like a caress. "As I'm sure you already know, men are far less complicated. In polite society or otherwise. All we need do is anticipate the needs of the ladies around us, and we've accomplished everything society expects."

"Then perhaps you need to revisit such a lesson, Ian," she whispered, "and anticipate the needs of the lady you're dancing with."

"That, Meggie, is exactly what I've been trying to do all along."

Meg would have thought to blame some mysterious ingredient in the punch for her light-headedness, but she hadn't consumed any. What sort of flirtation was this between them? They acted the typical couple at any society soiree, when they were anything but.

She must collect herself and get down to business, the business in which she was so eager to prove herself capable. "Did you know Mr. Brewster is here as well?"

He nodded curtly. "Second-tier charity balls lure nearly every kind of patronage, even the lowest." He lost the frown he'd sported at mention of Brewster's name to wink at her. "Myself excepted, of course. And this—or top tier—is where you belong, Meg. Any one of the gentlemen present would be a fitting choice for your happy future. You could be the one to take him to the top tier."

"Is immediate company excepted in that choice as well?"

"Absolutely. In fact, if your father were here, he'd make sure of that."

"Not only is he gone, Ian," she whispered, surprised at her own ferocity over a matter she refused to take seriously, "but *were* he here, I would do exactly as I'm doing now. Proving to him, and to you, that he shouldn't have shut me away all my life. I came here with a mission, one I intend to see through. With you or with Mr. Brewster."

"Stay away from him." His growl matched the tone she'd set, but barely a moment later he smiled—a forced smile, but a smile nonetheless. "What did he say to you just now?"

"He wanted to know if I've learned anything in regard to the reason I've come. And to suggest I might look for something a bit less obvious than the—" she dropped her tone even lower—"gold."

"Such as?"

"A seal of some sort. With a flourished *P*. Unique to the Pemberton family."

"Used on banknotes—and the gold bars themselves, or so it's said." Ian's gaze wandered the room, but it was clear he wasn't considering their surroundings. He was likely imagining what Brewster would do with such a seal.

"He said if I find it, I might be able to smuggle such a thing away without it being missed, at least initially."

Ian smirked. "I doubt they leave it lying around the house. Have you seen it?"

She shook her head.

"Look, Meg, I still think this is foolish. Why don't you return to Kate's? I'm sure she would appreciate your company. Perhaps she's planning to take a trip. She'd welcome you as a travel companion."

"Alas," Meg said, more confident now because it was clear this seal was of interest to Ian, too, "I'm otherwise occupied." Then, sliding a sideways glance at him, seeing he still glowered at her, she gave a smile far more sincere than the one he'd offered. "It might be quite simple to see about that seal."

Ian's grip on her hand increased, though he did not miss a step in their dance. "It may."

"It wouldn't be so hard to work with me, would it, Ian?"

He looked none too pleased over whatever struggle raged inside of him, if indeed one did. It certainly appeared to be so. "I'd like to arrange another meeting. Tomorrow, perhaps? Two o'clock? In Central Park."

Meg nearly held her breath with anticipation. "Claire and her sister go to the park every afternoon except Tuesday, when they receive callers. I always accompany them, but of course I won't be alone."

"That's fine. I'll look for you tomorrow. I don't want to over-stay my welcome tonight, so I'll be leaving before supper is served. Brewster has left, so you won't be troubled by him again."

"Then . . . we *are* working together?"

He held her gaze, and some of the grief she'd seen in his eyes after the death of her father momentarily reappeared. "I don't see that I have much choice."

She'd won! The music of his words sent her feet to floating with the dance. But when he squeezed her hand, she let him catch her gaze again.

"Don't look so happy, Meg. Our partnership could be the worst thing that's ever happened to you."

She shook her head. "No, Ian. I'm sure it's the best."

Ian allowed himself to look at Meg longer than he should, especially when images of partnering with her—in every sense of the word—came to mind.

Seeing Brewster here had changed everything. Clearly the man was intent on swaying her to his kind of life—and Ian would only transfer the blame to himself if he allowed Meg to work with him rather than Brewster.

Yet . . . he knew exactly what Brewster had in mind for that seal. Any number of lucrative deals could be had with such a thing. It was just the kind of tool Skipjack would have welcomed: taking from a family who wouldn't miss a few thousand here, a few thousand there. If it was cleverly used and with enough restraint to prevent the victim's wrath, in all likelihood no charges would be pressed. Embarrassment over being hoodwinked came in handy from those who could afford to lose now and then.

It would be an easy mark.

"If we go forward, Meg, things will get far more complicated for you, no matter how simple the circumstances appear. So far you've been relatively honest in your visit with the Pembertons, haven't you?"

"Mostly."

"Every day will birth a lie if we work together. Can you do that? Lie to people you've been sharing a roof with these past weeks?"

"Don't think I've changed my mind, Ian. I haven't. I am my father's daughter."

"All right, then." He softened his voice. "There is an art to lying, Meg. One I'm sure they never taught at Madame Marisse's."

"No, not formally. I believe they called it polite conversation."

"This is no light matter. When you introduce me to the Pembertons, you cannot give away anything except what we want them to know. It requires a certain sophistication. Not everyone has a knack for it."

"Did I not just tell you I am my father's daughter?"

He squeezed her hand again. "Listen closely, and don't interrupt. We haven't much longer to speak. When you introduce me tomorrow at the park, don't feel the need to give too much information. Novices at lying sometimes hope to cover their deceit with unnecessary details. Don't let yourself embellish in the false hope that it'll make your lies more believable. Be less specific, not more."

As he spoke, each word drew down his heart, lower and yet lower. But he couldn't stop himself. "Don't speak too quickly or fluctuate your tone. Don't stutter or let long pauses hamper the way you speak regarding me. You've spent considerable time with the Pembertons already, so they know your mannerisms. If they're different when you're lying, they'll notice. And by all means make sure the emotion you feel is consistent with whatever you're talking about. Because of that, I'll be known as your cousin. I don't think we could be believed as casual acquaintances."

"So many rules! I think it'll come more naturally if you just trust me."

"And don't tap your toes or drum your fingers. Those are signs of emotional stress."

"The sort you're feeling at the moment, by telling me all of this?"

He didn't acknowledge her attempted interruption. "I'll be using the name Ian Vandermey. We've known each other all our lives, but not so well that we know all about one another. I can help fill in only what's necessary to share. Nothing more. Do you understand?"

"Of course, Ian. I'm so glad you're recognizing my potential. In these past few weeks, I've felt as though I've gotten to know my father better just by knowing his past. I want to do this. For him."

Those were the first words she'd uttered with a trace of kindness toward John. Too bad for her he saw right through them to the truth. "You act as though what you intend to do would make him proud of you." He shook his head. "You were more correct—and I suspect more honest—when you said you were trying to prove how wrong he was to shut you away. It's revenge spurring you on, Meg. Not some kind of belated love for him."

Before she could defend herself or deny his words, the music ended and Ian took a step back, bowed, then politely excused himself. He wasn't sure which of them he despised more at that moment: her for deceiving herself or himself for using her.

Every bit of elation that he'd agreed to work with her abandoned Meg upon hearing his words. What right did he have to tell her how she felt? She ought to know. . . .

Just then Geoffrey came to claim his second dance of the evening, the single waltz she'd allowed him. But her stubborn gaze never stopped following Ian around the room.

Ian seemed entirely at ease, first laughing with Dex Markingham, then asking Dex's sister to dance. She watched him twirl the other woman around the floor, surprised when she found herself wishing he'd looked at her that way. Happily, without any concern except to enjoy the dance. How grand he looked, so strong yet graceful. So handsome.

"Someone you know well?"

She'd nearly forgotten she was dancing. "Yes, my cousin. I'll introduce him to you if you like."

Geoffrey turned his gaze back to her. "Yes, I would like to meet your cousin. I'd like to meet everyone in your family, or anyone at all who is important to you."

She smiled, but only briefly. "It's a very small group, actually. I have no siblings, and my parents are both gone."

"Then I imagine you're all the more eager to establish yourself in a new family—through marriage. With a husband whose family will welcome and love you. And then children of your own so you'll have a private portion of society to celebrate with, to hide away with, to enjoy every day of your life with."

His face was so friendly, so purely hopeful, as if everyone everywhere wanted exactly what he proposed. And why should they not?

But as appealing and natural as Geoffrey made a family sound, as much as Meg might secretly admit she'd wanted that all her life, she'd never allowed herself to dream of one. Not when the only family she'd ever known consisted of staff at a remote, if exclusive, school.

"You're a wonderful man, Geoffrey, with wonderful dreams about how a family should be. I hope you find just the right woman to share those dreams."

He leaned closer, nearly scandalously so, and spoke in a whisper. "Perhaps I already know her."

Meg laughed as if he'd shared a jest, but from the corner of her eye she caught Ian again. His gaze on her both intrigued and surprised her.

Such a frown! Perhaps he was jealous.

She laughed again, knowing it was foolish to think so. More likely he didn't trust her discretion. He probably wished she wouldn't talk to anyone but the Pembertons. And him.

Ian finished the dance, going so far as to kiss the fingers of the woman he'd just danced with. Then he returned her to Dex's side, where he'd found her, thanked them for a lovely evening, and said his good night. Their protests over his early departure assured him his identity would never be questioned.

After collecting his top hat and refusing the footman who offered to summon a carriage, Ian walked down the street as if he hadn't a forlorn thought in the world.

While inside he called himself the idiot he was—at the same time unable to ignore an inescapable, accusing voice.

This is my daughter, Ian. The child I gave up so she could have a better life—without me or my ways. You're going to make a fallen woman of her without even touching her.

It didn't matter that Meg was pushing him into this endeavor or even that it was the best way he could think of for her to be free of Brewster's interference. If Brewster refused to be cut out of their lives, Ian would be the buffer between them, shielding her until they were both free of him.

Even the fact that it was the *Pemberton* coffers—including gold John himself had coveted for years—seemed dwarfed by how monumental a mistake this felt.

A fine mist permeated the air, but there was more than that dampening Ian's spirit. Surely his soul didn't sag because of the way he'd allowed himself to be manipulated by her. As much as he'd tried not to think of Meg in these last few weeks, he'd suspected all along that he lacked as much control over his own heart as he apparently lacked over Meg herself.

If Skipjack were here now, he'd knock Ian off his feet and be right to do it. Any feeble protest Ian could muster—that he was only trying to stop her from going to Brewster—was nothing more than a weak excuse.

But Ian knew there was more even than that. It wasn't the dance she shared in that other man's arms. It wasn't even her laughter. Rather it was the *kind* of laughter she'd enjoyed. It had made its way straight to Ian, piercing through his heart and into his soul. Laughter that bubbled out of pure enjoyment, honest and true, the kind that made it past the mouth, up to the eyes. He hadn't needed to see it, though he had tortured himself and looked anyway. And there it was, in her eyes, just as he'd expected.

Such thoughts had nothing to do with anything so simple as jealousy. They came from the sure knowledge that not only was the man she'd danced with far better for Meg than Ian could ever be, but he was also no doubt the kind of man Skipjack himself would have chosen for his daughter.

Because John had made one thing absolutely clear before he died: he'd never have chosen Ian. Not for his Meggie.

21

It is an utter violation of good breeding and training to speak
or to behave in a way that disrespects, embarrasses, or otherwise
denigrates another human being; in so doing, you denigrate
yourself as well.

Madame Marisse's Handbook for Young Ladies

"BOTH OF YOU walk slower than Nomi." Evie's pace quickened as
she uttered the words. "I'm going ahead and will meet you round
the bend, at the *usual* settee."

Meg was familiar with Evie's disdain for Claire's favorite iron-
and-wood settee in the park. Although she hadn't been told the
entire story, Meg knew it was the spot Claire had most often shared
with her first and only love, the neighbor who'd left her behind and
eventually taken his entire family with him.

Just now Claire didn't seem to possess a hint of the wistfulness
she often held when nearing that spot. She looked ahead to where
Evie soon disappeared, a troubled frown on her otherwise-perfect
forehead.

But Meg wasn't in the least worried about Evie. She had other
thoughts on her mind as she continued to scan the area for a
familiar figure. Because the weather was so fair today, they'd left
earlier than usual. Meg was in no hurry to get to the park settee. It
would be at least a half hour before Ian expected her on this end

of the vast parkland. She must draw out their visit for as long as it took him to find her.

"I'm hoping to see Ian here," Meg said, perhaps a bit too eagerly. Was her manner as it should be? Her tone ordinary? Heaven knew it wasn't the first time she'd lied in her life, but doing it so calculatingly might be harder than she thought, particularly in light of all Ian's instructions. "Do you recall that I mentioned him last night? I don't think you saw me dancing with him. My cousin."

Claire nodded, but her mind was clearly still on her sister, who was beyond sight altogether now.

"I do hope you'll like him. He's a very distant sort of relative. I'm actually not even sure how we're related. He mentioned he would make a point to walk this end of the park today and hoped to spot us." Perhaps she'd said too much. . . .

"It's a fine day for a walk."

Meg obviously had little to worry about regarding Claire's scrutiny. "You're worried," she said.

"Yes, I am."

Meg put her arm through Claire's as they strolled along. "About what?"

"The usual. But today I worry for your sake, I'm afraid."

"Mine! Whatever for? Evie has been especially nice to me. She picked up the glove I dropped before we left, and this morning she noticed when my juice glass was nearly empty and asked for it to be refilled."

"Yes, that's just it. She's only nice when she has something up her sleeve."

Meg waved away Claire's concern. "Evie and I have been getting along well. Nothing's changed that. She knows I'm not interested in Geoffrey."

Claire continued to stare ahead as if she could still see the young troublemaker. "Last night Geoffrey danced with you twice.

He brought you punch three times. He stayed by your side whenever he wasn't obligated to dance with someone else. For all practical purposes, Geoffrey was your escort rather than Nelson and I."

Meg refused to be concerned. "You kept track of what went on as well as Evie might have, had she been there."

"I told you she's figured out a way to lay hold of what goes on at every party Geoffrey attends. I was watching him because I wanted to know if we should expect trouble."

"I'm sure Evie is clever enough to find out anything she wants to know. But have you forgotten I danced with a number of other gentlemen as well? My . . . cousin, of course, and I danced with Nelson twice. I even sat next to Nelson at supper. It wasn't as if Geoffrey were at my side the entire evening."

"But her spies only report what *Geoffrey* does, not anyone else. She would have been told only that Geoffrey brought you punch three times and danced with you twice and was very attentive."

Meg wished she had the heart to laugh, but in truth she was weary of Claire's fear of her own sister. "I'll speak to her again, then."

Relief flooded Claire's face. "Will you? Whatever you said soon after you first arrived was so effective, I know she'll listen again."

"It's ridiculous for her to expect Geoffrey to wait for her. I noticed there were a number of young ladies eager to dance with him, and whenever he approached, he received nothing but smiles. Sooner or later, someone closer to his own age will catch his eye."

Claire sighed. "Not while his eye is on you, I'm afraid. And you know Geoffrey is only nineteen years of age. Not so very much older than Evie herself, which is why she thinks it's logical for him to wait."

"I thought he was young! Why hasn't he gone off to college, then, and ended all of this nonsense? If he were no longer constantly around, perhaps Evie would outgrow this infatuation."

"Perhaps. Or perhaps absence will make the heart grow fonder, as they say. When Geoffrey said he was delaying college for at least a year, I think Evie convinced herself he didn't want to leave her side."

They turned the bend in the pathway where the trees grew dense behind the pond. It wasn't the most secluded location in Central Park because of its relatively close proximity to the edge, but it hinted at privacy with overgrown foliage, a swell in the land, tall granite ledges, and fewer places to sit along the way.

Meg looked for the usual settee, only to find it gone entirely from its spot.

"There she is," Claire said. "Whatever has she done now?"

Evie must have been on the lookout for them because she hastily grabbed something off the wooden seat nearby, then put whatever it was behind her back, awaiting them with the friendliest of smiles. All of which made even Meg suspicious.

"Why isn't the settee in its usual place?" Claire asked.

"I don't know," Evie said. "It was like this when I arrived." She spread out her arms as if to embrace the area, revealing nothing but a handkerchief in one of her hands. "I think it's a lovely improvement, so snug among the trees. I saw a frog just a moment ago. Why don't you sit and enjoy it awhile?"

"Let's push the settee back to its regular place," Claire suggested.

"Oh no!" Evie turned to Meg. "Aren't you positively exhausted of the same view every time we come to the park? At least this way you can see some of the setting from a new angle. Perhaps it'll inspire images for the garden."

Meg looked around. The trees were taller here, but other than pine needles and leaves decaying from last fall, there was little to see that might inspire a garden. "I can't imagine why someone thought the seating would be better here. You can't even see if someone is coming along the pathway."

"Of course you can, if you just glance over your shoulder," Evie said. "Now sit, because I really don't think hauling a Central

Park settee around is something Madame Marisse graduates should be doing."

Meg exchanged a glance with Claire. That was certainly true.

Claire neared the seat first. "All right, but I plan to tell our driver about it when he comes for us. He'll either set it right or find someone from the city to do it."

"We could find another settee," Meg suggested. She wasn't sure she wanted to cock her head around every few seconds, in search of Ian.

"No, positively not." Evie's voice was all confidence. "This is the one Claire's precious Jude sat on last. She won't sit on another."

No sooner were Meg and Claire settled than Evie stepped back toward the path. "I've just had a wonderful idea! Since the weather is so perfect today, why don't we walk home instead of that tedious carriage? I for one could use the movement. I wish I could positively *run* today!"

Claire tsked. "Run. No lady ever does such a thing, particularly in the city, and most assuredly not in the kinds of dresses any of us are wearing."

Evie snapped her arms into a folded position against her chest. "Well, I won't run, then, but I *will* walk home. Short of wrestling me to the ground—something *else* none of us are dressed for—you cannot stop me."

She marched back in the direction they'd just come, leaving Claire and Meg behind.

Claire watched her sister leave, the frown back on her face. "She brings out the absolute worst temper in me. I'm always saying no to her, but more egregious than that, I seem to look *forward* to saying no. She makes me dislike both myself and her whenever we're together."

As she spoke, Claire pulled the strings on her reticule. She was in the habit of carrying a small book of sermons, and often when they sat in the park, she read portions aloud. Meg had believed the spiritual content was for the sole benefit of Evie—though it seemed to have produced little in the way of results—but evidently even with Evie's absence, a sermon would be read.

Despite a preference for one of Evie's novels instead, Meg sat back to listen to Claire's pleasant voice. Meg had heard many sermons in her life, since church attendance was mandatory at school. More than once, she'd shifted in her seat, wishing some of the goodness of the words would seep into her soul and make the behavior she knew she needed to maintain come more naturally. But it never had.

At least now she understood why it had always been so difficult: she truly was her father's daughter, as she'd reminded Ian only last night. Instead of trying to please her father all these years with her false goodness, she should have embraced the rebellion she'd given up when she was fourteen. Perhaps then he might have loved her enough to want her company.

"Oh!"

The startled sound made Meg jump, and she looked around, expecting to see Ian coming straight toward them. She'd been so lost in her thoughts that she hadn't been diligent about trying to spot him.

But there was no one around. Claire pulled a handkerchief out of her sleeve and dabbed at what appeared to be a bird dropping on the cuff of her dress. "That Evie! I knew she was up to something."

Meg couldn't help but laugh. "You can't seriously blame her for that, Claire. Unless you think she brought Pindar out here somehow and trained him to wait until just now to . . . ?"

"I know you're right. You see how eager I am to blame her?" She glanced at Meg angrily. "You would be too, if you were her victim as often as I've been." With the mark as clean as it was likely to get with just a handkerchief, Claire picked up the book again. "I suppose I'm not exactly the picture of virtue, reading from this book one moment and in the same breath casting blame my sister's way."

"If it's any comfort, I'm sure I'd think the same if I were you. She did leave suspiciously quickly, and here we sit under all these trees. Only it's really impossible, isn't it? I know she loves birds, but she can't train those out here in the wild."

"She studies them enough to make me wonder."

Then Claire laughed, and Meg joined in. It was just too outlandish an idea.

Claire resumed reading, eventually passing the book to Meg to carry on at the halfway point as she often did. Meg took the book, hiding her reluctance to read about a God who wanted her best, who sent His Son so that they could spend an eternity in heaven together. Such thoughts poked at her conscience, despite her confidence that none of it should matter.

She glanced up now and then to see if Ian might be approaching on the path nearby. Surely he was looking for her by now, and this was the edge of the park she'd told him they frequented. He could be here at any moment.

But there was no sign of him, and so Meg's eyes returned to the sermon—only to freeze on the page in front of her.

"Oh!"

There, in exactly the middle of the book, was another dropping from above. Meg held the book away, tilting it for Claire to see what had happened.

"That Evie!" Claire exclaimed. "It *must* be a prank!"

They both sprang from the settee.

Meg looked up in search of some sort of cage, impossibly but intentionally placed in the trees by Evie. But there was nothing, just the sound of birds hiding among the new green leaves.

Then she looked at the settee, seeing for the first time where several splotches had been wiped away. Because of the faded paint on the wooden slats, the blotches hadn't been readily visible before they'd taken their seats.

She looked at the back of Claire's gown, seeing more than a couple of dabs that must have transferred from the settee to the material in her bustle. The same must have tainted Meg's own gown, although she wasn't about to attempt looking. At least Claire's dress was white; marks on Meg's dark-blue gown were probably even more noticeable.

"We've both been spattered, I'm afraid." Meg faced the settee again, tipping it back. "Would you look at that?"

Claire came up behind her. There, speckling the natural carpet of twigs and leaves, were bird droppings of various size, shape, and color. The settee had been set directly in line with a habitual droppings path.

"Evelyn Annabel Pemberton," Claire said between gritted teeth.

She stomped around the settee, bending down to pull back some of the ground cover that, upon closer inspection, appeared to have been deliberately thickened. New rows of leaves looked to have been brushed into place along where the settee now sat.

"That wicked girl dragged this settee over here on her own. Look at those tracks!" A fuming Claire started off toward the walking path, but Meg caught her hand. They couldn't leave! Not before Ian arrived. And yet, how could they stay, soiled as they were?

"Perhaps we both ought to wait a bit longer, Claire."

Claire looked at Meg as if she'd lost all sense, and Meg patted Claire's hand even quicker.

"First we might find someone to move the settee so it won't be in line with the bird droppings any longer. And then . . . well, we're both so angry at the moment, I don't think either one of us should see Evie until we're less . . . irritated. Madame Marisse always said never to act in anger or haste. Remember?"

Claire exhaled a long breath. "You're right, of course. You're as good at handling me as you are with Evie herself. Let's go to our driver and tell him about the settee."

She started to walk away, but Meg didn't follow. She took an uncertain step forward, then stopped. "I—I'll wait here, to be sure no one else sits here in the meantime."

Claire nodded and attempted to smile, but the frown still marring her forehead didn't allow the smile much room. "You're so good, Meg. God has blessed you with a pure heart." Then she hurried off down the path.

Meg looked around. Though she heard sounds of others enjoying this end of the park—a child's laughter, a dog barking—she saw no one through the abundant foliage. She wished she had a timepiece to know how much longer it would be before she could hope to meet Ian. Had something detained him? Ought she worry there had been some repercussion from his bank scheme?

She'd been so eager to see Ian, she'd hoped that getting here earlier would make the moment of seeing him come all the quicker. Perhaps it was Meg herself who had hurried them from the start.

And now it appeared she wouldn't see him at all. How would he find another opportunity, if it didn't happen today? Surely he wouldn't get away with a bold tactic like joining a society party again. How was she to contact him without the Pembertons becoming suspicious?

Meg wrung her hands, pacing along the pathway, well away from the settee beneath the birds' preferred branch. The more she worried, the more set her anger became. That Evie!

Just when she despaired over ever seeing Ian again—at least without entirely compromising her position with the Pembertons —a male shadow rounded the curve. The tall hat, the slender cut of a jacket, a single man walking purposefully along . . .

But it wasn't Ian. It was Nelson.

Hiding her annoyance, Meg met him on the path. He took her

hands in his and held tight. "I understand you and my sister have suffered another of Evie's antics. I'm so sorry, Meg."

She shook her head. "No, it's nothing. Only . . . the settee . . . As you can see, it's in the line of fire, so to speak."

She hadn't meant to be glib—in fact it was all she could do not to complain, and bitterly so, about Evie's deplorable conduct. But when Nelson laughed and squeezed her hands, the moment of anger passed. He went to the settee to drag it to its usual spot, then rejoined her and took one of her hands, placing his other along her back to lead her in the direction of the carriage.

"How did you know what happened?" Meg asked, though she didn't really care. She must follow Nelson. There was no possible reason to linger even a moment longer.

"I was on my way to my office when I spied Evie walking home—alone. She claimed she just wanted to take some air, but I recognized immediately that little glint of humor in her eye. I know it means trouble. So I took her home, gave her strict orders to wait, then came to see for myself what she'd done. I told our driver to take Claire home in the other carriage, and I'll take you in mine."

She made the attempt to look at her dress from behind, the glance doing double duty by allowing her to search for Ian. No sign of him.

"I hope my dress doesn't soil the upholstery."

"Yes, Claire warned me about that. Don't worry; I have a kerchief for you to sit on."

They soon reached Nelson's carriage and driver, and with a final look at this corner of Central Park, Meg allowed them to take her away.

Ian stepped outside the parkland shadows, letting go of Roscoe's collar. The dog had been remarkably cooperative, as if he'd sensed his master's need for cover. But now he romped free while never straying far, running forward, then back to Ian, encircling him as if his own sheer happiness could envelop Ian.

Ian had first spotted Meg when she was alone and had been immediately pleased she'd found a way to visit the park by herself. She was as resourceful as she claimed. Ian would have no trouble speaking to her. But no sooner had he quickened his pace toward her than the other gentleman had arrived. One Ian soon recognized as Nelson Pemberton.

Meg looked as though she'd been expecting him, the way she'd accepted his grasp of her hands.

Ian should be neither surprised nor dismayed over the apparently unlimited male attention Meg was receiving here in New York. What else had he expected? Place her in society—the very society for which she'd been groomed—and she not only fit, she attracted just the sort of man her father always planned for her to marry.

He should want her to have a choice, but why did she have to be so friendly with Nelson Pemberton, of all people? It hadn't taken the newspapers long to report the names of those lawyers and politicians who'd saved the bank so much money.

Ian put a hand on either side of Roscoe's massive head and scratched behind the dog's ears. Despite the dog's eagerness to please, solace wasn't to be found.

There was something else that irritated him about Nelson Pemberton. Everyone knew the philanthropy of the Pemberton family stemmed from an outspoken faith, one that Nelson was especially fond of making known in any public interview. It was that which pricked at Ian now, since it was the same faith his father had lived. Meg's desperation to please her own father—or prove him wrong—had unveiled a hole so massive in Ian that he could scarcely believe he'd lived with it so long without notice.

Ian walked the path again, in the direction he'd first come. He would manage seeing her somehow, even if it meant waiting in the park for her every day of the week. It wasn't his fault if she wanted to work with him. Pemberton pockets were deep, so dipping into them was a prospect he need not resist.

Between the ghosts haunting Ian and his fears for Meg's welfare, he might have been surprised the Pemberton gold still had the power to dazzle him.

But dazzle it did.

22

True reform is not the immediate result of punishment; rather reform is bred in the heart through remorse, repentance, or fear. Threat of incarceration can incite that fear.

ESSAY: "REASONS FOR INCARCERATION," 1832

MEG ENTERED THE Pemberton home just in front of Nelson, who followed close on her heels. She briefly wondered if she should go upstairs to change her gown immediately, mindful that the longer a stain sat on material, the less likely it was to be easily brushed away. But voices from the parlor didn't allow her to go past, and with little more than an exchange of glances, she accompanied Nelson into the room.

"Don't add lying to your crime, Evie," Claire was saying. "How long did it take you to find that spot? Or was this a prank you've been planning for a while, to be used at just the right time, so you might strike two victims instead of only me?"

"I haven't any idea what you're talking about! How could *I* control the birds of Central Park?"

Claire looked ready to speak again, but Nelson held up one of his palms, first to silence them, then to entreat them. "Come with me, both of you." On his way from the room, he asked, "Come along, will you, Meg?"

The three of them followed, silently, though Meg did glance

at Claire and saw a look of eager vindication on her face. Nelson took them to the other side of the foyer, to the hall leading to Mr. Pemberton's office.

Upon entry, Nelson said, "I want you to look at the painting, Evie. Look at it."

"I've seen it before, Brother dear," she said, singsong, refusing to do as told.

"No, you haven't. Not really, or you wouldn't use your considerable talents to hurt anyone. That painting—this room—is ample evidence of all we have to be thankful for. As a reminder to use our gifts for good, not ill."

"I didn't! How many times must I defend myself? I didn't know Claire and Meg would be bird-cannoned. I shouldn't have to remind you, Nelson, that you need evidence to persecute someone."

"Prosecute," he corrected, but Evie was already shaking her head. "It feels like persecution to me."

"If I may say something?" Meg asked. She shouldn't become more involved, but her own anger at Evie was much like Claire's. Because of Evie, Meg had no idea how she would contact Ian again. "I agree you need evidence. Evie, where is your handkerchief? The one you had at the park? Is it in your sleeve?"

The girl took a step backward, the self-assured smile on her face fading just a bit. "Yes, I have it. But it's soiled. I used it to wipe something off my shoe on the way home."

"Bird droppings, by any chance?" Nelson asked, standing not two feet in front of her, palm outstretched. "Give it to me."

She put one hand to a sleeve, then to the other, coming up empty. "I must have dropped it."

Claire approached her sister. "Really?" She grabbed and twisted Evie's left arm. "Then what is this lump under the fabric?"

"Ouch!" Evie tried to wrench her arm free but failed under

Claire's grip. Meg heard a slight tear of fabric, and in a moment the handkerchief fell to the floor.

Nelson picked it up, his frown deepening. "Do you know why I wanted us to come in here, Evie?"

Pulling her hand free of Claire, Evie rubbed her wrist and nodded. "Perhaps you might explain it to our guest, then."

Evie glanced to the portrait of Jesus on the cross; then her eyes shifted briefly to an opposite corner of the room before her gaze fell to the floor. "It's the room where Father reminds us of how much we've been blessed. The g—our blessings and the picture."

"Yes, the painting. But it's not just for you—it's for us, too. For you as the guilty party and Claire and Meg as victims, and me, too, since I'm inconvenienced and delayed by all of this. Your punishment is for us to decide, but we'll do it in here, where we remember what Christ did for all of us." He turned to Claire. "What's it to be this time, Claire? Do you offer Evie grace, mercy, or justice?"

"Justice!" Claire's answer was stern and quick.

Meg felt Nelson's eyes now on her with the same question in them. "I—I'm afraid I don't understand," she said. "Well, I do understand justice, and I must admit it's always tempting to see a person get what they deserve. What I don't understand is the difference between grace and mercy."

"Claire?" Nelson asked softly. "Would you like to explain?"

Claire sighed and closed her eyes a moment. When she opened them, Meg noticed they went to the portrait, not to any of them. "Mercy . . . is being spared the deserved punishment. The painting—the crucifixion of Christ—shows God's mercy. Grace is depicted, too." She pointed upward to a corner of the huge painting, toward a single ray of light shining through the raging clouds. "Grace is more than mercy. It's a gift, completely undeserved. Like heaven."

"So," Meg said slowly, "we should either extend punishment, justly, or let her receive no punishment—mercy. Or . . . go beyond that to give her something completely undeserved—grace?"

"Yes, like an embrace or a kind word," Nelson said. "Not a reward for her behavior, but an example of the sort of love God gives us."

Perhaps it was being in this room again, such a quiet, peaceful place with a cross on the desk and light shining down from windows high above—a meek but natural replica of the ray depicted in the portrait. The light even now touched the top of Meg's head and made it seem, once again, as if God was watching her.

Or perhaps it was the curious reference to their blessings this spot represented, blessings that didn't stop at what the painting portrayed.

More likely, though, it was the painting itself. It had a sort of life about it, something drawing Meg to it, keeping her there. Not as witness to the pain or suffering but to the love in the scene, the undeniable and incredible sacrifice.

Meg shivered when she looked around the rest of the room, recalling that she'd wondered if there was some kind of secret safe in here. Hidden behind a wall, perhaps in the very corner Evie had glanced toward when she'd mentioned their blessings?

The truth was, should any of the Pembertons know why Meg was here, why she pretended to be their friend, she would surely want grace for herself, or even mercy. Definitely not justice.

"Is this a democratic process, then?" Meg asked. "Each of us has a vote? Or must I go along with what Claire says?"

"We all get a vote, the three of us as offended parties. Do you vote with Claire, then? Justice?"

Meg slowly shook her head. She could do no differently, despite her previous anger. "I only wanted to make sure of the process. I would rather extend . . . mercy."

God help her, she might have said *grace* out of pure fear for herself. Evie's head shot up, and she looked at Meg with wide eyes.

"All right, then, Evie. I extend mercy as well." Nelson turned to Claire. "You have the right to exact justice, though, Clairy. What will it be?"

She leveled a long stare at her younger sister. "You'll ask Cook to be assigned in the kitchen after supper today, to clean the dishes. Each and every one of them, even the cooking pots."

Evie opened her mouth to protest but evidently thought the better of it before a word was uttered. Even Meg was about to question that particular punishment, having learned at school that putting Evie in a kitchen was like assigning an arsonist to a match factory. There were endless pranks to be had in such quarters.

"I'll see that you're closely monitored until the job is done to Cook's satisfaction," Claire added as if she'd read Meg's mind. "And you might thank me for not assigning you to empty chamber pots instead. That's all the mercy I'll extend."

"Very well, Evie," Nelson said. "Justice will be met regarding the prank that likely ruined two articles of clothing. Now for the lies, the one I overheard as we entered the parlor—your denial of the prank—and the one you told me when I asked if you'd caused any mischief. I suggest you apologize to all of us."

She did so, although Meg was sure she wasn't the only one who doubted the sincerity. Evie used the correct wording, however, and that was all they could expect.

Then Nelson stepped closer to Evie. He was much taller and more pale than she, with her rosy cheeks and wide, somewhat-relieved green eyes. "For God if not the rest of us, Evie, will you give up these pranks, once and for all?"

She nodded but then hurried out of the room so fast that Meg knew the girl was afraid Nelson or Meg would change their vote to justice.

23

There's rules inside the Tombs and there's rules outside. Neither set got nothin' to do with the law.

Maisie "Mad Doll" McCready
    Incarcerated for pickpocketing
    Code of Thieves

Roscoe's whimper alerted Ian to someone at the door before the first knock. Given the dog's wagging tail, it was likely someone they both knew. Still, he was cautious—only Pubjug knew Ian was staying in this gimcrack hotel, and for the time being he didn't want company.

"Ian, open the door."

Particularly not Kate's.

For the merest second he considered not answering. Let her think Roscoe was here alone, since there was no hiding his scratch and cry. There was only one reason for Kate's arrival—to remind Ian of what he already knew.

"It's too early in the day for a polite visit, Kate," Ian said, opening the door to face her despite his reluctance. Delaying the inevitable rarely served him. "So I'm assuming there will be nothing polite about it."

She walked past him into the room, her face somber. "I came

for your own sake, Ian. Keys just told me to stay away from you for a few days. You know what that means."

Too well. Ian brushed his chin with the back of his hand, considering the warning in Kate's words. Brewster liked to isolate his prey and avoid much damage spilling onto others. Resent Kate though he might, Ian knew Brewster thought enough of John's memory to want her spared any unpleasantness.

Brewster had no doubt heard about the bank fiasco, and the natural conclusion would be the truth: Ian needed Meg now—and what she could bring to him. If they were going to work together, Brewster wanted to make sure he wasn't cut out.

"If you use Meg to get to that gold," Kate said, proving she'd figured out the situation too, "you'll shred the memory of friendship with John that you claimed so important."

Ian should lie to her, assure Kate he wasn't taking that next step, no matter the truth. He *did* need Meg if he wanted the biggest heist of his career. But when he turned away from Kate's accusing face, unable to hide what he intended, something filled him that he hadn't felt in years—or if he had, he hadn't given the room to acknowledge it. Shame.

"Oh, Ian," she whispered, coming up behind him and putting a hand on his shoulder. A hand he wanted to shrug away but forced himself to endure. "You wouldn't do this to John's daughter, would you?"

"It's me or Brewster, Kate. Meg won't have it any other way."

"Then it's your job to *find* another way." She came around and looked at him earnestly. "And you know it."

Kate walked back to the door, adding quietly that she would do all she could to protect Meg. "If you know what's best for you," she added, "you'll leave the city right now, before Brewster's man shows up for you. I'll pray you do the right thing."

Then she left.

Ian looked at the closed door. To his own amazement, it was the first time one of her promises of prayer didn't fill him with anger. If Brewster was concocting a plan to inspire the kind of fear he used in his favor, then Ian needed all the interference he could find. Heavenly or otherwise.

With so many of the city's elite away for the eight-week summer season, morning calls to or from the Pembertons had been rare. Even Mrs. Mason, who had reminded Claire at the dinner party some weeks ago that she was happy to fill in for Claire's absent parents, had visited only twice. So when a card embellished with a simple, single flower and the name Lady Kate Weathersfield was delivered to Meg, Meg's surprise that she had a visitor couldn't have been more sincere.

"A friend?" Claire asked after Meg's gasp no doubt drew her attention.

They were in the parlor waiting for Evie for their daily trip to the park. Until this moment, Meg had been eager to go. But perhaps the park wasn't the best place to find Ian because of its vast size. Despite the unfamiliar last name, Lady Kate could only mean one person—someone most definitely connected to Ian.

Meg wasn't entirely sure how to answer Claire's inquiry. "Yes. . . ." She stood, ready to receive the caller just as soon as the maid could lead her into the room. "This is a most unexpected visit, and I know you only receive callers on Tuesdays, Claire. But I'd like to see her." *Needed* to see her was more truthful, even as fear over the reason for Kate's visit started to take shape.

Claire hardly looked rattled. "Of course! How would a friend of yours know the Pemberton schedule? Please have her come in, and I'll gladly delay our visit to the park if you like."

Meg was about to insist Claire keep to her schedule and go to the park anyway, but there was Kate, so astonishing a sight in the Pemberton parlor that Meg forgot what she'd been about to say.

"How good of you to see me," Kate said as she swept into the room. She was lovelier than ever in a princess-line tea gown of crisp red floral damask, topped by a bonnet of lace and ribbon over tightly woven black straw. She held out her lace-gloved hand, while a small beaded reticule hung from her wrist. "I've only just arrived back in New York but simply couldn't wait another moment to see you, Meg!"

Meg let Kate take both of her hands. What was she to say? Because no doubt every word pouring from Kate's mouth was a lie—polished and prettied with an entirely phony English accent.

"It's very nice to see you . . . Lady Kate."

Kate turned to Claire, but only partially so. She kept one hand on Meg's but held the other out to Claire.

"Do permit me to introduce myself, won't you, darling? I'm Lady Kate Weathersfield, originally of London but lately of Baltimore and visiting New York, where I knew this lovely child's father, John Davenport, simply years and years ago. When I learned through Meg's school that she would be spending the summer with the Pembertons, I ventured out without a single companion, I was so eager to see her. But do tell me—Claire, is it?—could you be related to Henshall Pemberton? The first Pemberton I thought of was dear, dear Henshall!"

"I'm afraid I'm not acquainted with a Henshall Pemberton. My father is Arthur. He does have a brother, but he's in Chicago. Hugh Pemberton?"

Kate—Lady Kate—waved away the lack of connection, and Meg watched as she so masterfully demonstrated how to be a confident and sophisticated liar. Meg almost believed the exhibition herself.

"Oh, never mind, then, darling." She dropped Claire's hand to replace her own atop Meg's. "But it's so lovely to see you! I'll be staying in the city for a while and would love to spend time with you. Shall we make a date for a dinner? Or something rather longer than that? How about an excursion! Oh yes, you simply must visit me for a picnic. We have so much to talk about! How fortunate that you're not away at that school for the summer or off to Newport like many of my other city friends."

"We can visit now for a while," Meg suggested. Evie entered the parlor just then, a look of curiosity on her face as she took in Kate. Meg looked at Claire. "Perhaps you and Evie might go on to the park as scheduled, and I'll stay behind."

"And who is this lovely child?" Kate exclaimed upon seeing Evie. "But you must be a Pemberton! You've your sister's eyes, only in green."

Evie's brows rose. "I never thought Claire and I resembled one another."

"Of course you do! You have only to grow into the look a bit. In a few years you'll be every bit as captivating, just wait and see. Beauty can be learned, of course, but you've been given it naturally. True beauty."

Evie's smile almost proved Kate's words to be true. For the moment she possessed a look of near serenity, making the beauty Kate predicted seem a reality. But Meg knew Evie too well to believe it for long.

"Perhaps we all ought to go—or stay," Evie suggested.

But Claire was already pulling her sister along. "It was very nice to meet you, Lady Weathersfield. I hope we get to see you again. But we'll leave you with Meg for a visit so the two of you can do a little reacquainting."

"Thank you ever so much, darling!" Kate called after them.

No sooner had the sound of a closing door echoed through

the parlor than Meg opened her mouth to speak. But nothing came out.

Kate put a finger atop Meg's lips. "Don't waste time," she whispered. "Is there somewhere we can speak—where you're sure we won't be overheard?"

Meg thought a moment, then nodded. "The garden."

She led Kate from the parlor, refusing an offer of tea when a servant met them in the foyer. It was too early for tea anyway, and she didn't want the interruption of its delivery.

Meg closed the doors once they were outside, for a moment seeing the garden as Kate might see it. Nearly untouched, making her effort toward improving it so scant as to be embarrassing.

But Kate didn't appear interested in their surroundings. She faced Meg, clutching her reticule as if she needed it to steady herself. "I came to talk sense into you."

"I already know you never wanted me here, so why this pressing visit all of a sudden?"

One of Kate's hands lifted from the reticule to curl into a small, tight fist, which she pushed against her lips as if to stifle what she'd been about to say.

Her obvious worry renewed the fear inside Meg. "Tell me, Kate. Has something happened? To Ian? Because of how the bank job turned out?"

"Not yet."

"What do you mean? Is he going to be arrested?"

Kate uttered what might have been a laugh, but it was choked into a moan. "If only it were that easy. No. It's Brewster. He sees Ian as a wounded pup. Now is the time to either convince him of his place or be rid of him altogether. He knows Ian will work with you now."

Meg wanted to swallow but found she couldn't. Her throat had turned to stone. "What does that mean? Be rid of him?"

"Oh, he won't kill him—if nothing goes wrong. But he'll scare him enough to hope he leaves town for other territory. Unless he agrees to cooperate with Brewster."

Meg turned on her heel back toward the door, only to be caught in Kate's firm grip on her arm. She tried breaking free, but Kate held tight.

"We've got to stop him, Kate! Come with me or not, but I won't stand by and let this happen. I'll see Brewster myself, and—"

"And what?" Her fingers dug into Meg's skin. "Do you think your words will stop Brewster from doing as he pleases? This is exactly why your father never wanted you to know the kind of life he lived!"

Meg stared at Kate as words Brewster had spoken to her came back in stark detail. "He warned me, Kate, only I didn't know what it was."

"Who warned you? When?"

"Brewster, at a charity ball. He said he had a way to convince Ian to work with him. This must be what he meant." She tugged on the arm Kate still gripped. "Now let me go."

Kate loosened but did not give up her hold on Meg. "Even if you'd known it was a warning, it wouldn't have made any difference. Brewster would still go through with whatever he has in mind, and what do you think Ian would do? Leave town? Leave you to Brewster? Do you think he's going to be scared off?"

Meg shrugged out of Kate's grasp and left the garden without looking back. She wound her way through the Pemberton home and out the front door without stopping for her hat and gloves or to let anyone know she was leaving. The coach Kate must have arrived in waited at the curb. Meg jumped inside, calling to the driver the name of the St. Denis Hotel.

Kate barely had time to join her before the carriage rolled down the street.

Ian could have waited in his rented hotel room. Or he could have tried hiding, and in a city as vast as New York, he might have succeeded, at least for a while. He might even have caught a train back to Peekskill with the faint hope that would be enough to show capitulation. Let Brewster have Meg because Ian stepped out of the picture.

But he did none of that. He knew he would have to get this over with, this next step toward independence. He only hoped nothing went wrong. Brewster's thugs weren't among the most careful when it came to enforcing an order of intimidation.

He went to a nearby bar with the idea of administering some anesthesia but thought better of it after a single drink. There was no sense in leaving himself utterly vulnerable. He'd need a bit of wit if he hoped to defend himself—and could at least look forward to the anesthesia once it was over.

When it was over.

Knowing John wouldn't have approved of Brewster's method afforded Ian some comfort, but even so he hoped Meg wouldn't find out. The last thing he wanted was anybody's pity, and for some reason the thought of hers was especially distasteful.

"It does no good to see Brewster," Kate insisted from her seat opposite Meg.

Her words might have been foreign for all Meg understood. She knew only one thing: she would stop this, no matter what it took.

"If you're really intent on getting involved . . ." Suddenly Kate threw her hands up in obvious frustration. "Oh, all right, then!

Driver!" She banged on the roof of the carriage in the most unlady-like manner Meg had ever seen. "Not the St. Denis!" she yelled. "Take us to Washington Square."

Then she settled back in her seat, eyeing Meg with something between irritation and fear. "There's only one way to make any possible difference, and that's to stick to Ian like two flies on a spiderweb. Brewster has just enough respect left to protect the women John loved from witnessing what he's planning to do. I'm not sure it'll work, but at least whatever's going to happen won't happen today. If we can delay it long enough, maybe we can think of a way to prevent it altogether."

Meg twisted out of her seat, balancing on one knee for her own turn at banging on the carriage ceiling. "Hurry, driver! Hurry!"

"Hey, Maguire."

Ian heard the voice, but it was the last one he'd expected.

Evidently this was to be Keys's test of loyalty too.

Ian didn't turn toward the carriage that slowed at his side, but from his peripheral vision he saw two drivers instead of just the one who normally drove Brewster's carriage. He also saw Keys leaning out the open window. "Better get in on your own. Save us the trouble."

Ian stopped, and so did the carriage. Other than the two atop, Keys appeared to be alone. He wondered if Keys thought Ian a more worthy opponent than he was at fisticuffs, if he'd brought two others to hold Ian down.

"This isn't your normal job, Keys. Been lowered in rank?"

"Yeah, all for the big fat nothin' your bank job brought in. Thanks." He opened the carriage door. "Get in."

Ian did so, seeing he'd been right about Keys being alone. That was good, although the man had a solid thirty pounds on Ian. His police training probably enhanced whatever natural ability he'd had for fighting. This would be no tomfoolery, particularly when one—or both—of the burly drivers participated.

"You have someplace special in mind for this little dance of ours?" Ian asked once he settled across from Keys. He'd hoped talking instead of dwelling on the stone in the pit of his stomach would help him ignore that weight, but it didn't.

Keys looked out the window at his side as if he couldn't stand the sight of Ian. "You'll know when we get there."

Ian looked out the other window, surprised that his breathing was steady, his pulse even. Didn't he believe Keys would go through with it? Maybe not. Or maybe Ian was as much an idiot as Brewster believed.

Without another word, the carriage continued on its way to the unknown destination away from the square, in the direction of Battery Park. There were plenty of scenic spots in that neighborhood. Stinking warehouses, run-down taverns and bunkhouses offering the first welcome to the poorest of immigrants coming through the fort, piles of landfill made up of rocks and stumps and debris cleared from the rest of the city to make it suitable for building.

A little blood sprinkled here or there would hardly be noticeable.

Ian shot a quick glance at Keys, wondering how he felt about spilling some of Ian's blood.

Just then noise erupted from the street.

"No!"

"Stop!"

The protests came from a confusing source. Certainly outside the carriage, but closer than expected—from empty walkways. Shouts quickly followed, calling Ian's name. Female voices.

At first Brewster's carriage picked up the pace, until it was obvious another carriage, the one containing the objecting voices, was behind. Just as Ian spied activity through the window behind Keys, Keys himself turned as well. It didn't take long to spot the hired carriage on their tail, with two women reaching out, waving frantically from each side.

One was Kate.

The other Meg.

Another man might have been hopeful, but not Ian. Far better to be beaten to a pulp than rescued by either one of them.

Yet rescue was not to be had, at least not easily. Suddenly the carriage holding Ian stopped, and the horses behind, so close in pursuit, whinnied at the abrupt obstruction. Before Ian considered seeing himself out, Keys landed a restraining grip on one of his forearms, and Ian saw Brewster's driver stomp toward the hired carriage behind them.

The sound of the horses, still complaining but perhaps now in fear rather than indignation, muffled the shouts between the men. In a facile movement, Brewster's driver leaped to the cabbie, effectively pulling him from his seat. With one soundly landed punch, the man fell past his perch all the way to the uneven Dutch bricks that paved the street below.

Then the driver waved at the man who must have remained on Brewster's carriage and drove off, carrying away both women squawking with dissent.

"He told you to stay away, Kate."

The man Kate said was Brewster's driver had each of them by the hand, as if they were two wayward children needing to be taught a lesson. Once the carriage had stopped from its dangerously rapid pace—in front of the familiar facade of Kate's French flats—he'd hopped to the side so quickly, Meg couldn't have escaped even if she'd thought of it. He'd reached in and grabbed each by a wrist, then hauled them out without delay. Meg could see Kate was nearly cooperating, perhaps in fear of being seen by one of her tenants.

"You have no right to do this!" Meg insisted, though she saw from Kate's face that continued protest would be fruitless.

The man said nothing, just kicked open the door to the building before Kate had a chance to reach it. Once inside she hurried ahead in time to open her own door.

Even as Meg had visions of her and Kate going right back out, the man followed them inside Kate's flat. Then he closed the door, folded his arms, and stood before it like the guard he was.

"This is outrageous!" Meg fumed at the man, her face only inches from his placid one. He stared past her with a gaze so steady it was as if she weren't even there. "Not only are you guilty of kidnapping; you're standing in the way of preventing a crime. I have every reason to believe Ian Maguire is being accosted this very moment, and you're doing nothing to stop it! Have you no hint of conscience, no shadow of human decency?"

Though the man clearly breathed a bit heavily—he was a bulky sort and likely expended a good deal of his energy jumping up on the hired coach, then pummeling the cabbie—he stood so still he might have thought himself invisible to anyone or anything around him.

"It's no use," Kate said. "He won't leave until he knows whatever happens to Ian is done and finished."

Meg wanted to scream, but all that came out was a garbled moan of pure frustration.

Ian felt himself dragged. He tried picking up his feet, but like a drunkard's, they wouldn't obey. His brain was indeed confused and slow, though it wasn't from anything he'd ingested. It was from his skull being slammed from side to side, then bashed against the brick wall behind a fish market.

He thought he'd have the chance to defend himself. He thought he'd be able to get in at least one punch or have the wherewithal to raise his arms in defense. But the slug who'd accompanied Keys made sure that didn't happen. He held Ian back while Keys battered him in a one-sided boxing round.

And now they were dumping him. He had only one more hazy thought. If they threw him in the river, that was the end of him.

"If Brewster thought for a moment I would help him now," Meg said to Kate, seated across from her on the settee in her parlor, "he'll know soon enough I'd rather turn him in than give him a whisper of information about the Pembertons."

Kate stole a quick glance the thug's way, as if to remind Meg of their "guest." "I've said all along it's foolish for you to be involved in anything regarding the Pemberton gold," she said. "Maybe now you'll listen."

"Oh, I haven't changed my mind. I've just decided whom I want to help, that's all."

"And what if after today Ian is working with Brewster, just as Brewster wants?"

Meg clamped her mouth shut. This was impossible!

"The only thing that should happen now is for you to tell both of them, Ian and Brewster, that you want no part in looking for the Pemberton money. You know now that you're risking your entire future. The rest of your life could be ruined because of this ridiculous scheme."

Meg was in no mood for a lecture. "Coming from someone

who calls herself Lady Kate, I find your caution more than a little disingenuous."

"Believe me, I hated to introduce myself in such a way this afternoon! But I had no choice if I was to see you in that neighborhood." She sighed, looking so worn that she seemed to have aged a few years in the past minutes of their confinement. "I was once known along Fifth Avenue as Lady Kate Weathersfield, so visiting there requires me to be her again." Her gaze rose to Meg's, this time defiantly. "I sit before you as proof that youthful mistakes can haunt a person the rest of her life."

"I'm sorry, Kate, but your life doesn't seem so bad to me." Meg raised one of her palms to indicate their surroundings. "You have a comfortable home, fine clothes, and apart from having my father's death break your heart, what have you to complain about? Brewster doesn't control you; he won't control me, either."

"Perhaps. But guilt can be a heavy burden." An impassioned plea filled her eyes. "Please, please, Meg. Bid the Pembertons goodbye and come back here to stay. We'll carry on together, you and I. We can get away from Brewster and his ways. We could travel— anywhere we please. You're bound to meet someone upstanding and honest if you only look in the right places."

Meg rose from her seat, but instead of nearing the man who'd stationed himself at the door, she went to the window that overlooked the street. Surely someone would show up soon to let them know it was over? What must Ian be facing this very moment? Her heart ached to know, fearing whatever pain he suffered was at least partially her fault. If she'd agreed to work with both of them from the start, perhaps she could have made sure Brewster had nothing to fear about being left out. Not that she wanted him to have any part of her cooperation now!

She faced Kate, offering her attention again. "You talk as though I can have a normal life, Kate. I can't. With my lineage I have no hope of marriage to anyone 'upstanding,' as you put it. I'm like you in that."

"Sit back down, will you, Meg? For a moment?"

Meg did as she asked, though stiffly. Nothing Kate could say would change the truth.

Kate's face was solemn. "Marriage is holy in God's eyes, a symbol of loyalty that mirrors God's loyalty to us. It's a union that will make one man and one woman better together than they can be apart. And although I loved your father in this way—just as he loved me—I've come to believe that our marriage might not have made us better for the rest of our lives."

She looked as if she was grateful to be sitting, as if she couldn't bear herself on her own strength. Then she continued. "Together, your father and I represented a formidable couple. But there were too many years when our partnership was strong for the wrong reasons. For selfish reasons—to cheat people and to get something from them. God Himself only knows if somehow, someday, we might have slipped back to those ways."

In her eyes Meg saw a desperate unhappiness. "It's what I worry most for you, if you were to work with Ian. Repeating the mistakes your father and I made. I think that's why Brewster wants to ensure he won't be left out. He sees the potential match you and Ian could be."

"Kate . . ." Meg wanted only to comfort her, but Kate quickly went on.

"Please, Meg, think about what I'm saying. Won't you? You're trying to recapture a past with your father that can never be. And Ian is reaching for a future he can never have. One with enough money for him to feel secure—only it's an empty hope because it will never be enough."

"No, Kate. You're wrong. I'm not looking for a future with Ian. Not the way you had with my father."

"Aren't you? Isn't that what's driven you to his defense today? Concern for him that makes you more than . . . whatever it is you thought you were? More than acquaintances, more than friends. No simple familial affection for you."

Meg didn't want to listen to such talk, yet it was clear nothing stood in the way of her uncompromising fear for Ian's welfare. Of course she cared about him! Resent him she had, nearly all her life. But the fact was she'd seen firsthand why her father had loved Ian. He was as flawed as her father had been—a thief. But he was also loyal and smart and capable of loving someone else. He'd loved her father; Meg had seen that in his grief.

Just as noise outside Kate's door began demanding her attention, Meg had one fleeting thought. Perhaps Kate saw more clearly what Meg didn't want to admit: she was falling in love with Ian Maguire.

24

The coming destruction can never touch us, for we have built a
strong refuge made of lies and deception.

ISAIAH 28:15

IAN HAD TO BE DREAMING. Or maybe he was dead. An angel min-
istered to him, her soothing voice a balm to his soul and her gentle
touch cooling him wherever it landed.

He struggled to sit, and the sharp jab—like a knife to his
insides—called him back to his senses, at least enough to feel the
entirety of his pain. Every inch from his face to his gut cried for
attention as he looked through swollen eyelids to see who was
helping him now.

Meggie.

He gave up all effort to sit, turning his face away as she reached
with a white cloth to one of his brows. "Go away."

"And leave you here? I don't think so. Now quit moving. I only
ever failed in one subject at school, and that was nursing."

He lifted a hand, surprised at how much it hurt to do so—and
not just in his arm, but from somewhere beneath that. Ineffectively,
he brushed her hand away and looked beyond her, horrified to see
they were in yet another alleyway, secluded from the street amid
the stench of garbage. Without another breathing thing in sight.

"What are you doing here? Are you alone?"

"Keys came to Kate's house to tell her where we could find you. He had such a smug look on his face, as if he wanted to show us what he'd done hadn't cost him a scratch. Oh! How I wanted to claw his eyes out. Kate went for Pubjug, but I couldn't wait. I came straight here. With this."

She held up the bottle containing whatever it was she used on his cuts and bruises, something that smelled not quite sweet and slightly antiseptic. That explained the coolness of her touch.

"And she let you? Do you even know where you are? Dressed like that, you might as well flag down the nearest hoodlum."

"I have nothing to steal but the gloves Kate loaned to me. Now sit still and let me help you."

He shifted in one agonizing move to sit upright with his back to the brick wall, holding his side the whole time in the hope of keeping steady what was no doubt at least one broken rib. "It isn't safe for you here, Meg." He tried to stand, ignoring his dizziness and another shocking pinch in his ribs. He had to get her out of this neighborhood. "Let's go."

"But you can't walk like this! You were out cold a moment ago."

"Come on."

"What about Kate and Pubjug? They'll come here looking for you."

"We'll go to Kate's. They'll look there first."

"Ian—"

He walked—wobbled—toward the street. Once there he knew he'd have to straighten up, not appear as weak as he felt. He brushed back his hair, and even that hurt. Meg must have cleaned away whatever blood had been on his face, because after a tentative scrub, he found it to be dry.

Standing as tall as the pain in his upper side allowed, he took the one free hand she had—the other still held the dark little bottle—and placed it over his forearm.

Assessing his whereabouts, he knew which direction to go. They'd be lucky to find a hansom cab in this neighborhood. More likely they'd have to walk the entire way to Kate's.

Meg wanted to hold Ian's arm rather than the other way around, but each time she tried, he shifted so as to look as if he were escorting her and not needing help. She finally gave up, imagining his struggle was a greater effort than her own in letting him walk unaided.

When she'd seen Ian crumpled and broken amid that garbage heap like a discarded mass of flesh and blood, her heart nearly stopped with fear that he was dead. But he'd flinched at her first touch, gentle though she'd meant it to be.

At last, still walking, they reached a respectable neighborhood. It wasn't long before a hansom cab could be hailed. She boarded first because Ian waited, but she could see the grip of pain on his face as he heaved himself to the seat opposite her.

"I—I'm afraid I don't have any money left," she said, embarrassed to reveal her lack of forethought. "I took only enough from Kate's bureau to pay the driver who brought me here."

Ian offered her a grim half smile. "I was beaten, Meg, not robbed."

It wasn't long before they reached Kate's apartment house. After Ian gingerly withdrew from a pocket enough money to pay the cabbie, Meg let him present himself once again as her escort. But inside the privacy of Kate's hallway, she grabbed his arm and helped him up the stairs. He didn't shrug off her help this time.

Kate's door was unlocked, and neither Meg nor Ian bothered to knock. Their entrance, however, drew the attention of Ada, Kate's maid. She'd been conspicuously absent the entire time Brewster's thug had detained Kate and Meg, although she now appeared instantly concerned at the sight of an obviously battered Ian.

"Oh, sir! It's bad, what they done to ya!" She grabbed his other arm, and between the two of them, Meg and Ada bore him through the parlor.

"He'll need to stay at least the night, Ada," Meg said. "Let's take him to the room I occupied when I was here."

In the hallway Ian attempted to pull away from them both, but Meg held tight all the way to the bedroom.

"There, that wasn't so bad, was it? Letting us help?" Meg said, seeing from Ian's face he thought it was. "Ada, chip some ice out of the icebox, will you? And after that, perhaps some tea."

She was glad when the maid left them alone. Meg knew she didn't have much time before Kate showed up, and there was something she needed to say without interruption.

Helping Ian out of his jacket, she then piled the pillows behind him so he could sit more comfortably. Thankfully there was no sign of blood on his shirt except what had spattered from a broken lip and pummeled nose; most of the visible damage had been suffered by Ian's face. One eye was already black, the other swollen.

"Anything broken?" she asked.

"A rib, maybe," he said. Then he put a hand to his jaw, opening and closing his mouth without wincing. Afterward he ran his thumb and forefinger along his nose. "Nothing else. I got off easy. Keys must have some leftover affection for me after all."

Meg huffed. "It doesn't look like it to me." She sat along the edge of the narrow bed and, ignoring the slightly alarmed look appearing on his bruised face, took one of his hands in hers. "I know it was Brewster who ordered this done to you, Ian. I want you to know I'll never, ever cooperate with him." She'd meant to stop there, but something made her want to do more. Maybe it was nothing more than thoughts Kate had inspired. Maybe what she felt at that moment wasn't any more real than that. But she leaned closer to kiss the side of his face, on a spot free of either bruising or any remnant of blood.

His lopsided grin was just enough to restart a trickle of blood from one of his wounds. He must have felt it because he lifted his sleeve to wipe it away. "You think you have a choice about working with me instead of Brewster?"

She gasped. "He would never do to me what he's done to you! My father was his friend."

"Yes, friendship holds so much value for people like Brewster." Ian looked away. "And Keys."

"There must be some way for us to be free of him."

Ian turned his gaze back to hers. One eye was bloodshot, but both were still blue as ever as he narrowed them her way. In contrast to the hardness in his gaze, he raised one of his hands to allow a finger to gently trace her lips.

"You leave that to me."

25

Cleverness and ingenuity should be employed in such things
as hostessing, gift giving, and the manner in which one offers a
compliment. Ingenuity should not be applied in fashion, home
décor, or prying. In such things as the former two, it is usually
best not to step too far outside the accepted norms, and there
is of course no excuse for prying, clever or otherwise.

Madame Marisse's Handbook for Young Ladies

IT WAS ALMOST THE dinner hour by the time Meg returned via a
hired carriage with Kate respectably at her side. Their story of a
drive along the Hudson seemed readily received, enhanced by tales
of how quickly time had flown while their laughter and conversation were nonstop.

Although Kate did refuse an invitation to dinner, citing another
obligation, she promised to return the next day, when she would
be pleased to dine with them.

Meg knew Kate was anything but eager to keep up her performance as Lady Weathersfield. But she'd agreed even before
stepping foot back inside the Pemberton mansion to return at
least once more, to let Meg know how Ian was recovering. Until
his bruises eased, Meg knew she could have no contact with Ian
"Vandermey."

Keeping up appearances of being carefree proved a heftier

assignment than Meg imagined. Each of her thoughts was invaded by an image of Ian, mauled and bloodied. She was more determined than ever to succeed in the plan she'd offered to him—because she knew Ian would think of a way to use it against Brewster. Somehow.

Between her lack of sleep and nervous aftershocks from the day before, Meg decided she would skip yet again a ride to the park the following afternoon. Her new determination made her regret all the time she'd wasted thus far. So she feigned a headache and waved off Claire and Evie as they left for their daily romp to Central Park, adding that she wanted to be sure she'd be home if Kate came by earlier than promised the day before.

Once alone, she took immediate advantage of the time. Although Nelson had invited her to use any room she chose, she found herself treading carefully to Mr. Pemberton's office. She didn't bother trying the door from the library, expecting it still to be locked.

Instead she went to the foyer, tiptoeing down the private hall. Only to find this door locked as well.

So much for an open invitation into any room of the house.

Perhaps she could still investigate an idea that had piqued her interest in the last few days. She faced the wall at the very end of the hall, measuring six steps past the door. Was that the same distance to the end of the house, where the high windows allowed light to fill the room? It seemed the office stretched farther than the distance between the door and the boundary of this hall.

Meg turned, aligning herself with the edge of the wall and counting off her footsteps to the foyer, to the very edge of the front door. If there was some kind of secret room in that office—someplace Nelson might have been hidden when she'd first discovered the crucifixion painting, in the very corner Evie had glanced toward when mentioning their blessings—then it stood to reason the distance from the outside end of the house would be different from what it appeared in this hallway.

In hopes of her effort at measurement not appearing blatantly obvious, Meg quietly opened the door and, seeing the pavement empty, walked outside. Marking the spot from the front door, she started walking, silently counting the paces to the edge of this front portion that halted at the white cornerstones.

Four extra steps farther from outside than from inside that hall.

Of course she couldn't be exactly sure of her guess, but she'd been careful to take the same approximate stride inside as out. There seemed to be a corner of the office unaccounted for, allowing at least the possibility of some kind of secret room. Surely whatever was hidden couldn't be a very large area. Perhaps only large enough to host a safe or a closet of some kind. Large enough for Nelson to be inside when she'd first entered the library.

Short of counting off closer to the actual length of the wall along the house—where a stone fence stood in the way—Meg had done her best. There was certainly reason to suspect a corner of the room was hidden from the casual observer. She turned back to the house.

"Change your mind?"

Meg looked up to see Geoffrey, top hat and gloves in place, though he removed his hat with a courteously friendly bow once he stopped in front of her.

"Weren't you going to the park? Or were you? It's a long walk from here."

"I—did think about it. But I've forgotten my gloves."

"And your hat," he said. "Are you sure you were going somewhere? Or did you just come outside to catch my eye?"

"I didn't see you at all," she said, instantly wishing she hadn't sounded so cross. "Were you out here the entire time?"

"No, I saw you from my office." He pointed. "From upstairs. Of course, I call it an office, but I don't actually work there. Mother wants me to keep up on my studies so when I leave for college, I won't be too far behind others my age."

Setting aside both annoyance at being caught and relief that he mustn't think her presence outside too odd, she took advantage of the opportunity for casual conversation. "Why haven't you gone off to college, Geoffrey?"

"Because it seems like a silly ritual to me. My parents will pay a small fortune to a college to let me do as I please because no college would refuse access to my father's money. Then I come home with a degree that means absolutely nothing, to *do* absolutely nothing. It seems like a lot of money and trouble . . . for absolutely nothing."

"Don't you like school?"

"To be perfectly honest—as I always am with you, Miss Davenport—no."

"Perhaps you just haven't been to the right school."

"Perhaps."

"Well . . . I really must return inside. Claire and Evie won't expect me at the park, anyway, and they have the carriage. Nelson has the other. I don't want to drive the pony cart. So I'll wait for them inside."

"I'd be happy to take you."

She shook her head. Wouldn't that be just fine to spur another prank from Evie!

"All right, I'll let you go back inside," he said, but first he stepped closer. In a swift movement he took off one perfectly fitted glove and captured her hand in his. Holding her palm, he let his thumb caress the top of her hand.

"I knew your skin would be soft," he whispered.

Before she could protest—surely she should have—he turned away, covering his ungloved hand by switching his hat from the other. Then he disappeared into his house, leaving Meg to do the same.

Kate arrived for dinner, as expected, and she thoroughly charmed all of the Pembertons, including Nelson when Kate mentioned a series of books she was reading by George Müller, whom Nelson had evidently long admired.

She managed only a few moments alone with Meg, long enough to assure Meg that Ian was recuperating nicely and had decided to take up residence closer to the Pemberton home, provided he could find a hotel willing to take a dog the size of Roscoe. The admission came with both sadness and censure, since it was obvious that Ian and Meg were now working together.

Something from which Meg would not be deterred, not even when the following Sunday's sermon about a prodigal directly contrasted Meg's determination to help Ian steal from the Pembertons. When the pastor went on about how the bitter brother's protest highlighted the father's grace—not justice as the brother might have demanded—Meg felt like she was a child again, squirming in her seat.

You made me the way I am. You gave me the earthly father whose blood I share. What else do You expect of me?

No answer came, and eventually the torturous sermon ended.

That same afternoon heralded rain, but a visit from Mrs. Mason prevented them from going to the park anyway. Sunday was the only day of the week the park drew many and various crowds, when working-class New Yorkers had the day off to enjoy it. Evidently that was an occurrence Mrs. Mason thought they needed to avoid.

On Monday, when they were about to set out despite the continued presence of rain clouds, a thick envelope arrived from Europe and even Nelson stayed home to hear news from their parents. They invited Meg to the library to listen as well.

The multiple-paged letter was filled with their mother's descriptions of Paris—the weather, the people, the food, including recipes for the Pemberton cook to accustom herself with in advance of their return. Mrs. Pemberton had ordered gowns made for herself and her daughters, as well as suits for both Mr. Pemberton and Nelson and included full-color drawings of each from the designers. She promised to bring home new ideas for gala parties sure to please everyone on Fifth Avenue.

"I think Mother will be hosting more parties than ever this fall," Claire said sadly, "to make up for a lost summer season."

Nelson leaned against one of the bookshelves. "We knew our freedom wouldn't last. Mother said as much when she gave us permission to skip Newport this summer. It was on the condition that we won't complain when she sends us into battle in the fall."

"I don't know why you want to escape all the parties anyway," Evie said. "I can hardly wait!"

"Tell me that again when you're wearing a corset," Claire murmured.

"That doesn't explain why Nelson doesn't like the parties. I don't know which of you is more dull."

"You won't think us dull when we tell you about our plans to host the first annual Blue Moon Picnic," Nelson said with a wink.

That stirred Meg's interest. The Pembertons were hosting a picnic?

Claire smiled. "Oh, Nelson, you haven't forgotten!"

"What are you two talking about?" Evie demanded. "What is a Blue Moon Picnic?"

"I'd like to know that myself," Meg said.

"It's something Claire and I jested about after taking Mother and Father to the ship. We pledged to spend an exorbitant amount of money on a party only for the household—the servants, the entire staff. And that we would host it in Central Park, where everyone can see it."

"You don't plan to attend it yourself, do you?" Meg asked, ready to recite a direct quote from one of Madame's handbooks about keeping servants happy but not fraternizing with them. Although, couldn't such a party be a delightful way of breaking rules?

"That's the entire point," Nelson said, "for all of us to have a party together. Eat together. Dance together."

Meg laughed. "Dance! Oh, that ought to go over well with your neighbors. They'll send out the army to bring your parents home immediately."

"When are we having this party?" Evie asked.

"We haven't decided yet." Claire was looking again at the pages in her hands, and she spoke without looking at her sister.

"I think we should do it soon," Evie said, but then her gaze followed Claire's to the letter. "Is that all Mother says?"

"Isn't an eleven-page letter and five drawings enough?" Nelson asked.

"I meant is there anything about when they're coming home?"

Claire read the rest of the last page, which offered fond endearments and promises of many gifts, but no specific date for their return.

"And nothing from Father?" Nelson said, obviously surprised.

Claire turned over the last page. "Oh—yes, here it is. He's wondering about the project you began for the immigrants, Nelson, and hopes the soup pavilion is going well. And a verse. Oh, how funny! It's the same passage Pastor read yesterday, about the prodigal."

Nelson reached for the page with one hand but tousled Evie's hair with the other. "He must miss you, Evie."

She tried pushing his hand away but missed, smiling in spite of his teasing.

"I'll start a letter to them," he said, "although I guarantee it won't be half as long even if all three of us write something. I don't know how it will find them with all the places they intend going."

"We'll send it to their hotel in Paris," Claire suggested. "It'll be waiting for them when they return to pick up all the fashion Mother ordered."

"Very good." Nelson walked toward the door leading to Mr. Pemberton's office. "We'll put it on Father's stationery."

At the office door he paused, reaching up to a brass bookend shaped like a woman's high-heeled boot. From under the heel he withdrew a key.

Meg watched with a bursting pulse and unexpected glee, pushing away a silent accusation of treachery so opposite the trust with which he revealed such a secret. All the while she wondered why she'd never thought of looking in so simple a spot for so simple a solution.

She spent the rest of the afternoon reading a book while the siblings composed a letter of respectable length. Occasionally she glanced out the single window, imagining their trip to the park tomorrow. Central Park was the only spot to "casually" see Ian again. By now he was likely healed of the most obvious of his injuries. Knowing how to access that office, she could do exactly as she hoped. Perhaps by the time she saw Ian, she would have something important to share with him.

God speed the time until then!

But she wasn't sure God would listen to her.

Meg lay in bed, her eyes fixed on the bronze clock that she'd moved from the mantel to the small table beside her bed. She missed her clock and windup key from school. It had offered an alarm, and if placed under her pillow, the noise would have been enough to wake her but muffled so as not to alert anyone outside her room.

Not that she believed she would sleep. How could she rest knowing tonight she would follow through with her plan?

Although soggy ground had kept them from the park another couple of days, Meg hadn't despaired. For the last two nights she'd opened her bedchamber door and listened as long as she could force herself to remain awake. Sounds from other bedrooms taught her some of the sleeping habits of those who shared this considerable roof. Claire was the first to sleep, the light from under her door extinguished by eleven. Evie sometimes fell asleep with the gaslight in her room still up, but any noise from her room quieted around midnight. Nelson was the most unpredictable and hardest to decipher, since his room was farthest from Meg's. She had to venture to the hallway to see when the light from under his door went out, usually not long after midnight.

There was a third story to the mansion, where servants slept. Those noises quieted the earliest, and she had little to worry about with them so far from downstairs. Only Mr. Deekes, the head butler, whose quarters were near the kitchen, presented much concern. The main stairs were directly over his room, but in daylight hours she'd calculated the stair and floor squeaks and learned that staying close to the walls allowed both stairs and foyer floor to accept her slight weight without protest.

Meg had determined that waiting until two thirty in the morning would provide the least chance of being caught. The scullery maid roused at four to stir fires for heating water, followed soon after by the kitchen maid with preliminary preparations for the cook's entry some time later.

No one must see Meg wander the halls at night, although she'd prepared herself for the eventuality. If caught in the library, she would say, "I had such trouble sleeping, I needed a new book to pass the hours." Or if caught downstairs in Mr. Pemberton's study, where she intended spending most of her unusually timed visit, "I was feeling like praying and knew the painting would help me feel closer to God. I'm happy to say I noticed where the key was kept and let myself in."

She must remember to be bold in her lie; she had yet to become as accomplished as Kate, but determination would make up for her lack of experience.

Although she barely slept, she was startled into wakefulness by fretting over the time. She'd left her curtains open tonight, glad to have the return of the moon whose light confirmed it to be the perfect night for her nocturnal investigation.

It was two fifteen. Close enough.

Throwing back the light cover, Meg stood. She donned her robe, made of a dark-burgundy silk that was impossible to see in the darkness. Putting her feet into slippers, she went to the bedroom door and opened it carefully. She waited for any sounds to warn her.

As expected, the night was quiet but for the occasional creak she'd come to expect. Evidently a contented household left little reason for sleepless nights. She heard not even the flutter of a wing from the aviary.

Cautiously, she made her way down the hall. Past Claire's room, past Evie's. The stairway was nearer Nelson's room, but that, too, was dark and silent.

Creeping close to the wall as she'd learned to do when no one was watching, Meg found her way to the first floor. Her embroidered, quilted slippers made not a sound on the marble floor of the foyer, nor upon the carpeting that led into the library. The door was ajar, and enough moonlight filtered into the room that she didn't have to light a candle to find her way amid the chairs, sofa, and tables.

Standing at the shelves, she reached up to the third bookshelf, finding exactly what she sought. The key.

Heart pounding, nearly breathless from exhilaration, Meg stilled her trembling hand to fit the object into the lock. It opened easily, with the barest sound of a metal lever sliding from its place. She returned the key, then pushed open the door, moving it slowly, ever so slowly, because in the day-lit hour when she'd seen this door used she hadn't thought to pay attention to any possible squeak.

Silence.

Surely this was the easiest way to investigate, knowing the entire family and staff were in the secure arms of slumber.

Stepping into the office, she first thought about where *not* to look. In fact, when she'd envisioned this exploration, she forewarned herself to keep her eyes only on the suspicious corner. But the windows that during the day shed beams of sunlight now opened the way for the glow of the moon. It shone a shaft of light that led nowhere but to the portrait.

Her feet would not move as quickly as she bade them. Nor would her eyes obey her; they sought the vision of Christ as if pulled there by a force not her own. Her heart stuttered.

But she pressed on. The desk was neat, offering only a stack of stationery, blotter and ink, pens and tips. Opening the middle drawer, she searched first for the seal Brewster had mentioned, then for anything that might identify a bank used by the Pembertons. It didn't take long to find a book of checks, which she eagerly opened and read. The Bank of New York!

Slipping the record book back where she found it, she looked around the room again and settled her gaze on the corner Evie had glanced toward when mentioning the family's blessings. It was easy enough to imagine Nelson emerging from there, when he'd appeared so unexpectedly while Meg's attention had been arrested by the portrait.

The wall looked ordinary. Another picture hung there, this one far smaller, one she'd barely noticed before. Just a simple country scene, a landscape. Obviously it would not stand in the way if there were a secret behind this wall.

She ran her palms along the suspicious wall, going in a pattern so as not to miss a single spot, starting as high as she could reach.

Nothing seemed unusual on the smooth, stained paneling—no levers or even so much as an indentation. Getting down on her hands and knees, she felt along the baseboard and floor, looking for a release button or a break in the woodwork.

The wood did reveal a slanted cut . . . but was it only because the woodworker did not have a length to measure the exact width of the room? Or was it the spot where a door opened?

She felt along the wall again from that spot, but it revealed nothing more than what might simply be another panel joint covering the walls.

Yet she was sure this room was more than it presented itself to be. Where had Nelson appeared from that day? Had Meg been so engrossed in the portrait that she hadn't heard him approach in the normal way, down the hall?

She thought back to that moment. She'd been staring at the painting, but she'd been too close to the door not to notice someone entering from that angle. Surely he hadn't come through the library; she would have seen that out of the side of her vision. There *must* be a hidden spot in this office.

Sudden noise made her heart leap to her throat. She scampered away from the spot of her investigation, knowing the safest room in which to be found would be the library.

Just as quickly as the noise appeared, it silenced. It had been nothing more than a carriage traveling on the street outside.

Breathing in a deep gulp of fortifying air, Meg set about her task once again. She couldn't recommend Ian risk breaking into the Pemberton home if the prize he sought wasn't here.

She faced the wall again, looking up and down and around. That same light she'd resented a moment ago for calling attention to the portrait now aided her in the study of the questionable corner.

Surely there was a secret here; she had only to find it.

26

If a young lady is to be introduced to someone of the male persuasion, it is of utmost importance to ensure that the gentleman be not only of impeccable character and unsullied reputation, but unimpeachable integrity.

Madame Marisse's Handbook for Young Ladies

As Meg anticipated, the following day produced sunny skies. And though Claire told the driver they would stay in the open carriage and forgo the still-wet pedestrian paths, Meg was so eager to look for Ian that she refused to worry over details. She had every reason to hope she would see him soon—perhaps even today.

The driver took them through the menagerie, past the bear cage and the swans in the pond, past the peacock that unfolded its colorful tail. It was as if Central Park had come alive again, and the animals had missed showing off for their visitors after so many days of inclement weather.

Perhaps because they ventured past their regular spot, Meg saw signs of neglect in the park for the first time. Trees untrimmed, once-lush lawns gone to weed in spite of old signs warning people to keep off, pathways rutted with running water from the recent rain. When they passed the ruins of Mount St. Vincent—the chapel, conservatory, art gallery, and restaurant that had burned to the ground the year before—the park's gradual decline seemed even more noticeable. Nelson had complained only the day before about how city politics threatened the pastoral escape, but since his plans for the park's improvement supported allowing Sunday concerts, he hadn't been able to gain much help from Fifth Avenue neighbors or even the church. Saturday concerts were quite enough for them, when working-class folks were unable to attend because of the six-day workweek. He lacked the church's support because they hadn't yet decided if a concert accommodated proper Sabbath rest.

Meg's eye was drawn to a dog loping along the path nearby. The animal's muddy paws and filthy tendrils of wet fur made her wonder why the dog hadn't been kept from the shadier paths that took longest to dry or why he wasn't at least leashed. The owner called after it affectionately from atop a horse, and from the mud streaking both the horse and the rider's pant legs it was obvious they'd come from a similarly unwise route.

Her heart fluttered. That owner was *Ian*.

"Please stop the carriage!"

"Whatever is the matter, Meg?" Claire asked as the carriage came to a halt nearly as sudden as Meg's entreaty.

"It's . . . my cousin, Ian . . ." What had been the name he'd chosen? *Maguire* was on the tip of her tongue. "Ian Vandermey. I wondered if he was still in the city, and there he is."

It took only a moment to catch his eye, as if he fully expected to meet them at this traditional spot where pedestrian, carriage, and equestrian trails converged. Or had he simply been following from a distance?

She greeted him with a smile, noticing that he was nearly as spattered with mud as the dog. Perhaps he hadn't minded the smudges to his face, if they hid any remaining evidence of his recent encounter with Keys.

"How nice to see you, Ian!"

She would have started the introduction, but Roscoe

approached first and threw up a pair of thoroughly soiled paws to the edge of the carriage. That dog!

Evie screamed but followed so quickly with a laugh that Meg was unsure if she was afraid or delighted. "Oh, may I pet him? He has the friendliest eyes!"

"If you can find a clean spot to touch," Ian said, "he'd welcome any attention you have to spare. We were just headed to the pond to clean him off."

Evie folded and set aside the parasol Claire insisted she use and raised an uncertain hand, at last touching a spot directly on the top of the dog's massive head. The animal pressed as close as he could, making Evie laugh again. Meg was relieved only that the dog wasn't as smart with door latches as Pindar was; otherwise she was sure he'd have crawled right inside and settled atop all of their laps.

Ian reined in his horse beside the carriage, removing his hat to greet Meg. She saw then that the mud *did* seem strategically placed. "How nice to see you, Cousin Meg."

Meg tried to calm her fast-beating pulse by recalling her manners. "Claire, permit me to present to you my cousin, Mr. Ian Vandermey. This is Claire Pemberton and her sister, Evie Pemberton."

Claire nodded her greeting, holding her own parasol to the far side so as not to get in the way. "How very nice to meet a relative of Meg's. I've known her for years and have yet to meet a single member of her family." Leave it to Claire to politely ignore the state of Ian's personal attire.

"Our family is a rare breed," Ian said, flashing a smile that did nothing to help Meg control her heartbeat. How white his teeth were! "Nearly extinct, in fact."

"Then you both ought to get married and have lots and lots of children," Evie said. "At least then your children will have plenty of cousins."

"Evie." Claire's cautious voice was tinged, for once, with what sounded like amusement.

"You're no doubt right, young lady," Ian said. Then he eyed Meg again. "I would enjoy an opportunity to visit with you while we're both here in the city. Will you be attending Saturday's concert in the park? Provided the fine weather holds, of course, and the grounds continue to dry?"

"Yes," Meg said. "We attend the concerts regularly."

He replaced his hat. "Then I hope to see all of you there. Good day." He directed his horse onward—a careful walk, no doubt due to Ian's recovering ribs—then whistled for the dog, who scampered away, leaving behind paw prints on the top edge of the carriage.

Saturday. Leaving her less than two days to search for a clue to what was hidden in the office corner.

The concert on Saturday was to be a ballad event, blending instruments with soloists. Meg had looked forward to the performance for its own merit, but now that she knew she would see Ian again, she found herself all the more eager to attend.

The only possible source of trouble was Geoffrey Mason. He'd started the habit of going to the grounds early to claim prime locations along the iron seating that circled trees and foliage, protecting park landscaping while doubling as chairs. A service for which Claire seemed grateful even while Evie was always quick to grab a seat beside him. Though he allowed Evie to sit on one side, he'd come to expect Meg to sit on the other—and often filled every gap in the concert with conversation that demanded her attention.

Perhaps it was just as well for Geoffrey to meet Ian; Meg would make it clear that Ian was only the most distant sort of relation and let Geoffrey draw his own conclusion. If he watched Meg as closely as he usually did, she intended to leave the impression her heart was already taken.

An impression that seemed more honest than so much else about her these days.

The afternoon was warm, and so Meg chose the lightest of her white muslin dresses, the sheerest lace gloves, the smallest hat of straw with the tiniest paper-flower embellishment. The trees were still young in the Ramble, where the concert was to be played, so there would be little shade. In deference to the close proximity of seating, she would bring her most petite parasol of brushed chiffon, the one trimmed simply in lace rather than fringe that might otherwise impede the view of someone nearby. A delicately carved white wood fan was an absolute must.

Geoffrey waved to them as they approached, and as usual Evie drew near to him first.

"Good afternoon, Evie," Geoffrey greeted her. "You're looking very happy today."

Evie had refused to wear braids, opting instead to keep her hair free but for the pearl hairpins that loosely held back her light-brown waves. Meg had to admit that though Kate's visits had been an uncomfortable balance between truth and lies, she had produced an astounding result in Evie. The girl had thrown her energy into trying to look older and, in so doing, displayed some of that beauty Kate claimed she possessed.

Geoffrey was not alone today. He'd brought with him his parents and Nomi as well, so only Nelson was absent from this gathering of neighborly households. Nelson had claimed too much work to be able to go to the concert, something Meg noticed Claire tactfully omitted when Mrs. Mason asked about him.

"You're looking especially lovely today, Miss Davenport," Mrs. Mason said with a twinkle in her eye when she looked from Meg to Geoffrey. Her approval of Meg—based solely on Meg's friendship with the Pembertons and her attendance of Madame Marisse's—had come to be as much an annoyance to Meg as Geoffrey's interest in her.

No one was seated as yet, but Evie squeezed between Geoffrey and his mother. "Won't you sit beside me and Geoffrey, Mrs. Mason?" she asked. "I wanted to show you my new hairpins. The pearls are from England. Look closely at this one—the left. Its color has a bit more luster than the other, don't you agree?" She shifted her head from side to side to offer a better view. "I was reading just the other day about a famous pearl one of the English kings wore at his beheading simply hundreds of years ago. The tale goes that the crowd rushed forward to claim the single earring—you know, since he no longer had need of it— and the jewel disappeared. I would guess *any* pearl from England might be that one. Imagine! This very pearl could have been worn by a king."

Mrs. Mason gasped, though she did make a belated attempt to cover her horror for kindness' sake.

Meg suppressed a laugh, resuming her search of the area for any sign of Ian.

Ian stared at Kate as she made herself comfortable on the chair in the fancy room at the Glenham Hotel registered to Ian Vandermey. He'd had to leave Roscoe with Pubjug at a hotel room less fussy about accepting animals—at least ones Roscoe's size.

At first he'd refused to let her in, stating he would be late. It took Kate's announcement that she intended to be his companion to the concert and her threat to confess all to the Pembertons to make him listen.

"You won't go through with a confession, Kate."

She stopped smoothing the wrinkles from her red dress and sent him a confident smile. "Won't I?"

"No, you won't. Because telling everyone Lady Weathersfield is a figment of your imagination might send you to jail as well as me."

She shook her head, lifting one elegant hand to assure her hair was still in place after unhooking the mesh veil that had shrouded her face. "The crimes I committed are in the past, perpetrated against carefully chosen men wealthy and proud enough not to admit they'd given me money they must have suspected I had no intention of returning. In any case, no charges were pressed against me. I was as good at that as John was."

"Still, it's a risk you'll take to admit who you are. And what about Meg? You'd ruin her socially just by your association with her."

Now Kate leaned forward, the confidence replaced by earnest entreaty. "I don't want to cause trouble for any of us, Ian. Not for you or for myself, but especially not for Meg. And I suspect if you let yourself think about it long enough, you want the same thing."

He took a seat across from her, avoiding her gaze. He didn't have a reply because he'd done exactly as she hinted: not allowed himself to think of it. Especially lately, while he'd been concocting a plan to use against Brewster that unavoidably utilized Meg and her connection to the Pembertons. He didn't have to see evidence that Brewster was watching them both; he just knew it.

"Ian, the Bible says that the laws of the governments are here to execute revenge on those who do evil. This stealing, you know it's evil. To resist the power of the rightful law is to resist the ordinance of God."

"God has nothing to do with plenty of the laws out there, Kate. And He has nothing to do with this. All I want is to be free of Brewster."

"And ruin Meg's life in the process? You don't care that you're using her?"

He stood in a surge of annoyed energy, pleased when the sudden movement caused only a trace of pain to his healing ribs. "If that's the only way to keep her from Brewster, why not?"

"I know your father taught you to believe in the Bible, Ian."

So John had told her even about that! Kate might have used a gentle tone, but each word stung him—because they were true.

"Do you know that it says it would be better for you to have a millstone tied round your neck than to cause an innocent to fall? Do you want to be a stumbling block to another? To Meg, of all people? You couldn't have loved John and not loved her, too."

"That's enough, Kate." He gave her his back as images assaulted him. Not just recent ones of John, speaking to Ian in his dreams, but others of Ian's own father, starker than ever though it had been more than a dozen years since his death. *There is nothing worse, laddie, than to cause another to fall away. . . .*

"No, it isn't enough," she persisted. "Why must you do this? To be free of Brewster or for revenge? Or maybe it's something else. Maybe it's far simpler than any of that."

She paused just long enough to make Ian look at her. "This desire of yours—" Kate used the softest of voices because she'd neared him, and he easily heard her—"this desire for money can never be satisfied because that isn't what you really want. You'll always want more because money cannot satisfy you. Not when it's your father's faith that you're missing."

Ian turned so violently that Kate took a step backward, away from him. But Ian didn't apologize for frightening her; it was her fault his thoughts made his mood so ugly. "God let my father, my mother, and my brothers die on that ship! And left me, the most useless of the bunch. Why, Kate? To torment me? Well, He's done that, all right."

Kate gently shook her head. "No, Ian. Not to torment you. But to wait until you were ready for Him, the way the rest of your family was."

If she'd kicked him in his sore rib cage, he wouldn't have felt less assaulted. The truth, his father had once told him, could cut like a sword.

He turned again, tearing both hands through his hair. It had taken years for Ian to conquer the echo he'd carried with him after the death of his family. Their voices used to haunt him, but his pain over their loss led eventually to associating that pain with God, making it easier to ignore Him as well as his memories.

Somewhere along the way the voices had eased, eventually disappearing. Until lately.

The irony was not lost on Ian: Meg wanted so badly to join her father's legacy that she was willing to break the law. For Ian to join any legacy of his own family, he must do the opposite.

But if he did, his plans didn't have a chance—and he wasn't about to give them up just yet.

Once the concert began, Meg both welcomed and resented the performance. Where was Ian? Her mind was so preoccupied she was barely able to enjoy herself. She gazed as much at the surrounding crowd—looking for just one face—as she did the gazebo where the musicians sat and the soloists came to perform.

Meg was the first to her feet during intermission. Surely he was here somewhere! She might not have specific evidence of how to reach the Pemberton treasure, but she had plenty of suspicion she was eager to share.

"Our Mr. Plowden should be here with the refreshments shortly," Geoffrey said, referring to his butler. "He knows where to find us."

"That's very kind of you," Meg said, still searching the crowd. She barely listened as Geoffrey went on about which songs thus far had been his favorites, noting various qualities about the vocalists who had performed.

Soon the Mason butler arrived with a basket of refreshments, from rolled cheese-and-cucumber sandwiches and pickled peppers to plum cakes and fresh oranges offered in their own silver bowl, accompanied by orange knives or spoons as desired.

Meg accepted a glass of *tea à la russe*, sipping its sweet, lemony flavor. Everyone chatted around her, Evie demanding Geoffrey's attention with her questions and, when he drifted away, seeking his mother. Moments went by so slowly Meg could scarcely contain herself from setting out on a search of her own.

"Oh! Look, Meg, there is your cousin." Evie, facing the other direction, was full of excitement. "And he's with Lady Weathersfield!"

Meg turned so quickly she nearly spilled her tea. It was true: there they were, as unlikely a couple as Meg had ever seen. Kate was dressed in her trademark red, her hair swept up beneath a matching feathered hat with a lace veil hooked from one side to the other, effectively shrouding her entire face. This time, only her gloves were black.

Her arm was looped with Ian's, whose image took Meg's breath away. With neither that dog nor any remnant of his attack, there was nothing to diminish his portrayal of a perfect gentleman. In a light frock coat and vest, tan trousers, and a brown silk top hat, he looked as crisp and fresh as if they hadn't been seated through the entire first half of the concert. Evidence of her father's pocket watch glistened from his vest, and she found a surprising sense of satisfaction seeing him wear it.

"There you are, you darling!" Kate greeted Meg. "How many times have I said to this dear boy that I simply will not let this concert end until we've found you? I see you're not alone."

While Claire made introductions, which not unexpectedly resulted in a trace of awe on Mrs. Mason's face, Meg found her way to Ian's other side.

There were plenty of refreshments left to offer, although Meg knew she couldn't swallow another thing. Ian accepted a glass of sherry while Kate received currant wine, and the conversation picked up again about the music, the city, the state of the park. As they talked, Meg linked her arm with Ian's.

Mrs. Mason undoubtedly noticed but was clearly so impressed by Lady Kate that she ignored the attention Meg had for her "cousin."

When the musicians returned to the stage, warning the audience the concert was about to resume, Geoffrey's father invited Kate to take his seat.

"Oh no, Mr. Mason," Meg said, knowing she was breaking more than a couple of rules by standing in the way of a gentleman's offer of a seat. "Lady Kate may have my place. I absolutely cannot sit again, and I'd like to continue stretching my limbs by enjoying a brief walk with my cousin." Two more rules broken: referencing her limbs and intending to walk away, relatively alone, with a man of mysterious relation.

"But, my dear Meg," Kate said, "I don't mind in the least accompanying you and Ian."

Meg shook her head at Kate's attempt to save her from such a breach of etiquette, taking Kate's hand long enough to lead her to the vacated seat. "I insist you enjoy the second half of the entertainment. Ian and I won't walk far, only down the path toward the shade, where we won't be in the way."

Surely Mrs. Mason's estimation of Madame Marisse's graduates had sunk a peg or two, but there was nothing to be done for it.

"That's very generous of you, Meg," Ian said with a smile. "Lady Kate was just saying how she looked forward to sitting again, after our stroll."

And so it was done. Meg let Ian lead her away, and she felt nothing but triumph.

Ian's heart went unexpectedly light, considering his confrontation with Kate only minutes before. For the first time since John's
death—no, Ian couldn't remember ever feeling this way—he was
flooded with hope. His resolution to end any ties to Brewster
would come to fruition, mainly because he had more incentive
than ever. His partnership with Meg virtually guaranteed it, even
if the only job they worked on together was this one.

"Oh, Ian! I have so much to tell—"

"Wait," he whispered, glancing over his shoulder. That Mason
fellow was far too watchful. He was, in fact, observing them now,
just as Ian had expected.

A trickle of hope escaped when Ian glanced again at Mason.
Who was Ian kidding? He'd once hoped not only to protect
Meg from Brewster, but to protect her from herself. Now he was
using her, but it still didn't mean Ian could claim her for himself.
A memory of how Mason had made Meg laugh still pricked his
pride. While it might be true Mason was the one doing the pursuing, Ian wondered if Meg would stop resisting if he stepped out
of the way.

"Is your visit with the Pembertons going well?" he asked at last,
once they were well away from the group.

"Remarkably well." Her eyes were filled with such delight that
his stubborn doubts about working with her diminished. "I have
information. The Pembertons bank at the Bank of New York—"

Perhaps she'd expected him to be more interested—or at least
pleased—by her information. Even though he was careful not to
frown, it came as no news. Anyone with an interest in banking knew
which institutions the Pembertons used and that they were expanding their interests as far as Chicago, St. Louis, and even Denver.

"Oh," she said, "did you already know that?"

"Where they do the majority of their banking doesn't matter," he said, "because they likely don't keep all of their gold in one spot anyway."

Her smile unexpectedly reappeared. "I believe the Pembertons have a safe inside their own home. Perhaps the gold bricks are there—right inside the house where I'm staying!"

This suspicion came as no surprise either, given the relative ease with which so many banks could be robbed. Still, perhaps she'd learned something to confirm what he already believed. "Why do you think so?"

"There's a mysterious corner in the Pemberton office—a few square feet of space I cannot account for. It would be a perfect spot for a safe."

He pondered the thought. "If the safe is of any size, it would require a specialized spot. Safes are heavier than you'd guess."

"This spot is near nothing less than a cornerstone! I've measured the office as closely as I can, and I'm convinced the room is not all it appears to be."

"It wouldn't be the first hidden closet I've heard of," Ian said. "But even so, it would take some time for me to investigate. Burglarizing a home isn't what I do."

Now her lovely, delicate brows came together. "But if I found out how to access the safe—if it's there—it would be the same as getting into a bank safe! I'm trying to find all the information you need; I've even gotten up in the middle of the night to go over every inch of that wall. For the life of me, Ian, I don't know how the corner is opened. And yet I'm sure, positively sure, something is there."

Admiration mixed with surprise, and only belatedly did he think to worry she might have gotten caught before this whole thing went any further. "You've done that in the middle of the night? Undetected, of course?"

She nodded. "I spent a few nights listening for sleeping habits, to be sure I would be safe. And if I am discovered, the room is next to the library, where I can claim I came for a book."

"It's an office, you said. There must be a desk."

"Yes, a large one near the center of the room."

"And is the floor bare wood or carpeted?"

"There is a carpet, but only beneath the desk. The floor is tiled."

"I once saw a design from a safe manufacturer that might be exactly what they have. Look beneath the rug, under the desk, where it would be relatively easy—yet perfectly hidden—to access a small trapdoor. If there is one, it may hide a release lever connected underneath the floor to a door in the wall. It could be beneath the desk or on another wall—anywhere, really, inside the room."

"I hadn't considered looking very far from the corner," she said.

"I wouldn't ask you to take the risk again, Meg, but I'll have to know not only that it's there, but more importantly what kind of safe they have. I need the brand, the approximate size, and what the handle looks like. I'll know how to open it if I know that much."

The directions came of long habit, as if there were no doubt about going through with this plan that would forever alter Meg's life. Even as Ian was certain she would comply to the best of her ability—an ability he found impressive—he squashed the voices that threatened his hope. The doubts, the condemnation that wanted to bombard him from within. The fact was he needed what Meg so freely offered.

He'd just have to forget she was John's daughter.

The concert soon ended, and Meg and Ian rejoined the group to say polite farewells. Kate grasped Meg's hand a bit too long, and through the veil covering her face, Meg saw a silent but earnest plea. Meg stared back without flinching, pushing away the warning in Kate's eyes.

As Ian led Kate away, Meg couldn't help but pity her a bit. She knew what it was like to feel entirely ignored. Meg had felt the same from her father nearly all her life.

"Let me escort you to your carriage, Miss Davenport," Geoffrey said.

Before she could refuse, before she could offer even the slightest glance of apology to Evie, Geoffrey claimed her hand and led her away.

"I see now why you were so distracted during the first half of the concert," Geoffrey said quietly. His tone held something akin to sadness. "You were looking for your cousin, weren't you? Hoping to see him here today?"

She let her gaze meet his, knowing that a lack of denial said enough. Still, it wasn't easy to withstand his unhappiness. He'd only been kind and friendly to her, and if she were anyone but her father's daughter, she might have enjoyed his company.

"It's difficult to compete with someone who's had a place in your heart for any length of time," he said as he set a slow pace beside her, "but I don't intend giving up."

Meg grabbed the hand that rested on hers. She wasn't sure it was right letting him think that Ian held more a place in her heart than he did. She knew only that they were partners; the rest was too confusing to sort out just yet. But it served her purpose to rebuff Geoffrey. He only complicated what she'd come to do. "Please do, Geoffrey. I cannot be what you want me to be."

He leaned in on her, so close she was afraid he would kiss her. He stopped only inches away. "But you already are."

Then Evie joined them, and any more such talk was tucked away.

It is essential for the young hostess to provide an evening of effervescent pleasantry, fit for fond memories. Vulgarities in any form are to be avoided at all cost, so as not to cause dyspepsia in her guests.

Madame Marisse's Letters to Young Wives, NO. 5

"YOU CANNOT BE SERIOUS!"

Evie's protest over the proposed dinner procession echoed from one end of the parlor to the other. The three of them, Evie, Claire, and Meg, sat planning an event that was still four days away—days that hopefully would not prove to be four more filled with quarreling. Perhaps it was a good thing they'd forgotten about planning the picnic Nelson and Claire once mentioned; that would no doubt be a source of as much contention as this dinner party.

"Don't imagine I'll be any more pleased to walk in with you, Evie," Claire said, "but it's only one evening, ten feet from here to the dining room, and there is simply no other way."

Meg looked between the bickering siblings, afraid Claire was correct. She was hardly thrilled with the arrangement herself, but if they were to follow decorum as set by London—and really, no company dinner did otherwise—then they must do it by rank.

Of course this issue would have been avoided altogether if they hadn't invited Kate, but Evie would hear nothing of that. Or it could have been solved with something as simple as the truth. Kate was not nobility and as such didn't need to be given preference. But as it was, Nelson, being the temporary head of the household and therefore the host, would escort "Lady" Kate into the dining room. She would sit at his right hand. That much was not in dispute.

Nomi was the eldest and therefore next in line of importance. This was some cause of concern, since it would have been simple for Claire to act as hostess and expect Ian to escort her. On the other hand, the whole purpose of the evening was to allow Meg to enjoy Ian's company in front of Geoffrey, a plan which Evie fully endorsed. But because they'd agreed to allow Evie to join them, it meant one less seat available for another gentleman, leaving Ian the only available escort for Nomi.

It also meant putting Mr. and Mrs. Mason together, an obvious social mistake in a setting that was designed to expand one's chances at diverse conversation. But there was nothing to be done for it.

In Claire's display of humility that seemed to rankle her only because it meant walking in at her sister's side, she suggested she and Evie go after everyone else. It wasn't being last that seemed to bother Evie, but rather the irksome idea of Meg walking in with Geoffrey.

"Don't forget we're allowing you to dine with us as a favor to you," Claire said to Evie's continued scowl. "You're the one so eager to grow up."

The frown did not ease. "You couldn't set a table with only nine people. I'm as necessary to the evening as either of you."

"We could always invite one of Nelson's associates and leave you off the list entirely," Claire suggested. "That way I could at least walk in on the arm of a man instead of a child."

"You won't do any such thing. Not that you would hesitate to thwart me, but being a dinner partner to some other man would mean being false to your silly memory of Jude."

Meg cleared her throat. "I think you're forgetting, Evie, that this dinner was practically your idea." Or at least that was what Meg wanted everyone to think. She'd done nothing more than make a suggestion to Evie, and the child had taken over just as Meg had hoped. "You haven't been properly introduced into society as of yet, and even though this is a simple dinner party for neighbors and friends, it's still stretching the rules to include someone your age."

"Oh, all right, I won't argue anymore." Her glare softened somewhat when she turned to Meg. "Except having you sit with Geoffrey through the entire meal spoils the whole idea."

Meg shook her head. "But I don't plan to charm him, Evie. I plan to convince him of the truth: I have no intention of marrying him or anyone." Perhaps if she told herself that often enough, and pronounced it publicly, she would believe it.

"Or anyone?" The shocked question came in unison from both Claire and Evie.

"Well, at least not anyone I know."

"Not even your so-called cousin?" Evie asked.

Meg felt warmth scroll up from her heart to her forehead. Why did everyone insist she felt more for Ian than she wanted to admit? And yet it did no harm to let Evie think what she wanted.

"It's true Ian is only a distant sort of cousin, honorary rather than blood. My friendship with him began when my father died and is on my father's behalf." Establishing anything more would no doubt make her create a labyrinth of lies too complicated for her to keep straight, so she wouldn't try. "Just know that I'm no competition for Geoffrey's attention, Evie."

Claire was shaking her head, setting aside the list of menu ideas—another area of dissension they'd visited earlier. "I'm not at all sure this idea is a good one. For one thing, we're practically encouraging her infatuation with Geoffrey. Anyone can see he's too old for her and still considers her a child."

"For now!" Evie insisted.

"When he leaves home for college or to travel again, he may come home with a bride, Evie. One his own age. I'm only trying to spare you future heartache."

Evie was clearly unconvinced.

Meg picked up the paper Claire had set aside. She needed this dinner party to take place for altogether different reasons. Claire might resent her little sister, but in this case she was entirely correct about the evening lacking any element of protection for Evie's young heart. Something Meg would rather not dwell upon too long.

"Getting back to the menu," she began, "did we decide on three courses? We ought to have at least that many for ten of us and perhaps four *quelque chose* to start with."

Evie laughed. "You can call them kickshaws around here, Meg. Claire isn't much better than I at French."

"All right, then," Meg said. "What shall we have for the kickshaws? Shrimp? Or oysters? Both, perhaps, and celery, too."

"Oh, Claire, can we have Cook make some candied fruit, the way she did at Christmastime? And a centerpiece of sugar flowers and figurines!"

Claire frowned. "We told Cook this was a simple dinner, remember?"

"Then we can order in for a confection centerpiece. I saw an advertisement for table ornaments in the newspaper just the other day. It'll save ever so much time but be fitting for Lady Weathersfield. I'm sure she's used to fancy dinners. We don't want to disappoint her or disgrace our house, do we? And beside that, think how Mrs. Mason will appreciate it. She likes a fuss to be made over her."

Claire nodded. "Very well; I'll see about ordering something."

Meg listened, wishing she could ease some of their eagerness for the designated evening. Kate, in all likelihood, had never graced her own table with sugar figurines. And Mrs. Mason . . . well, there was something about her that inspired Meg to remind her that even though half the families along Fifth Avenue could afford to pave the streets with gold, this was not the footstool of heaven.

The evening was set for Thursday, and invitations had already gone out. She had four days left—more importantly three nights—to discover more information about how to access the office corner. If it housed a safe as she suspected, she would supply Ian with access to the house, a floor plan he would be familiar with after this dinner party, and instructions on how to reach the safe that she would describe as he'd requested. He would know what to do after that to complete their plan.

The clock from the library struck three. Meg stood in the office, desperate to find what she was looking for. She had only tonight left; the last two nights had proven fruitless.

There was little light without a moon to shine through the two high windows. She was forced to use a candle. It was a risk, of course, but she would keep it well away from the windows. She closed the door to the library to prevent any shadows from escaping that way. The paraffin candle Meg had borrowed from the dining room earlier would leave behind no scent, unlike the bayberry in her room.

Keeping her back to the painting, she stared at the desk. That cross, the one that stood on the edge—was it only decorative, a symbol of Mr. Pemberton's faith? But why have it when the painting did the same thing? Had she missed something as obvious as what this cross might be?

Meg touched the carving, tipping it forward, then backward as if it were the secret lever Ian had described. But nothing happened, not even when she lifted it.

Almost nothing.

The cross in her hand, so smoothly carved, so stark a representation of the painting she'd turned her back on, beckoned her to look at what she'd vowed to ignore. But Meg refused to turn around.

She returned the carving to its spot, then rounded the desk and got down on her hands and knees. She'd searched here already, but if there was a lever behind this desk, Meg would find it—without a moment wasted staring at a portrait that was nothing more than canvas and paint.

Meg settled the candleholder on the floor behind her and pushed the chair out of the way. Then she rolled back the carpet as far as the heavy desk allowed and ran her hands along the smooth, cool tiling.

Nothing.

Surely if there was a secret lever, it couldn't be too difficult to access, if one was to open the corner with any regularity. But repeating the action, lingering over tile edges, pressing and pulling at the lines of grout lest any seam conceal a hinge, she still found nothing.

At last Meg sank back on her feet, a soft moan escaping that she hadn't realized was trapped inside. Perhaps she was wrong. Perhaps the room had been designed with the hall in front of it for the very reason she'd first assumed: the occupier of this room wanted no distractions, thus the only windows were up high for the benefit of light, but no view or compromise of privacy. Perhaps the measurement shortage in the hall meant nothing at all.

Still, it made no sense. The parlor, on the opposite end of the house, had no such secret corner. She'd measured that just to be sure. It appeared only this corner, in this room, was inexplicable.

She looked around the room again. The only place she'd steered away from was the painting. She didn't want to go near it. Even as she turned away to restore the rug and chair to their original placement, the struggle waged within her. Superstition. Irrational fear. Omens.

Which was, of course, ridiculous. She knew God wouldn't approve of what she was doing, but did she honestly believe He cared? Surely if her father or Ian were here, they wouldn't let misplaced guilt or premature remorse prevent them from doing whatever they needed to do.

With that thought, she strode forward, candle high in one hand and the other hand outstretched. She touched the edge of the picture's frame, half-expecting some kind of shock—like the jolt from a metal stair railing or a fireplace poker after walking across a carpet on a dry day. But nothing happened; the portrait accepted her touch as if it had expected it. Welcomed it.

She slid her fingertips behind the frame, starting high, barely disturbing the way it hung so solidly from the wall.

And there it was, high enough to be hidden by any work of art—something much smaller could certainly have accomplished what this massive portrait did with such excess. Her fingertips brushed against a narrow but smooth indentation. Sliding her fingers in as far as it allowed, she felt the lever. Like the ceramic beneath her slippered feet, it was cool, made of steel or iron. She pulled it; it lowered only as far as the edge of the indentation, so the painting hiding it was in no danger of damage.

Instantly she heard a dull click and she spun around, still holding the candle. A shadow appeared that was not there before—a long, straight line near the corner. It beckoned her. She went to it, pulling wider the gap.

Thrusting her candle into the darkness, she realized the wall hid neither a room nor a safe. Looking down, she saw the narrowest of stairwells—plain, unadorned wood steps with metal sidings. Gingerly she tapped a toe to the top stair; it was sturdy and would accept her weight.

Still, she hesitated. She lifted the candle again, looking at the walls. They were plain block without so much as a spiderweb in sight, and yet fear accompanied her excitement. It was one thing to face the insects she knew in the garden, another to face the unknown in pitch black.

But she knew what she must do.

There was no railing, nothing but the stark, cold wall to provide balance on the narrow stairs. Three of the four walls were easily within reach, making her feel closed in, trapped, even with the secret door left open. The steps were steep, little better than a ladder. As she descended, the air grew cooler. And though the walls likely did not grow any closer than they'd been at the top of the ladderlike stairs, it was as if they engulfed her with each step she took.

Meg stopped, lowering the candle to see what waited at the bottom. How much farther could this squeezed staircase go?

Dank air licked the candle's glow as if threatening to extinguish it. Though unsteady, the flicker remained intact all the way to the last stair, where she paused to look around. Her eye caught on a line in the wall in front of her, her candle's glow reflecting what appeared to be a narrow bead of dampness between the cement blocks. A rag of some kind had been wadded on the floor below to catch the seepage.

There wasn't much space; the walls down here in no way matched the room above. But the flame did its job—it revealed what she most wanted to see. There it was, behind the stairway.

A safe. Nearly as tall as Meg, made of some kind of metal. The handle was of the lever kind, with a dial above it. From her spot on the stair it was too dim to read the brand, but she could see there was lettering etched or painted in an arch on the very top of the door. She would have to approach the safe for a better look.

So she did, holding the candle high as she stood before the safe. The brand was Madison.

That was all she needed.

Like a trapped animal darting to the only way out, Meg nearly dropped the candle on the way up the stairs. But she settled it back on its holder, lifted her nightgown and robe out of the way, then rushed to the office with her feet moving faster than her heartbeat.

She shut the door—it closed as quietly as it had opened—then extinguished her candle and ran as fast as her quest for silence allowed, nearly full speed through the office, slower through the library, and finally, steadily but quickly up the stairs, all the way back to her room.

It was some time before her breathing returned to normal. She removed her robe, kicked off her slippers, and went to the window, first glancing at the clock still at her bedside.

Three thirty.

How, oh how, was she to calm herself enough to sleep now? She'd done it! She'd gotten what she needed and could tell Ian everything. Would he be amazed at her accomplishment? Proud of her? Surely she'd proven herself her father's daughter.

She held back her laughter with both hands over her mouth. Oh! How glorious it felt to meet a challenge and conquer it. She knew Ian hadn't really believed she could go through with it. Nor had Kate. But Meg had!

With a renewed burst of energy, Meg twirled toward the bed, kicking aside her slippers on the way.

That was when she spotted it. The soil on the bottom of one of her pink quilted house shoes.

Her heart plummeted from its heights to the depths of her

stomach. She snatched up the slipper and felt the spot, tossing it aside to examine the other. Worse!

Why had she rushed up here so quickly? Why hadn't she thought to remove her slippers? She'd seen the damp in that secret cellar. Spots on her slippers no doubt left footprints—leading exactly to her doorstep!

Plucking her robe from where she'd so joyously tossed it aside only a moment ago, she put it back on. She stopped only long enough to retrieve two handkerchiefs and once again her candle. First she bent low to inspect her own floor. No sign of footprints here.

Nor in the hall.

She was thankful she'd kept to the edge of the stairway, where the carpet did not reach. Just in case there was a trace or smudge from her slipper where she could not see, she wiped each stair all the way down. Then, retracing the path she'd taken through the library, she felt with her bare feet for dampness in the foyer and on through the library carpet. In the office, it was difficult to identify any moisture because the tile was so cool.

But sure enough, there were several wet spots on the floor nearest the hidden door. She wiped them clean, going so far as to retrace her path between the secret corner and the library door.

The sound of the ding-dong striking the three-quarter hour nearly made her vomit. How much time did she have before the scullery maid rose? Less than fifteen minutes!

Meg knew she had no choice but to go back inside the secret stairway. Although those stairs had likely been marred before she'd stepped on them, it would be odd indeed to see the pattern of a quilted slipper on either the stairs or the cellar floor.

She must erase all evidence, and do it quickly.

28

I only took what I needed. You know, to make me pretty?
JANE "JOLLY" HIGBIE
    Incarcerated for shoplifting
    Code of Thieves

MEG DID NOT MAKE it in time for the morning meeting, since she did not fall asleep again until after the sun rose. Somehow she would survive the day after her exhausting triumph. Tonight when Ian arrived, she would supply him with everything he needed. She could hardly wait to see the look of appreciation in his eyes—perhaps even a touch of awe—the moment she was able to speak to him alone.

Details for the evening had been thoroughly planned and ultimately agreed upon, from the kickshaws of salmon with green peas in one dish to shrimp, asparagus, and oysters on the half shell in others. All of that would be accompanied by soup, then lobster *farci* and fillet of beef in mushroom sauce. Finally they would partake of the sugared fruit Evie had wanted, along with frozen pudding and the *eau sucrée* to be served one hour after *café noir*.

Meg joined Nelson and Claire in the parlor at seven thirty, approximately half an hour before dinner was to be served, fifteen minutes before their guests should arrive. Meg wore a gown she hadn't yet displayed, of pale-blue silk edged in white lace. The scooped bodice was trimmed in tightly gathered white sheer, a tiny silk rose set in its center.

Claire, in the customary gift of humility from a hostess to her guests, wore a modest dark gown of forest green; her cuirass bodice with square-cut décolletage was filled with frilled lace that was matched at the end of elbow-length sleeves.

"Is Evie not down yet?" Meg asked, looking round the parlor. "I'd have guessed she would be ready first."

Claire glanced toward the hall behind Meg. "I expect she'll arrive just when the bell rings, so if we have any objections to her dress, it'll be too late."

Nelson, presenting himself as the usual man of status in a black square-cut evening suit with a single-breasted white waistcoat and small white cambric bow tie, frowned. "You didn't supervise her for this evening?"

"She refused to let me into her room and short of having someone break down her door, I saw no alternative but to let her make a fool of herself if that's what she chooses to do." At her brother's continued disapproval, Claire went on. "I admit I haven't seen the dress, but I gave strict orders to the seamstress overriding any inappropriate ideas Evie might have suggested. I can't imagine it'll be too outrageous."

Nelson walked toward the hallway. "I intend to make sure she won't embarrass us, or she'll not be joining this little soiree."

"No, I'll go," Claire said, although her reluctance was clear and she made no move to leave. "She's my responsibility."

Meg stepped forward. "I'll see to Evie. The guests may be here any moment, and you'll both need to greet them first."

Nelson agreed with a word of gratitude, and Meg retraced her steps upstairs, only slightly irritated over her task. Although she wanted the evening to go smoothly, she still carried more than a bit of guilt at how easily manipulated Evie had been. She was an eager innocent in tonight's particular game.

She tapped on Evie's door, and a moment later her maid opened it no wider than a few inches. "Is Miss Evie ready?" Meg asked.

The maid nodded, although she did not look Meg in the eye. Nor did she open the door any farther.

"May I see her?"

"I'll be down shortly." Evie's voice was breathless and nearer than Meg had expected. Probably right on the other side of the door.

"I'm afraid I need to see you."

Evie met Meg's words with a moan. "I must pass muster, is that it? Make sure I don't embarrass the family name?"

"I wouldn't have to do this if you'd been a more exemplary student at Madame Marisse's. May I come in?"

The maid looked relieved to open the door, so relieved that Meg wondered what Evie had done now. Evie was still behind the door, and Meg leaned around to see her.

If her goal had been to look older, she'd succeeded. But in so doing she looked like something between a circus actress and what Madame had once defined as an immodest woman of the night.

"Evie." As Meg issued the name, she knew she sounded just like Claire. But at least her exasperation was mixed with a touch of sympathy. "Do you . . . do you honestly think you're prettier this way? What have you used on your eyes? And that lip color . . . Don't you remember what Lady Kate said about you? That you have natural beauty? You've hidden it completely."

"But don't I look all grown-up? Old enough for Geoffrey to notice me?"

"Oh, he'll notice, but not in the way you hope." Meg turned to the chest of drawers that sat next to a full-length mirror. On the chest was all the evidence of the maid's ministrations: powder, rouge, black candle wax, and a needle that had obviously been used to apply the wax to Evie's lashes. "Where do you keep your handkerchiefs?"

The maid quickly obliged, opening a small drawer at the top of the dresser. There was water in the nearby washbowl, and Meg went to it immediately. They didn't have much time.

"No, Meg . . . ," Evie said when Meg approached her, but the plea was halfhearted. With a final glance in the mirror, Evie must have seen what Meg did: administrations to her face that weren't an improvement.

"If you'd been able to stay at Madame Marisse's," Meg said as she scrubbed Evie's face, "you would have learned the art of beautifying, better known as cosmetics. It's meant to draw attention to your natural features. To reveal health and genuine beauty. Genuine beauty that is, of course, more than what any of us were born with."

She had trouble removing the stain from Evie's lips and had to send the maid to the kitchen for hot water, along with a touch of Vaseline, to remove as much of the wax as she could, but she succeeded for the most part in uncovering Evie's face. She only hoped the redness would ease by the time they walked downstairs, even if they had to be a few minutes late. Such was an inexcusable offense according to Madame Marisse, who taught that being late for a dinner party gave the chance for hungry people to gossip about the one keeping them waiting. It was, she had said, better to send a note of apology and not attend at all than to be grievously tardy.

Thankfully, Evie's dress was acceptable. It was a trifle long to be worn by a child but did not reach the floor. Rather it topped her white shoes to reveal matching stockings that showed off what would no doubt remain slim ankles. The gown itself was pale yellow with short, puffed sleeves adorned with white ribbons. While the style was made for youth, it also offered a ruche at the back that resembled a bustle closely enough to show the inspiration of a gown fit for a young lady rather than a girl of fourteen.

There was little time to do much about Evie's hair, styled in an obvious attempt to duplicate the way Claire wore hers. It was still parted in the middle as Evie always wore it but swept up at the back amid curls and a single diamond comb.

"Perhaps we might let down only part of your hair," Meg suggested gently. "So Claire will know you've made an effort to look your age."

"I can do that easily, miss!" the maid volunteered. "It's what I had in mind when I suggested the style. I'll have it down in no time, and she'll look as pretty as ever."

"But . . ."

"Evie, we haven't much time," Meg reminded her. "It's better to comply than to be sent back up here by your brother, isn't it? And miss the party altogether?"

"Oh, all right."

By the time the maid had adjusted Evie's hair, the girl's face was no longer red from the washing. Still, she cast a glow that was more from the petroleum jelly than nature.

Meg picked up the powder puff. "A trace will be all right," she said, meeting immediate approval from Evie.

Finished, Meg hurried to the door—only to stop when Evie went instead to the mirror. Eyeing herself, she tilted her head to one side. Then she nodded and followed Meg from the room.

When they walked down the stairs, a mix of new voices could already be heard from the parlor.

Ian listened to Kate while she chatted with the others, silently amazed at the consistency of her false accent. She was easily the most popular person present. They'd been introduced again to the Masons from next door, recalling their first meeting at the park.

The two women of that family had barely given Kate a chance to speak to anyone else.

The only person apparently not interested in impressing Kate was Geoffrey Mason. He, in fact, glanced more than once Ian's way, and Ian knew why. Competition was easy enough to spot. The man's obvious disdain for Ian had a surprising effect. Instead of feeling proud that the boy thought Meg had chosen Ian, all Ian felt was guilt.

At last he saw the two latecomers from upstairs. Ian's gaze glided easily past the child. Had he felt guilty over wanting to claim Meg as his own, knowing full well the other young man in the room was far more suitable? How foolish to allow anything but delight in Meg instead.

The gown she wore enhanced her beauty: light blue that nearly matched the color of her eyes. He'd seen how the same blue eyes on John had effortlessly captured the interest of women, particularly in contrast to the same dark hair Meg possessed. Now Ian knew firsthand just how powerful those qualities had been.

"How wonderful to see you, Ian," she said softly. Leaning closer, she dared to kiss his cheek as if he were a brother and not some other vague and distant sort of relative. "I'll need to see you privately, in the library," she whispered.

His pulse skipped forward. She must have important information or she wouldn't be so eager to see him alone. Did that mean she'd gotten away with collecting the information he needed?

"Wonderful to see you as well," he replied to her greeting. Then he knew he had to let go of her hand, as other greetings were in order. He'd forgotten the child's name and was glad to be reminded. When Meg extended her welcome to the Mason chap, she was cordial at best, even a bit cool. Something Mason seemed to notice, since he shot a quick, almost-embarrassed glance Ian's way.

Mason's face changed altogether a moment later, however,

when Claire Pemberton whispered something in his ear. Once dinner was announced, Ian figured out what Claire had said as partners were assigned for entrance to the dining room.

There was a time Ian would have welcomed the prospect of getting to know someone with Nomi's wealth. Tonight, however, he had all he could do not to scowl.

The meal passed without mishap. Nomi was easy to amuse, and although during the brief before-dinner interval, he'd guessed she was only interested in someone of Kate's perceived social value, he discovered something else during the quiet conversation they shared. She viewed Meg a worthy target for her grandson's affection.

"My daughter is eager to see Geoffrey married well. They look fine together, don't they?"

Ian studied the pair, caught up in a conversation of their own. "They're young and attractive. I assume each would look fine with anyone equally attractive at their side."

Nomi smiled, but it was the kind that said she knew more than she revealed. "Such as yourself, Mr. Vandermey? Should I be cautioning my grandson about his attention to Miss Davenport?"

"Miss Davenport is entirely free to welcome his attention," Ian said, then added with a smile, "or mine."

She gave a wispy little laugh before reaching with her blue-veined hand for a glass of Sauternes that had been served with the salmon. "Things were easier in my day, when young people relied on their parents to help choose a spouse."

Such a prospect wouldn't have allowed Ian much hope. "I'm sure parents wouldn't have taken the responsibility lightly. But what if they chose the wrong mate, someone who wouldn't be able to make their child happy?"

"Who can tell what is best better than a loving parent?"

Ian took a sip of his wine, determined not to dwell on her words.

Meg could hardly wait for the meal to end. Why had they chosen to serve so many courses? She'd barely had a chance to speak to Ian, except about the food and the weather. And he was farther away than she'd expected, the table was so long. Geoffrey demanded almost all of her attention, and Nomi on the other side of Ian seemed to be doing the same with him. She was about to despair that time would ever move forward when Evie's sugared fruit was finally moved from the center of the table and served.

Soon after, they returned to the parlor for the after-dinner interval. Claire had suggested reading poetry from Elizabeth Browning and Emily Brontë, but Nelson had recommended more general conversation.

Meg took a seat near the window, seeing Ian headed that way. Rather than joining them, Kate took a place in the center of the parlor.

"Ladies and gentlemen," Kate said after everyone had gathered. "Do allow me an indulgence, won't you? I've had the most fascinating discussion with Mr. Pemberton, and I must tell everyone how very impressed I am. Now, Mr. Pemberton, I don't mean to embarrass you, but I simply must tell everyone what you shared with me over dinner. About your new project."

Nelson's fair skin went a bit pink in the cheeks, something Meg hadn't seen in all the weeks she'd lived under the same roof with him. Everyone but Kate and Nelson had taken seats, with Ian in a chair near Meg's. Nelson remained standing at Kate's side as she expounded on his virtues and shared about his efforts to improve the lives of immigrants through work and food kitchens, along with attempting to remove a massive elevated railway that went down Third Avenue in the Bowery—a noxious iron roof that on occasion spewed ash or cinders from the trains that ran above.

Meg glanced at Ian. The Bowery—his territory.

She watched Ian's eyes come to rest on Nelson, his expression somber yet interested. She'd known, of course, that Nelson was involved in myriad good works. She knew, too, his heart for others. If she thought about God more than she allowed herself, she might conclude He'd been wise to entrust a great deal of gold to this family. Something Kate might be trying to prove.

But these were thoughts Meg was training herself to ignore. Surely Ian did the same. He had even more incentive than Meg to carry out this plan; it hadn't been her who'd been left in an alley on a pile of refuse.

Somehow she must find a way to take him to the library—alone—so she could show him where to find the key to the office. Not easily done while Kate demanded and directed everyone's attention.

Ian felt Meg's growing anxiety. Did she sense Kate's capacity to manipulate the evening?

After a short session of general admiration for the virtues of Nelson Pemberton—something Ian was half-tempted to endorse himself—Kate did not give up playing the hostess.

"Now, darlings, I went to a party recently in Boston and they played the most delightful game. It's called Composition. Who wants to play?"

At Kate's bidding, Claire produced enough paper and a mix of decorative metal- and cedar-encased pencils for all who cared to join in. Geoffrey's parents and Nomi opted to be spectators, the same status Ian himself would have claimed. But he knew enough about parlor games to realize there must be a winner. Perhaps he could do a bit of manipulating himself, with the library as his prize.

"First we must choose fifteen specific words all of us are required to include in our little essays. There is no limit to other words, but to earn the first point, each composition must contain every single one of these fifteen words. Points are deducted if we fail to use all fifteen words, but extra points are earned by a single grammatically correct sentence using the most words from our list. Understood?

"Let me see," Kate continued. "Since there are seven players and we must choose fifteen words, each of us should suggest at least one word of our choice, and we must agree on the rest. Words like *sacrifice*." With a glance at Meg, she added, "Or *deception*."

That was enough for Ian's suspicions to resurface. Just what was she up to with this game of hers?

Nelson and Claire added more words Kate would no doubt welcome—*trust*, *love*, and *home*. Ian knew he would have less trouble winning if the words were more mundane, and so he suggested *train* . . . and *library*, to mirror Kate's maneuver. He needed to stir interest in that room if he was to demand his reward when he won.

Once the remaining words were agreed upon—making one exception for Evie's choice of *sugared fruit* to be considered a single word—Ian set about the task of winning without delay. He was less concerned about beauty of content than about receiving the highest score, and so when he finished first, he held up his sheet.

"Did you offer an extra point for fastest completion?" He was glad to receive amused laughter from Nomi and the Mason couple.

Kate, who'd been busy at a nearby side table, shook her head. "Rules have been stated, dear. No extra point for that, though I should have stipulated extra points for loveliness of prose. Something that takes more time."

He cocked his head and grinned at her. "But alas, you said it yourself: rules have already been stated."

"I for one am relieved about that," Nelson said. "This isn't much like writing a legal document."

When all the participants had finished, Evie was the first to volunteer to read her composition.

The girl stood, apparently without a trace of shyness or awkwardness many children her age might display in adult company. Certainly Ian would have been unsure of himself, as a boy. At her age he'd still possessed a lingering Irish brogue and been spindly of body and brash of mind. It wouldn't have taken anyone two minutes to show him to the door—not even the Pembertons' kindness would welcome the kind of youth he'd been. And the Masons? They'd never have let him in.

Evie stood in the center of the room and read, "'At a *luncheon* in the *garden* the other day, I noticed many *birds*. The *glasses* on the table were not safe from above, nor was my *hat*. When I left for the Bowery, I heard the noise of the *train* and wished to be back *home*, where I am the only *person* who will always *love* to eat *sugared fruit* in the *library*. I'm very glad to *trust* that *God* made a *sacrifice* of His Son because of my bent toward *deception*.'"

Evie clearly enjoyed her reading, perhaps more than anyone else in the room, and when the others clapped and congratulated her on successfully using each of the prescribed fifteen words, she curtsied as if she'd just pleased an audience in any of the Bowery theaters.

"I have seven points; is that correct, Lady Kate?" Evie asked as she handed her page to be counted. "I used six of the fifteen words in one sentence and one more point for using all the words. No deductions."

Luckily for Evie, Kate did not consider content flow, since her essay jumped from one topic to another with nearly every sentence.

The young Mason stood next, and Ian settled back in his chair.

The man did not take the spot Evie had vacated; rather he stood before Meg as if he'd designated her the only one worthy to be in the audience.

"'I fell in *love* with a *person* I met in the *garden* belonging to the *home* next door. Songs of *birds* around us were as sweet to the ear as *sugared fruit* is to the tongue. I removed my *hat*, then asked the lady to *trust* my absence of *deception* and willingness to make great *sacrifice* for her. I hoped we might share a *luncheon* or at least two *glasses* of lemonade, but she was otherwise engaged reading a book from the *library*, and so I implored *God* to *train* her heart to accept mine.'"

The Mason family clapped and sighed, and even Kate, Ian noticed, complimented the man's prose. Ian only smirked. No extra points for that.

Meg followed, and Ian was relieved to hear she did not return any of the sentiment young Geoffrey had been so eager to reveal to one and all. Rather hers contained some of what Ian expected, a reference to the *library* as her favorite room and a statement that stories of *sacrifice*—and *deception*—were as sweet to her as *sugared fruit*.

After Meg finished, Nelson invited his sister to go next. Claire read quietly that only the *love* of *God* was without *deception*, something Ian found curious. Did that mean she viewed human love as deceptive? But he had little time to contemplate the question, because Nelson began his reading.

His prose contained no hint of the legal tones he'd admitted to struggling with. Ian listened politely, all the while wishing he could find something to detest in the man. Reminding himself Nelson had played a part in having the bank bonds declared worthless did little to expel a growing respect for him. There was something about him, something Ian could describe only as "soulish," that Ian wished he could better understand.

Nelson's composition extolled *God* for His *love* and *sacrifice*, claiming His Book to be the most precious in the *library*. After a description of heaven, Nelson ended his prose with a promise to wait patiently because even on earth the *glasses* on his table overflowed with blessing.

Ian volunteered to go next, hoping to forestall Kate altogether. If each composition was to reveal something about its author, might she take a chance and reveal something he had no desire to let be known? He prepared to read his essay without flourish but with confidence, knowing he'd followed the rules and so far had accumulated the highest number of points.

"'I've heard it said that *deception* does not come from *God*, that we should *trust* in His *love* and *sacrifice*. But a *person* without a *home* must live with the *birds*; he hasn't even a *hat* and possesses nothing more than dreams of a *luncheon* with *sugared fruit* or a *train* ride to a *garden* where he will read many books from the *library* while enjoying several *glasses* of wine.'" He looked up, letting his gaze challenge Kate's. "I believe that's eleven points, Lady Kate. The winning total."

"But we haven't heard from Lady Kate!" Nelson reminded him. He approached Kate, gently taking her paper and holding it up. "We're all good for the forfeit if you're the winner, Mr. Vandermey. But I for one would like to hear what Lady Kate composed, whether or not it earned a winning score."

"Thank you ever so much, Mr. Pemberton," Kate said. She smiled Ian's way, one brow slightly raised as she scrutinized his sheet to verify the points. "And I'm not entirely certain you deserve all those points, with such a cumbersome sentence and your use of a semicolon."

"Prohibition of a semicolon was not previously stipulated," he countered, "therefore permissible."

"Then I shall read mine anyway. If you don't mind, my dear?" Ian stepped aside, returning to his chair. He waited, more fearful than ever that Kate was about to do something he would regret. It was one thing to have Meg ousted from the Pemberton home before she encountered any real trouble, quite another to have all of them found out for the frauds they were.

"'*Deception*,'" Kate read in her perfectly faked British accent, "'like *sugared fruit*, is something a *person* can *train* himself to *love*, proving *God* alone is worthy of our *trust*. Each day at breakfast, *luncheon*, and supper, I lift up a *sacrifice* of prayer that flies faster than *birds* up to heaven. I cannot keep the truth under my *hat* much longer because even without eye *glasses*, I see more clearly than others. I know this: a *home* belongs to those who live in it, whether or not it has a *library* or a *garden*.'"

Amid everyone's praise, Ian stepped forward again to examine her paper. He must not allow anyone time to dwell on her words of secret warning. "Like some of the other compositions, it's fortunate for you that no points were deducted over lack of subject continuity. Or for the questionable use of the word *glasses*. Wouldn't *eyeglasses* be one word? I won't even count your use of a colon, as you did with my semicolon."

"Yes, we have a few things in common, don't you agree? Using words to win something?"

He wouldn't allow such banter any more time. "True enough, although I remain the winner."

"And what sort of forfeit would you like us to pay?" Nelson asked congenially. "For us to identify an item of your choosing, blindfolded? Or perhaps sing the entire score of 'The Star-Spangled Banner'?"

"Oh!" Evie chimed. "What about making everyone imitate a pig or a cat?"

As tempted as he was to see young Mason on all fours and grunting like a sow, Ian reined in such a dishonorable thought. He had something else in mind.

"My demand requires only a spare number of forfeits. A moment of my cousin's time, and permission from you, Mr. Pemberton, for her to take me on a tour of the famous Pemberton library Meg boasts about."

"Why don't we all go, then?" Evie asked. "The library is just across the hall. It's not much of a prize if you ask me."

If Ian didn't know better, he would've thought he saw a twinkle in Nelson's eyes as he refused his sister's suggestion. Obviously he knew Ian's request to see Meg alone was something of a social risk, but Ian could tell already he would get what he wanted.

"Meg can show you a number of rare and original volumes," Nelson said. "Take your leisure in enjoying the collection." He glanced at the clock ticking on the nearby mantel. "Five minutes?"

Ian didn't contain his own smile. Five minutes was enough. He offered Meg his arm. The fact that Nelson had made this so easy should have made Ian proud of himself. Ian could say this job—one that would not only provide him more gold than he'd ever beheld but also freedom from Brewster—had thus far proven the easiest in terms of groundwork. Thanks to Meg.

He dared closing the library doors once they were inside. Meg's nervous laughter drew him to her side.

"You're so clever!" she told him. "I couldn't imagine how I was to bring you to this spot without calling attention to such a wish."

She held out her hands to him, which he immediately moved to accept; then she willingly complied when he pulled her close.

"I have so much to tell you, Ian."

"Have you?" Only two words, but issued with the leisure of someone enjoying the moment he was in. And he was. He couldn't help adding a smile that broadened every bit as slowly.

With his arms securely around her, he was in no hurry to hear her news. She had only to catch his gaze to return it with the same kind, one that said she didn't want to look anywhere but at him, think of anyone but him. She nodded in response to his unnecessary question, though it was clear neither one of them cared about words just then. Then she let him kiss her, even as he wondered if she knew the kiss wasn't merely a prize required for the social gamble he'd won.

Her lips beneath his were soft, inviting. Willing.

But five minutes . . .

Ian pulled himself away. "What have you to tell me?"

"Oh! Ian, wait until you hear!"

Meg broke free of his arms to lead him to one of the bookshelves, one nearest an inner door he noticed for the first time. Reaching up, she placed her hand beneath the heel of a brass bookend and pulled out a key. "This opens the door to Mr. Pemberton's office, right here, where I'm sure they're hiding their gold. I saw the safe myself."

Ian couldn't help but gape at her. The last thing Meg's father would have wanted to believe was that she'd inherited all the talent necessary to follow in his footsteps: cleverness, bravery, and a way to ignore self-reproach that was necessary to carry out a plan against the Pembertons. But the smile on her face convinced him.

God help him, Meg made doing the right thing a near impossibility.

He smiled despite himself. "That's my girl."

Then he kissed her again.

29

There comes a time in every young lady's life when right and wrong are not easily defined. It goes without saying that a lady's behavior must be exemplary in all things. But when confronted with two choices, both of equal merit, how does she choose? The answer to this starts of course with prayer, but she may also consult those around her, those older, wiser mentors God has placed in her life.

Madame Marisse's Letters to Young Wives, NO. 7

MEG'S HEAD—AND HEART—spun. She wished they had more time. She wanted nothing more than to kiss Ian again, and again after that. There was no denying it now—she wanted far more than a simple business partnership with him, and she hoped his kisses meant he felt the same way.

There was, however, more important business to attend to. Meg could see on Ian's face that she had his full attention. "The office is fairly square. Just inside of this door, to the left, a large painting hangs. Go to the far edge of the painting, reach about this high—" she raised her hand even with his shoulder—"and slip your fingers behind the frame. There is a small lever in the wall, which must connect down the wall and under the floor, just as you suggested. The door is in the opposite corner, the one toward the front of the house. When you shift the lever, a door in the corner will pop open. It leads to a stairway, and at the base is a safe. It's a Madison, Ian. Almost as tall as I am, with a combination wheel and a horizontal handle."

"Meg," he whispered, drawing her close once again, "you've done it. Guaranteed success."

She smiled, pleased with his praise. How she wanted to extend those five minutes that were too quickly passing.

"There is just one more thing we need to do," Ian said, calling her attention from his mouth to his eyes. "Set up a date when the house will be as empty as possible. Do you know of any plans for the family to be away—overnight, even? Perhaps when the staff will be minimal?"

Her breath caught with renewed enthusiasm. "Oh, Ian! Not all that long ago, Nelson mentioned something about a Blue Moon Picnic in the park. I can easily encourage them to proceed with it."

"I'm not familiar with Blue Moon Picnics. Are they something new connected to high society?"

"It's something Nelson concocted with Claire, a sort of picnic that should never happen on Fifth Avenue. But it's exactly what we need. A party given by the Pembertons for the household staff *and* the family to enjoy. Together."

"Hmmm . . . an evening picnic, under the moon?"

"It hasn't exactly been scheduled," she admitted. "But all I need do is remind them of their idea and foster it." She offered all the surety and willingness anyone could ask from a partner, and the look on his face told her he'd noticed.

"It sounds like the perfect opportunity. Do you think they'll go through with it?"

"I'll do my best to see that they do." She believed her own words and added with confidence, "I'll see that you receive an invitation as my special guest. Practically one of the family."

"And you'll succeed, just as you have already. Now, about your garden. I'd like for you to plan some kind of wall, something made of bricks. Can you do that? I'll give you the name of the brick supplier to use, but when the bricks arrive, you'll discover they're not to your liking after all. A messenger will arrive at the specified time to pick them up. *After* I've visited the safe, of course. I'll have hidden the gold bricks among those garden bricks, and no one will notice when they're taken away."

"Do you mean you won't take the gold immediately with you? You'll just take it up to the garden—and wait for someone from the brickyard to carry it away?"

"Not just someone. Pubjug! Even if I were to come here during the middle of the night, someone might see me toting heavy bricks to and from the house. It's important to go in and out without attracting attention. Besides, I'll replace the Pemberton bricks with ones that look just like the real ones we'll take."

"Replace—but why?"

"To give you enough time to get safely away," he said. "They likely won't know the safe has been compromised until they have need of checking it. With that kind of safe I can cover my tracks, at least a bit. Even if they do discover the tampering, if they think nothing has been stolen, they won't have anything to charge you with if somehow you come under suspicion. Everything will appear to be intact."

"But where will you get something that looks like gold bricks?"

"Lead bricks plated with inferior gold—but gold nonetheless, at least in a thin layer. It's an old swindle. The best provided a true golden nugget that customers could take to any assayer of their choice to have verified, just to be certain the gold was authentic. They returned later to buy the entire brick—which, of course, was phony. It's a scheme as old as gold itself."

Even as he spoke, Meg already had an idea. "I can draw up a sketch for a settee in the garden—a fine brick settee. It'll be easy." Her voice was nearly breathless from seeing their plan so close to fruition. She grabbed both of Ian's hands, crushing any doubts, leaving only anticipation. At last, she truly would be Ian's partner! "We're going to do this, aren't we?"

He kissed one of her hands. "You are the only one who can stop it, Meg. Say so, and I'll end it right now."

"I won't stop it."

Still holding her hands, he kissed them again before letting her go.

"If we succeed—and really, with all of this information, it's impossible to fail—then Brewster will mean nothing anymore. Our success is the surest way to be free of him. But," he added and kept her gaze in his, "you'll be held as responsible as the rest of us if we get caught. That means going to jail. Are you sure you want to risk that?"

Jail seemed as unlikely a possibility as stopping this whole plan now. She'd come too far to turn back. "I'll risk it. My father would have."

Ian knew the gold scheme he described to Meg had worked in the past because he'd done it himself. He'd hoarded every bit of the cash he'd earned back in those days, protecting it like it was some kind of lover. He'd counted it; he'd admired it. Eventually he'd purchased an entire house with it.

Meg's groundwork promised even greater success. Gold the likes of which he'd never seen before, provided the Pembertons were foolish enough to keep the bulk of it in one location.

Soon it would be his.

Gold. The purest that could be found.

Like the streets of heaven . . .

He shut away that last thought; it had come unbidden. God had no part in his life, and that wasn't about to change now.

30

The tone of the household is reflected from mistress to staff.
A tyrant at the top will only create tyrants in the staff. Do not be
fooled into thinking servants cannot ultimately manipulate from
the kitchen. It is best all around for you to be kind and generous
with your staff, if you wish to have a happy household.
Madame Marisse's Letters to Young Wives, NO. 3

THE FIRST DINNER PARTY without their parents had proved so
enjoyable to the Pemberton siblings that when Meg mentioned the
Blue Moon Picnic, Claire's enthusiasm bubbled up all on its own.

Between Claire's eagerness and Nelson's willingness, compounded by Evie's hopefulness to be part of the planning, the
event seemed bound to happen.

Plans for the Blue Moon Picnic took up nearly all of Claire's
time, and Nelson's, too, when he was at home. Meg was relieved
Claire had found something for Evie to be involved in as well; she'd
worried, at least for a while, that Geoffrey's display of affection for
her at the dinner party would result in repercussions. Evidently
the prize of five minutes alone with Ian had shown both Evie and
Geoffrey where Meg's attention rested. When Evie wasn't searching
for recipes with Claire or practicing her dancing skills under Mrs.
Longford's direction, she kept to herself.

All of which left Meg free to be busy in the garden, overseeing the removal of several plants and the addition of many more. She reserved a spot for the addition of a brick seat, a bench that would extend from the privacy wall at the garden's edge. It seemed such a natural part of the plan that she wondered why she hadn't thought of it before.

Meg was just measuring where it would be erected when a maid announced the arrival of Lady Weathersfield.

Meg turned, so startled she nearly dropped the spring-loaded measuring tape Mr. Deekes so prized. Clutching it to her, she forced a smile but refused the offer of tea from the maid, waiting for her to close the leaded door behind her and leave Meg alone with Kate.

Kate stood before Meg for what felt an interminable moment before closing the gap between them and taking Meg's free hand into both of her own.

"You're not really going to do this awful thing against the Pembertons? It's the last thing God would have you do."

Meg pulled her hand away, setting the measuring spool on the nearby table. "Ian and I are partners now, Kate. The same way you were with my father." She turned, noting as she did that a bee had joined them and was even now alighting on a thistle in a search for nectar.

"But you can't want to take from them, when they've been nothing except kind to you."

Meg refused to consider Kate's words. "I am what I am: my father's daughter. I can't help but do what comes naturally in taking care of myself."

Kate laughed. "Everyone struggles against selfishness. That isn't what you inherited from him; you have that just by being human. Why does your connection to your father have to include breaking the law? Why can't it be the fulfillment of what he wanted for you—a better life than he had?"

Meg's gaze went once again to the bee to keep track of its presence. It was a shame the same flowers attracted them as drew the butterflies.

"I think you'd better go . . . *Lady* Kate." She turned only partially, giving Kate nothing more than her profile. "And please . . . don't visit here again."

Meg heard no movement for such a long time that she feared Kate wouldn't go. But then, slowly, came the soft swish of the gown Kate wore. She moved to the door, which opened and closed. Then there was silence.

Broken only by the bee buzzing over a blossom.

Kate's visit haunted Meg each and every morning that followed. Because she wanted to keep abreast of at least some of the plans for the picnic, she decided not only to attend the morning prayer gatherings that Nelson conducted, but to arrive early enough to listen in on any specific exchanges of information between the Pembertons and their staff. Although the picnic fare would be a gift of the Pembertons to their household—prepared by the kitchen at a nearby hotel—Meg did not want to miss any unexpected details that might arise.

Which meant suffering through prayer time. And suffer Meg did, through each kind word, each moment she witnessed of sweet surrender to a loving God, each whisper of concern they spread out before a God fully immersed in their lives. Every prayer pierced Meg's soul, but she withstood the attack.

It was not difficult to remind herself why she must carry out her plans. This had turned into something far more than proving to everyone in her father's world that she could have been valuable to him. This single event would tie Ian to her. They would be partners forever after this. Something she was only beginning to understand.

When Meg inquired if an invitation to the picnic for Ian might be permissible, she received immediate affirmation. Claire also suggested extending one to Lady Kate, but Meg told her she was unsure if her friend was still in the city. She hoped the discouragement was enough to forestall an invitation, but if it wasn't, Meg planned to do what she could to prevent the invitation from being extended at all.

Nor were the Masons invited, though that had been a universal decision. Since this was not the kind of party Fifth Avenue was likely to condone, and even though Geoffrey might have defied his parents to attend, Evie was persuaded they shouldn't put him in the position to choose.

Meanwhile, the bricks for the garden were delivered two days before the picnic. They stood stacked and bundled neatly together with sturdy rope, brought in on a dolly through the servants' entry via the kitchen. Meg spent a good deal of her afternoon hours in the garden, pretending to consider how best to use the bricks without daring to even loosen one of the ropes that bound them.

In fact she watched over them, knowing in the center of the stack were fraudulent golden bricks that would soon be used to replace the famous Pemberton bricks hiding under the house. She'd been tempted to sneak a peek at the fake gold but forbade not only herself but Mr. Deekes from freeing them of their ropes under the false claim that she wasn't yet sure she liked the shade. She would want them to remain undamaged and ready should she choose to send them back.

The day of the picnic quickly approached. While working-class folk throughout the city would return home on Saturday exhausted from another six-day workweek, the entire Pemberton household would set out to enjoy dinner *together* in the park.

All they needed now was fair weather. A storm would change the venue from the park to the Pemberton house itself and, in so doing, end the plans Ian and Meg had for the Pemberton gold, at least for the time being. Although Meg did not pray for clear skies—she wasn't foolish enough to depend on God's help for such a thing—she let herself hope for it with every unused thought during the long wait until Saturday.

Ian sat on the veranda of his home on the Hudson, overlooking the river with Roscoe at his side. Instead of growing in confidence that he and Meg were doing the right thing, or at least the best thing to be free of Brewster, he was no less plagued by doubts and fears than he'd been since the moment Meg had shown up at his door. The consternation had made him flee the city entirely, at least temporarily. Out here on the Hudson he'd hoped to find peace.

Peace wasn't to be found, though—not the peace he used to have. He'd once settled for a lack of imminent danger and satisfaction of knowing he had plenty of money. Now he wasn't sure what peace really was, only that he didn't have it.

Particularly when he knew he'd been followed from the city. He had half a mind to go to the hotel in town, the one that overlooked the train station where Brewster's thug would spot his departure. Perhaps he should just invite the man to the house. Ian might persuade him to switch loyalties.

But soon enough Ian's plans would begin; he needed only to get some information across to Brewster—something he knew would be easy between himself and Pubjug. Before escaping the city, he'd laid needed groundwork. He'd first arranged employment for Pubjug in the brickyard, explaining to a trusting Pubjug that his investment in the fake golden bricks hidden among the Pemberton delivery would be worth every penny. Real gold covered that lead, and each one had cost a bit of money to produce. Far less, of course, than the real thing, but an investment nonetheless.

Ian had also visited the Madison safe manufactory in New Jersey to assure himself he had the correct safe in mind from Meg's description. A trip that turned out to be most beneficial, since a new model had indeed been designed. Luckily he hadn't needed to purchase one to be familiar with its idiosyncrasies, to decide the drill requirements or putty color; it was similar enough to another model Ian knew so well.

He'd done everything without Kate's knowledge. She was, in fact, part of the reason he'd bolted from the city. Her frequent visits and references to the commandment about not stealing weren't very effective, but when she gave up harping and simply reminded him that a loving God wanted Ian to do the right thing—especially in regard to his innocent partner—he'd once again had to fight the feeling of being hunted.

Ian turned away from the river, catching as he did the view of John's gravesite. "I have no choice but to take advantage of the opportunity," he said quietly. But even as he spoke, he told himself John couldn't hear him anyway.

When Saturday dawned fair, Meg let her eagerness for the final part of the plan rise—until another thought struck her as she ate breakfast with Claire and Nelson.

This was likely one of the last times she would share their table. Enjoying peaches, fresh strawberries, and dropped eggs on toast, she couldn't help letting her gaze fall first on Nelson, then on Claire with more than a touch of sadness. She could no more deny affection for them than she could deny that she wanted everything to be over. An end to this game that she needed to win if she was to prove herself capable of being her father's daughter. Of helping Ian.

Thoughts of both her father and Ian were all she had to keep her life going on this course.

Tonight, if all went well, Ian would arrive just a bit late to the party in the park. She would assure everyone he would be there shortly, that something unforeseen must have detained him.

Knowing the front door to the Pemberton mansion was unlocked—Meg would see to that—he would let himself into the empty house. He would take whatever gold he could manage and swap it for the fakes waiting in the center of the stack of clay bricks that had already been delivered. Bricks that later this very day she would deem unworthy of the project she had in mind, arranging for their return just as soon as possible.

Pubjug would arrive before dawn to take those bricks away, gold and all. Before breakfast tomorrow, before anyone was awake, before anyone would have a chance to notice the safe had been tampered with, the Pemberton bricks would be gone. Replaced with the phony ones that waited in the garden.

At any time after tonight, Meg would be free to leave the Pemberton home.

"Is everything all set for tonight?"

Nelson's question made Meg's heart skip a beat. She clamped her lips shut.

"Yes, it'll be such fun," Claire said serenely. She glanced toward the window. "It's a lovely day and promises to be a lovely evening, too."

"Have Evie's spy servants mentioned anything from the neighbors?" Meg asked. Better to participate in the conversation than entertain more thoughts and worries. "About the nature of the party, that is?"

Claire sipped her tea. "Yes, actually. The Masons have decided to take a short trip out to Saratoga, for fear of any uncharitable glances they might have to endure from their own staff tonight."

Meg's heart soared with relief at the news. The Masons had been her only worry. If Ian were spotted replacing the phony bricks with the real ones—and only from the Mason house would that view be possible—the entire plan might have been unveiled. It was part of the reason they'd needed to wait for cover of darkness.

Now, it appeared, they had nothing whatsoever to worry about.

If Meg didn't know better, she'd have thought the entire plan had been supernaturally ordained.

But however much she wanted to believe that, instant conviction made her think otherwise. No, God certainly had no part in this plan.

She ignored the heaviness of such a thought pulling on her heart.

Late Saturday morning, Ian went into town to await the train back to the city. Pretending to read the newspaper he'd purchased from the boy on the platform, he studied the others who waited with him. It didn't take long for Brewster's man to arrive. Ian couldn't remember his name, but the man made no attempt to hide the fact that he'd been assigned to follow Ian. He nodded Ian's way with a cocksure smile.

Ian stood, leaving behind the paper. If tonight's plan was to be the kind of success he hoped for, the action started right now.

"I don't think we can wait any longer," Claire said gently to Meg. "We told the servants to go ahead nearly half an hour ago. Your cousin will likely come directly to the park. Perhaps he's already there."

Meg nodded. Ian's tardiness was all part of the plan.

Another benefit to Ian's delay was that Meg would easily be the last to leave the house, making sure the latch that normally locked the door was not flipped. Following Claire from the house to the carriage where Nelson and Evie already waited, Meg only pretended to secure the door.

Then off they went, to the first annual Pemberton household Blue Moon Picnic.

One that very well might be the last.

31

The revision of criminal laws in recent decades has prompted this essay to firmly state that we have gone far enough in our sympathy for villains. While I do not suggest we return to such punishments as burning at the stake, I implore the legislators to keep in mind that hangings are justified in most cases of murder and theft.

"REASONS FOR INCARCERATION"

IAN WATCHED THE Pemberton carriage roll down Fifth Avenue. He'd seen Meg, as the last to leave, join the Pembertons in their carriage. From where he stood on the other side of the street, behind a lamppost surrounded by tall foliage, he was far enough away that he couldn't see her features, but he would know Meg anywhere.

Ian kept his head down, knowing in the absence of complete darkness his hat would shadow most of his face. His dark suit and black scarf covered the only white he wore, the shirt and cravat. Careful movement helped him blend into the surroundings. He didn't have to look up to find his way to the Pemberton door. As expected, it was unlocked.

Good girl.

He let himself in, locking the door behind him once he was inside. No sense leaving evidence that he'd been so easily allowed in.

Only the slightest of house creaks greeted him. Quickly, he

walked through the foyer and rounded the hall to the back of the house. It didn't take long to locate the kitchen and, through that, the servants' entrance, which he opened to find Pubjug already waiting. From under his jacket, Pubjug withdrew the drill and two different points, only the round drill crank rattling in the otherwise-silent exchange.

Ian found his way to the library, while Pubjug followed.

The key to the office was placed exactly where Meg had shown him. She was, indeed, the perfect partner. He opened the door, then replaced the key, careful to leave it just as he'd found it.

Then he stepped into the office. It, too, was exactly as Meg had described. Square; a desk slightly to the right, beneath high windows that offered light from the setting sun. He eyed the farthest corner, where he guessed the secret stairway to be housed.

Stepping forward, he looked for the first time at the artwork that, as expected, covered nearly the entire wall to the left. Light shone through the windows like beacons on its subject.

Pubjug must not have expected Ian to stop short, because the older man bumped into him. But Ian didn't care. He was seized by the painting: Jesus, the Lamb of God.

Ian's knees nearly failed him.

Why hadn't Meg warned him?

But of course, why should she? Had the image no impact on her, that she thought its subject so inconsequential?

From its inception, Ian had wondered if he could go through with this plan. Even as he stood on the street just now, doubts had muddled his intentions. Of every job in Ian's life, this one would likely offer both the largest haul and the best opportunity to pay back Brewster—not just for the beating Ian had taken, but for his belief that he deserved Ian's allegiance just because John had died.

Yet this same job could result in Meg's endangerment.

As he stared at the painting, taking more time than he knew he ought, all those memories of his father, all the times John's presence had haunted him, all the impressions that God Himself was closer than he'd ever imagined, became clearer and stronger than ever.

He swallowed hard. That gold was guarded by more than just a safe.

The thought crossed his mind to pray—nearly an urge—but Ian feared it might be too late for that. Or maybe it was too soon, with just the faintest remnant of a faith he'd abandoned so long ago trying to work its way back into his heart.

He shrugged away the thought and found the concealed lever, pulled it. Pubjug reached the secret opening before Ian did and held the door wide to let Ian through first.

Without a word, Ian went down the narrow, sturdy stairwell. Pubjug carried a lantern, which he lit only after the door was shut behind them.

There it was, just as Meg promised. Under the light Pubjug supplied, Ian set about his work without delay. He cranked the drill, boring a hole as small as possible. Three would do it, before he was able to pull aside a steel triangle just large enough to insert his mirror. Then, leaning aside to allow the maximum light from Pubjug's lantern, he gently twisted the combination wheel until the reflected image revealed which numbers tumbled into place. The lock was open in less than a minute.

Ian turned the handle and pulled open the door to reveal the safe's contents.

He had trained himself to work in silence, but neither he nor Pubjug could withhold a gasp. All that gold in one spot was something to see.

All that gold . . .

So the rumors were true. Each brick was stamped on the top and short edges with the famous Pemberton seal, a *P* with a flourish.

Each brick four hundred troy ounces. The purest gold this country had to offer. At twenty-one dollars an ounce . . . How many were there? More than a dozen, at least.

He knew Pubjug must be wondering what was taking so long. The plan was for them to carry the bricks up to the garden, to exchange the phony ones for these. Of course they'd have to take the seal first, use the additional melted gold Pubjug even now had simmering in the covered bed of the brickyard's wagon. They would stamp the phony gold bricks with the Pemberton seal, and no one would be the wiser about which was which—at least at first glance.

They had enough counterfeit bricks to take some with them, all dressed up in that fancy *P*. The real bricks would be stored in a compartment below the wagon bed, while extra fakes would be waiting above for Brewster to do what he did best: steal them, now that he'd been fed information Ian had spread.

But an image of Meg stopped Ian short. Exchanging with Pubjug the drill for the lantern, Ian held the light close. He couldn't help admiring the gold that glimmered so warmly, so invitingly. Would it be cool to the touch or warm? He feared any contact as much as he desired it, wondering if even the briefest contact would make him cave in to temptation.

Ian forced his gaze past the gold. There was also a considerable sum of cash, yet another temptation. Banknotes as well as greenbacks. He looked past all of that, too, without more than a guess of the value before him. A copper-and-silver box made him wonder what kind of jewels he might find as well. But Ian didn't have time to investigate. In fact, he'd wasted precious seconds already just coveting the considerable wealth before him.

There it was: the Pemberton seal. Exactly what Ian needed if he was to salvage any bit of this job.

He snatched the lead seal; it was heavy and solid. He knew lead and gold were similar in weight, but what a difference it would be to simply hold one of those gold bars.

How he wanted to close the safe's door without another glance. He should flee this temptation as surely as a saint flew from a demon.

And yet he couldn't. Because Ian was no saint, and he knew it.

He took a step back, his gaze still captive to the gold.

"Ain't we gonna move it, Pinch?" Pubjug whispered. "We best get to it."

Pubjug reached for the uppermost bar of gold that crossed the other two stacks beneath it.

"No!" The word was little more than a blurted croak, as weak as a dying man refusing the inevitable.

Pubjug stared at Ian. "No? You mean we ain't gonna take it up to the bricks we got waitin'? You know, to exchange 'em? You know, the plan?"

That *was* what they'd come for. And staring at the riches, unable to do otherwise, Ian wanted to do exactly what they'd planned.

But somewhere in all of that gold he saw something else. The shimmer of Meg's hair under a golden sunset. The warmth of John's memory. The words of his own father, about not loving money more than God. The streets up in heaven.

Everything that painting hanging just up the stairs brought so vividly into focus. A painting that washed Ian with something he'd never felt before: the love it would've taken for someone to do what Christ had done.

Love.

God's love.

In the same moment he realized another kind of love. If he stole this gold, he'd do what John's love had shielded Meggie from all these years.

And Ian knew now that he loved Meggie too. Enough to do the right thing. For her, if not for himself.

"Shore up the hole, Pubjug." The words, breathless and feeble, barely made it past his lips.

Then, still clutching the seal, he fled temptation the only way he knew how: by running to the steps and scurrying ever upward.

He stopped in the library just long enough to rearrange the key on the bookshelf. Everything made sense now, what he had to do. If he was to leave all that gold in a broken safe, the compromise needed to be discovered sooner rather than later.

Meg watched the household staff eat and mingle with the Pembertons, a laugh rising now and then amid the sound of violins playing near a table laden with everything from watermelon to cold slaw, ham sandwiches to roasted turkey, iced currants to fine fruit sweetmeats.

Meg knew she would have to eat, although her stomach was in such a knot she wasn't sure how she would manage. She'd expected Ian to be late but didn't know how late to expect him.

"There you are, darling!"

Meg turned round, the knot in her stomach twisting tighter at the sight of Kate.

"You—you're here!" She shouldn't be here at all, since Meg had destroyed the invitation she'd found on the outgoing silver tray a few days ago.

"Of course, dear. Where else would I be tonight of all nights?"

Meg nearly pulled Kate aside to demand she admit why she'd come, but Claire was already calling them over to the banquet table. Kate *knew*—surely she must—the significance of the night. What did she plan to do with the information?

"Oh, you did come, Lady Kate!" Claire's smile was always infectious, though tonight Meg was immune. "I'm so glad. Meg was afraid you'd left town. Tell me, did you receive two invitations for tonight or just one?"

"Just one, darling. Was that enough, or should I have received more than that to be fully invited?"

Claire laughed. "It's only that I left the first invitation on the tray to be posted, and when I checked on it, our Mrs. Longford said she hadn't seen it. So I sent another. I cannot imagine what happened to the first!"

Kate spared Meg a glance before speaking. "Well, no matter. Here I am, delighted to share the evening."

"Did you . . . happen to see Ian, Lady Kate?" Meg asked.

Kate looked around with a frown. "Isn't he here?"

Too late, Meg realized the foolishness of having brought up Ian at all. Kate already looked suspicious. "Just detained, I suppose."

Nelson approached from behind Kate. "Where are these frowns coming from on a night like this, ladies? This is an evening to enjoy."

Claire looped her arm with her brother's. "Meg is wondering what could be keeping Ian."

"I'm sure he'll be here soon," Meg said, squashing her nervousness, hoping her tone sounded as lighthearted as she meant it to be.

"Perhaps he went to the house first. I was pondering going back there anyway," Nelson said. He patted his sister's hand. "Claire and I worked on a little speech to thank our staff, and I've just discovered I left my notes behind. I'm not sure I can do without them."

If the ground of Central Park had suddenly opened to swallow her, Meg would not have felt more unsteadied than she did at that moment. "Why don't I fetch the speech for you, Nelson?" Was her voice too eager? Nervous? "I don't mind going, since if he did go to the house, it's likely my fault for poor communication."

"Yes, darling," Kate said, and Meg was sure her face was as

fraught with tension as Meg's own. "Why don't we both go so Nelson won't be an absent host?"

"No, no, no," Nelson said with a smile. "I insist you both stay here and enjoy the party. Go now, and enjoy yourselves. I'll take the carriage and be back with Ian, if he's there, and my notes as well."

Meg watched Nelson leave, sick at the thought of him discovering Ian. When Kate took her arm to turn her toward the buffet, the sight of the many varieties of food made her stomach roil.

"Calm down," Kate whispered. "Ian will know how to handle himself, and it's best if you're not involved." Then she laughed Claire's way and said, "You won't let us eat alone, will you, Claire? I believe your staff has already partaken."

Meg turned a seething glance on Kate, who obviously cared not a whit that Ian might be found out. Kate had likely come to stop them anyway. This way only Ian would be caught. Was that what she wanted? Or would she confess to the Pembertons that she was a fraud too, along with Ian—and Meg? Once Ian was caught, Kate would indict them all at once. What did she want more than seeing God's justice done?

Could anything else go wrong?

Another drop of sweat tickled Ian's scalp, but the heat he felt had nothing to do with the pot he helped Pubjug return to the back of the wagon. With it safely returned to its spot, Pubjug climbed up to the driver's seat.

The job was nearly done. Inside that pot had been enough hot coals to keep melted the gold they'd needed for the fake bricks they'd just rehidden among the delivery inside the garden. The melted gold eagerly accepted the image from the Pemberton seal. Thanks to false information supplied to Brewster through the man

Ian had sat with on the train from Peekskill, he would monitor that pickup. All they needed was for Brewster to act true to himself by stealing from the thieves he believed had stolen the gold first.

The only difference in the plan was the empty compartment beneath the wagon, something Pubjug clearly did not understand. This job had ended up costing them instead of bringing in a penny of profit. But the thought of Brewster believing he'd outsmarted Ian, then learning he hadn't, was worth every cent of Ian's investment. It might not free him—it might inspire another beating—but it would be worth that, too.

He stepped back from the covered cart and took a deep breath of evening air as Pubjug drove the wagon out of the covered Pemberton parkway. Ian hadn't been sure he could do it. But he had. Best of all, it would be done without a whisper of trouble Meg's way.

Maybe God didn't think Ian so useless, after all.

He had just one thing left to do. Return the seal.

Ian let himself back into the Pemberton home through the servants' entrance. The prospect of facing that safe this second time hardly frightened him at all. He'd done the right thing once; he could do it again.

A noise at the front door froze him into stillness, choking back his confidence along with his breath. Someone was there—with a key.

Silently, Ian retraced his footsteps. He listened at the kitchen door, only to be sure someone had indeed entered. He heard the front door open, then close. It was no use. He would have to find another way to return the seal.

Ian left the kitchen, shutting the servants' entrance and locking that as well, knowing that doing so meant he would be unable to get back inside without some measure of trouble. Hang it all, this was why he never took the chance at home burglaries. They were too unpredictable. Too personal.

Ian pulled the black scarf from around his neck, wrapping the seal inside. Searching for a place to hide it, he chose a spot close to the delivery porch, well beneath a thick and prickly bush so no one—not even a curious dog—was likely to investigate.

Then, brushing off his jacket, straightening his cravat and hat, he walked around to the front of the house, glad Pubjug was long since gone. Ian was just in time to see Nelson Pemberton emerge.

With a wave, Ian joined him at his driverless carriage. Evidently the man had come back entirely on his own.

So much for thinking God might have blessed what Ian had just done. He'd very nearly been caught, and until that seal was returned, he wasn't free of trouble yet.

Meg hadn't expected the height of her performance to begin until after the theft was discovered. But behaving as if nothing were wrong while everyone else celebrated an evening of entertainment was surely as difficult as acting innocent.

With each passing moment of Nelson's absence, she grew more and more fretful that he had found Ian in the most compromising circumstance.

The music, instead of soothing her, grated on her nerves as each note pounded into her head. Rubbing her eyes, she wondered how much longer she could endure the wait. She'd left Kate with Claire, preferring instead to sit off to the side by herself so she could play with the food she had no intention of eating.

"That looks especially delicious."

She nearly dropped the plate from her lap at the sound of the familiar voice nearby. Next to Nelson stood Ian, as tall and handsome as ever, a twinkle—of triumph?—in his eye.

Meg rose, but there was nowhere to put her plate. So she

clutched it in hopes of keeping steady her hands and offered instead the most welcoming of smiles. "Oh! I'm so glad you've made it to the party."

Relief over seeing him gave the first hint of unfurling the knot inside. Surely nothing had gone wrong. Did it mean that even now the golden bars were hidden among the bricks in the garden? Entirely unprotected, innocently waiting for Pubjug?

Refusing to dwell on any number of dire possibilities, Meg trusted the calm facade Ian presented.

"I found him just arriving at the house," Nelson said, "with apologies for his tardiness. But that doesn't matter, does it? We're all here now."

Ian looked around. "I must say you know how to plan a party. Everyone looks to be enjoying themselves, and the violins are bound to attract more people than you've planned."

"Music should be for everyone, don't you think?" Nelson asked.

Kate joined them, smiling as easily as if this were any other day, as though she and Ian were the true friends they pretended to be. All of which steeped Meg in confusion. Not knowing what Kate was about to do only added to the tension this night had already brought. At the same time she marveled at their self-control. It required more than composure to do what they did just then, in their elegant grace—each wanting the opposite outcome. How did they do it?

She'd expected her fears to subside once Ian arrived, yet his presence did not ease her anxiety after all. If anything, her heart pounded harder, and she could not even look at Claire.

The rest of them sat chatting while Meg watched silently, barely keeping up with the topic at hand. Her best training couldn't keep her mind on what was being said. It all seemed so mundane and unnecessary.

Why had Claire proven herself so fully capable of being a

friend? Even Evie, who just now laughed with the scullery maid, as troublesome as she could be, possessed not one ounce of true malice. Youthful self-centeredness, yes, but though she had yet to show a trace of the piety both her siblings demonstrated, she crossed class barriers far easier than any one of her Fifth Avenue neighbors might.

The violins played nearby, low enough to allow conversation but loud enough to cover a quiet voice. Meg leaned closer to Ian while the others continued to eat and talk.

"Is everything . . . all right?" she asked.

"And why shouldn't it be? I'm only a bit late, not absent altogether. I hope to speak to you, though. There is something that must be said."

"Yes, I have so many questions. Did everything—?"

"It's fine, Meg." His gaze held hers, and she wanted to stare into the dark-blue depths far longer than she should allow. There was something new there, a sort of peace that she could not recall seeing since the day she arrived at his home on the Hudson. Was that what came of completing a challenge? It was exactly what *she'd* expected to feel. Triumph. Joy, even, that she'd proven herself to be her father's daughter, fully capable of working with Ian and thus with her father. She'd proven he was wrong to have shut her away all those years.

Yet she didn't feel peace at all.

They ate in silence for a while, even as Meg grew more restless for answers. This was neither the time nor the place for a discussion, and yet somehow they must have it.

Not long after Nelson delivered his speech—one that only compounded Meg's guilt because of his goodness—the chairs were rearranged and the musicians relocated off to a corner, leaving free what appeared to be a makeshift dance floor. Because of the music, and because it was a Saturday evening in a public place, others besides the Pemberton staff were attracted to the sounds just as

Ian had predicted. Soon there was dancing both within the circle of chairs and beyond it.

Ian asked Kate to dance first. Meg watched him holding her in a polite waltz, yet a closer look revealed their conversation seemed anything but polite. It was quiet but earnest.

Perhaps Kate could be convinced not to bring Ian or Meg any trouble. She was no squealer, after all. Was she?

Meg wanted to be relieved when both Ian and Kate smiled her way after their dance ended. They'd obviously come to some kind of agreement for the very first time. But complete relief was not to be found. This was likely the last function in polite society Meg would attend. Her life as a thief had already begun, and if her part in the crime was discovered, it would be the end of any welcome except by other thieves like her.

Ian could hardly wait to hold Meg in his arms. It was likely the last time he would be able to do so.

He'd wanted her to be the first he danced with but knew he needed to speak to Kate, just in case her presence meant any trouble. What he'd told her forestalled any of that. She'd been only too happy to hear what he'd had to say. Meggie was safe; that was all that mattered. She'd agreed to keep quiet about all of it, to not even tell Meg what he'd done to protect her. No sense risking her reaction until everything else had gone according to plan and Ian's goal to see Brewster made the fool was complete.

On his way here, he'd wondered how he would feel when he saw Meg. If she knew the truth, would she hate him? Be disappointed? And which would be worse to withstand?

The force behind his love for her had surprised even him. If he'd doubted himself before tonight, he would never do so again. He was capable of loving someone more than gold, after all. Enough to do what was best for her . . . even if it was not best for him.

At last he was able to lead Meg to the dance circle. He wished he could lavish her with a gaze of admiration, but he looked at her only when he thought she couldn't notice. Tonight, for the first time since landing in this country, Ian had conquered the loss he'd carried with him since disembarking from that ship without his family. He hoped it would make what he was about to do easier or at least bearable.

"You're lovely, Meg," he whispered, because in spite of his intention, he couldn't keep the words inside or stop himself from holding her close. Let this dance be as unconventional as the rest of the party. "But then I've noticed your loveliness ever since you were a child. From the first time I saw you."

"Have you?"

The two words came to his ears in breathless happiness. Yes, he would savor that. He wanted to tell her he loved her, that he'd loved her since that first moment—even before that, from the moment John had told him about her. He wanted to ask her how it was possible she hadn't seen his love the moment she'd stepped off that carriage in Peekskill all those weeks ago.

But instead he must keep that to himself, if tonight's job were to be considered nearly complete. Soon she might remember this night as one she'd spent dancing with a man who'd lied to and humiliated her. If that must be what she believed in order to secure her future, so be it. A future without him or his ways.

"You should be dancing under these stars with someone like Mason," he told her. What an accomplishment, to make his voice sound so sincere.

She was surprised by his words; he saw that immediately in the lift of her brows. "I thought it was already clear I'm hardly fit for permanent residence on Fifth Avenue."

"You're fit, Meg. More than fit for such a life. Mason himself would be all too eager to convince you of that. You ought to consider letting him."

Her lips tightened, changing that look of surprise into anger. "If I didn't know better, Ian, I would say you're trying to be rid of me before we've split whatever spoils you garnered tonight."

He laughed at the words that proved what she thought of thieves like him. "Perhaps I am."

She still looked at him through narrowed eyes. "Kate once said you would never be satisfied. That I might be reaching for something I can't get from my past, but that you'll always reach for more to secure your future."

His gaze left her briefly to land on Kate, who was dancing with Nelson. "She may be right." Then he looked again at Meg. "Tell me, did you think nothing of the painting that hangs in the Pemberton office? Of Christ with the two thieves?"

She looked away rather than facing him straight on, and when she did not speak, he knew the truth. It had affected her as well. That was the best sign he'd seen all evening. Maybe this evening's turn had been worth it from more angles than he'd hoped.

The dance ended too soon and Ian bowed, then squeezed her hand. "I've always wanted what was best for you. Never forget that, Meg."

He excused himself, found his way to the Pembertons, thanked them for the evening, then bid good night to Kate.

He would see Meg once more, just to be sure the consequences of the break-in went exactly as he had planned.

And after that, he would never see her again.

Meg watched Ian go, troubled by his early departure but more than that by the words he'd spoken. The dance had begun so promisingly. He'd told her she was lovely, that he'd thought so since she was a child. She'd held her breath at such words, fully expecting them to be followed by a declaration of love. In that moment she realized she'd have easily and eagerly returned such a declaration. She loved him. How could she have ignored it for so long?

But he'd gone on as if she were nothing more than an inconvenience. Someone he wanted to pass on to a man more willing to share her future.

She found her way to Kate, who was sitting next to Claire. Meg waited some time to speak alone with Kate.

"What's changed your mind about your confession?" she whispered. "Did you make some kind of deal with Ian? That he would give up his partnership with me if you don't endanger our plans?"

"What a lovely idea!" Kate said. "But no, I hadn't thought of it. Why do you ask?"

"Because Ian acted so strangely this evening, and you . . . I thought you were going to tell everyone your real identity. And yet you haven't."

"I cannot make my confession without jeopardizing your entire social future, Meg. And I once promised your father that if ever you and I were to meet, I would love you with all the love I held for him. How could I do anything to hurt you?"

Meg watched the others who were dancing: Claire with her brother, Evie with one of the stable boys, the servants with each other. She knew the evening wouldn't last much longer, but it had ended for her the moment Ian departed.

32

The truly elegant young lady always remains in control over her inner sentiments. She does not compromise grace by exhibiting melodramatic behavior that commands attention, whether she finds herself in the heights or depths of emotion.

Madame Marisse's Handbook for Young Ladies

MEG HAD ONCE believed her nights of investigation in the downstairs office resulted in the greatest loss of sleep. That was no longer true. From the moment she arrived home from the picnic, she was beset tenfold with anxiety.

Would the robbery be discovered? Sooner or later it *must* be. But when?

Once inside the Pemberton home, nothing happened.

No one went into the library or the office at such a late hour. There was no chance for anything amiss to be discovered.

All she had to do now was wait for Pubjug to retrieve the bricks from the garden. She saw them from her bedroom window, a neat, square stack that looked as untouched as it had since the moment it had been delivered.

Pubjug would come for them in just a few hours. The job would truly be complete then.

And if by the end of the week Nelson had no cause to go into his father's office, if by next Sunday the missing gold had not been discovered, Meg would hint at her departure anyway.

Then, perhaps within a few days of that, she would leave without the slightest suspicion. Perhaps by then she would have learned to live with the fear of discovery. Perhaps that could even begin by dawn, after the bricks had been taken away.

Meg did not go to her bed at all that night. She watched the bricks. Before she heard the first bird welcoming dawn, she paced, waiting for Pubjug. Her restless heart picked up a beat when she heard him arrive at the servants' entrance and the scullery maid let him in. He never looked up, never wavered from his task. He secured the rope-bound bricks to a dolly and wheeled them away. She watched, tears in her eyes that he had made it look so simple. The gold had been taken away without a noise, not even a grunt.

Meg sat silently, listening to the birds just waking. The garden below had only one spot left in need of attention. Soon the new, innocent bricks would be delivered and Mr. Deekes would hire someone to build the bench to her design. Then the garden would truly be complete.

Meg wanted to say it would be lovely. In the pinkish hue of the early morning, it might have been—to any other eye but hers.

"Where are your hat and gloves, Evie? It's almost time to go."

"I don't want to go to the park today, Clairy."

"What?" Claire's surprise was followed with an enlightened nod. "Just because Geoffrey and his family haven't returned from Saratoga doesn't mean you should avoid the fresh air."

Meg slipped into her gloves as she watched the exchange. She could tell already that Claire would lose this battle; Evie had that not-going-to-budge look on her face, and of the two sisters, Evie was clearly the stronger.

"I had enough fresh air last night, but I'll sit in the garden if I want any more of it. What I really want is to spend the afternoon in the aviary or the library."

"All right, then." Claire followed her capitulation with a glare. "But don't get into any trouble."

Evie offered a smile that would have been at home on the most innocent child. "Why would I cause any trouble? You won't be here to enjoy it."

Claire tsked but was clearly in good humor anyway. "We'll be back early, then, just to make sure that you won't miss us for too long."

Then Claire forged the path through the foyer and out the front door, which was hurriedly opened by the butler, Mr. Deekes.

Meg glanced up at the sky. Myriad layers of clouds skidded along, white and gray, some wispy, some thick. All moving on something more than a gentle breeze.

"She may be right about staying at home today," Meg said. "The fair weather looks to be changing."

"We won't stay long."

The Pemberton driver paced the carriage at a healthy clip, as if knowing he raced with the weather. He gained entrance to the park at the familiar Scholars' Gate. While Meg noticed the air didn't hold the scent of rain, she realized her worries about something so mundane as a soaking seemed nearly a pleasure compared to the anxiety that had plagued her since last night.

Meg could think of nothing to chat with Claire about, not with her secretly burdened heart pulled firmly downward. She'd been alternately sympathetic and unaccountably irritated with Claire all morning. Sympathetic because of her own guilt, but irritated for the same reason. If Claire hadn't been so easy to like, Meg wouldn't feel nearly as guilty. Would she?

In the rare moment Meg's mind drifted from the plague of her remorse, she strove to think of other things. But the strain was never truly pushed aside; it hovered over every thought she tried putting in its place.

You're a thief, a liar, a fraud. If Claire knew the truth about you, she would demand justice as quickly as she'd demanded it of Evie. Every naughty thing Evie had done in her life did not add up to the grievous wrong Meg had helped perpetrate.

Meg continued to summon the image of her father, hoping his face would dispel some of the oppression. How had he lived with himself all the years that he had? Knowing he'd cheated people? Had he known any of his victims as well as Meg knew hers?

Perhaps she'd gone about it the wrong way; perhaps she shouldn't have allowed herself to become so fond of the Pembertons. She would know better next time.

Next time! Her heart whirled painfully in her chest. Somehow the thought of doing such a thing again wasn't as exciting as she imagined it would be. But that had been the goal, hadn't it? To set herself up as Ian's partner? That undoubtedly meant this was only the beginning.

When the driver left them at the usual footpath, Claire told him not to go far, that their walk would not be long today.

The park seemed different than it had just last night, when it had been the unlikely location for a servants' ball. Meg glanced at the spot where the grass was still somewhat trampled—the keep-off-the-grass signs set neatly back in place. A moment's reminiscence of dancing in Ian's arms nearly took Meg's breath away. But even that brought little comfort, remembering most of their conversation had been less than romantic despite dancing under the moonlight.

A glance at Claire and her guilt settled back into place.

Perhaps Meg's fortitude against this oppression would build, in time. She might become immune to it, desensitized. Surely she couldn't live this way without developing a callus against the shame.

They took the usual path toward the usual park settee, but as they rounded the wooded curve, Claire stopped short. Meg looked ahead and stopped as well.

The settee was occupied.

That occupant, however, stood as if he'd expected them, waited for them. He was a stranger to Meg, though obviously not to Claire, whose breathing became irregular in her hurried step—which she cut short not ten paces from the man.

He was of generous height, thin but broad in the shoulders, and handsome in a rugged way. Despite the fine cut of his morning coat, he didn't seem the Fifth Avenue type. He looked as if he should be on a trail out west or at the helm of a sailing vessel. Just now he held his hat in one hand, a walking stick in the other, shifting each from one hand and back again as if he couldn't decide what to do with either item.

"Claire."

"Jude."

Meg's eyes widened. Was this why Claire made a point of visiting this same settee every single day the weather permitted? Had she come here day after day with this secret hope?

Yet as the two stood staring at one another, Meg wasn't at all sure Claire's hopes had come true. She looked every bit as fearful as she did hopeful.

A surprising swell of protectiveness washed over Meg's heart. If this man was the cause of the pain Claire had borne these past few years, Meg wouldn't hesitate to sharpen her tongue and send him on his way.

"I'm sorry, Claire." His gaze was intent on hers. "I'm such a sorry idiot. It was all my pride, every stupid decision I made since the day we parted. I've wronged you, and I came to ask your forgiveness."

Claire's hands went forward as she issued one tremulous word: his name. Meg seemed to have been forgotten as the two closed the gap between them. In an instant Claire was in the man's arms, he with the most profound look of relief, she with such longing that he couldn't possibly misread her forgiveness and acceptance.

"I ask that you deal with me in the Pemberton way," Jude said. "I haven't forgotten, you see? I know I deserve justice—"

"Grace, Jude." Claire laughed her verdict. "Most definitely grace."

He kissed her then, the kind of kiss that ought never have been performed in public, not even by married folk, but Meg couldn't blame either one. She doubted Madame Marisse herself, had she seen the look on Claire's face, would have condemned the action.

Meg, uncomfortable with witnessing so private an exchange, took a step back, drawing their attention.

"Oh, forgive me, Meg! I—I'm so . . . just aflutter! This is—"

Meg held out her hand as she finished for the flustered Claire, telling the man her name, then saying, "I can guess that you must be Jude Johnson. Claire—and not to mention Evie—have both spoken of you."

"Evie!" He looked past Claire. "Where is the little mischief maker?"

"At home. And won't she be sorry not to have come along today!" Claire clutched Jude's hand. "You'll return with us to the house, won't you? Are you staying in New York?"

"Only long enough to . . . to ask you to marry me, if you'll have me. It means coming with me to Chicago, but it's not so terrible a place, really." He tossed his hat to the settee nearby, dropped his cane to the ground, and put both of his hands around one of Claire's. "I know Chicago isn't New York, Claire, and I haven't nearly the money your father has or even what my own family once had. But I offer you all I do have, with a promise to take care of you the rest of our lives."

Claire was fully sobbing now. "Oh! Jude! Of course I'll marry you."

If either one of them had dreamed of such a moment, it surely hadn't included Meg as a witness. Nonetheless she felt hot tears stinging her eyes. When her dance with Ian had begun last night, she might have dreamed of him asking that very same question. But he hadn't.

A cold thought struck her. Her father had only asked Kate to marry him after Kate had no doubt insisted, with her recently found faith. Was that the way of thieves? Not wanting to commit to something as mundane as marriage?

Perhaps she would *never* hear Ian say such a thing to her! Last night he'd told her he only wanted what was best for her. Suddenly, in comparison to what she'd just seen between Claire and Jude, Ian's words sounded like a good-bye. Especially when she remembered his words about Geoffrey. All Ian had ever hinted about marriage was for her to consider someone else.

She must send him a note immediately or, better than that, go to the Glenham, where he had been staying. Even if it meant humiliating herself with a demand that he clarify exactly what kind of partners he expected them to be.

Meg knew she'd agreed to stay with the Pembertons through the next week or two, long enough so the exact date or time of the robbery would fade among many more nights that followed. But she couldn't wait. She wanted to leave now.

"Claire," she said, glad when her voice sounded far calmer than she was, "would you like me to take the carriage home and send the driver back for you? I'm sure you'd like a little time alone with Mr. Johnson."

Claire blushed but shook her head. "Of course I'd like to, but how could we? Half of Fifth Avenue might still be in Newport, but the half who stayed behind have tongues just as active. Evie used to be our chaperone, as unlikely as it sounds." She turned to Jude. "Will you come back with us?"

"Yes, I'd like to speak to your father anyway."

"He's traveling with Mother, but Nelson will be home soon. . . ." She grinned. "Jude, everyone in my family believes me to be in danger of becoming an old maid. I don't think you need my father's permission or my brother's if you want to ask for my hand. They'll both be only too happy to see me wed."

By the time the carriage let them out at the Pemberton home, Meg couldn't decide which was worse: waiting for the robbery to be discovered or for confirmation of what she'd just figured out. Ian might have wanted to be her partner, but such a partnership never included any hope of him becoming her husband.

Ian downed the rest of his beer just as Pubjug entered the bar.

"It's done," Pubjug said, low. "Not one of the phony bricks ever made it to the yard, just as you expected. Our tips for Brewster went straight on up the line."

"Was it Keys who stole them?"

Pubjug nodded grimly. "He pulled a gun on me. Never thought I'd see such a day, not from him." Then he grinned. "Didn't show no surprise about me bein' willin' to hand 'em over. He just took 'em like they was gold. I seen Brewster's carriage a ways off, waitin' for Keys to bring them over. I even helped."

Ian took a moment to relish an image of Keys delivering the gift to Brewster's feet, of Brewster looking at the "golden" bars with that familiar gleam of greed and triumph. Had he touched them the way Ian wanted to touch the real bars? As tenderly as he'd have touched a woman?

How long had it taken before he realized he'd been fooled? Ian nearly laughed with the thought.

He slipped a coin across the counter to pay the barkeep, along with a generous tip. It was a good day, no matter what else happened from here.

Ian stood and patted Pubjug's back, although the man hardly looked pleased. He hadn't understood this job at all, but then what had Ian expected of a man who'd been a thief nearly his entire life? Ian had hardly planned for the outcome of this job himself, not until the moment he'd succeeded.

He had one thing left to do as a thief, and that was the reverse of all he'd ever done before: make sure the seal was returned to the right hands. To do that he awaited only the right moment, when the broken safe was discovered.

"Well done. Now go home. Roscoe will be happy to see you."

Pubjug hesitated. He looked older than ever today; when he was unshaven, the gray of his beard added at least a dozen years to his leathery look. "You *really* want to do this, boy?"

"I made the decision longer ago than I realized, my friend. Getting the best of Brewster confirms it. It's a fine way to say farewell." He shook Pubjug's hand. Next to John, Ian hadn't cared for any other man as much. But if Ian were to follow the leading of the faith he'd discovered, he wouldn't be working with Pubjug anymore. He needed to start anew, away from every nefarious contact he had, which meant just about everyone he knew. Away even from Meg, for her own good. Even if she somehow gave up on following her father's path, she could do far better than someone like Ian, who might very well struggle to do what was right for the rest of his life.

"Good-bye, Pubjug. And thank you. Be careful of Brewster— he won't be pleased to discover what we've done."

Pubjug looked as if he might say something but evidently couldn't decide what. He only nodded, then turned away.

"Pubjug?" Ian called after him.

The man looked back.

"If anything happens to me, take good care of Roscoe, will you?"

He nodded again and walked out of the tavern.

Leaving Ian to do one thing. He might have bested Brewster today, but that didn't mean Ian would get to enjoy any freedom he'd gained from the man. He'd spent the better part of the afternoon composing, destroying, composing, then destroying again a letter to Meg. Ultimately he'd decided it was no use. She'd have to figure out for herself why he'd done what he'd done.

Regardless, he must return that seal in the only way he could do it without any of them getting into trouble—or letting Brewster cause any.

Ian only hoped he succeeded.

Evie was, as expected, disappointed at having missed the astounding reunion of her sister and Jude. Leaving them to chatter about everything from how long he'd been gone to the exciting prospect of the first wedding in the family, Meg drew away to her room to compose a note to Ian. Short, cryptic, but enough to convey her eagerness to join him. Would he wait for her at the Glenham, or should she meet him at his home on the Hudson?

She addressed it to him at the Glenham, which was not so very far from Fifth Avenue in miles but seemed immeasurable in distance between them. She would send someone with the note that very afternoon.

When Nelson arrived home, the atmosphere became festive again, with laughter and chatter echoing from the parlor and into the dining room once supper was served. Jude told them what had taken place in his life since he'd left New York, after explaining to Meg that his family made a bad investment and lost most of their fortune. How they'd gone to Chicago with enough to start a modest business there. How he'd tried moving his heart along with him, but it had remained behind in New York. With Claire.

All in all, the day's events were almost enough to take Meg's mind off her troubles.

Evie sighed. "Months and months, years and years of suffering that silly park settee and I wasn't rewarded at all. It isn't fair."

Nelson, sitting near her at the dinner table, patted her hand. "Yes, life is like that sometimes."

"I stayed in the library nearly all afternoon. Which reminds me, Nelson, you ought to be more careful about the key to Father's office."

Meg felt the sudden drop of her heart at mention of the key.

"Why do you say that?" Nelson asked.

"Because it wasn't in its proper place. After how many times you've lectured me and Mrs. Longford or Mr. Deekes about returning it to its place, I don't think it's fair that you didn't return it properly."

Her words brought every bit of temporarily forgotten guilt crashing back upon Meg's head. Only now that guilt was accompanied by stark fear. Terror, in fact, of being caught.

Nelson frowned. "I haven't used it since . . . let's see, not for weeks, since we wrote that letter to Father. You saw me return it. You did check with Mr. Deekes, though?"

"Yes, and Mrs. Longford, too, but both said it was in its place the last time they went in to see that the room was cleaned. That's why I assumed you'd been the one to use it again."

They both turned to Claire, who shook her head.

After a moment, the inevitable happened. Evie first, then Nelson, and finally Claire . . . even Jude followed their lead until they all looked at Meg.

Meg had never been subject to swooning, but in that moment

such a wave of light-headedness washed over her that she was grateful for the chair beneath her. In the next instant it took every fiber of her strength to remain seated, not to flee such stares. To act as if nothing were wrong.

"If it was moved, it was not I." How could such true words be so thoroughly a lie?

Evie's laughter made Claire, then the others, look her way. "You look as if you swallowed vinegar, Meg! All pasty white."

Meg told herself to join in with the laughter, but the effort produced a sound that seemed anything but natural. How could Ian have made such an amateur mistake? Even Meg, each and every time she *had* used the key, returned it to the exact spot in which it was always found. Under the heel of the brass button-up shoe bookend on the third shelf.

"I'll check again with the staff, Evie," Nelson said. "But thank you for pointing it out to me."

"You see? I'm not the cause of trouble all the time."

Claire narrowed her eyes. "How do we know you didn't make it up, just to garner credit for replacing something that wasn't even moved to begin with? You do like to be the center of attention, and that's been lacking this afternoon."

"I did no such thing!"

Jude put a hand over Claire's, his eyes merry. "I see nothing has changed between you and Evie these last years."

"*Please* take her to Chicago, Jude," Evie said. "The sooner, the better."

Meg was relieved the topic had moved on, yet the fact remained that Ian's visit had not been as invisible as he'd assured her it would be. She needed to talk to him more than ever now. How could he have been so careless?

She'd never been his partner before, but based solely on the fruit of his past successes, she guessed he wasn't careless at all. Did that mean a servant *had* somehow misplaced the key, coinciden-tally just after Ian's visit? Preposterous.

That left only one option: he had purposefully left it out of place so the robbery would be discovered sooner rather than later. But why? So she would have the opportunity to offer a quick, convincing performance of innocence and leave without further inquiry?

The only way to know was to ask him.

"Meg, what do you think? Will you?"

Startled and dismayed that she hadn't been listening to the conversation, she looked at Claire apologetically. "Forgive me, I was lost in thought. What did you say?"

"Will you stand with me at my wedding? Act as my first bridesmaid?"

"I . . . I would be honored." Another lie. While she was indeed honored, she had no idea if she would remain in New York—at least in this circle of society—long enough to perform such a dis-tinguished task. She squashed an immediate feeling of regret. She would have been delighted to stand next to Claire on that happy occasion, if Meg hadn't proven herself so thoroughly unqualified to be Claire's friend.

Meg left most of her dinner untouched, and what did end up on her fork was simply moved from one side of the plate to the other.

Had Ian been right when he'd first met her—that she didn't have the stomach for life as his partner?

33

Once guilt is established, a swift and harsh punishment is the best deterrent for other would-be criminals.

"REASONS FOR INCARCERATION"

MEG APPROACHED her bedroom door after hearing a gentle tap—a sound that stirred immediate concern considering Jude had left an hour ago and everyone else had retired for the night. "Who is it?"

"It's Claire. I'm so sorry to disturb you, but Nelson thought it important enough to gather tonight rather than before the meeting with the staff in the morning. Could you come to his office with me, please?"

Meg glanced at the clock, which she had long since replaced on the mantel. Near eleven.

Donning her robe and slippers—she'd just about managed to remove the stains—she opened the door to see Claire's concerned countenance.

"Has something happened?"

"I'll let my brother explain."

Meg followed Claire across the hall to Nelson's study, where the gas lamps had been turned high to brighten the room. He sat behind his desk with such a grave expression that Meg's heart, already beating erratically, picked up its pace and sent new fire throughout her body with every pump.

He stood when they entered, as if he'd been about to speak, but stopped when Evie raced in behind Meg and Claire.

"I thought I heard voices!" She looked from her sister to her brother. "You *were* going to call me in, weren't you?"

"We didn't want to burden you," Nelson said, "but since you're awake, you might as well stay. Close the door, please."

She did so, but no one took a seat.

"There was a fracture in our security here at home," Nelson said. Then, catching sight of Claire's face, he added, "Actually it was more than a fracture; it was a complete break." He rubbed his eyes, which looked red and tired already, not even an hour since he'd happily bid them good night. "To be honest I'm glad we'll have this cleared up before Father returns, or he might never leave us alone again, Clairy." Then he shook his head as if reminding himself of the day's events. "I should say he might not leave *me* in charge again, since you'll be leaving home when Mother and Father return for the wedding."

"Do you mean to say someone *did* use that key?" Evie asked, leaning over the opposite side of Nelson's desk. "And I'm the one who found the first clue?"

Nelson nodded. "I've sent for the police chief tonight rather than waiting until morning, and I didn't want any of you to be alarmed when he arrives. We're safe; I'm sure of that. It's just—"

"Not Grandfather's gold!" Evie nearly shrieked. "Was it—was it taken?"

Nelson patted the air in front of him, air that was full of Evie's worry. "Now, now, hush. Something was taken, but not the gold."

"The thief—or thieves—wasn't able to open the safe, then?" Claire asked.

"As curious as it is, yes, they were. I noticed as soon as I saw the safe that it had been tampered with. Only the Pemberton seal was taken—an item thoroughly worthless now that I know it's gone. Whoever did this actually did us a favor."

Meg nearly covered her mouth but settled for knitting her lips tightly together. A favor, indeed. What would happen when they discovered the gold left behind was fraudulent?

"A favor?" Evie repeated. "Why is it a favor? I'm frightened, Nelson! Someone—a stranger—came into our home!"

"It's a favor because he proved our security is lacking. The safe, for one, was obviously too easily opened."

"But how did they know where the safe could be found?" Claire asked.

"They must know everything about us to know our biggest secret," Evie said, her voice tremulous. "Only Mr. Deekes and Mrs. Longford even know where the key is kept, and only Mr. Deekes knows about the safe. Isn't that right?"

Nelson nodded, still deep in thought. "The chief of police knew about it; he was the one who gave advice to Father about updating the safe."

"Have you ever mentioned the safe to anyone, Evie?" Claire asked, though she did ask the accusatory question somewhat gently. "To any of your friends? Perhaps you were overheard."

"No!"

Nelson rubbed his chin. "It's true the only member of the staff to know of it is Mr. Deekes, and we all know it wasn't him—he's one of the family. But if it wasn't any of us and couldn't possibly be the chief of police . . ."

Meg kept silent, even as confusion poked questions at her. Should she pretend to be entirely in the dark? Ask where the safe was? Ask . . . anything?

Soon Mr. Deekes himself opened the office door, quietly announcing the police chief had arrived.

"I'll see him in a moment," Nelson said before turning to Meg and his sisters again. "There is nothing any of you can do. I only wanted to inform you of what was happening should any noise have disturbed you. You might as well go to bed."

"All alone?" Evie asked. "In a house where a stranger can come and go?"

"Don't be silly, Evie," Claire said. "They couldn't have been here when we were all home."

"It likely happened when we were out," Nelson said. "Perhaps at a party, or more likely during the picnic when the entire house was empty."

"Just last night!" Evie's words were breathless. "Oh, please don't send me to my room alone, Nelson! I'd rather stay up with you."

He shook his head, then glanced at Claire, who looked none too pleased by his silent entreaty.

"Oh, all right, she can stay in my room," she said.

"Can I bring Pindar? He'll squawk if anyone comes in—or flutter his wings and wake me."

"Absolutely, positively not. I'm not sleeping in the same room as that creature. Not even in his cage, since he knows how to get out of it."

"But—" Before Evie could form an argument, she turned her attention to Meg. "Could I stay in your room, then? Me and Pindar, too? I promise you he won't make a bit of trouble. I'll bring a blanket to put over the table, so if he happens to . . . Well, he won't make a mess like the last time because he's calmer when I'm with him."

Meg knew Evie had nothing more to worry about tonight than she had any other night, but logic wouldn't let her say so and compunction wouldn't let her refuse the request. She nodded.

"Oh, thank you! Will you come with me to the aviary to get him? I don't want to be alone, not for a moment."

Meg uttered a somber good night to Nelson and Claire, hearing her friend say that she wanted to send someone to the hotel where Jude was staying, but Nelson discouraged her from sending for him this late. Then Meg was out of the room, unable to hear more.

Claire was clearly as upset as Evie. Fearful, even.

But they had nothing to fear! Ian wouldn't hurt anyone; he was entirely incapable of such a thing. And certainly they weren't afraid of *her*!

Yet she was responsible for their unease.

The bird did not appear at all ruffled at the visit, but Meg reminded herself of Evie's late nights in the aviary, so it was little wonder Pindar welcomed her company as if he'd been waiting for her. He probably didn't expect to return to the guest room he'd been banished from so many weeks ago, but as Evie promised, he made no noise while sitting on her shoulder as she spread a blanket on the table near the window overlooking the garden.

She spoke quietly to him, soothing words Evie herself probably needed to hear more than the bird did. Meg removed her robe and slippers, then pulled back the covers of her bed. It was certainly large enough for two, although a thought unsettled her as she climbed in. Once, when she was a child, one of her schoolmates told Meg she'd spoken in her sleep. What if she did so again, only said something incriminating for Evie to hear?

Perhaps she shouldn't have let her guilt force her into accepting Evie's request after all.

"Can we sleep with the light on?" Evie asked.

"Yes, if you like," Meg said. It was just as well; she didn't plan on falling asleep until well after Evie did anyway. If at all.

Evie crawled into the bed beside Meg. "Thank you so much for this, Meg. You know, I'm sorry I ever played any pranks on you. Here or at school. I honestly like you."

"Thank you, Evie," Meg said, but rather than welcoming the words, her heart went leaden. "I like you, too."

Meg woke with a start. She hadn't realized she'd fallen so thoroughly asleep, though she must have dozed more than once during the night. The sun shone brightly through the open window.

Then she remembered Evie, but the bed was empty.

Meg sat up. Pindar was still there, the bird's outline sharp against the light through the open curtains. He eyed her unflinchingly, a cold-eyed, accusing stare.

"Good morning," Evie said. She was at the dressing table, fully dressed. Meg's robe had been neatly cast aside and her slippers were nowhere in sight. Meg saw instantly that in the light of day Evie did not look at all as timid as she had last night.

With a glance at the clock, Meg realized it was later than she'd assumed. Past ten.

"Is Nelson meeting with the staff?" Meg threw aside the covers. "I must get dressed."

"The meeting already happened," Evie said. "I didn't want to wake you." Her voice sounded strangely cold.

"I wish you would have," Meg said. How could she have slept so soundly? Then she eyed Evie again, who stared back in a peculiarly intense manner. There wasn't a trace of leftover fear, which was a relief, but next to her reestablished self-confidence there was something else. Curiosity?

"Will you be all right on your own this morning?" Meg asked, but the moment the question was uttered, Evie broke her stare. She went to Pindar, put him on her shoulder, took up the blanket that had covered the table beneath him, then walked silently from the room.

Evidently she would be fine.

Meg dressed quickly in the first gown she grabbed, one of blue-and-green gingham. There hadn't been any reason for her to attend the usual Pemberton meeting, but she wished she'd been there to hear what was said. Had the police returned—had anyone other than the police chief arrived? Surely they weren't going to allow all that gold to be unguarded in a broken safe, gold they didn't know was worthless. Perhaps they'd moved it already this morning!

After pulling up her hair into a set of combs, Meg emerged to a quiet upstairs hall. She heard voices below and descended. The foyer was empty, but she caught a glimpse of shadow, someone going into the office.

Meg was about to follow when someone called her from the parlor. She turned to see Nelson and Claire. Claire had obviously been crying, and Nelson's brows were drawn, his mouth set in a grave frown.

Behind them was another man. Although he was dressed in a plain suit of clothing, he had a look of calm authority about him. The police chief?

He stepped around Claire and Nelson to stop in front of Meg.

"Permit me to introduce myself, Miss Davenport. I am Detective Cambridge. And you, young lady, are under arrest on suspicion of burglary."

34

MEG THOUGHT SHE might faint. The edges of her vision seemed to fade, as if preparing her for a complete blackout. But just then someone twisted the bell at the front door, sufficiently calling her attention back to consciousness.

Perhaps it was Ian! Perhaps he'd come to take her away—could they run? Was it possible they could elude the police detective standing not three feet from her?

But it wasn't Ian at the door. The butler let in Jude Johnson, who went to Claire's side after only the quickest greeting extended to Nelson.

"Oh, Jude, I'm so glad you've come," Claire said. "It's just awful! Our safe was broken into—drilled right through the metal. And they think my dearest friend had something to do with it. I cannot believe it!" Then, as if stronger with Jude at her side, she stood a bit taller and faced the detective. "In fact, sir, I do not believe Meg could have been involved. And what does it matter, anyway, if only that silly lead seal was stolen?"

"I concur with my sister on this, Detective," Nelson said. "I cannot believe Meg would have anything to do with this, despite the evidence."

"I . . . don't understand," Meg said, her voice as feeble as she felt. "Why do you think that I was involved?"

Neither Nelson nor the detective answered. Rather the detective called for someone and two officers responded, dressed in traditional police uniform. He said something to Mr. Deekes about showing them to Meg's room; then the butler and the two officers went up the stairs.

"Your room will be thoroughly searched, miss," Detective Cambridge said. "We've only waited this long on orders from the Pembertons. If there is any evidence, or if the missing item is in your room, we'll find it."

"But I don't have anything that doesn't belong to me." She hadn't thought herself so capable of meekness, yet here she stood, the very picture of it.

"There, you see?" Claire said, now coming to Meg's side and taking her hand. "I told you she wasn't responsible. It's ridiculous. I've known her for years, and a graduate of Madame Marisse's simply wouldn't do such a thing."

The detective, a man with a fair complexion made fairer by white hair and a matching white mustache, appeared only skeptical. "We'll see about that, then."

Nelson stepped to Meg's other side. "Even if the missing seal does turn up in her room, Detective, there was no real harm done." He eyed Meg. "We'd like an explanation, of course, but we have no intention of pressing charges."

Meg wished she could find comfort in his words. What would happen when they learned the gold bricks were fake? That Ian had replaced them with look-alikes?

Part of her was tempted to confess to it all, except that it would endanger Ian—and that she wouldn't do.

If only she hadn't been foolish enough to be caught! But how had she been found out?

"What is your evidence that I was involved?" Perhaps this time she would receive an answer.

"Evie found your slipper," Claire said. "It's stained with the rust from our old safe. We can't imagine how, except that you must have been in the cellar. But how, Meg? How could that be?"

Meg's head was so light she feared all strength would abandon her. Why, oh why, had she thought herself capable of going through with this if she couldn't pay the price of being caught?

The bell at the door sounded again, but this time it was Jude Johnson who answered the call, since Mr. Deekes was still with the officers upstairs. Two more police officers came in. Evidently both Nelson and the detective had expected them, since the detective introduced them to Nelson.

Nelson then led the two officers from the foyer to the office, while the detective excused himself from Claire to move toward the stairs. He sent Meg a somber glance before speaking as he ascended. "I trust you'll still be here when I return in a moment, Miss Davenport."

She nodded. Where could she go under so much scrutiny?

"Nelson is having the gold moved to a safer location," Claire said, "until we decide what to do with it. I suppose we'll have to send word to Father, to see what he thinks best. I wonder if they might cut short their trip?"

"I never knew your family kept so much of the gold here, Claire," Jude said. Then he looked at Meg. "How did you?"

Meg swallowed hard, and the effort pierced her throat. "I . . . didn't."

"But the stained slipper, Meg," Claire said. "It's obviously from our cellar, from the unusual color. How did they become stained?"

"I . . . I . . ."

Claire leaned closer. "Meg, if you're innocent, just say so. I want to believe you. But there is a footprint in the cellar that matches the quilt of your slippers. I don't know how you could be innocent, but I want very much to believe that you are."

Part of Meg longed to confess, thinking it might help. But fear wouldn't let her.

"Unless . . ." Claire's voice sounded curiously hopeful as she scanned the hall and what was visible of the parlor. "Unless this is one of Evie's pranks! Where is she, anyway? She's been skulking around all morning." Claire turned to Jude. "Do you suppose she could have done this? She could have taken Meg's slippers and worn them down there. We've never shown her how to open the safe—she's still too young—but she's been in the cellar on her own. She's been wanting to cause trouble for Meg ever since our neighbor first laid eyes on her."

For the barest moment Meg wanted to latch on to the slimmest thread of hope Claire was so eager to cast her way.

But she couldn't. She would not lay blame where it didn't belong.

She opened her mouth to confess, but nothing came out. Not a word.

How could she confess without implicating Ian? She couldn't do that any more than she could get Evie into temporary trouble.

"If nothing of value was taken," she finally managed to say, her voice so raspy it hardly sounded like her own, "then can we not forget this whole thing?"

Jude was already shaking his head. "With the police involved, it's not likely to be entirely excused." He looked at Claire. "Didn't you say the safe was broken open by a drill? How would Evie have drilled into that safe? I don't think she's strong enough to turn a drill crank through metal as substantial as a safe would require."

"If Evie isn't strong enough, then neither is Meg."

Meg felt tears warm her eyes over Claire's staunch defense. She looked again toward the hall that led to the office. If Nelson brought that gold up from the cellar, would the light of day reveal the bars to be the frauds they were?

Then Claire would know; they would all know.

And she would go to jail, even though she hadn't the faintest idea where the real gold could be found.

Ian stepped up to the Pemberton door. If he was to be sure Meg's reputation remained intact—allowing hope of a future her father would have wanted for her—this part of his plan needed to succeed every bit as much as everything else had thus far. If the break-in had been discovered, as surely it had based upon the activity surrounding the house, they would soon have an explanation. At least the explanation Ian wanted them to believe.

A man he didn't recognize—clearly not a servant by his fashionable set of clothing—answered the door at Ian's ring.

Ian removed his hat. "Ian Vandermey."

"Ian!"

The man could not even step aside before Ian heard Meg's call—her tone a mix of horror and relief.

He moved past the man who'd opened the door, directly to Meg's side. Her color was high, her blue eyes dismayed—though still lovely and clearly glad to see him. He knew she would have come into his arms had he offered such comfort, but instead he held out his hand for her to clutch. That was all the contact he could afford and still have any hope of carrying through the rest of his plan.

"I came to call on you, Cousin," Ian said, as jovially as possible, "but I see you already have company."

It was then he noticed Claire Pemberton. She stepped closer, putting her palm on the arm of the man near her. She had a look of distress on her face, an expression not unexpected, but he saw that the man beside her was someone from whom she drew strength.

"I'm afraid we're facing something of a crisis, Mr. Vandermey. Our safe was broken into."

He put on a frown. "Was it? Did you catch the perpetrator?"

Both Claire and the man at her side looked at Meg. They suspected *her*? But how? Surely she hadn't confessed, when she'd shown such fortitude so far!

Meg confirmed the horrific notion with a small nod. "They think it was me."

Ian knew immediately he must hasten with the rest of his plan. He bowed as if an actor at a performance. And truly, he was. "It was I who broke into the safe."

"You!"

Meg did not look pleased by his admission, though it should have eased the worry on her face. He would soon have all of this cleared up—at least as far as Meg went.

He handed Claire a card he pulled from his vest pocket.

"Vandermey Securities," she read. She looked at him, her brow ruffled. "What is this?"

"That, Miss Pemberton, is the name of my business. I believe I proved my services are required by successfully breaking into your safe. I assure you I can prevent such a thing in the future with as much expertise as I used to carry out this violation."

The man beside her took the card from Claire's hand, looking at it, then at Ian. "So you broke into the safe to prove your necessity?"

The man was every bit as tall as Ian himself, only he was a bit sturdier than Ian's slim build. The kind of man Ian had learned long ago to avoid inciting. "Yes, of course. Obviously my services *are* needed."

"You realize you could be arrested for doing what you did?"

"Not if I can convince the Pembertons they need me. Soon I intend having all of Fifth Avenue looking at that same little information card." He looked at Claire with hope in his eye.

He knew Meg must be confused; he didn't have to see her face to know that. She still believed he'd switched the gold bars. But he refused to look at her, partly from the sure knowledge that he wasn't the actor he needed to be when it involved her, and partly because it fit so exactly into his plan not to give her the comfort she obviously would find in his reassurance.

"I think all of us need an explanation," Meg said.

"Wait," Claire said, holding up a palm. "Let me get my brother, or we'll be forced to repeat it all for him. You'll wait, won't you?"

Ian nodded, then eyed the glowering man at her side. "I imagine your friend here will make sure of that."

Claire disappeared, and Ian could not ignore Meg when she leaned into him. He tried avoiding her eyes but found he couldn't after all. He was never so weak as when it came to her.

Meg needed Ian to be anything except what he seemed at the moment—evasive and cool, even toward her. Did he think this security business would give them enough time to get successfully away before the Pembertons discovered their gold was gone? But how? She only knew she intended to keep close to his side.

She knew one other thing as well, and there was no sense denying it any longer. Ian had been right at the outset. She didn't have the stomach for thievery. Perhaps if she'd been raised at her father's side, as he had, things would be different. The truth was she'd been sick at heart since imagining the results of their crime against the Pembertons. People she'd come to love.

But why did he act just now as if he barely tolerated her touch? Did he know how close she was to breaking down, confessing all? If he knew, surely he should offer her comfort instead of this confident reserve. Perhaps this confrontation between thief and victim was part of the fun for him, but it had ceased being that for Meg. Longer ago than she wanted to admit.

There was no time to ask him anything, not with Jude standing right there and with Nelson's return. Nelson appeared pale again, more so even than earlier. He studied Ian with what looked like a mix of distrust, curiosity, and a touch of anger.

"Mr. Vandermey," he said, "my sister tells me you've just confessed to breaking into our safe. The other night, I presume, when the house was vacant for the picnic."

"That's right. And did she tell you why?"

"Something about a security business." He sent a stare Ian's way that Meg thought possessed nothing short of an accusation. "If that's the case, you might consider returning the missing brick."

Meg's breath caught in her throat. Brick? Had he referred only to one? Had he discovered, as she'd feared would happen in the sunlight shining through those two windows of the office, that the bricks were not the ones that had been in his family for three generations?

She glanced at Ian, who suddenly lost the cocky, devil-may-care look on his face.

"A missing brick?"

"That's right. We're in the process of transferring the gold to a safer location, now that the storage space is rather public knowledge and the safe compromised. In so doing, we discovered that we're one short."

She saw Ian's gaze dart from Nelson to the direction of the office. "Are you sure? Quite sure?"

"I ought to know my family's inventory, Mr. Vandermey. I assure you we are missing one brick. An approximate value of eighty-four hundred dollars."

Ian shifted on his feet, and the grip on his hat seemed to tighten. "I'm afraid there has been some sort of mix-up, Mr. Pemberton. I broke into your safe on Saturday night but removed only an unusual seal with the *P* on it. Worthless, but unique enough to prove what I'd done. It will, in fact, be on its way back to you in a secure and nondescript carton via the postman, along with my calling card."

"That's quite a daring feat, Mr. Vandermey," Nelson said.

Ian didn't look offended by the disdain in Nelson's voice. "I assume you discovered the breach . . . yesterday or this morning?"

"Last night, actually."

"And is it possible anyone else might have had access to the safe—besides myself, of course, and yourself—after you checked on it?"

"No. I spent the night in the office, and it's been guarded throughout the day."

"Although," Claire said, "just before you left to transfer the gold, Nelson, the office was empty. Aren't the two men who'd been guarding it upstairs, searching Meg's room?"

"Yes, but we were all standing here. No one else could have had access to the room without our seeing it. We were standing right here before the front door."

"I hate to ask this yet again, Mr. Pemberton," Ian said, "but when you first noticed the safe had been compromised, did you count the bricks?"

"No, I did not. But just now when we went to move them I did, and we're one short."

"And it's not possible that it's still there, just out of place?"

"I searched. It isn't to be found."

Ian appeared more than a little uncomfortable. "Well, it's not my finest moment as a security expert, I admit, but I'm afraid I have no explanation. I do not have the brick, Mr. Pemberton."

Nelson looked immediately to Meg.

"Nor I!"

Just then the two men who had been sent to Meg's room with the detective came down the stairs. The detective, in the lead, shook his head.

"You found nothing?" Nelson asked. "Nothing at all?"

"That's right. No sign of the missing seal."

"I'm afraid that's not all that's missing, Detective," Nelson said. "One of the bricks was stolen as well."

The detective frowned, then looked from Nelson to Meg and back again. "I suppose that means you'll be pressing charges after all."

"Yes, but not against Meg," Claire said. "This man has admitted to breaking into the safe."

The detective assessed Ian. "And you are?"

Ian introduced himself, although Meg's head was spinning so fast she could barely hear anything until Ian said her name.

"Miss Davenport had nothing to do with this. I did, however, extract information from her, information she unknowingly provided. I finagled an invitation through her to this home and compromised the room on my own. My goal was merely to ignite a reputation for security services on this famous avenue, but somewhere along the way the plan went awry if one of the bricks isn't there."

"Until that brick shows up, Mr. Vandermey," Nelson said, "you will be responsible for its absence."

"So you'll allow me to arrest this man?" the detective asked. "But not the girl? Even though a good thorough questioning of her, too, might bring in more information about all of this?"

"Oh no, Nelson!" Claire said, nearing Meg to put an arm about her shoulder. "I'm sure Meg is innocent."

Nelson looked to be considering something before speaking. "This is a most unusual case. It's more than a little odd that only one brick should be missing."

"Exactly!" Ian said. "If I *were* a thief, I can tell you I wouldn't have stopped at one. And I say this again: Miss Davenport had nothing more to do with my activity than to be naively used."

"Nonetheless, one brick was a hefty sum to run off with for a single night's work." The detective took Ian's arm. "You'll be coming with me, sir."

Meg watched the detective march Ian outside to a waiting police wagon. Complete with bars, like a cage to house an animal in the Central Park menagerie.

Ian never even looked back at her.

Ian threw himself onto the bench that ran along the inside of the patrol wagon. Blast it all, where was that missing brick?

He thwacked his forehead.

Pubjug.

It *must* have been him. He'd been the only one with the opportunity when Ian left him to apply the putty to the safe. Ian himself had been so eager to flee temptation that he hadn't thought what it must have done to Pubjug. The man had been a thief far longer than Ian had been!

He'd never felt like such an idiot. Despite the feeling of betrayal—for a single brick!—Ian couldn't blame Pubjug. It was Ian's own fault for subjecting the man to such irresistible bait.

Staring at the bars surrounding him—the first time he'd ever had to surrender his freedom—Ian tried shaking away his anger.

An arrest wasn't unexpected, was it, sooner or later? The only surprise was that Vandermey had come to this. Ian Vandermey was innocent as a lamb, but if they learned even half the things Ian Maguire had done, he might be forced to pay his debt to society.

Maybe that was what God had in mind.

35

Don't let nobody tell you bein' a thief ain't hard work. It's hard, all right, and not without plenty a risks, too. Still, it's better'n workin' for somebody else. I don't like nobody tellin' me what to do with my time, see?

BILLY "MOOSEFACE" BUSHNELL
Incarcerated for selling stolen goods
Code of Thieves

MEG WANTED NOTHING MORE than to run to her room and let out the tears burning the rims of her eyes. Yet what would she find up there? She was sure each one of her personal articles had been manhandled by the New York police.

She looked at Claire, who still had her arm around Meg. Meg could barely withstand Claire's sympathetic, guileless gaze.

"I'm so sorry you were fooled by him, Meg," Claire whispered. "He's a handsome rogue, but you're well rid of him."

"I—I'm so confused!" Meg admitted, though she could not explain why.

"I don't doubt you are," Nelson said. "No one likes to be used in such a devious way."

That was enough to nearly break her. Meg stepped back and the tears began to fall. "But that's what I've done to you!"

Then she ran up the stairs, the coward she was, knowing she should have been carted off in that awful cage along with Ian.

No longer caring what she would face in her room, Meg didn't stop until she reached her door.

"Meg!"

Evie's unexpected voice sounded from the other end of the hallway. She'd just emerged from the aviary and stared at Meg with wide, nervous eyes, looking surprised to see her.

"I'm not feeling very well, Evie," Meg managed to say. "Please excuse me."

She opened the door to her room, finding it surprisingly neat in spite of the search, and threw herself on the bed.

Meg refused to leave her room for the rest of the day, politely declining the invitation to lunch. She didn't care if she ever ate again. She deserved far more punishment than simple deprivation.

All afternoon, thoughts of the Pembertons' kindness replayed in her mind: Claire's loyalty, Nelson's disappointment. They didn't deserve to be victims. She'd never once entirely realized that was what she'd doomed them to become all along.

How could she have done what she did? Plotted against such lovely, faith-filled people?

Somehow their faith only made Meg's condition worse. She was sick at heart, sick to her very soul over what she'd helped accomplish. Even if the theft hadn't gone entirely as planned, the Pembertons still had every right to hate her. She hated herself.

Yet the details made no sense, and neither did Ian's attempt to cover it up. There was only one explanation, one that added weight to her already-laden soul. Ian truly had not stolen the gold. If that was true, surely God must be protecting the Pembertons if somehow Ian hadn't gone through with their plan. Thoughts of God Himself working against the theft suddenly made Him far more personal, as though He were against *her* as well. And why shouldn't He be?

There could be no other explanation. Nelson seemed so sure the bricks were all intact, except for the one that was missing. But if Ian had a change of heart, why take only one?

If God did have anything to do with the outcome, she wondered if He'd used that painting. Ian had referred to it at the picnic. What a fitting deterrent, showing the rightful punishment of two thieves. Who could deny it affected everyone who set eyes on it? Even Meg had felt God's presence from it.

In a way she couldn't understand, Meg almost longed to see the painting again. To torture herself. Somehow, though, she knew that painting wasn't meant to represent condemnation, or it wouldn't be drawing her to it even now.

But she didn't have the courage to leave her room, though she knew she must eventually. She must go downstairs, find Claire and Nelson, and confess her involvement. She mustn't let the Pembertons believe her to be innocent, and she must take whatever punishment they—and society—meted out.

When she stood, dizziness assailed her again, but this time it was as much from hunger as worry. She stopped at the mirror and saw circles under her eyes and a gaze that even in her own company darted nervously about. She attempted to make herself look as presentable as possible, then left her room.

The parlor was empty, and so was the nearly finished garden. Awaiting only the new bricks. . . . She swallowed away the thought.

She went to the library and thought it, too, was unoccupied until she spied Evie in one of the corners, reading a book beneath a lamp lit to supplement the fading afternoon light.

Evie looked up but didn't say anything, simply putting one finger over her lips. She pointed toward the office.

Low voices came through the open door.

Meg approached but stopped short of entering. She could decipher only some of the words, about love and truth and guidance and thankfulness and protection, but it did not take long to realize they were spoken in prayer. Peeking inside, she saw Claire, Jude, and Nelson all sitting together, heads bowed, the painting behind them.

Perhaps it was the prayer or the painting or the dregs of her guilt pushing her, but as soon as the voices quieted, Meg found the courage to step inside the room.

"I came to tell all of you the truth," she said softly. "You certainly deserve that much. And I deserve . . . far worse than your prayers."

All three of them stood, but it was Claire who approached. She took Meg's hand and led her to the seat she had vacated. Would she still want to offer such kindness when she knew?

"I'm not as innocent as Ian led you to believe."

Claire still held one of Meg's hands even though Meg had taken her seat. "You couldn't help that he used you."

Meg shook her head, fighting tears she thought spent. "My father was a thief. Like Ian." She heard Claire's gasp as she let Meg go, but instead of looking at any of them, Meg turned to the painting. Unexpectedly, rather than a flood of shame, gratitude filled her. She no longer saw what the thieves had done. She saw only Christ's sacrifice—for her father . . . and for her.

"My father could have been one of them, at Jesus' side." Regret was still there, along with her overpowering gratitude, but in the painting she found the strength to continue. "I didn't know he was a thief. He sent me away when I was a child, too young to have learned the truth about him. I thought he didn't want me with him. I didn't know—" She pressed her fingers to her mouth in a feeble attempt to hold back another sob. "I didn't know he loved me. I didn't believe it the way I do now. He sent me to be raised at Madame Marisse's, to be sheltered from a life of lies and dishonesty." She sniffed again, and Claire produced a handkerchief.

Meg looked up at her friend. "I came here trying to prove to myself that I was my father's daughter. I thought by breaking the rules, by doing as he did, I would prove that he shouldn't have shut me away all those years. That he could have trusted me, could have . . . loved me. But now I know that he did. He wanted me to be free of the kind of life he had, only I didn't believe it until now."

"So you knew Mr. Vandermey planned to breach the safe?" Jude asked.

She nodded. "I told him where to find the key to this office. I told him about the secret cellar."

"But how did you know about it?" Nelson asked.

"I guessed, from the way you appeared in this room when I first admired the painting. Then I snuck down here when all of you were sleeping, until I found the secret latch. That's how my slippers became stained."

"Oh, Meg," Claire whispered.

Meg offered a dispirited smile. "But I'm afraid I don't know where the missing brick is, Claire. I did give all of the information to Ian, and I knew he was going to break in."

"But to take only one makes no sense," Nelson said. "If he was willing to risk so much, why do it for a single brick when even taking only half the gold would have yielded so much more?"

Meg shook her head. "I don't know. A reluctance to see me get into very much trouble, perhaps. He didn't want me to follow in my father's footsteps, not from the start. Ian was very loyal to my father." She couldn't say more, that he'd tried protecting her because of feelings he harbored for her. Meg didn't know if he had any.

"But a theft is a theft. If he wanted to spare you from harm, why even take one?"

"Perhaps he couldn't help himself. He's a thief and a gambler. He came because I knew Claire from school and because I offered a way to your gold." Then she added, although she knew it wasn't enough, "I'm so very, very sorry."

"Oh, Meg," Claire repeated, taking the seat beside Meg that Jude had left free when he stood. But it wasn't judgment in her voice; she sounded sad and disappointed. Meg wasn't sure which was harder to withstand.

"Then you ought to be in jail along with Mr. Vandermey!"

Those words came from behind Claire—from Evie, who must have been listening at the door.

"Now, Evie," Nelson said calmly, "let's not get carried away."

"She didn't do the actual stealing," Claire said.

"But she made it possible for him to do it! And as Nelson and Claire have so often reminded *me*," Evie said, "intentions are part of the crime. I for one don't want to offer grace or mercy or even justice. I want revenge!"

Meg might have thought it amusing, or at least appropriate, that of all people Evie should demand such a thing. But she hadn't the peace of mind to feel anything but deserving of every bit of wrath any Pemberton cared to issue.

Nelson was the first to shush his sister, followed by Claire.

"Revenge, as we've always said," Nelson told her, "is the sinner's response to being wronged."

"And you know that, Evie," Claire added.

"You can't be the judge this time, Nelson," Evie insisted. "I'm going to the police if you won't."

"You'll do no such thing." Claire stood and grabbed Evie's arm. "The fact remains Meg did not take the brick, and as you can see, she isn't exactly dancing with happiness over what she's done. We must consider all of the facts, and that includes everything about her father. I suspect she was trying not only to connect with his memory, but with Ian himself." She looked at Meg.

Meg nodded again, every bit as miserable as she'd been a

moment ago. She loved a thief, one who was in jail. There was no future for her, none at all. She might as well be in jail beside him.

"I certainly cannot tell someone to stop loving another," Claire said, sending a quick smile Jude's way, "but, Meg, he's clearly not good for you. You see that, don't you?"

"I know that I should see it that way. I hoped . . . oh, I don't know what I hoped. I know after this I never want to be involved in anything remotely illegal, and unless he's changed his ways, I don't see how I could ever . . . love him."

"Meg, listen to me," Nelson said. "I'll talk to him and find out his side of this story. There must be a reason he stole only the single brick. Perhaps he meant to be honest from now on and start that business he talked about. Someone with his history would have a unique perspective on how to prevent burglaries."

"Nelson might be right," Claire said. "Ian didn't want you to get into any trouble. That must mean he cares."

Meg sniffed again. "It's inconceivable to me that you should be standing here trying to comfort me, after what I've done."

Evie crossed her arms. "Don't think I have any part in it." She stomped from the room, back into the library.

"I'll go to the jail and speak to him right away," Nelson said. "I planned to do so at any rate, but I won't put it off, not even until tomorrow."

Then he, too, left the room, by way of the door that led to the foyer.

Claire smiled at Meg. "Heaven knows I'm far from perfect, but I've learned offering grace brings peace. And I do offer you that, Meg. Grace. Just so you know."

When Meg burst into tears, Claire returned to her side, and she and Meg clung to one another. Never before had Meg believed God loved her, not until this moment when He'd sent someone so precious to show her that His grace went beyond mercy.

Ian leaned back on the cot, though he was convinced a comfortable spot was not to be found. He'd been in the cell less than an hour, the first two hours of his stay having been spent waiting for, then being interrogated by, the police detective and another officer Ian hadn't met before. He told them everything he did at the Pemberton mansion, leaving out Pubjug's name entirely. He might have betrayed Ian, but Ian was no snitch.

In the hours since he arrived, he'd been thankful for only one thing: in here, he was safe from Brewster's revenge. Not that he'd be safe for long, not if he found the courage to admit who he was, how he'd evaded arrest despite his many crimes in the past.

The damp permeated the dark hallways and narrow cells, and straw on the floor did little to absorb either the dank or the stench.

No wonder they called this the Tombs.

"Vandermey!" The bulky guard, easily twice as wide as Ian himself, rattled his keys before fitting one into the lock on Ian's bars. "Visitor. Come with me."

Ian had trouble following the pace set by the guard, hampered by the shackles on his ankles. Perhaps humiliation was part of the punishment, since Ian felt like a toddling child behind him. And for what? Who could be visiting him, anyway? Common sense told him it couldn't be Meg, and Ian didn't care to see anyone else.

To Ian's surprise, it was Nelson Pemberton.

The visiting room was starkly lit with gas lamps. Narrow tables formed rows, and this late in the afternoon all were empty. Ian had heard someone say visiting hours had ended, but somehow he wasn't surprised they'd bent the rules for a lawyer of Pemberton's status.

Ian sat, letting the manacles he wore around his wrists clank on the marred wooden table between them. "I'm surprised to see you."

"Are you? Don't you imagine I'm having a hard time figuring you out? Why steal only one brick, for example. Why, in fact, come back to my home at all, after the deed was done. You must have known that security business story was useless once the missing brick was discovered. Were you just revisiting the scene of the crime?"

Ian didn't answer.

"And another question," Nelson said quietly. "Why bother to steal the seal?"

"Isn't it obvious? Have you any idea how many cons a thief can concoct with a seal as well known in banking as yours?"

"But only until the theft was discovered. Now that I know about it, the seal is worthless. We'll issue a new seal and notify our holding managers not to honor anything with the old one. It doesn't make sense that you should return to my home today." Nelson paused yet again, eventually shaking his head at whatever thoughts he had. "My sister said you admitted to the break-in only after she told you Meg was under suspicion. If you truly hoped that security business story would work, then why wouldn't you have come to us immediately? The morning after the break-in, for example?"

"I'm afraid I don't have an answer for any of that."

"Were you working alone—other than with Meg, of course?"

"I'd hardly call Meg a partner."

Pemberton's gaze was a bit too intense for Ian's comfort, and he began to wonder why the man limited his services as a lawyer to banks. He'd make an effective criminal prosecutor.

"It seems to me you're protecting her as much as yourself."

This wasn't going as well as Ian had hoped. "Look, when I knew there was real trouble, I pulled out the same old con I've used before, about the security business." He sneered. "Even rats like to keep their head above water when everything around them is sinking. Whatever protection I offered was for myself. Meg wasn't involved."

Pemberton shook his head. "She told us the truth. She admitted she supplied you with the whereabouts of the key, the location of the latch, the safe, everything. I'd call that something more than someone you negligibly used."

Ian shifted in his seat and the chains rattled again. "All right, I used her blatantly. But it was all my doing. I took advantage of her when her father died. I made her think she could be just like him, to get the information I needed."

"Good grief, man, have you no shame at all? To use a woman floundering after the death of a loved one?"

Ian sent the man a cynical smile. He must use this opportunity to accomplish what he'd been unable to finish earlier. To send Meg to a better future. "I'm a thief and a liar. What else would you expect, except that I mistreat women, too?"

"So now you admit to having stolen the brick?"

He shrugged.

"And you don't care that Meg might have gotten into considerable trouble had she not become so dear to my sister and me?"

"That's why I took only one of the bricks," he said. "I could have taken more—I wanted to take them all—but I have a certain amount of loyalty to her father's memory, so I restrained myself."

"Loyalty to her father? Not to her?" He appeared less confused but more irritated with Ian than ever. "If you return the brick, I'll see that any charges against you are dropped. You'll be a free man in no time."

Ian shrugged. "There are only two things wrong with that idea. One, I really am a thief. And two, I have no idea where the brick is."

"But if you stole it—"

Ian had been about to pound his fist on the table, but the clatter of the chains proved satisfying enough. "I don't have it!"

Nelson studied Ian for a long moment. "You may be a thief and a liar, but even your lies don't add up correctly. I'd like to know why."

Ian leaned forward, never more earnest in his life. "Keep your charges against me; I don't care. Go back to Meg Davenport, Pemberton, and tell her whatever you want about what a rat I am. She's well rid of me, wouldn't you say?"

"Yes, I would. I have little left to say to you, except to tell you one day you'll face a Judge far more fair than any you'll find here on earth. Think about that day, sir, and see if you don't mend your ways."

"Then why don't you pray for me?"

Ian had intended the request to sound as sarcastic as the man he meant to portray. But he was afraid a touch of sincerity seeped into the question—because prayers spoken by this man, whose faith seemed so like Ian's father's, were exactly what Ian desired.

He stood with a shove to the chair he'd been sitting on, leaving as quickly and steadily as the iron around his ankles allowed.

Meg stood eagerly when Nelson arrived in the parlor. It was already dark outside. Although he hadn't been gone long, the minutes had ticked slowly, even with Claire and Jude trying to make the best of it.

The moment she saw Nelson's face, Meg knew she wouldn't welcome his news.

Nelson refused an offer of coffee from Claire.

"You can say it, Nelson," Meg said. "Whatever it is that's making you frown."

He sat on the settee beside her, taking her hand gently. "He confessed to taking the brick and that he's every bit the scoundrel he seemed to be. He admitted his security company idea was some sort of scheme."

Meg nodded, unable to look at him or anyone else in the room. "I knew that it was. I knew he was a thief."

"He said that he used you, though why he only took one of the bricks remains a mystery. Something about loyalty to your father's memory and not wanting you to get into too much trouble."

"He's not worthy of you, Meg," Claire said, "but at least he cared that much."

Nelson shook his head. "I'm afraid he made a point to say he restrained himself out of respect for Meg's father, not for Meg." He patted her hand. "You're well rid of him."

Meg nodded, feeling more tears prick at her eyelids. "I'm sure you're right. If you'll excuse me . . . I . . . I'm very tired."

Then she found her way to her room, where she once again burst into tears.

36

If a young lady has mistakenly offered her tender affection to a man who, upon closer acquaintance, proves himself to be a boor, she may quietly withdraw herself from his attention. It is better to learn this before marriage than after, when it is too late.

Madame Marisse's Handbook for Young Ladies

MEG DID NOT LEAVE her room until the following morning, well after the meetings and breakfast. How she'd longed to go to the parlor to pray with Nelson and the rest! But knowing the depth of deserved loyalty from each and every person in the Pembertons' employ would surely make them hate her all the more, she stayed hidden in her room, where she prayed alone. She begged God's forgiveness again, though in her heart she knew she already had it, and she wept once more with gratitude. Finally she asked direction and guidance.

She knew she must leave the Pemberton household, but she wasn't sure where to go.

She'd always intended to go to Ian's home on the Hudson. Had all gone according to their misguided plan, they would have met there and continued as partners. But the more she pondered what Ian had done, how ignorant he'd kept her, the more she realized one thing: he'd *never* wanted to be her partner, not even when he'd pretended he did.

She must find a new life, one without schools or thieves or high society. If only she knew what that new life should be.

Kate was likely the only person on earth who might welcome her company, especially if Meg confessed to her what had become so clear: not only had Meg's earthly father loved her, but so did her heavenly one.

She went to the stairs, intent on looking for Claire. She would talk to her about the decision to join Kate if she was still in the city, and to travel with her. Although it might mean unveiling yet another liar. . . .

A servant was just leaving the parlor but stopped at the foot of the stairs when she caught sight of Meg descending.

"A visitor for you, Miss Davenport. In the parlor."

Her first thought went to Ian, but she knew it couldn't be him. Kate? Had she known about Ian's plan, that it would leave Meg without him? Perhaps she'd come to pack Meg's bags. This time, Meg might even help her.

Instead, she found Geoffrey Mason. He stood at the window, his back to her.

"Geoffrey, so you've returned from the country."

He rotated to face her, then closed the gap between them with a few quick steps. "I've heard what happened. We expected to come home to servants buzzing about a picnic they felt deprived of, but instead they cried tales of police carts and missing gold. I'm so sorry, Meg."

She eyed him curiously. "You're sorry? For what *I've* done?"

He took one of her hands. "You've done? But they said it was Vandermey who was arrested. Just because you introduced him to the Pembertons doesn't make you guilty of anything at all."

She pulled her hand away, shaking her head, turning from him. "No, Geoffrey. You've always been honest with me, and for once let me return the favor. I came here under false pretenses. My father was

MAUREEN LANG

a thief. I didn't know it, of course, but when I learned the truth, I thought I could prove I was just like him. That I could have fit into his world, if only he had let me. And so I volunteered to make the Pembertons victims. I was wrong about so many things. Not only in doing what I've done, but also in believing myself fit to live as he did."

Geoffrey stepped around her, putting a gentle hand beneath her chin so that she had no choice but to look up at him. "If anything, Vandermey must have taken advantage of you, misled you."

She gently pushed his hand away. "Do you honestly think me naive and featherbrained as well? That I would have allowed myself to be so misled?"

"Then you must have misled yourself. I cannot believe you capable of malicious intent. I won't."

"Then you don't know me because that's exactly what I did. I may not have known how much gold the Pembertons possessed, but I was willing to allow someone else to take it from them. Illegally, unfairly, and yes, maliciously."

Her voice crumbled on the last few words, filled once again with remorse. Perhaps she'd been better off hating her father rather than trying to be like him. But she knew that was wrong, too.

Even as she wanted to refuse allowance of any more tears, they appeared anyway. Geoffrey took her into his arms.

"Someone as coldhearted as you claim to be wouldn't be standing here this way," he whispered. "I know you well enough to believe there is true goodness in you, Meg. Enough so that I hope you'll agree to marry me. Your tears prove you don't fit into the world you think your father would have provided. But you do fit into mine. This summer held evidence enough of that."

"Oh, Geoffrey," she said quietly. Sadly. Perhaps this man before her was exactly the kind her father would have chosen for her. Even Ian had said so. But the choice was Meg's, not either of theirs. And as fond as she was of Geoffrey, she did not love him.

"That wasn't exactly the kind of sigh attached to my name I'd hoped for, but I'm willing to be patient."

Meg wouldn't let him wait for something that could not be. She didn't know what her future held, but she would not agree to marry someone only because it was the best of her few unwanted choices.

"Geoffrey!"

Meg had no chance to voice her refusal. Mrs. Mason's call for her son preceded her appearance only by seconds—and close on her heels was Evie, a look of glee sparkling in her eyes.

Geoffrey dropped his arms from around Meg, and they both faced his mother.

"Geoffrey, you are to come home this instant." Mrs. Mason stopped at the parlor entry. Her hair was not quite coiffed, and she wasn't wearing any gloves. "I'm terribly sorry, Miss Davenport," she added, her tone hard enough to reveal a lack of sincerity in the sentiment, "but certain information has just been revealed to me, suggesting you might not be all you've presented yourself to be."

Meg glanced at Evie again before speaking to Mrs. Mason. "Yes, I'm afraid whatever you've heard is true."

"Geoffrey, you'll come home with me. Now."

"No, Mother. I was just waiting for Miss Davenport's answer. I've asked her to marry me."

Dread reached both Mrs. Mason and Evie at the same time.

"But, Geoffrey!" Evie said. "Don't you understand? She's a fraud. She came here to help a thief!"

"A thief who is entirely responsible for all of this trouble, so what harm has Meg done?"

"But she helped him from the start!" Evie insisted. "That makes her a thief too."

Mrs. Mason took another step closer to her son. "The degree to which she was involved hardly matters. She was associated with *criminals*, Geoffrey. She is a liar and a fraud. Do you know what everyone will say this fall? Oh, what a laugh they'll have over the summer antics of those unfortunate enough to have stayed in the city. All fooled by nothing more than an actress!"

"She was as much a victim as any of us, Mother. Persuaded by the wrong man."

"Geoffrey," his mother said with such steel in the single word no one else dared speak, "if you disobey me in this, your father and I will write you out of our will. You've been foolish enough to put off the rest of your schooling. You won't go far without a penny to your name."

"Now, Mother, you don't mean that." He might have meant to issue the words forcefully, but even to Meg there was something lacking. Not in volume, but in conviction. She could tell this was not the first time he'd feared his mother.

"I most certainly do mean every word I've said. I'll not have people snickering behind my back over the choice you made for a wife. Choose carefully because I will not change my mind, and your father will most certainly agree with me. We'll leave everything we have to charity rather than to you. At least our name will be attached to something worthwhile rather than an ungrateful offspring and a woman who creates scandal."

Meg saw on Geoffrey's face that he did indeed believe his mother's words. Still, he hesitated. He looked at Meg, then at his mother.

"Of course you can't go through with marrying *her*," Evie said. "It would mean turning your back on everything! On Nomi! Your father! Me and Pindar!"

"I believe I do have to think this over," he said quietly. Then he turned back to Meg, allowing his gaze to meet hers for a fleeting moment. "I'm terribly, terribly sorry, Miss Davenport. I hope you'll find it in your heart to forgive me."

In spite of his mother's fierce scowl, Meg brushed the side of Geoffrey's face. "There is nothing to forgive, Geoffrey. You've made the right decision."

She watched him walk quietly from the room, his mother following with her chin held high, leaving Meg alone with Evie.

The look of triumph Meg expected to see on the girl was strangely absent. There was even a glimmer of guilt there, if Meg wasn't mistaken.

Perhaps there was hope for her yet.

37

Every time I get caught, it's the same old thing: they ask me questions I don't want to answer. Why don't they just show me to my cell and forget the wasted interrogation?

MAISIE "MAD DOLL" McCREADY

Code of Thieves

MEG WENT TO the stairway, intent on staying in her room until Claire returned from her errand. What Evie had done might be understandable, even justified—hadn't she only wanted to spare Geoffrey from Meg's dishonest clutches?—but facing her wasn't getting any easier.

Before Meg went very far, the front door swung open and Claire called to her.

"Meg! I just saw Mrs. Mason fairly pushing Geoffrey back home. Was he here?"

Meg turned but did not descend the few stairs she'd mounted. Jude had come in beside Claire and was just removing his hat after setting aside a package and his walking stick.

"He was here, but he . . . left."

"He made a visit so early in the day? It's barely past noon!"

Though Meg did not look at Evie, she saw the girl emerge from the parlor and slink by on the stairs, evidently on the way to her own room. "The Masons heard about the theft."

Claire climbed two of the bottom stairs, her eye on her sister. "They couldn't have arrived home any sooner than last night! Did Evie tell them?"

"It doesn't matter," Meg said, grabbing Claire's hand even as Claire hoisted her skirt as if to march up the remaining stairs in Evie's wake. "The news was bound to travel anyway. Everyone on the block saw all of the police activity."

"That's no excuse!" Claire said. "She didn't have to help speed the news along."

Meg cast an imploring look at Jude, who stood uncertainly at the foot of the stairs.

"Please come with me, Jude," Meg said when Claire broke free. "You have such a calming effect on Claire. I don't deserve her defense and I don't want to be the cause of an argument."

It took no more than a moment for Jude to sprint up the stairs along with Meg. They were in time to see Claire emerge from Evie's bedroom, leaving the door ajar, then burst into the aviary.

"Evie!"

Only the squawk of several birds answered.

Evie stood near Pindar's cage, but the bird wasn't in it. He was on his favorite perch, Evie's shoulder.

"You will apologize this instant for causing trouble between Meg and the Masons," Claire demanded.

"I didn't! She did that herself." She stroked the belly of the bird. "I only made sure they knew about details their own staff couldn't provide just yet."

Meg stepped closer to Claire, who had stopped not two feet from Evie. "She's right, Claire. The Masons would have refused all contact with me once they learned the truth—learning what my father did would have been enough, let alone the rest."

"No one needed to know any of that. She made matters worse!" Claire's anger wasn't cooled, either by Meg or by Jude's presence. "We've never encouraged gossip, and she's done that with pure and selfish malice, in hopes of ending Geoffrey's interest in Meg."

"Claire," Jude said gently, "Evie might have wronged Meg, but it's Meg's choice to be angry or not, isn't it? Not yours?"

"But Geoffrey was Meg's best chance at happiness!"

"No, he wasn't!" Evie said, so loudly that the bird on her shoulder fluttered his considerable wings. One of them hit the edge of his cage, sending it swinging.

"Put that awful bird in its cage, Evie," Claire said.

"No, I won't." Evie took a step backward, but she must have lost her balance from the bird fairly bouncing on her arm. She nearly fell, catching herself on the bar that held Pindar's home.

"Another prank," Pindar said. "Pretty bird. A prank."

Then he hopped from Evie onto the top of his enclosure.

"No, Pindar!"

Evie reached for the bird, but as she did, the entire metal structure crashed to the floor, the racket sending off immediate cackles and screeches from a dozen other creatures in various cages only half-visible in the verdant room.

Flapping nearly two feet of wing, Pindar refused to go down with his cage. He latched on to Evie with his beak. First he used her sleeve to pull himself upward to her braid, effectively swinging toward his open stand, which sat close to the window and well away from the fallen hardware.

With a cry and a hand to her pulled hair, Evie seemed relieved to be free of the large bird. Then she turned and flew at her sister, stopping almost nose to nose. "See what you've done! Go away, all of you!"

"How is this my fault?" Claire demanded. "I didn't know the

cage was so precarious. We'll have someone fix it or bring in something bigger. Not that Pindar is ever *in* it."

"Leave here!" Evie shrieked like one of her birds, her color high, eyes filled with anger. The birds around her refused to be quieted, joining in the pandemonium. "All of you! This is my place, and I don't want any of you in it."

"Just a minute now," Jude said, bending over the fallen mess. "Here's the reason the cage fell, Claire. It was holding weight it was never meant to hold—not along with the bird, at any rate."

"No!"

Despite Evie's cry, Jude opened the cage door and reached past old newsprint near the bottom. Then, twisting his wrist to hold it just so, he withdrew a shiny, rectangular object stamped with an embellished letter *P*.

A brick of gold.

38

When a young lady feels she has been wronged or insulted
by a peer, she must first consider the wisest of advice before
contemplating her reaction: do unto others as you would have
them do unto you.

Madame Marisse's Handbook for Young Ladies

"I WAS GOING to return it!"

Evie pulled her hands close to her chest while sliding behind
Pindar, her wide-eyed gaze darting between her sister and Meg. The
bird prattled again about a prank, in between loud French words.

"*You* took the gold?" Meg asked.

"I only moved it! It's mine anyway." She stole a glance toward
Claire. "Partly."

"But why? And when?"

Evie's breathing had increased rapidly, but even as her gaze still
bounced between Meg and Claire, she slowly regained control
when neither came any closer. Her hands dropped to her sides. Her
shoulders rounded and her head hung low. She came away from
Pindar's perch as if exhausted, then plodded to the nearby chair.
Once seated, she covered her face and burst into tears.

Claire lunged at her, grabbing one of her sister's wrists. "Do
you know how much trouble you've caused this time, Evie? We had
the *police* here! We told them we'd been robbed when we hadn't!"

Meg stepped closer, taking the chair next to Evie's, the same one she'd sat upon not long after she arrived, when she'd promised no interest in Geoffrey. She gently touched the grip Claire had on her sister. The moment the two separated, Evie covered her face once again.

"She wasn't willing to show you any mercy, Meg," Claire reminded her. "She deserves to be punished."

Meg looked at Claire, feeling the first smile in days cross her face. One of affection and admiration, but also sympathy. "Oh, Claire, you're so eager to be kind to me but just as eager to judge your sister. Why is that, when the two of us are so much alike, Evie and I?"

Evie slowly uncovered her eyes to look at Meg.

"We're both passionate about what we want," Meg told her. "And clever but not very wise, I'm afraid. We made choices and never considered consequences."

"Are you going . . . to give me consequences?"

Meg shook her head.

Evie clearly did not believe her. "But when it was my turn against you, I chose revenge."

Meg put a hand on one of Evie's shoulders. "Maybe when you're older, you'll be able to extend a little mercy to someone else because of what you've done. Because you'll remember what you're feeling right now."

Claire, still frowning, tapped one foot. "Just why did you take that brick, Evie? And when?"

Evie sat up straighter, wiping away the last of her tears. "Yesterday." She glanced Meg's way again, but not for long. "I wanted her to get in trouble for it, but all I heard you and Nelson say was how innocent she was. She didn't get in any trouble at all so long as only that silly seal was missing. So I waited in the library yesterday morning, until I could get to the safe without someone seeing me."

"And made sure something of value *was* taken," Claire finished.

Evie nodded, looking at the floor. "I only wanted to be sure Geoffrey found out she was a thief. That's what she wanted to be, so I made sure everyone knew it. Especially Geoffrey."

"That would have happened without the added intrigue," Meg told her.

The girl looked at Meg, her eyes filled with renewed tears. "No, he didn't lose interest in you at all. His mother just said he couldn't have you and his family at the same time. I thought if he really believed you were a thief, he wouldn't want to love you anymore."

She leaned away, sinking lower into the chair and covering her tearful face. Perhaps Meg should have comforted her, having so recently felt the relief of forgiveness herself. But two thoughts stopped her: doubt that Evie would welcome her touch and knowledge that Ian sat in a cell that very moment—because of Evie.

Nor did Claire offer any consolation.

Jude, holding the brick, turned it over in his palms. "I'll see that Nelson adds this to the others." Then he looked at Meg and said, "I'm sure he'll want the charges dropped against Vandermey."

Meg stood. She wanted to feel hopeful, but if the authorities knew anything of Ian's general pursuit of illegal gains, he wasn't likely to be free anytime soon.

None of that changed another important fact: Meg wasn't a suitable partner for a thief.

Not even one she loved.

39

My dear young ladies, I remind you that etiquette must be applied
to each and every situation. However, never use etiquette to judge,
to excuse, or to impress. Most especially, never let such rules
be a replacement for the right and wrong you already know in
your heart.

Madame Marisse's Handbook for Young Ladies

CLAIRE SENT A MESSENGER to Nelson's office and he was home
within the hour, joining Meg and the others in the parlor. Upon
learning the whereabouts of the missing brick, he spared no more
than a regretful glance upward, where Evie had been hiding in the
aviary ever since the discovery.

He then looked at Meg. "We'll let our mother and father
decide what's to be done with Evie this time. But right now I have
a client to see."

"A client?" Meg said.

Claire, standing next to Meg, put an arm about her shoulders.
"If I'm not mistaken, I believe he means Ian."

Nelson smiled, then retrieved the hat he'd carelessly tossed
aside on a nearby chair and left the house once again.

"Maguire!"

Ian looked up from the gruel on his plate. He would welcome any interruption to this meal.

The burly guard pointed a fist with a plump thumb sticking out of one side. "Visitor. Come with me."

Ian followed.

"It's your lawyer," the guard said without looking back at Ian.

That he had one was news to Ian, although he supposed a lawyer would have been appointed to him. He just hadn't expected to have one so soon. When he'd confessed his real name and a list of his crimes, he assumed the city would let him stew awhile before inching toward their version of justice. Although to his knowledge he didn't have a single arrest warrant against him, it wouldn't take long to connect Ian's confessions to evidence of crimes.

But instead of seeing a young, unproven image of inexperience, he once again found Nelson Pemberton. Ian stopped, not even bothering to take a seat when Nelson pulled out the chair on his own side of the table.

"There must be some mistake."

"No, no mistake," Nelson said without looking up. He'd brought with him a satchel, from which he withdrew paper and a pencil. "Sit down, Mr. Ian Maguire. We have a lot of work to do."

Ian took a step forward. "So you know who I am. And you want to help me?" Though he issued the words like a question, he didn't believe it for a moment. He didn't even allow himself to hope it was true. What was the point, anyway? One of his potential victims defending him in court might make for sensational news—the kind Fifth Avenue normally sought to avoid—but it wasn't likely to make a difference in the end. Ian was guilty, and soon everybody would know it. He was willing to pay the price; it was the right thing to do.

There was only one court that should matter to Ian now. If he could just keep his mind on that one, maybe he could withstand the time he'd have to wait for it.

"Before I arrived, I spoke to one of the officers who said you made a confession," Nelson was saying. "Of course you'll need to share that with me as well so we can formulate a case just as the prosecution does the same. But I'm hopeful we can avoid court altogether with a nontrial procedure. It means pleading guilty to whatever misdeeds—"

"Which I am." Ian shoved the chair far enough from the table on his side to take a seat, but not to join Nelson, who hovered over papers scribbled with various notes.

Nelson looked up. "I'll need your confession, Ian, to make sure it matches what the authorities will bring against you."

"You mean if I leave anything out—on either end?"

"Mistakes are made every day," Nelson said as if oblivious to the idea that someone might think Ian would intentionally leave something out. Didn't Nelson believe, like so many others did, that lies were hard to keep straight?

"I don't understand," Ian said. "Why are you doing this?"

Nelson set aside the pencil and leaned over the table, staring at Ian in a way he couldn't escape. "Was I mistaken, or did you not sincerely ask me to pray for you yesterday?"

Ian pulled his gaze away. "Anybody can have a moment of weakness in a place like this."

Nelson was still staring, as if he could discern Ian's thoughts despite his bravado. "Sometimes prayer changes the one who's praying as much as the one being prayed for."

"I don't think God needs to do much to change you, Pemberton. From all accounts, you're a saint."

"Hardly. I was ready to leave you in here to rot, even though I still had doubts. Now let's get back to my question. Was it a sincere request when you asked me to pray? Which is the act? Your words now or your request yesterday?"

Ian knew this was a moment as powerful as the one when he'd stood in front of this man's gold. Steal it, and stay the same thief he'd been since leaving that sugar factory so long ago. Refrain, and prove he was capable of loving Meg more than himself. He knew he hadn't conquered that moment on his own power or even through his love for Meg.

Nor would he conquer this moment on his own. For once and for all, he needed to set aside his resentment that God had left him behind when He'd taken his family. He needed to let go of his pride and declare his faith publicly. It would be a declaration that could change his life even more than it already had.

Pulling his chair closer to the table, Ian looked again at Nelson's powerful stare. "The truth is, Pemberton, I might as well be one of those two thieves hung next to Christ, like in the picture you have in your home. But I want to be the one looking at Him, not the one who turned away. If it wasn't too late for him, I'm hoping it's not too late for me."

Nelson issued a quick but nonetheless pleased nod, then stuck his hands once again inside his case.

Evidently finding what he sought, Nelson smiled and pulled out a leather-bound book. "That's good to hear. Now let's get to work on your defense. This city has been known to extend mercy in the right courts, and I intend to find one. Let's start with why you broke into my safe at all, if you didn't intend stealing anything. And tell me where my father's seal is at this moment."

Telling the truth wasn't nearly as hard as Ian thought it would be. Not even when he confessed what he'd done with the seal—perpetrated a fraud against another criminal—and where Nelson could find it now.

It was that part of Ian's confession which turned their conversation in a direction he never thought it would go. Somehow Ian suspected such a test might be condoned . . . by the Author of the Bible Ian took back to his cell.

There was no sign of Nelson that entire day. Meg spent much of her time in the library, trying to take her mind off of what was happening to Ian. Would Nelson really defend him? A thief who might be innocent in one case but guilty in so many others? That would go against everything Nelson had stood for so far. Why would he do it?

Meg might not be able to figure out why, but she couldn't help filling her brand-new prayers with pleas for Ian. Not only for protection in whatever place of detention they kept him, but for him to turn from his ways. If he did that, perhaps . . .

It was no use hoping, though such thoughts refused to be ignored.

Finally an unusual and uninvited evening visitor stole Meg's attention. Kate arrived, her face awash with both hope and concern.

"My dear, dear girl," she said with an embrace—and her accent entirely absent, even though Claire stood at Meg's side. "I had no idea things would take such a turn for Ian when he did the right thing for once! After he told me what he was planning, I waited for either one of you to come and give me the good news together. I didn't know he'd been arrested until this morning!"

Meg pulled herself away. "You'd be justified in saying 'I told you so' because you were right all along, about everything. I know that now."

Tears sparkled in Kate's golden eyes. "You've no idea how blessed I am to hear it!"

Meg took one of Claire's hands along with one of Kate's. "I'm afraid we have yet another confession, Claire."

"You're not Lady Weathersfield?" Claire asked. When Kate shook her head, Claire laughed. "Oh! If only Mrs. Mason were here, to realize she'd been tricked as well."

Meg knew she ought not have laughed, but another visit from Mrs. Mason that afternoon had pushed her already-fraught nerves too far. The neighbor had arrived to apologize for not fulfilling her duty as surrogate parent, following quickly with a demand to know why Meg was still under the Pemberton roof. It was obvious no household in New York would welcome her now. Claire had quickly shown the woman to the door, afterward assuring Meg that she welcomed any changes to the fall season. In fact, Claire would be forever grateful if obligations to attend every party of the season disappeared.

Claire showed no hesitation now about inviting Kate into the parlor, waving away Kate's apologies for deceiving her.

Kate took a seat beside Meg. "You know, don't you, darling, that you're welcome to come home with me? I confess the only talent I've cultivated nearly all my life has been duping generous people, but all of that is far and well behind me. As it turns out, my French flats are providing me with more than enough income, and we can live there comfortably without worry."

"Oh, Kate, that's so very generous of you. I only wish I could accept."

Kate's brows rose. "You had something else in mind?"

Meg nodded, seeing both Claire and Kate looking at her curiously. "I have only one asset. My education. I intend using it to teach others." She looked down at her hands. "Not in New York, of course. I must go where my reputation will not follow."

Claire leaned forward, excitement bursting through her bright eyes and wide smile. "Chicago is far from what happened here, Meg. I would love to have a friend there with me."

Meg reached for her friend's hand and squeezed it. "Oh, Claire, you are ever generous."

"But New York is a big city!" Kate protested. "Surely you can teach here?"

Meg shook her head. "I know you'll understand better than anyone that memories can be precious and painful all at once. I think . . . I may have to leave New York if Ian . . ." She stopped because she knew Kate would never approve of her love for him. Not while she feared the two of them together would be as unhealthy a match as Kate had been with Meg's father. "We wait, even now, for Nelson to bring news of him. I know he's likely to be . . . away . . . for some time, but I can't help loving him. I don't think there could ever be another man for me."

"Yes," Kate said, though her face had not taken on the censure Meg expected. Rather she looked as hopeful as Claire had a moment ago. "He might have begun protecting you for your father's sake, but I know he's loved you since the day he learned of you. How could he not, the way your father spoke of you?"

"He—he never told me that."

"Oh, Meg, haven't his actions said it well enough? Pubjug told me that Ian ran out of that cellar as if something were chasing him. I know what it was. His fear that the theft might hurt you. He did the right thing out of love for you."

Meg's heart thrummed against her chest, in desperate longing for the words to be true. She'd refused to consider such a thing, believing he'd done everything in revenge against Brewster. But that never had explained why he hadn't stolen the gold for himself.

Yet she knew that until she heard such a confession from Ian himself, she couldn't believe it.

It was nearly midnight by the time Nelson returned. Kate had remained in their company, eager to hear news even though the hour grew late and their conversation dwindled until all three showed traces of drowsiness. Meg was the only one to hear the front door open, but when she stood and called Nelson's name, the other two roused. He'd nearly passed them by, evidently not expecting anyone to have waited until so late into the night.

"Lady Weathersfield!" He looked surprised to see Kate, though pleasantly so.

Kate stood, taking the hand Nelson proffered. "Please, just call me Kate."

"We'll explain all that later," Claire said, addressing his instant confusion. "We want to hear news of Ian—and quickly for Meg's sake, Nelson!"

"He's doing well. Better, I think, than he has in a very long time, from what I gathered through speaking to him. He'll be out on bail by tomorrow."

Meg's heart pounded so painfully that it seemed to demand all of the blood from her head. "Out—do you mean free?"

"We're hoping to avoid a trial in order to end all of this quickly, but until he sees a judge, we won't know what's to happen. In the meantime, I've been given custody."

"I . . . I thank you, Nelson." Meg could barely muster more than a whisper. "Your generosity is beyond compare."

"You might think me as foolish as generous when I share with you what Ian and I have decided to do."

Any trace of fatigue had long since disappeared in Meg, but she saw that curiosity on both Kate's and Claire's faces had rid them of their sleepiness as well.

Nelson turned back toward the foyer. "Come with me, will you?"

Meg followed in step, and so did the other two women. To Meg's surprise Nelson led them to the kitchen and through the service door. He stopped only when he'd descended the few stairs outside and turned back to the house, looking at the bushes on each side of the porch.

To her astonishment, Nelson fairly dove into one of the thorny bushes. A moment later he pulled himself out, holding some sort of object.

When they returned inside, a nightcapped and obviously groggy butler greeted them.

"May I be of any service, sir?"

"No, Deekes. It's a family matter, nothing to concern yourself about."

The butler followed them from the kitchen, but only as far as his room beneath the stairs. Nelson led Meg and the others through the foyer and into his father's study, turning up the gas lamp on the innermost wall. Afterward he offered a look at what he'd carried inside by unwrapping it on the center of the desk.

The Pemberton seal.

Looking at Meg, he said, "I arrived home the other night before Ian could return it."

"So you do believe he had no intention of stealing from you, then?" Meg asked.

"Yes, that much was obvious when he left everything intact. The interesting fact is, if Ian is right, there is a certain Mr. Brewster who thinks Ian has this seal."

Meg was intrigued. "Something Mr. Brewster wants."

"Exactly. And you're going to hand it over to him."

Ignoring Claire's gasp and Kate's sudden grasp of her arm, Meg smiled. "And why would I do such a thing?"

"Because all he has to do is use it once and I can have him arrested."

"But won't your seal be suspect by the banking industry?"

"The moment I discovered it missing, I started proceedings to have a new seal made, and every note we hold is to be kept aside awaiting new authentication."

"But Brewster must know you would do such a thing," Kate said.

Nelson shook his head. "With Ian in jail and he the only one Brewster thinks knows the whereabouts of the seal, he can be led to believe I think the seal is still safe to use. How can it be used fraudulently, if the one who stole it is safely incarcerated? Any thief would always have known the seal's worth would be short-lived. We only need Brewster to use it once to be guilty as charged."

"But how do I give it to him?"

"You'll say Ian told you where he'd hidden it, but that all he wanted you to do was return it so he can be released, innocent of the charges against him. And this is where you might think me mad, Meg. You must convince Brewster that you chose the wrong partner in Ian and want to work with Brewster instead."

Meg swallowed hard. She'd seen what Brewster did to those who betrayed him. Memories of Ian in the alley, broken and bruised, were still vivid. "Did . . . Ian think of this?"

Nelson shook his head, holding her gaze steady. "After hearing about this Brewster fellow, I was the one who suggested it. As a matter of fact, Ian insisted I keep this to myself. He liked the idea of setting up Mr. Brewster for arrest, but he wanted to be the one to hand over the seal. I disagreed; I believe no one with any sense would fall for it, after what Ian already did to the man. But you won't be in danger. I plan to have men following you to see that you're not harmed, and you'll hand it over to him in as public a place as possible. A restaurant, perhaps."

"I can accompany her," Kate said.

But Nelson shook his head. "No sense risking more than necessary—not only your safety but any opportunity this man might have to interrogate two of you rather than one."

Meg picked up the seal, surprised by its weight. "Of course I'll do it."

Nelson smiled grimly. "It'll have to be first thing in the morning, before Ian is released on bail. It'll have to appear as if you've turned your back on him."

"So . . . I can't even see him?"

"No, not until Brewster uses that seal."

40

A young lady is more blessed to inherit from her parents their
virtue rather than their money.
Madame Marisse's Handbook for Young Ladies

THOUGH THE CARRIAGE came to a smooth stop before the St. Denis
Hotel, Meg's heart still pounded as if in rhythm with the fast gait
of a racing buggy. She waited for the cabbie to open the door and
help her alight, offering him her free hand and using the step he
pulled out onto the curb. In her other hand she carried her reticule,
heavier than usual though it contained only one item. The seal.

The neighborhood was busy enough for late morning, for
which Meg was grateful. Perhaps Jude, who'd insisted on being
one of the men on her trail, would not be readily spotted.

Walking into a hotel unescorted would have been deadly to
Meg's reputation, but as she'd assured Claire that morning, such
a thing hardly mattered anymore. She went directly to the desk
and without a word retrieved from her glove the card she'd held
on to all these weeks from Brewster himself. She handed it to
the clerk.

He barely glanced at it before raising a surprised gaze to Meg.
Then he studied her with a glint in his eye. "You don't look his
type, miss."

It was easy to ice her stare, since it readily claimed some of her nervous energy. Though it was too early in the day to meet in the dining room as Nelson had hoped, she had another idea. "Can you ask Mr. Brewster if he will meet me across the street, at Grace Church?"

He laughed. "You don't know Mr. Brewster, then? He isn't likely to darken the church door."

She pursed her lips. "Then ask him to meet me just outside, on the steps in front of the church. I have something he'll be interested in."

With far more confidence than she felt, she turned away and exited the hotel lobby, dodging carriages and horse-drawn trolleys full of shoppers to cross the street. Once there, she dared glance around. Jude was just outside the hotel, a newspaper in front of him, but she could tell he watched her. Another man was closer, just to the side of the church. She was sure he was no ordinary loafer, though he might be a bored husband waiting for a wife to finish her errands.

She hadn't been there more than a few minutes before a familiar figure crossed the street. But it was not Brewster. It was Jamie, dressed in as showy a jacket as ever, this one the color of an overripe tomato.

"Well, if it ain't Miss Davenport!" he said. "You make the sun pale in the sky."

"I want to see Brewster, Jamie. I have something he wants."

"And what's that?"

She clutched her reticule. "I plan to show only him."

"There some reason you won't come up and share a cup a tea or something? This is a bit unfriendly, standing here on the street."

"You tell him I'm giving him the opportunity to prove himself a friend to me. Until then, I don't trust him any more than I did Ian Maguire."

He folded his arms and grinned, assessing her with what

appeared to be new appreciation. "So you and Maguire had a parting of the ways?"

"That's right. I gave him the opportunity of a lifetime and he threw it away because he didn't think I could be like my father. Well, I'm every bit like my father, and it appears I should have trusted Brewster to believe me because Maguire obviously didn't."

He looked at the purse she held. "What's that you got in there, anyway? Can't be much of that Pemberton gold. Too small."

"It's something better than that. The gold has been dispersed to several banks in the city—the Bank of New York and others. With what I have right here, a banknote can be drawn up to demand the withdrawal of several of those bars. You tell him that and see if he won't come down to these unfriendly streets." How her heart pounded with each word, but her voice didn't give her away.

Jamie unfolded his arms, more serious than ever. He glanced across the street, up to one of the windows. "Here's the way it'll be, little lady. You see that open window on the second floor?"

She did.

"Just inside that curtain is a man with a gun on you right now. He can shoot you dead and before anybody figures out where the bullet came from, he'll be gone. So either give me what you've got there or come on upstairs and give it to Brewster himself. But he ain't coming down here."

The idea of having a gun aimed directly at her dizzied Meg. Never, ever, had she imagined the courage she would have needed to associate with the people her father must have dealt with every day of his life.

"I—I need some assurance that you'll give this to Brewster. How do I know you won't let him down, the way Maguire let me down?"

His brows met in surprised confusion. "You don't double-cross Brewster, Meggie Davenport! You think I'm addlepated?"

"I need to see him, then. So I can be assured he knows I'm giving you something."

Instead of leading her back across the street, somewhere Meg assuredly did not want to go, Jamie saluted toward the open window. A moment later the curtain was brushed aside to reveal Alwinus Brewster. On his face was a friendly smile.

With a puff of his cigar, he waved at her.

She had one more piece of advice for Jamie to feed Brewster—though she hoped her urgency wasn't recognized as the desperation she felt. "You tell him this prize won't be good for long. The Pembertons think Maguire still has it hidden somewhere. If they find out I took it when everyone was so busy counting those gold bricks, they'll make it as worthless as the lead it's made from."

Meg handed over the seal, reticule and all, then turned to walk down the street, hiding herself in the growing number of shoppers filling the walkway.

41

There is no greater tribute a woman may receive than a man's pledge of eternal love.

Madame Marisse's Handbook for Young Ladies

MEG COULD BARELY keep herself from the window, in hopes of seeing Nelson arrive home—this time with Ian at his side. So distracting must her pacing have been that Claire suggested the three of them—Claire, Meg, and Kate, who had stayed the night—move to the garden.

"You've made it so lovely out there, we really ought to enjoy it. Perhaps the air will soothe you."

Although Meg didn't want to go, she knew it was silly to choose one spot to wait over another. The garden was not so much farther from the front door, was it? What did a few seconds matter, anyway, once Ian arrived?

It had taken Alwinus Brewster no more than three hours to employ the Pemberton seal. Like the coward Meg believed him to be, he did not go himself but sent Keys to the Bank of New York, with a fraudulent banknote demanding the withdrawal of three of the famous Pemberton bricks. Once the theft was completed, Keys was arrested before he'd made it out the front door of the bank.

It might have been challenging to indict Brewster as well, having only Meg's assumption that he'd been the true recipient of the seal used to make the withdrawal. But Keys had been so eager to lighten his own sentence that he'd been happy to cast the blame on Brewster. Evidently having awakened the considerable resources of the Pemberton family had intimidated Keys enough to know they were a greater danger to his future than Brewster was.

Now, with Ian free on bail, Meg could barely withstand the wait.

The garden was indeed lovely, with tiers of colorful plants, a nest of exquisitely designed orchid pots, and the prized focal point, a monkey puzzle tree newly imported from as far away as Chile. It was just unusual enough to have become the most fashionable of the exotic fauna in any modern garden. Beside that, flowers had been especially chosen throughout to attract butterflies and their larvae for years to come.

Only after they'd settled did Meg realize the wisdom of Claire's suggestion. The quiet of the garden made it seem as if they were far from any worries, particularly when a butterfly glided in from above. Sunlight touched his purple-and-black wings, and after landing on the tip of a thistle, he fluttered as if knowing he was on display. There wasn't a bee to be seen.

Kate and Claire, obviously intent on helping to keep Meg's worries at bay, asked question after unnecessary question about nearly all the plants and flowers. It was an effective ploy, one Meg cooperated with gratefully.

When at last the door leading to the garden opened behind them, Meg was almost afraid to turn around. What if Nelson stood there alone and they hadn't let Ian go? But a glance at Kate's pleased face gave Meg the courage to look.

Nelson stepped out of the way to let Ian emerge from the house. Before a word was spoken, both Claire and Kate abandoned their spots, joining Nelson to leave Meg alone with Ian.

He stood before her, hat in hand, gaze holding hers transfixed. He wasn't wearing the suit she'd seen him in a few days ago. Rather he wore what looked like something new, a navy frock coat and matching trousers. A tan waistcoat stood out, along with the navy cravat over a stark-white shirt. He sported the look of an honest gentleman.

It seemed as though their first glance went on forever. It wasn't that Meg was at a loss for words. It was that too many came to mind at once.

"I want to know only one thing," she said softly. "Why did you stop yourself from stealing the bricks?"

The relief on his face made her wonder if he'd doubted his welcome. He took a step closer but made no effort to touch her. "I would say I wanted to protect you, but that's only partially true. Until seeing the painting that hid the lever, I wasn't sure I had it in me to do the right thing. With God's help, I did."

Heart hammering in her chest, Meg wished she could see even farther into his eyes. She'd once marveled at how easily she could read him, but at the moment she was too afraid to believe what she saw. The peace she'd thought rose from a job well done, an illegal job . . . she knew now it wasn't that kind of satisfaction at all. It was the kind of peace she herself had experienced; she was sure of it. An honest peace.

He took a step closer so that he was mere inches away. "You deserve better than me, you know. You deserve someone with a long, trustworthy history. Not me."

"Perhaps we're exactly what we need for each other, Ian. Someone who knows what it's like to have been forgiven."

He nodded, a grateful smile touching his lips. "I have much to make up to society for and much to prove to you. But with God's help, I can do it. He's already taught me I could love someone more than money. And I do. I love you, Meggie."

Meg was in his arms the moment he'd uttered her name, knowing that from him she wanted to be called nothing else.

EPILOGUE

These are the kinds of marriage proposals that should rarely be considered:

The first, even from the man a young lady fully intends to marry. However, the lady should never refuse him a third time lest she be considered too difficult to please.

A written proposal, lest a young lady wonder if the man might have wrestled with submitting such a note to the trash before allowing it to be delivered.

Under moonlight, lest the mood of such surroundings be responsible for the question rather than the sincerity of his sentiment.

Upon a full stomach, lest his contentment with life in general fool both the gentleman and the young lady into thinking too quickly ahead. This is particularly true if he believes the young lady planned or prepared any of the dinner.

From a man who has little security to offer.

Madame Marisse's Handbook for Young Ladies

MEG SAT WHERE FEW women of Fifth Avenue ever had, in an anteroom at the courthouse adjoining Tombs Prison. Even here, well away from the cells that housed everything from pickpockets to murderers, she felt the damp from a building that, they said, was sinking into the mire upon which it had been built.

Although Nelson was in the courtroom with Ian, Meg was not alone. On one side sat Kate, and on the other Claire, despite Meg's insistence she not trouble herself by accompanying her to such a place. But Claire would hear no protest, particularly when Jude announced he'd been recruited by Nelson to help in the case. He'd been mysterious about why, but that had made the decision about whether or not Claire would accompany Meg that much easier. Mr. Deekes stood off to the side so the women would not be unescorted.

A good portion of the time the three women waited had been spent in silent but heartfelt prayer on Ian's behalf.

Nelson had been able to arrange the nontrial procedure he'd hoped for. Not so much a miracle, he'd assured her, as the eagerness of negotiators to deal with someone willing to plead guilty. Since there had been no doubt of Ian's plea, the court had been persuaded to avoid the extra time and expense necessary for a jury trial.

The risk came with the judge assigned to Ian's case, but Nelson had assured them this judge was not only fair; he was as immune to corruption as possible in a city like theirs.

Meg had been forewarned about allowing herself any hopes of grace. They would find justice at worst, a touch of mercy at best.

Part of the deal Nelson had been able to procure included Ian's agreement to give up his home and fortune as recompense to those institutions he'd victimized in the past. Because of the sub-dued nature of Ian's crimes, knowing there were no formal charges against Ian and that he'd confessed rather than been coerced into the truth—a rare occasion in this courthouse—Nelson had let Meg dare hope Ian could be spared prison altogether. Instead, they would agree to probation of not less than five years, with the stipulation that Ian would use his knowledge and experience in favor of banks instead of against them. All that was required was a bank willing to trust him, and that, Nelson assured them, he could provide.

At last the door to their small waiting room opened. Nelson came in first but was quickly followed by Jude and finally by Ian. For the barest moment Meg could read none of their faces. Did they bring good news or bad? And yet how could it be bad if Ian himself stood before her?

She rose to her feet, unable to guess what the judge had decided. Was Ian's presence in this wing of the Tombs only a brief reprieve from a cell down one hall or another? Or had he been given probation?

"Mercy won," Ian said, his eyes meeting Meg's, alight. "I'm free—at least, relatively so." He glanced unexpectedly—if uncertainly—toward Jude. "The measure of that freedom is due partially to Jude."

Jude grinned, then looked at Claire. "We've been awarded custody of Ian, so to speak."

"Custody?"

"We're to deliver him safely to his probation officer in Chicago, where he'll spend the next five years working for a Middle West bank recently purchased by your brother."

Ian nodded. "I'll be in securities at last. Starting over the honest way."

Tossing all etiquette aside, Meg threw herself at him, tears warming her cheeks.

Ian must have misread the source of those relieved tears. He held her at arm's length with nothing less than concern on his face.

"Don't worry, Meg. They didn't take everything from me. I still have my faith, my wits, my ambition, and some newly acquired integrity." He drew her into his arms. "And Roscoe! They let me keep him, too."

Meg laughed through her tears.

That dog.

AUTHOR'S NOTE

Dear Reader,

I'm convinced God surrounds us with inspiration to match the gifts He gives us. Talk to any writer and they'll tell you the ideas behind their novels can come from a variety of sources. People we know might inspire us. Events we've heard or read about can evoke entire plotlines. Even songs that strike an emotional chord can make an author want to explore the human condition through characters of all kinds.

Those are just some of the sparks that many authors, myself included, have experienced to ignite a full-length novel. But for the first time, at least for me, the inkling of *Bees in the Butterfly Garden* came from the title. Let me tell you how.

One afternoon as I was writing at my desk, I happened to look out at the garden in my yard. I'd purposely planted flowers known to attract butterflies, but unfortunately many of those same plants also bring bees. From where I sat, I had a clear view of which visitors I received that day. Two large bees.

Taken momentarily out of the story I was writing at the time, I sat there feeling sorry for myself. *I plant a butterfly garden and all I get are bees. Bees in the butterfly garden.*

I recall speaking the words aloud, and the moment I heard

them, they struck me as fit for a book title. Since I'm normally title-challenged, I abandoned my self-pity about the garden visitors to feel nearly proud of myself. I'd thought of a title that was fit for a book! All I needed was a novel to go along with it.

That was how this book was conceived. With the insight of my Tyndale editors, Stephanie Broene and Sarah Mason, and my agent, Rachelle Gardner, my first attempts at the story were vastly improved and polished to what you have read here.

Creativity is a gift that God has given to all of us simply because we're made in His image. From believers to nonbelievers, from culture to culture, from youth to old age, each of us possesses this part of God's nature inside of us. How fun it is to tap into it!

I pray you enjoy your own gift of creativity and that you may offer up a thought of thanks to the One whose likeness your creativity reflects.

Maureen Lang

ABOUT THE AUTHOR

Maureen Lang has always had a passion for writing, particularly stories with romance and history. She wrote her first novel longhand around the age of ten, put the pages into a notebook she had covered with soft deerskin (nothing but the best!), then passed it around the neighborhood for friends to read. It was so much fun she's been writing ever since.

Her debut inspirational novel, *Pieces of Silver*, was a 2007 Christy Award finalist, followed by *Remember Me*, *The Oak Leaves*, *On Sparrow Hill*, *My Sister Dilly*, and most recently, the Great War series. She has won the Romance Writers of America Golden Heart award, the Inspirational Reader's Choice Contest, the American Christian Fiction Writers Noble Theme award, and a HOLT Medallion, and has been a finalist for Romance Writers of America's RITA, the American Christian Fiction Writers Carol Award, and the Gayle Wilson Award of Excellence.

Maureen lives in the Midwest with her husband, her two sons, and their much-loved dog, Susie. She loves to hear from her readers at maureen@maureenlang.com or via the mail at:

Maureen Lang
P.O. Box 41
Libertyville, IL 60048

Visit her website at www.maureenlang.com.

DISCUSSION QUESTIONS

1. Early in the story, what aspects of Meg's character hint that she might be more like her father than he would have liked, despite all of her proper training? In what ways does her naiveté show through?

2. Meg's father sacrificed his own relationship with her so she could be raised with the hope of a better future than one he could offer her at his side. Do you agree with his decision? Can you name a time when your motives were unselfish but misunderstood by others?

3. How did you feel about Meg's character? About her desire to take up her father's profession? What do you think she is really trying to accomplish by following in her father's footsteps?

4. What did you think of Ian's reaction to Meg's rebellion? Should he have handled it differently?

5. Kate has a habit of wearing red and even breaks the era's tradition of black mourning garb to carry a red handkerchief. Why? What do you do to remind yourself of God's love, forgiveness, or presence in your life?

6. As you read some of the advice given in *Madame Marisse's Handbook for Young Ladies*, did you find yourself relieved

our society no longer puts emphasis on such details or slightly nostalgic, wishing some of these traditions had survived? How do you think you would have fared if you lived during this time period? Do you think future generations will view some of today's customs and expectations as unnecessary or unhelpful? What might those be?

7. Near the end of the story, Meg feels "under attack" from God. What circumstances make her feel this way? Have you ever felt as if God was pursuing you? How did you respond?

8. Ian turned his back on God when he felt God had treated him harshly. Have you ever allowed disappointment with God to create distance from Him? How did you or could you overcome the chasm?

9. Despite the difference in their ages, Evie feels a strong sense of sibling rivalry with her sister, Claire. How might Claire have alleviated some of Evie's feelings of insecurity, rather than just being continually annoyed by her?

10. Meg's story is an example that death does not end a parent's influence on a child's life. Can you name a person, living or dead, who has influenced your behavior in a major way? How has your life or your character changed as a result of that person?

11. In spite of her faith, Kate forces herself to lie about her identity to the Pembertons and others in New York society because she knows to do otherwise would jeopardize Meg. How do you think God views such deception? Could she have handled the situation in a more honest way without bringing suspicion to Meg?

12. Even though Jude broke off his engagement with Claire long ago, Claire continues to hold out hope that he will return for her. What did you think of her decision to wait for Jude? If you were in Claire's position, would you be willing to forgive? Why or why not?

13. At one point in the story, Kate says Meg is reaching for a past that can never be recaptured and that Ian hopes to secure his future by filling it with money. Have you ever found yourself missing out on or impatient with the present, while memories of the past or hopes for the future take up your time? Have you looked to money—or to another person—instead of God for contentment? What were the results?

14. The Pemberton form of addressing family wrongdoings is to respond with justice, grace, or mercy. If you were faced with someone who'd wronged you, which option do you believe you would choose? Would it matter what the grievance was or how you felt about the person?

15. Do you think justice is served in the end? For Brewster? For Meg? For Ian?

Don't miss one thrilling moment of
The Great War Series

Look to the East

France, 1914. A village under siege.
A love under fire.

Whisper on the Wind

Belgium, 1916. She risked
everything to rescue him. But what
if he doesn't want to be saved?

Springtime of the Spirit

Germany, 1918. The consequences
of war force her to choose between
love and loyalty.

More great fiction from
Maureen Lang

The Oak Leaves
A legacy she never expected.
A love that knows no bounds.

On Sparrow Hill
A legacy she never wanted.
A love she'd only hoped for.

My Sister Dilly
Two sisters. One committed
the unthinkable. The other
will never forgive herself.

Engaging the mind. Renewing the soul.
www.maureenlang.com